Pra

"An engrossing novel, well told. DS Gabrieli is a detective to cheer for and Morganti has immersed him in a clever and engaging plot. *The End Game* is just the beginning to an addictive new series."

Robert Dugoni, New York Times Best Selling Author of *The Tracy Crosswhite Series.*

"It just doesn't get much better than this. Sharp and pitch perfect, *The End Game* is by turns heart thumping, heartbreaking, deeply human, and wryly funny. Gabe Gabrieli is a smart and engaging character. I look forward to spending time in his company again."

Linda L. Richards, award-winning author of *Endings* and *Exit Strategy.*

THE END GAME

A D.S. Gabrieli Mystery

CHARLOTTE MORGANTI

Cover image: evenfh/iStock/Getty Images

Cover Design: Laura Boyle Designs

For John, my own Indiana Jones

OCTOBER, 2009

THE FIRST SATURDAY

Chapter 1

ROCKY SWIPED a gloved hand across his forehead. One-thirty in the morning and balls-on-a-brass-monkey-cold at this altitude, yet he was sweating like he was in a sauna. Not because he worried about the explosives. The Forcite was new and dry. Primo. If you want to steal something, he always said, snatch the best.

No, what made Rocky's nerves jump was the gasoline. Explosives he could control. Gasoline—not so much. Ignition equaled instant flame. Plus, timing was vital. He couldn't risk someone investigating an explosion before the fire did its job, so the shack had to burn long and hot before he could set off the Forcite. Which meant he had to hang around, upping the risk he'd be seen.

He gulped air and told himself to calm down. Freaking out would only make him screw up. Again.

Following the Doc's master plan, Rocky tied several bundles of Forcite. He lowered some into drill holes on the exploration property and attached others to the drill tower. Then he unspooled thirty feet of fuse. Once he lit the fuse he'd have five minutes, more or less, to get the hell away before the exploration rig became pricey scrap metal.

1

He grabbed his two gas canisters, the glass bottle of gasoline and its wick, and hurried to the small wood building. Some core shacks were glorified carports, intended only to shelter mining samples from weather. Others, like this one, were sheds—walls, a door, windows—allowing the miner to catalog samples in comfort. Maybe have a sleep over.

Inside the shack, Rocky uncapped a gas can and poured its contents slowly, saturating the dead guy's clothing and body. Unfortunate it had come to this. For a brainiac, the guy was okay. But too smart for his own good.

The fumes made Rocky's eyes water and his breath catch. Coughing, he ran outside. He filled his lungs with clean mountain air, held his breath, and entered the shack again. He sloshed gasoline over the wood racks, walls, and concrete slab before backing out, his lungs screaming. Outside, Rocky sucked in fresh air. When his chest stopped aching, he closed the door and poured the second canister of gasoline over the shed's exterior.

Finally, with the glass bottle in hand, he took up a spot several yards away, facing the shack's door. Here goes nothing, he thought, and lit the wick. It flared nicely. Imagining himself thirty years younger and back on the mound, Rocky wound up and fired the bottle at the door. Center of the strike zone. The bottle hit, the glass shattered, the gasoline ignited, and flames leaped and danced up the door and siding.

He grabbed the empty gas canisters, ran to the end of the fuse line and sat, staring at the fire. Nothing left to do but wait. Make sure everything burned nicely and Brainiac became a crispy critter. Then he could light the fuse to the Forcite and leave.

The flames roared, devouring the shack's dry wood.

Chapter 2

BUTT-SORE AND BLEARY-EYED, Gabe pulled into Cheakamus, British Columbia midway through a sunny October morning. He needed coffee and breakfast. He angled his F-150 into a shady spot in front of a café called Tiffany's, one block past the traffic light on Main Street, and sat there. Not yet willing to shut off the engine.

Thinking.

It wasn't too late to turn tail, head home to the foothills and wide skies of Alberta.

Of all the places Gabe wanted to spend time, Cheakamus ranked lower than courtrooms. Lower than a salad bar. Barely above a church social. He had nothing against small towns, even when, like Cheakamus, they were clutched in a fist of mountains and had a wacko sabotaging nearby gold exploration sites. Gabe would even admit the place had a couple draws—his best friend Harris was the town's mayor, and recently Gabe's kid brother Jack had moved here. Two years ago, those positives would have been enough to convince Gabe that Cheakamus was worth checking out.

But not today.

Because Cheakamus was also where his horse Tornado

Callie now lived. And she brought memories of his darkest year raging to the surface.

He blew out a breath and rubbed his neck to ease the lengthy trip's accumulation of cricks. At the sound of rustling overhead, he raised his eyes to the open sunroof. Three feet above, give or take, a magpie perched on a branch, head cocked and one black eye peering down. Gabe knew The Frikkin Comedian, the *bête noire* who loved to mess with him, would seize the opportunity. He hit the sunroof button and the glass slid closed, a nanosecond before the bird shit splatted.

He reached to turn off the engine but hesitated, once more considering bailing out. Unbelievably, this upcoming commitment spooked him more than his worst case ever had. Until today only three things had ever terrified him: confined spaces, dealing with nutjobs, and the worry his marriage might really be over. And now, Gabe admitted as he stewed in his truck, perhaps a fourth: the thought of being some kid's godfather.

That was the trouble with a promise, especially one made to your oldest friend over a few double Scotches the night before his wedding. You'd likely regret it if called on to deliver. And when the friend was Harris Lancaster Chilton III, you'd definitely get that call. Gabe flicked the small silver spur on his key fob. Who'da thought Harris's wife Kate would go along with it?

He studied the bird-crap Rorschach on his sunroof. It looked exactly like a rubber chicken. "Sticks and stones," he said aloud.

A promise was a promise.

He shut off the engine and hauled his sore body from the truck. He was here. The christening was tomorrow. Hanging around Cheakamus for a couple days wouldn't kill him. And not even The Frikkin Comedian would mess with a baby's christening.

On the sidewalk, Gabe flexed his bum knee and watched a fire engine roar by, siren wailing. Then he opened the door to Tiffany's Café, releasing a blast of energetic voices and steamy air, laden with the aromas of bacon and real maple syrup. He pushed his way through the customers bunched by a commercial espresso machine, all of them watching a teenaged version of Katy Perry pull their shots. A sign inside Tiffany's entry directed: "Seat Yourself. No Fighting or Whining." Gabe cricked the right side of his lips upward and mentally filed the café under "Attitude, awesome."

He claimed the only empty stool at the counter, scanned the menu, and spotted an egg-sausage-pepper-cheese scramble named Ain't No Dude Ranch Special. After a nine-hour drive from Alberta, Gabe was heartened by the menu's guarantee the Special would kick-start his day.

While he waited for service, he placed a call to Jack. An automated voice informed him, "This mailbox is full. Please try again." Gabe sent a text: "Call me. I'm here. Looking to see if I'm still taller than you."

A fortyish woman, who resembled the barista but was shorter and rounder at the edges, deposited cutlery on the counter. When Gabe glanced up at her, she studied him for a beat, her eyes lingering on his. "Welcome to Tiffany's," she said over the clacking espresso dispenser. "Famous for more than breakfast."

Gabe put his phone down and smiled. "Are you Tiffany?"

She guffawed. Throaty, joyful, and loud, momentarily quieting nearby conversations. "Kee-ryste. Do I look like a Tiffany? Nope."

He had to agree with her.

"I'm Rhonda Zalesko," she said.

"D. S. Gabrieli. Call me Gabe. Everyone does. I'll have your Dude Ranch Special. Hot sauce. Coffee, black."

"One Special coming up." She pointed to a rack of thermoses by the entrance. "Self-serve coffee over there."

He heaved himself from his stool and limped to the rack. While he studied the list of "Today's Oso Negro Beans" inked on the antique mirror above the thermoses, Gabe shifted his weight off his aching knee and fingered the small bandage on his forehead. The sutures were a week old and beginning to itch. His shiner, the same age as the stitches, formed a tasteful lime-green pouch beneath his right eye. Compared to last week, he looked refined and felt fit. Relativity was a brilliant concept.

He poured a large mug of Mudshark, advertised on the mirror as "swift, efficient, and deep," and reclaimed his stool. He'd barely sat down when his phone rang, the display flashing "H. Chilton."

"What's your ETA?" Harris said without preamble when Gabe answered the call.

"I'm here. Tiffany's Café. Apparently famous for more than breakfast."

"Pick you up outside in two minutes." Harris clicked off.

Gabe's stomach rumbled. He hit the call return button and sipped his coffee. The Mudshark was as complex as touted and more. When Harris answered, Gabe said, "Hang tight. I just ordered breakfast."

"Un-order it. There's been another explosion at an exploration site. This makes three. We gotta check it out. Now."

Chapter 3

THERE WERE times a guy could blow off a friend, but from the sound of Harris's voice, this wasn't one of them. Gabe tossed money on the counter, poured his coffee into a to-go cup, and was leaning against his truck's tailgate in forty-five seconds flat. His latest record for time taken to vacate an establishment voluntarily.

When he scanned the Saturday morning traffic on Main Street looking for a Jeep, he spotted Harris's bar, The Peak, diagonally across the road. Its dark green awnings and windows were clean, and the wood doors gleamed in the sun. A realtor's sign in one window caught his eye. It was crisp and bright, obviously a recent addition.

What the hell, the bar was for sale? Why hadn't Harris mentioned it? Perhaps excitement about the upcoming christening pushed the sale from his mind. Perhaps the legendary Chilton memory had experienced a momentary lapse. Perhaps Harris had stopped wearing bolo ties and driving red Wranglers. Not a chance.

Two rapid horn blasts drew Gabe's attention down Main Street, where a spotless red Jeep poked its nose out from behind a dusty dump truck. When the vehicle came even with

Gabe, Harris leaned out the driver's window, did a double-take and yelled, "Great shiner."

Harris spun a U-turn and stopped behind Gabe's truck. He jumped out and rushed over, the strings from his bolo tie swinging in time with his steps. Grinning, he shook Gabe's hand and smacked him on the back. "Good to see you, man. Walk into a fist?"

"Minor mishap at home."

Harris raised his eyebrows.

"Not worth getting into."

Harris's grin widened beneath his blond mustache. "I'd bet it is."

Gabe shrugged. "Nope."

Harris glanced at the F-150. "Yours?"

"Oh yeah." Gabe caressed the tailgate's pristine black paint and then nodded toward the bar. "What's up? You're selling?"

Harris grimaced. "Yeah. The sign went up last week. It's too much for us right now." He turned away. "C'mon. I'll drive."

When they buckled in, Harris stared at Gabe's jeans and boots. "Levi's, cowboy boots, and black F-150s. Some things never change."

"One thing hasn't changed for sure. I was hungry and looking for breakfast when I went into Tiffany's and now here I am, not three minutes later, outside the café, still looking for breakfast. Still hungry." Gabe sipped his coffee. "Why's that?"

"I want to get there before Jacobson hears about it and shows up to tell me any mayor worth his pay could put a stop to these explosions."

"Who's Jacobson?"

Harris blinked. "If you had visited just once in the five years since Kate and I moved here, you'd know."

"Life conspired against me," Gabe said. "But I'm here now, so tell me about Jacobson."

"Brief story? He owns the local paper and thinks he should be mayor instead of me."

They stopped at the traffic light at the River Road T-intersection. When the light changed, Harris turned left and followed River Road as it veered gently right onto a bridge spanning the Rocque River. As the Jeep rattled along the metal bridge deck, Harris said, "The sabotage is getting worse. This latest one is more than an explosion. Our fire chief says the bombers have added arson to their repertoire."

"And you dragged me away from my Dude Ranch Special because…?"

At the end of the bridge, Harris turned right onto Highway 41 and headed north. "A couple reasons. I'm counting on you, the former excellent lawyer turned successful P.I. that you are, to take one look at the scene and know who did it."

"Hah. You're correct about the former excellent lawyer bit. But as for the P.I. bit, I'm so successful, I gotta tend bar to pay the bills." Gabe stretched his arms above his head and yawned. "And just saying, I'm officially on vacation."

"I'm not asking you to work. Humor me and check out the scene? Something might jump out at you. Fresh eyes, y'know?"

After his long trip Gabe's eyes were far from fresh. But as they sped along Highway 41, he scanned the nearby treed slopes. Furrowed and folded like a much-loved grandmother's face, unlike the Rockies near Eau Claire, Gabe's hometown in Alberta. *His* mountains were hard rock, feisty, in-your-face peaks that shot abruptly from the dirt. "I don't see smoke. How far away is this place?"

"The smoke's long gone. The fire chief thinks it happened during the wee hours. Trail riders found the wreckage this morning. The site's not far west of town, but quite a hike up Rimrock Mountain, above a closed gold mine called the Evergold."

Gabe rubbed his neck. "When the first bombing hit the news in Alberta, the reports mentioned vandals. Is that your take?"

"One incident, I'd agree. But three explosions? All at exploration sites?" Harris groaned and flicked a quick sideways glance at Gabe. "This could give the town a notoriety it really doesn't need. I need help figuring it out."

The appeal of a challenging case and Gabe's natural inclination to help his friend almost made him blurt, "I'm in." Then he remembered his vow not to stay in Cheakamus longer than duty required. He said, "That's what the Mounties are for."

Harris's shoulders sagged. He turned left off Highway 41 onto Timberline Road, a skinny two-lane that wound up the steep hillside. "Welcome to Rimrock Mountain," he said, "home of some of the best trails around for ATVs and mountain bikes." As they approached a viewpoint looking south and east over Cheakamus, Gabe opened and closed his mouth to clear his ears. The southern horizon was a mere hint between two distant peaks. In the viewpoint's parking area, a fire truck displaying a "Cheakamus Volunteer Firefighters" emblem sat amid roughly a dozen vehicles and ATV trailers.

"Busy place," Gabe said.

"Deception Ridge Viewpoint. The primary access for trails."

Gabe glanced at the mountains facing the area. "Which one is Deception Ridge?"

"None of them. Back in the day the locals gave the name to this ledge, after a miner who was conned by his partner jumped to his death."

Harris turned right onto a narrow, overgrown logging road and gunned the Jeep along rutted switchbacks. Gabe grabbed the roll bar and grinned, exhilarated. Off-roading in Wranglers was what the Head Honcho had in mind when He created Heaven.

A couple minutes later Harris pulled into a small turnout and parked. He climbed out of the vehicle and pointed at a break in the wall of evergreen and birch that bordered the road. "C'mon, we walk from here."

Harris was halfway to the trees before Gabe extricated himself from the Jeep. When he caught up to Harris, he said, "You left your key in the ignition."

"No one's gonna take the car. This isn't the big city."

The understatement of the year. Gabe shivered in the hazy air. "Cold."

"Winter comes early in the mountains," Harris said. "It's been snowing in the high passes and on the ski runs for the last couple weeks."

Gabe zipped his leather jacket and jammed bare hands into his pockets, resolving to find a fireplace in town and park his body in front of it for the rest of the weekend.

They hiked a steep trail through firs and chalky birch skeletons to a field half the size of a major league ballpark. Small bushes and the occasional sapling dotted the field. Charred remnants of a building formed a black heap almost dead center of the clearing. Off to the side, a drill tower had been reduced to a twisted mess of black metal that leaned against a boxy, Hummer-sized engine.

Three firefighters stood in the middle of the debris, using crowbars and long-handled axes to separate burned wood from the heap. The smoky air almost masked an unsettling smell. Sulfur and something more—cloying, sweet.

Harris pointed out a fourth firefighter. "Our fire chief, Chester Ubrowski." He waved Ubrowski over and made introductions. The chief lifted a sweat-and-soot-stained hand at Gabe. "I'll do you a favor and not shake."

"What d'you know so far?" Harris said.

Ubrowski tipped his helmet back and wiped his face with a handkerchief. "Looks like they used dynamite on the drill tower, consistent with the other two bombings. Burning the core shack is a fresh twist—they used gallons of accelerant, probably gasoline. The debris is cool enough now to touch, so the fire likely started around midnight and burned itself out in a few hours." Ubrowski wiped his face again. "I have a nasty feeling about this one."

"You called the Mounties?" Harris said.

"On their way."

"How about Aldercott? Isn't this the site he's exploring?"

Ubrowski nodded. "Yep. We tried. Got voice mail."

A female firefighter shouted, "Chief."

The tightness in her voice made Gabe's stomach clench. When he added Ubrowski's uneasiness and the smell in the air to the mix, he knew, but didn't want to know, what lay under the debris. They moved closer and watched the firefighter use her crowbar to hook a piece of charred wood and fling it aside.

She removed two more blackened planks.

And uncovered a coal-black, twisted corpse.

Chapter 4

THE BUNCH of them stood in a silent circle staring at the pitiful, blackened body. Gabe hoped the victim hadn't seen it coming.

"You think the body's Aldercott?" Harris said to Ubrowski.

"Could be." When two RCMP officers entered the clearing, Ubrowski said, "I'm gonna go tell them they'll need the coroner."

As soon as Ubrowski talked with the Mounties, the younger one, a constable, approached Harris, Gabe, and the firefighters, and directed everyone to move well away from the wreckage and body. Then he hustled back down the trail and a few minutes later, reappeared clutching yellow caution tape.

Harris and Gabe watched the constable string the caution tape around the area, attaching it to bushes and saplings to create a lopsided no-go zone that measured between forty and fifty feet per side.

Gabe's eyes were drawn away to the trail when a hefty, bearded man burst into the clearing, jerking his head as he looked from the cops, to the caution tape surrounding the wrecked drill rig and corpse, to Harris and Gabe.

Harris sighed. "Damn. Jacobson."

The man hurried over, his camera bouncing against his paunch. Halting in front of them, he stilled the swinging camera with his hand and glanced at Harris before focusing on Gabe's shiner and the bandage on his forehead.

"Bill," Harris said. "Meet my good friend, Gabe."

Jacobson touched his forehead in a small salute. "Bill Jacobson. *Cheakamus Journal*. Owner, writer."

Gabe saluted back. "D.S. Gabrieli. Renter, reader."

Jacobson's lips tightened momentarily, and then he jutted his chin at Harris. "Still think it's the work of vandals, Chilton?"

"Give it a rest, Bill."

Jacobson turned to Gabe. "This will be the third story I print about the latest blows to town businesses. The unanswered question in all of them is whether your *good friend*, our mayor, gives a damn."

When the RCMP constable spotted Jacobson's camera, he came over. "No pictures," he said to Jacobson.

"I'm the press," Jacobson said. "What's going on?"

"No comment. No pictures."

Jacobson swore under his breath and stomped over to the firefighters. Gabe watched him go and filed him under "Ass, pain in."

"That guy has a problem with you," he said to Harris. "What did you do to him?"

"Beat him out for mayor in the by-election two years ago." Harris pointed at the Mountie with three chevrons and a crown on his sleeve who stood just inside the caution tape. "Let's talk to Sergeant LeBlanc."

The sergeant watched Harris and Gabe approach, his expression unreadable. "Sergeant," Harris said when they halted at the caution tape, "this is my friend D. S. Gabrieli, visiting from Alberta."

LeBlanc was closing in on forty, stiff-spined, clean-shaven. Brown, serious eyes. A couple inches over six feet tall. He grimaced in what passed for a smile among cops. "Mayor Chilton. Mr. Gabrieli."

"D'you think this is connected to the other explosions?" Harris said.

"Too early to tell," LeBlanc said, arms folded and jaw set.

"Makes sense it would be, though?" Gabe said.

"Too early to tell."

On the effusiveness scale, LeBlanc tended toward negative numbers.

Harris said, "People were anxious when we thought it was vandalism. Now someone's dead. Aldercott's not a local, but there'll still be an uproar."

"Who's Aldercott?" LeBlanc said.

Harris gestured at the corpse. "Recent arrival from Vancouver, a miner exploring for gold around Cheakamus. This was his exploration site, so we think the body's him."

LeBlanc tapped his chin with his forefinger. "Or one of his crew."

Harris shook his head. "Maybe, but miners run their exploration operations real tight these days. One guy to run the drill, and the explorer logging core."

"Plus," Gabe said, "you gotta ask why the driller would be inside the core shack in the first place. So, that leaves the explorer, Aldercott."

LeBlanc shot Gabe a look.

Gabe shrugged and folded his arms. "But then, I'm no cop."

"No, you are not," LeBlanc said. "We'll check it out."

As Gabe and Harris returned to the Jeep, Harris said, "Help me out and investigate these explosions?"

Gabe's heart dropped. He'd solved every case he'd investigated except one, and it was reassuring to know Harris thought he could help, but for the first time since the sandbox Gabe intended to cut and run. The reason boiled down to a mix of horseflesh and regret. Rather than admit the truth to

Harris, Gabe said, "Nutjobs make me nervous. Explosives make me nervous. You've got both. Leave it to the Mounties. Their Major Crimes people are equipped to deal with wackos like your bad guy."

"The cops are spread thin. We don't have a local RCMP detachment, so we rely on LeBlanc's team in Trail. They cover a dozen towns in the area. Every time we need the police, they have to drive an hour to get here."

"We both know cops don't like civilians messing around in stuff like this. And LeBlanc doesn't strike me as someone who welcomes outside help, especially when there's a body involved."

"Then we won't tell him you're working on it." Harris dragged a hand through his hair. "I need someone people will talk to, someone who doesn't look like a cop. Like you."

"LeBlanc will call in the Major Crimes team, bring in reinforcements and undercover officers if he has to." The cold seeped through Gabe's leather jacket. He opened the Wrangler's passenger door. "Let's go, I'm freezing. And starving. Drop me back at Tiffany's?"

Harris blew out an exasperated breath as they settled in the vehicle. "I'd feel better if you looked into it."

Gabe shook his head. "I'm doing a cameo—gonna become a god-daddy and head home. Forty-eight hours. Not even Sam Spade could solve this in two days."

"Which brings me to the second reason I dragged you away from breakfast."

Gabe's stomach lurched as he registered Harris's tone of voice. It was the voice your accountant uses when he says you owe thousands in taxes. The Jeep plowed over the rutted logging road, and Gabe braced himself against its jerking. Perhaps against the coming curveball. He wasn't sure which.

"What?"

Chapter 5

"Reverend Beam was called away," Harris said. "He won't be back until Thursday. We've postponed Devon's christening to next Saturday."

The burn built deep in Gabe's gut. He'd hit the road at midnight. Drove all night. Spent most of the time worrying about how to be a godfather. His head pounded, his neck ached, his knee throbbed. He hadn't yet had breakfast, and Harris was saying it was all for nothing. "Are you kidding me? Why didn't you tell me this before I numbed my rear for nine hours and got bird crap on my sunroof?"

Harris made a left turn from the logging road onto Timberline Road. "He only told us this morning."

Gabe couldn't believe it. He hadn't wanted to make even one trip to Cheakamus. Now he'd have to make a second trip in a week's time. "Awww man, you're paying for my truck's wash job."

As the Wrangler sped along the two-lane road, Gabe thought again about the thrill of off-roading. An idea took shape: the perfect quid pro quo. He'd make the tiring trip to Cheakamus again next week. He'd put on his best suit and dress shoes, knot an impeccable Windsor in his most sedate tie, and smile at the minister during the christening. In return, Harris would hand him the keys to the Wrangler. Gabe would investigate the mountain trails Cheakamus was famous for. And he would be as close to the Head Honcho as a guy could get without dying.

Harris said, "I'll gladly wash your truck, if you stay and work on the investigation."

Gabe's laugh was sharp, edgy. "Not a chance. As I said before, LeBlanc won't want a P.I. snooping around. And I'm banged up enough without chasing over mountains. I'm into less violent cases these days."

"C'mon. I'm not asking you to do anything violent. Just talk to people. Use your famous intuition."

"My intuition's working fine. It's telling me to duck. I'm gonna grab breakfast, see Jack, and head out."

"You just got here. At least stay overnight. Get some sleep and see how you feel in the morning."

Gabe knew how he'd feel. He would have told Harris too, but a battered orange-and-white Volkswagen Vanagon sitting at a side road caught his eye. "Lordy, a shaggin' wagon."

Harris glanced at the vehicle. "It belongs to Solomon's Choice Ranch, a resort on the north slope of Rimrock, about five minutes up that road."

"Seriously? A dude ranch?"

"They deny it. But hey, horses plus trail rides…."

Gabe took in the van's dented and rusty side panel, missing hubcaps, and the way it listed noticeably lower on the passenger side. No trust-fund babies were coming out of *that* dude ranch.

———

AN HOUR after first dragging Gabe away from Tiffany's Café, Harris parked outside The Peak Bar. "I've got work waiting inside," he said. "Don't leave town without telling me. Promise to think about sticking around, at least overnight."

An easy promise for Gabe to make and keep. He fulfilled it while jaywalking across Main Street. Thought about it. Decided no. Opened the door to Tiffany's smiling.

He poured a mug of Mudshark, chose a stool at the counter and sent another text to Jack: "Where R U. Call."

Rhonda placed cutlery on the counter. "Mr. Gabrieli. Welcome back. I've had customers run out on the bill. Usually, they eat first. But you—you pay, don't eat, and split. Are you on some weird diet?"

"Nope. Had to go sightseeing. I'll have your Dude Ranch Special. Hot sauce."

While Gabe waited for his breakfast, he thought about the realtor's sign at The Peak. The bar was Harris's prize. Something he'd dreamed about for years. He'd relaxed between bouts of trial preparation by sketching floor plans for the perfect layout. He'd spent vacations touring craft breweries and haunting auctions in search of the just-right brass rail. When Harris opened The Peak four years ago, he sent out birth announcements. Gabe couldn't believe he'd sell his first child.

Rhonda plunked down a sizzling cast-iron skillet of scramble and cheese.

"Hot sauce?" Gabe said.

"Taste it first."

He studied her unsmiling face and wide-legged stance. No question where the café got its attitude. He lifted a forkful. Two seconds after he swallowed the first bite, the back of his mouth registered the heat. His sinuses opened. The skin above his eyebrows prickled.

Rhonda waggled a red bottle between her fingers. "Hot sauce?"

Gabe smiled and waved it off, not trusting his voice. His eyes teared. He swiped at them as his phone rang. He fished his pocket for it, fumbling. The phone was on its third ring by the time he wiped another tear from his eye and checked the display: J. O. Diamond. Finally, Jack had surfaced.

"Hey, Jacko. I was gonna head over to see—"

Jack interrupted, gulping, and whispering in quick snatches, "Gabe, help me. Cops—"

"Slow down. What's happening?"

Jack sucked in a breath; it trembled through the phone. "The cops...." He let out a sob, dragged in another shaky breath.

"What about them?"

"They're here, asking me where I was last night. Asking about bombs."

Chapter 6

Seventeen-year-old Jack Diamond perched on the veranda's top railing, his Yankees ball cap pulled low over his sunglasses, his hands jammed in the pockets of a dark green ski jacket and his long, skinny legs wrapped around the chunky spindles. In front of him the drive ran between split rail fences, slightly downhill to Stockman's Road. If not for the RCMP-issued SUV parked on the driveway and the constable leaning against its hood, Jack would be able to see the arched gateway that announced, "O'Malley's Preferred Stock."

Behind him the ranch rose and fell over seven thousand acres in the Rocque River Valley, stopping just short of the US border. On a good day, the trip from Cheakamus to O'Malley's was a relaxed fifteen-minute drive, south on Highway 41 to Stockman's Corner and then east on Stockman's Road.

Jack hoped Gabe and Harris would slash the average travel time in half. His heart raced, his head felt thick, and his eyes stung despite his sunglasses. But he stared at a distant hillside, telegraphing, "You don't scare me" to the cop. He heard the grumble of a muffler and swiveled his head toward the sound. A wave of dizziness, the fourth since the Mountie rousted him way too early this morning, made him grab the rail and clamp his legs more firmly against the spindles.

As he watched Harris's Jeep approach, Jack whispered a brief thank-you to whatever supernatural force made Gabe answer the phone when Jack had called in a panic. As soon as Jack had said he was at the ranch alone with the police, Gabe had gone into lawyer mode. He'd said, "Harris and I will be right there. Meanwhile, tell the cop O'Malley isn't home, and you called a lawyer who said to wait outside for him. Say lawyer, not brother. Don't let him snoop around. If he tries, tell him he needs a search warrant."

Gabe-the-lawyer was awesome.

Gabe-the-brother was another story. Especially lately: an annoying mix of lectures, babying, and indifference. Everything had changed when Bethany left Gabe. Before that, he seemed to enjoy hanging out with Jack. In the last year, however—Jack gritted his teeth and blinked against the threatening tears.

He uncoiled his legs and jumped to the ground. The jolt of the landing fired ice picks into his brain. Nausea overtook him. He grabbed the railing and focused on the ground, willing his stomach to settle. Then Gabe was hugging him. "Hey Jacko, how you doing?"

"Okay. Sorta scared."

Gabe stepped back and flashed a smile and a wink. "Relax. It'll be okay."

Jack sucked in a shaky breath.

Gabe gave Jack's shoulder a squeeze, then left his hand there, a protective, calming presence.

"Who's the lawyer?" the cop said.

Gabe opened his mouth, but Harris spoke first. "I am. Harris Chilton. This is D. S. Gabrieli. I recognize you from TEG's site earlier today but didn't catch your name."

"Constable Lambert." He looked at Harris quizzically. "I

understood from Sergeant LeBlanc you're the mayor of Cheakamus?"

"Correct. But that job doesn't even keep me in gas money, so I practice law too. What's happening here?"

"He thinks I planted bombs," Jack said. "He—"

Harris raised his hand. "Let Constable Lambert tell us what he wants. Then I'll decide if you can answer."

Lambert said, "We're talking to everyone who might dislike mining. Including environmental groups. I don't know how well you know young Mr. Diamond—"

"Pretty well," Harris said.

"Then you know he belongs to Green Dudes. I'm merely gathering information. I asked Jack what he knows."

"And what did he tell you?" Harris said.

"He *says* he doesn't know who'd blow up drill rigs."

"You have doubts?" Gabe said.

The cop smirked. "You know, it was an informal chat. Not like I was interviewing him formally, right? No reason to get skittish. Makes me wonder why someone who professes to be pure as the snow on Rimrock calls a lawyer the minute I ask a simple question."

Gabe glowered and started to speak, but Harris cut him off. "There's no such thing as an informal or off the record chat with the police, Constable. Stop being coy."

Lambert took a short step backward and flicked his hands in a "Me? Coy?" motion. He fixed his attention on Jack. "What have the Green Dudes been up to in the last week?"

When Harris nodded, Jack said, "Nothing much. Meetings, printing posters, a bake sale."

Lambert grinned—a quick, tight slash. "Nice video on YouTube of your meeting. Write your own stuff?"

Jack shrugged.

"What do you need the money from the bake sale for?" Lambert said.

"Supplies."

"Supplies. Like red spray paint?"

Harris jumped in. "What's your point?"

"Jack's friends say he paints slogans—like the graffiti we've found at the sabotaged exploration sites. We've also heard about his escapades in Alberta. He's been bragging about his skills in chemistry labs. Branching out now, Jack? Moving from stink bombs to the genuine thing?"

When Jack opened his mouth, Gabe squeezed his shoulder and whispered, "Shut up."

"He's not answering that," Harris said.

Lambert jutted his chin at the three-car garage. "Is that where you keep your *supplies*, Jack? Mind if I look?"

"We're done," Harris said. "You want to look around, get a search warrant."

Chapter 7

AFTER LAMBERT LEFT, Gabe sat at O'Malley's kitchen table, listening to his stomach growl as he tossed questions at Jack. They'd watched the YouTube video Lambert had mentioned. On it, Jack occupied center stage, exhorting viewers to join the battle for the planet.

"Did you have to use the word 'battle'?" Gabe said.

"It's only a promo clip," Jack said. "We're into passive protesting. Y'know, sit-ins, chaining ourselves to trees."

"Was Lambert blowing smoke about the graffiti?"

Jack shifted in his chair. "No idea what he's talking about." A tiny tic appeared beside his mouth.

Gabe shoved away from the table and moved to the back door. "Be back soon."

"Where're you going?" Jack said.

"Gonna tour the spread. Maybe check the garage, outbuildings. You just keep on talking bullshit to Harris."

"I'm not bullshitting anyone." Jack's voice rose an octave. "I'm not."

"Jacko. Hello? It's me, your big brother who knows you. You are a lousy liar. Always were. I'll find red spray paint in the garage. Or the barn. It won't belong to O'Malley. And if the cops test your clothes, they'll find traces of red paint. Am I wrong?"

Jack folded his arms and stared at the floor. Gabe gave him a few seconds to come clean. When that didn't happen, he opened the door and stepped onto the back porch.

"Okay, shit, okay," Jack said. "But it's got nothing to do with the explosions."

Gabe returned to the table. "Spill it. And watch the language. What would Mercy say?"

Jack glared. "Who cares? What's Mom gonna do? She already shipped me out here, put me in exile with Warden O'Malley."

"You blew up the chem lab and got expelled. What did you expect her to do, pat you on the head and increase your allowance? I would have sent you to juvie."

Jack glared. "Well, that figures. Just like Mom. Ship me away. Get rid of me."

Harris cleared his throat. "Calm down, guys. Fill me in, Jack. If I'm gonna be your lawyer, I need to know what's going on."

Jack paced the kitchen. "Okay, I sprayed a couple buildings. And maybe one or two signs. But not where the bombs went off. No way."

"Who knows you're into graffiti?" Gabe said.

"For shit's sake, I'm not *into* graffiti. I just sprayed a couple slogans. Y'know, to make people stop ruining things."

"What slogans?" Harris said.

"Stop killing trees. No mining. Like that. But I haven't done it for a long time." He leaned against the counter and folded his arms.

"How long is long?" Harris asked.

"A couple months."

"How many places have you tagged?" Gabe said.

"Maybe four?"

"Jacko. Really?"

Jack sat down. "I coulda underestimated. Probably closer to twenty."

When Harris asked who knew about the graffiti, Jack said a few Green Dudes. He was adamant he had nothing to do with the explosions. "I haven't messed with stuff like that since the chem-lab thing."

"Okay," Harris said. "From now on, no more graffiti."

Jack nodded, eyes on the table. "Sure."

"And no more protests. Until we figure this out, you need to be squeaky clean."

"Okay."

"Try to remember where you were when these explosions happened," Gabe said. "And if anyone was with you."

Jack's head shot up. "You don't believe me?" His voice was combative, but his eyes held a plaintive quality.

"We want to believe you," Gabe said. "But you just lied to us about the graffiti. So ..."

Jack dropped his head, raised his shoulders. "I'm not lying."

"Whatever. Lambert has a burr in his pants. If he comes around again, he might ask where you were when the explosions happened."

Jack snorted. "I don't know *when* they happened. So how do I know what I was doing when it counts?"

Harris said, "Minken's explosion happened last Sunday evening; the Fortune Gold one was this past Wednesday, late afternoon. Think about who saw you at school, did you run errands for O'Malley, did Kate talk to you while you groomed the Percherons at our ranch? Did you help the men here with the herd? Like that."

Jack looked morose. Gabe tried to lighten the mood. "Or if you snuck out after dark, which girl did you meet?"

Jack jerked his eyes at Gabe, a faint flush appearing on his cheeks.

Harris stood. "We should get back to town."

As they walked outside, Harris said, "If the RCMP return or call, say nothing, Jack. Phone me immediately."

Jack nodded. "Got it. I'll see you later. It's my day to groom Kate's herd and I want to ride Tornado Callie." Grinning, he turned to Gabe and blurted, "Wait till you see her. She's sleek and full of fire. Way better than …" The grin fell away. "Before."

Gabe's steps faltered as Jack's remark hit home and he remembered the lost months after his wife Bethany left. Was it only a year ago? He opened his mouth to speak, then thought better of it. What could he say, really? Instead, he merely nodded and headed to the Jeep.

Jack hung back for a second, then caught up and walked alongside Gabe. "Did you bring your truck?"

"Yep, a new one, a couple weeks old. Loaded. His name is Three. How about tomorrow you show me some of that graffiti? Maybe I'll let you drive."

Jack pumped his fist in the air. "Rockin'."

Harris said, "Does that mean you're sticking around?"

The minute Gabe had received Jack's phone call, all hesitancy about being in Cheakamus had vanished. "I thought I would."

Harris pounded Gabe on the back. "Fantastic!"

"Let's not advertise the fact I'm a private investigator. We need a cover story—something more than being your baby's godfather, something that will let me jaw with the locals, snoop around."

"I could hire you to tend bar," Harris said. Then he frowned. "Of course, we don't need extra staff."

Gabe thought for a moment. "Suppose I'm looking to buy a bar? Know of any for sale?"

Harris grinned. "Perfect."

"I'll work a few shifts and tell people I'm checking out the business and the town."

Harris punched a number into his cell phone. "I'm calling

the realtor to tell her I've got a live one. That will give the story legs."

Jack had been following their conversation like a tennis match. Gabe said, "D'you think that story makes sense, Jacko? Can you tell O'Malley to forget I'm a P.I. for now?"

"Got it. Not a P.I. Maybe buying the bar. Am I still your brother?"

Gabe tousled Jack's hair. "You'll always be my brother. I woulda told Lambert that too, until I realized that with my past, it won't help you if they know we're related."

Harris ended his call. "The realtor's ecstatic. She'll meet us around four at the bar."

"Fine," Gabe said. "Meanwhile, I'd like to find a motel and then, if we have time, go back to the TEG site and check it out, assuming the cops have released the scene."

"Kate and I hoped you'd stay with us at the ranch. It would give you a chance to reunite with Callie."

Gabe wasn't ready to face his horse again. Luckily their cover story provided an excellent way out. "Love to, but I don't think it would be smart. If I'm a buyer checking out the bar and the town, it makes more sense that I'd stay in Cheakamus."

"Yeah, you're probably right," Harris said. "Still, nothing stopping you from coming to the ranch another day, right? You can meet Kate's herd and spend time with Callie."

"Sure. I'll pencil it in," Gabe said, intending to do nothing of the sort.

Chapter 8

EN ROUTE to town Gabe said, "I heard Cheakamus is famous for off-roading."

Harris's knuckles whitened on the steering wheel. His eyes flicked sideways at Gabe. "Yeah. The town was once a booming mining center. Today, outdoor recreation rules. Still, mining's making a small comeback. Which some people oppose."

"I haven't been on backcountry trails in a Jeep for ages. Just saying."

Harris's head jerked a quick no. "My vehicle's off-limits."

Gabe studied him for a few seconds and then decided to press his agenda another day. He sighed. "Okay. About the bombings. Who opposes mining and exploration?"

"You name it. Environmental groups, outdoor adventure companies, hospitality businesses." Harris gestured at the farmland edging the highway. "Then we've got farmers here in the River Flats area and ranchers to the north and south of town. Some, like Kate and me, make extra money leasing land to mineral explorers for their operations. But others worry about endangering their herds."

Gabe took in the dense trees hugging Rimrock's slopes,

perfect for sheltering a myriad of illegal activities. "And I'm sure the survivalists and grow ops in the bush don't like anyone invading their space."

"Yeah, lots of potential saboteurs," Harris said. "So, do you think Jack was being straight with us?"

Gabe didn't worry so much about Jack's story as he did about the kid himself—pale, appearing close to passing out when they arrived—was he wasted, or ill? Gabe kept his concerns to himself and said, "I doubt he's a bomber or fire-bug. Back home he was a problem student—cutting class, earning money doing classmates' assignments, telling the truth on teacher evaluations. Then: stink bombs and several thousand dollars' damage, and he's expelled." Gabe huffed out a breath. "Still, he's not telling us everything. The graffiti and protests surprise me. I thought he was into horses and snowboards."

"First I heard about it too. Maybe Jack's love of horses and the outdoors explains the other stuff."

"Mom will freak when she finds out," Gabe said. "And O'Malley will say he's turning out exactly like his no-account brother."

Harris grinned. "I think Jack wants to be like you."

Gabe shrugged. "Two years ago, I would've agreed. Even six months ago. Today I'm not sure. Jack seems different."

"Of course he does. He's seventeen."

"He's furious that Mom sent him here to live with O'Malley. I know she and your father-in-law have been intimate for years, but she's bonkers trusting him to guide Jack. That, or deeply in love."

Harris chuckled. "I know which side you come down on."

"O'Malley is rigid, narrow-minded, and authoritarian. How did Kate end up so normal with him as a father?"

"She had a wonderful mother for thirteen short years. Listen, about Tornado Callie. Jack was right. She *is* doing great."

Gabe nodded and stared out the passenger window. He'd had Callie since she was a colt. "She comes from good endurance stock," Bethany had said when she gave him the colt as a wedding gift. "Guaranteed to go the distance. Just like our marriage, hey?"

That was six years ago and at the time he'd been positive their marriage would endure. Then Bethany left him, and Callie became a symbol of everything that was wrong in Gabe's life.

Now, he said to Harris, "You did both me and Callie a favor by adopting her. She's in much better hands."

"Only because the hands are Kate's. She's so good with horses they think she's one of them. It's eerie how she can get inside their heads. The Percherons follow her around like one-ton puppies."

"How many horses in Kate's herd?"

"Eight Percherons, and four other horses including Callie."

"How do you manage them all?"

"Rhonda Zalesko's kids, David and Roxanne, split the grooming and mucking with Jack. They get a small salary and all the riding they want. It was easier before the baby arrived. Now we may need to hire additional help."

"Lots on your plate. Is that why you're selling the bar?"

Harris shrugged. "Things have a way of piling up. Sometimes you don't notice until it becomes too much."

"No kidding. Apparently, the trick is to deal with it before it reaches a crisis. If I'd known that when Bethany left last year, you could've avoided being my personal nursemaid and butt-saver."

Harris laughed the comment away. "I've been saving your bacon since that day in kindergarten when you kicked over Mean Jeanie's sandcastle."

As they crossed the Rocque River Bridge heading back into Cheakamus, Harris said, "I'm taking you to a guest house in town. Greta, the owner, is the widow of Pierre Rocque, the guy who started the Evergold Mine. Pierre did many good things for the town, from building playgrounds to spear-heading fundraising for our hospital, so when he died about ten years ago, the townspeople petitioned the government to name this river after him."

Harris stopped on Main Street by Tiffany's and let the Jeep idle. "Get your truck and follow me."

Gabe flipped a U-turn and then followed Harris left at the light onto Lookout Road, which climbed in a steep curve north from Main Street. Near the top of the hill, they pulled over by a wooden sign: *"Rocque & Hound, a Guest House."* The solid two-story house had an unobstructed view of the mountains and valleys to the west and south of town.

When Harris joined him on the sidewalk, Gabe said, "This place looks hopeful."

A short, chunky woman with cropped silver and hot pink hair, and clad in leopard-patterned leggings and a voluminous black tunic, answered their knock. If Gabe ignored the hair and leggings, she reminded him of his first-grade teacher. He wondered if Greta also handed out milk and cookies during a trying day.

"Greta, this is my friend, D. S. Gabrieli," Harris said. "Goes by Gabe. He needs a place to stay."

She gave Gabe a sly grin. "You're the hunka-hunka burnin' love who never eats the meals he orders."

She's not handing out milk and cookies, Gabe told himself. Try a shot and beer back.

"No way he's hunka anything," Harris said.

"I agree he's no pretty boy," Greta said, casting an appraising glance at Gabe. "But he's got a definite va-voom going on."

She waved them inside and then turned to Gabe. "I hear

you've walked out on Rhonda's cooking twice. She's gunning for you."

"How ...?" Gabe said.

Greta tapped her temple with a manicured finger. "Cheakamus is all about three things: skiing, mountain biking, and gossip. Only two of those are seasonal."

A shaggy white standard poodle came down the hallway and tilted his head at Gabe. Greta scratched the dog's ears. "This is Hound. Harmless. Follow me."

She led them through the kitchen and stopped at the back door. "The best space is the apartment over the garage. Sunny."

Mercy's face flashed into Gabe's brain when he heard the word "sunny."

Harris nudged Gabe and mouthed, "suh-nee." Gabe grimaced. A part of him raged silently at his mother's penchant for what she called meaningful names. Another part of him wondered if Greta was clairvoyant.

They followed Greta and Hound along the garden path to the detached double garage. Greta unlocked the side door and waved them inside the empty space. "My car's in the shop for a while, waiting on parts. So there's plenty of room for your truck."

She led them up an interior staircase, and into the spacious sun-filled suite. When Gabe noticed the oversized skylights, he was sold.

After they settled on the rental fee, Greta said, "I hear there was another bombing."

Harris nodded. "The TEG Mines site. The core shack burned to the ground."

"Good grief! Ed was out there only last week."

"Who's Ed?" Gabe said.

"Ed Gwinn, my previous guest. He checked out a week ago. Ed's a geologist. He was kicking TEG's tires for a client." She shook her head and sighed. "Twenty years ago, people thought mining was wonderful. Now they're attacking everyone in the business."

Greta handed over the door key and garage remote to Gabe. "You can come and go through the garage privately. Not that I spy on my guests. Good grief, perish the thought. I might listen to gossip, but I don't spread it."

Gabe filed Greta under "Sources, likely."

It took a mere three minutes to move his truck to the garage and haul his suit carrier and duffel upstairs. As Gabe walked back to Harris's Wrangler, he searched the internet on his phone and found Ed Gwinn's website and a contact number. When voice mail cut in, he left a message, hoping Gwinn knew something that could help solve the case.

———

FIVE MINUTES out of town on their return to TEG's site, Gabe said, "Since I'm sticking around awhile, I've been thinking about quid pro quo. You know, for missing breakfast and for the postponed christening. And the bird shit on Three. Keys to your Wrangler would be a fair trade."

"No chance. You've wrecked four of my Jeeps. That's plenty. Speaking of numbers, I remember an F-150 called Two. What happened to it?"

"Two was replaced by Three."

Harris smirked. "When you state the obvious, there's a wild story you're not telling."

Gabe clenched his jaw and stared straight ahead. "No story. The truck got a couple scratches. You can never match the paint."

"You're aggravated."

"Never." Gabe folded his arms across his chest. "No big deal. The truck got dinged up. I replaced it."

Harris laughed. "What happens to you is never as simple as a few scratches or dings."

Gabe worked at relaxing his jaw. "You weren't there. I was. No story to tell."

"It's only a matter of time before I get it out of you. I'm a masterful trial lawyer. You're pigheaded, but I've wrenched the truth out of witnesses sixteen times as obstinate."

"Give up. Find something else to irritate me about."

Gabe smoldered for several minutes. As they gained altitude on Timberline Road, Harris said, "Good grief, *suh-nee*, lighten up."

Gabe laughed in spite of himself. "Go ahead. Give me grief over my name—I don't care. I've got va-voom. And I'm still not talking."

Chapter 9

JACK WASTED no time after Harris and Gabe left the O'Malley ranch. He set about upgrading his stomach from upchuck-city to merely queasy: two aspirins, four glasses of water, a three-hour nap, and reheated pizza. And presto, if not a new person he was at least ready to groom the herd at the Lazy C.

He was thinking more clearly too. When he replayed the morning's events, two warning flags waved. First, Harris had told the Mountie, "Get a search warrant." Second, Gabe had said the cops might return. If the RCMP were targeting him, Jack had housecleaning to do.

He grabbed a black garbage bag and drove his ATV the short distance to O'Malley's stable, where he opened his tack box and transferred six aerosol paint cans to the bag. He slammed the lid closed, then paused, remembering the look on Gabe's face as he stood by the veranda. Was Gabe suspicious? Definitely.

Jack reopened his box, shifted a halter to the side, and slid his hands under the saddle blanket. He removed two Smirnoff bottles, one empty. He studied the vodka in the second bottle and then took a drink before tossing both bottles into the garbage bag.

Jack carted the bag and its guilty cargo to the ATV. He had a safe place to stash it, well away from O'Malley's ranch. Let the cops come back with a warrant. They could snoop all they wanted. Gabe too, if he went into big-brother mode.

Within fifteen minutes Jack had deposited his paint canisters and vodka bottles at his secret spot in the trees bordering one of Harris's remote pastures. He'd avoided the workers at the exploration drill in the pasture by parking his ATV one field over and hiking through the trees. The drill made so much noise Jack could probably have driven right up to them without announcing his presence.

Now, he sat on his ATV on a rutted trail running south of Harris's ranch. Logging companies had long abandoned the makeshift road, leaving it to hikers and trail riders. Jack waited at a small turnout, far enough into the overgrowth that it hid him from the highway. Soon he heard an engine.

A dusty, beige pickup stopped beside Jack. The driver leaned out his window and scanned the area. He held out a small baggie. "Your order, sir. Prime BC bud. Twenty bucks. Worth forty."

Jack snorted and handed over a twenty. "No, Craig. It's worth twenty. I know the prices."

Craig shrugged. "Can't blame me for promoting what I sell. Gotta pay expenses. No way BAM's running kiddie bake sales like your group does. What're you called? Greenies?"

Jack mentally winced at the kiddie reference, but stared Craig down. "Green Dudes."

"You Greenies got any protests planned?"

Jack shook his head. "We're shutting things down. The cops came by, asking about the explosions. Have they been to your place?"

Craig shook his head. "We're not into bombs."

"Neither are we. But they still hassled me until Harris did his lawyer thing."

"Who?"

"Harris Chilton."

"You got a lawyer?"

"Not really. I work at his ranch sometimes. He told the cop to get a search warrant." Jack started his ATV. "Gotta go."

"Okay man. Enjoy the weed. You know where I am when you need more." Craig shifted gears, turned the pickup, and drove away.

Jack then drove his ATV to Harris Chilton's ranch and parked beside the barn. He stopped at a fridge inside the building long enough to grab some oat-and-molasses horse treats. When he entered the stable, Callie whinnied in her stall.

"Hey Callie." Jack fed her a cookie. "How's my girl?" The horse stared at Jack and chewed. Jack stroked her ears. "Best thing Gabe did was give you to Harris and Kate."

Callie blew air out in a chuff and bobbed her head.

She gets it, Jack thought. She'd been lonely too.

Chapter 10

Harris and Gabe parked in the logging road turnout on Rimrock Mountain and hiked to the TEG drill site. A shroud of silence wrapped the area, as though paying respect to the soul wrenched away.

"Mounties have left," Harris said. "If LeBlanc called in Major Crimes, they've checked things out and released the scene."

Gabe checked his watch. Two o'clock. "Quick service."

"Yeah, the nearest Major Crimes unit is only a couple hours away."

"Great, let's see what's what."

They circled the perimeter of the debris pile. Remnants of yellow caution tape on the ground warned the world not to cross. They stepped into the cleared space where a few hours earlier a charred corpse had lain.

Blackened wood littered the scorched concrete pad where the shack had stood. When Gabe toed the debris around, a dirty egg-sized rock flipped over, spots of purple glinting on its underside. He grabbed it and wiped its sooty surface on his jeans. The rock had the heft of a good paperweight. He thought of his sister Lucy's fondness for unique rocks. Fairly certain she didn't have a purple one in her collection yet, he stuck it in his jacket pocket.

A half-hour search revealed nothing more than glass shards, a mangled metal chair, and a potbellied stove with two pieces of half-burned firewood inside.

"Think the guy lived here?" Gabe said, pushing the stove door closed with his foot.

Harris shrugged. "Maybe he simply wanted warmth." He expelled his breath in a huff. "I'm worried the bomber's just getting rolling. I hope the explorers hire security."

Gabe studied the trees ringing the clearing. "How did our saboteurs access the site? Would they risk being seen by driving up Timberline like we did? Or would they sneak in via one of the trails?"

"If it was me," Harris said, "I'd want to avoid the roads." He glanced at his watch. "We have time to check a trail before we meet my realtor." He pointed south toward a narrow opening in the trees. "Let's try that one. You'll be able to see part of our ranch from the top."

"Assuming the saboteurs stick to exploration sites, how many are we talking about?" Gabe asked as they entered the trail.

"Seven, including the sabotaged ones."

"All on Rimrock Mountain?"

Harris shook his head. "No. The only ones on Rimrock are TEG's site here, and Minken Minerals' operation on my ranch. The rest are east or north of town."

The trail twisted upward at a steep pitch through the dense trees. After climbing several minutes, Gabe bent over, gulping air, trying to ease the sharp pain in his side.

Harris laughed. "Want to quit, old man?"

"I'm a measly three months older than you. I can still beat you where it counts. Lead on."

Harris moved ahead at a slower pace. Gabe huffed along behind him, not confident he could beat Harris at anything anymore. When they'd finished law school in 1999, he wouldn't even have considered the possibility of coming in second. It was the way things were, the way they'd been since kindergarten—when Harris and Gabe competed, Gabe won. In the ten years since law school, however, Harris had twice proved himself the better man when it mattered. The first, eighteen months ago, when Gabe needed a criminal lawyer and Harris saved his hide. The second, last year, when Bethany left and Harris picked Gabe up from the Eau Claire gutters and helped put his life back together, piece by shattered piece.

Gabe felt an icy breeze and heard a distant thumping as they exited the trees and their trail dead-ended on a wide V-shaped ledge. Crisp white snowdrifts swirled against Rimrock's face.

"How about that," Gabe said, staring at the curls of snow and thinking about crinolines flashing beneath square dancers' skirts. Or frothing upward when he scooped Bethany into his arms and carried her over the threshold on their wedding night.

"How about what?"

Gabe blinked, jerking himself away from crinolines. He pointed to the drifts. "Winter."

"We've climbed above the snow line." Harris pointed south where the view opened onto a range of dark green mountains, splotched with daubs of orange and red, and topped by solid white. "The US is about eight miles away through those mountains. Due east of here is our ranch."

"What's that pounding?"

"Minken's exploration drill in our far pasture." Harris moved closer to the edge and pointed east and downhill. "There."

A boxy engine and a drill mast sat in a field halfway down

the slope. Two men stood near the rig, watching the drill as it moved up and down through the tower.

Gabe swept his gaze over the area directly below the ledge they stood on: perhaps fifteen feet of sheer drop and then a football field-sized plateau scattered with outcrops. The mountain's rock face reminded Gabe of a ship's prow, its wedge cutting several yards into the field below.

Evergreens hemmed the south side of the plateau. Gabe counted six horses cropping the still-green grass on the field. A couple more munched on hay under a woebegone, sagging lean-to beneath an enormous pine near the western perimeter, where the plateau dropped sharply, perhaps three feet, to a shallow basin measuring about half the size of the plateau.

Gabe spied a trail emerging from the trees on the far side of the basin and tracked it as it snaked through the brush and undergrowth before petering out near a clump of birch. He couldn't see a trail connecting the basin to the upper plateau. Perhaps it was hidden from view. How else could the horses access the grass on this field? He tried to picture a bomber scaling Rimrock to reach this ledge. "If our saboteur hiked into TEG's site, I don't think they used this route, unless they're into climbing."

"I agree," Harris said. "There are many more trails to choose from."

A mix of snow and sleet began falling as they turned to leave. Gabe glanced at the herd. "How long before the snow line reaches that pasture and the horses?"

"A week, maybe less. But someone will round them up. Let's go. It's cold."

They hurried through the trees, downhill to TEG's site. By the time they reached the Jeep, Gabe felt like he'd played four hard quarters of football in a sleet storm. When Harris started the vehicle, the vents blew frigid air.

"Turn on the heat. I'm freezing," Gabe said.

"It is on."

"In that case, take me someplace warm where I can defrost. Then I'm going shopping. Gonna buy the town's entire supply of down jackets." Gabe rubbed his knee. "And painkillers."

"You can defrost in front of The Peak's fireplace."

"It will be good to see it in person. I'm sorry I missed the grand opening."

"New Orleans with Bethany, or a bar opening in Cheakamus. Weren't those your options? I don't blame you one bit. Still, I gotta say, The Peak's opening rivaled the best Louisiana soirée."

"I don't get why you're selling it. I thought it was a money maker."

Harris made a sharp left turn, and they bounced onto Timberline Road. "It is. But since Devon came along, Kate and I have almost no time for each other. I'm either at the office or the bar, and Kate has the ranch to run. Something's gotta go."

"Why not hire a bar manager? Wouldn't that free up time?"

"Not easy to find capable managers." Harris accelerated through the turn from Timberline Road onto Highway 41.

Gabe was quiet. Something didn't add up. If Harris needed to free some time, resigning the mayor's job was the obvious solution. Harris had implied the pay was minimal. Why would he hang on to a low-paying headache instead of a lucrative bar?

Before Gabe could ask, Harris said, "What's new with your investigation into Drake's murder?"

The question diverted Gabe's thoughts to the case that had kept him awake nights for the past year. Andover Drake, a misguided romantic, had stalked Bethany mercilessly until one day he turned up dead. Prime suspect: D. S. Gabrieli.

"The case is ice cold. I'm still digging, trying to find the people Drake pissed off enough to kill him."

"Why not let it go? Get on with your life."

"Because too many people doubt my innocence."

"Those who matter don't."

Gabe stared out the passenger window. Bethany mattered. He feared she was a doubter.

Chapter 11

HARRIS PARKED in front of The Peak, once more leaving his key in the ignition. "An easy walk from here to Greta's guesthouse."

Gabe eyed Lookout Road, dismayed by the thought of testing his aching knee against the steep pitch. "Yeah, a guy wouldn't even break a sweat."

Harris swung the main door open and waved Gabe across the threshold. "Welcome to The Peak."

Once through the door and foyer, Gabe paused at the entrance to the bar proper, cataloguing his first impressions: warm, intimate, roomy. He strolled the length of the room along the right side, between stand-up communal tables on his left and the benches and sit-down tables along the wall. The row of windows high above the bench seating caught the sun's last rays. Gabe nodded at a group of seniors seated at a table tucked into the back corner before making his way to the river rock fireplace in the center of the bar's rear wall.

Holding his still-frigid hands toward the fire's warmth, Gabe noted a wide, open entryway to his left. Above the arched entry, signs pointed the way to washrooms and the office.

He raised his eyes to the vaulted ceiling, trying to estimate the height by envisioning himself scaling the rocks fronting the fireplace to touch the massive beam running from the fireplace to the front entrance. How many body lengths? Four? So, twenty-five feet? Close enough.

He turned to study the bar from this far end, grateful for the fire warming his backside, and listening to the background sound of Fleetwood Mac. Grouped in front of the fireplace were three large couches and coffee tables. If Harris had thought to put a large screen TV on that river rock chimney, a guy could stretch out on one of these couches and spend some quality time with his favourite sports team. Then Gabe thought about how many beers six or eight men sitting on the couches could buy, compared to one lazy bum lolling around, and mentally removed the TV from the fireplace.

After a beat, he wandered back toward Harris, who still stood forty feet away at the entry, grinning like a proud poppa. Now the bulk of the stand-up tables were on Gabe's left, running down the center of the room. The business part of the room, the bar itself, occupied about twenty feet of the wall on Gabe's right. A sprinkling of patrons sat on the well-cushioned barstools, watching a baseball game on one of the television screens on the wall.

Gabe felt like he'd come home.

He rejoined Harris at the entrance. "Wow."

"You like it?" Harris said, grinning.

"If I owned this, I couldn't part with it."

They slid onto barstools at the polished mahogany bar. "Tom Mitchell," Harris said to the bartender, "meet my best buddy, D. S. Gabrieli. He might buy the place, so he's planning to put in a few shifts behind the bar to get a feel for the business. Don't worry—he knows how to tend a bar."

Gabe shook Tom's hand. The bartender was barely old enough to drink. Husky, fit, outdoorsman's coloring. Blue eyes.

A nose that said this kid might once have run into a door. Or a fist.

"Pleased to meet you, Mr. Gabrieli. What can I get you?"

"Coffee, black, and call me Gabe. Worked here long?"

Tom placed a mug of coffee on the bar. "About a year. Saving for college," he said, moving down the bar to collect empty pints.

Gabe sipped his coffee and winced.

"Want a burger while you're here?" Harris said.

Gabe's stomach growled. Afraid the food would be as bad as the coffee, he shook his head. "I'm good."

"Wouldn't you prefer a beer?"

"Yeah, but it's the annual Dreaded Month of Abstinence."

"You still do that?"

"Yep, just to prove I can. As they used to say in the barristers' lounge, if you can go an entire month without alcohol, you don't have a drinking problem."

Harris smiled. "Most lawyers choose a short month, like February."

"Yeah, call me a maverick. So, since the beginning of October, I've developed a taste for great coffee. The downside? I can't sleep."

Shortly before four o'clock, when Gabe was halfway through his coffee, a woman hurried in, waving at Harris, a wide, red-lipped smile on her face. Big blond hair; black, touch-me sweater; tight buns in smooth white jeans; a red leather tote slung over her left shoulder.

Harris introduced her as Cheryl McMillan, his realtor. She placed a manicured hand on Gabe's forearm. "*So good* to meet you. Buying The Peak is *the best* decision you'll ever make."

Gabe lifted his palms. "Whoa. I haven't decided anything. Still checking things over."

Rooting through her oversized tote, she breezed through his words. "You'll just *love* Cheakamus. There's *so much* to do here. Skiing, hiking, trail riding. Thousands of tourists visit in *both* summer and winter. We even have a dude ranch down the road. Are you an outdoorsman?"

If that included guys who planted their rears in lawn chairs and enjoyed a beer, Gabe qualified. "I've thought about hitting the trails."

"Oh, a mountain biker?"

"I'm allergic to things with pedals. I'm thinking more of an ATV."

"Findrich's Rentals has ATVs," Harris said. "Get one, and tomorrow we'll go out."

Cheryl handed Gabe her card and a pamphlet. "I *must* run. Here's a spec sheet. *Do* phone if you have questions or want to sign an offer. I'm available twenty-four-seven. Bye now."

Gabe watched her walk away; filed her under "Gusher, to be avoided."

When the street door sighed closed behind Cheryl, a short, balding fellow wandered over, beer in hand. "I heard about the body at TEG's site," he said to Harris. "Things are escalating. At least no one died when they blew up my operation."

That piqued Gabe's interest. He extended his hand. "Gabe Gabrieli."

"Horace Minken," the paunchy man said, shaking Gabe's hand.

"Horace owns Minken Minerals," Harris said. "He has that drill I pointed out on our pasture. Until recently he had another one at a site he leases on George Findrich's property north of town. *That* operation was the first one sabotaged."

Tom, the young bartender, approached with the coffee carafe. "Top up?"

Gabe shook his head and turned again to Minken. "Much damage?"

Minken shook his head in disgust. "Total loss. Blasted the core shack to smithereens, sprayed graffiti, trashed my core samples. The stupid amateurs even blew up some closed drill holes. They cleaned out my powder magazine."

"You lose much?"

"Exactly twenty-seven sticks. Enough to flatten several drills and core shacks." Minken's lips turned downward. "Cops have been useless. The day it happened they asked a few questions, took a buncha notes, some pictures. I've heard bugger-all since."

"When was this?"

Minken took a long pull of beer. "Last Sunday."

Tom Mitchell chimed in. "The next explosion was Wednesday at Fortune Gold's site east of town on Granite Mountain. Same thing. Core shack blown up, samples trashed. And their drill rig got blasted too. Horace here was luckier 'cause his driller had moved off site."

Minken snorted. "Luckier, Tom? Right. Now I gotta bring the driller back to re-do the core sampling tomorrow. It's gonna cost a wad."

Tom stammered. "I meant your guy's rig wasn't damaged."

"I know, kid." Minken sighed. "I'm just angry about everything. Whoever's doing this has it in for mining. It's tree huggers. No matter what we do, it ain't good enough for them."

Gabe said, "What makes you think it's an environmental group?"

"Two things." Minken raised his index finger. "First, they make a stink every chance they get, opposing permit applications, picketing exploration sites, you name it." His middle finger flicked upward. "Second, they plain look the type—pasty and geeky, like they spend all day in a basement building bombs. Huge clumps of too-long hair, stuck in ratty sausages, inviting God knows what to build nests."

After a slurp of beer, he added, "The sort of guys that if

my daughter brought one home for dinner, I'd go out to the barn and shoot myself."

Minken wore a grin as he spoke, but Gabe sensed steel beneath it. He knew the breed. Scores of crusty old guys like Minken hung out at his sister Lucy's bar back in Eau Claire, cursing millionaire hockey bums and federal politicians. He filed Minken under "Sources, definite."

"Let's hope she doesn't meet a tree hugger then," Gabe said, unconsciously running his hand over his close-cropped hair.

Minken studied him. "Don't know if you'd be any better, with that shiner and two-day beard. You look like trouble. I might not shoot myself if my daughter brought you home, but I'd be having a serious talk with her after you left. And make no mistake, you'd *definitely* be leaving."

Gabe raised his hands in mock surrender. "I'll check with you before I ask a woman for a date next time. In case she's your daughter."

Minken chuckled. "Deal." He turned to Harris. "Your buddy's okay."

"The best," Harris said.

"Must be interesting work, looking for gold, hey?" Gabe said.

"I think it is," Horace said. "Would you like a taste of it? My driller's coming back tomorrow, so I could show you how exploring for gold works."

Gabe mentally pumped a fist. Exactly what he'd hoped Horace would do—give Gabe an opportunity to compare the damage at Minken Mineral's site to the firebombed TEG site. "That sounds good. When?"

"Meet me tomorrow around one o'clock at Findrich Ranch."

———

AFTER MINKEN GAVE Gabe detailed directions to his exploration site on Findrich Ranch, Gabe and Harris strolled west along Main Street toward Findrich's Gear in search of a warmer jacket for Gabe. Through the windows of Tiffany's, Gabe spotted Rhonda behind the counter. The young ebony-haired barista and a teenaged boy cruised the tables, armed with bus tubs. "Rhonda's kids?" he said, gesturing at the café.

"Yeah. David is Jack's age. Roxanne's a year-and-a-bit younger."

Gabe sized up the crowd. "Is Tiffany's the go-to place for dinner?"

"There's also The Peak for bar food, the Red Dragon for Chinese, Ouzo for Greek and pizza. And, if you want a beer with your waffles, Jerry's Flapjacks & Lounge."

They crossed the intersection of Main and Prince Street and passed the *Cheakamus Journal* office. "Findrich's Gear is two doors ahead," Harris said. "George Findrich's on town council with me. Solid, business-headed guy."

"Same guy who has Findrich's Rentals?"

"Yeah. He'd be worth talking to—used to be the town doctor until he decided he'd rather deal with cars or skis. Owns several businesses in town, keeps his finger on what's happening."

The clerk in Findrich's Gear sold Gabe a black down-filled, water-repellent jacket, guaranteed for mountain wear. "Exactly what's needed," Gabe said, "when dragging one's butt around high, rocky places."

Gabe hitched a ride back to Greta Rocque's guesthouse with Harris and was halfway out of the vehicle when his phone rang, the display flashing "Andrews." His heart jumped. "Gotta take this, Harris. Call me in the morning."

He answered the call as Harris pulled away. "Ciao, bella."

"Ciao, is this a bad time?" Bethany said in her low, warm voice that made Gabe's chest ache with both desire and loss.

"Never. Are you still in Italy?"

"At the apartment in Florence. Packed and ready to catch the train to Fumicello. A week in London, then home and back at work."

"It's been a long year, babe. Can't wait to see you."

"Gabe?"

She spoke his name slowly.

Instantly he could see her, in the aftermath of the wild cow milking contest at a rainy Eau Claire Rodeo so many years ago, the backside of her jeans and shirt blue, the fronts streaked wet and brown with mud. "You shoulda dropped the rope," he'd said, "instead of letting the cow drag you."

She'd laughed and said, "Where's the fun in that?" Then she'd run full tilt and leaped on him, toppling him to the ground. They rolled in the arena's mud, the rodeo crowd cheering its approval. She straddled him, wiped a smear of dirt from her cheek, and acknowledged the crowd's applause before gazing at him, her expression soft. "Gabe? You love me?" His name came out then with the same slow cadence as it did now. And he'd answered, "Marry me, bella."

"Gabe? When I get home, let's talk."

The memory snapped away. "Sure. I hoped we could."

"Here's my cab. See you soon. Ciao."

"Okay. Love you," he said to an empty line.

Chapter 12

IF THE ROCQUE RIVER was named for Pierre Rocque, Gabe figured Lookout Road was named for Pierre's widow. Greta stood at her living room window, phone to her ear, watching him. He waved and continued along the side of the house, onto the garden path, through the garage side door, and upstairs to the apartment. Seven minutes and fifteen seconds later, he'd unpacked, beating his previous record of eight minutes and twenty-three seconds.

Concentrating on the mundane task of organizing his belongings calmed him, enabled him to seal away the jumble of want, frustration, and hurt that Bethany's calls always left behind. "I need space," she'd said. Space: a polite term for separation. It wasn't far from separation to divorce, the thought of which always took the sun out of Gabe's sky.

Now, however, for the first time in a year, their conversation gave him hope. A week, she'd said. They'd talk. Surely that was a positive sign.

Meanwhile, he was in Cheakamus with a case to solve. Unlike Drake's murder (and if he ignored the temperature at the top of Rimrock) this one was far from cold. He hummed a Dylan tune and opened his laptop, planning to do some online research before he went in search of dinner. He was grateful for the internet: it took the shoe out of gumshoe.

When he phoned Greta and asked for the wifi codes, she said, "The network is Rockhound, and the password is 'allthatglitters,' lowercase, no spaces. The wireless shouldn't give you problems. Ed set it up."

"Ed Gwinn?"

"The one and only. Call me biased, but that man is Indiana Jones. Suave, educated, travels to exotic, dangerous places. Once, they had to airlift him out of Hells Canyon after a fall. He still limps from the broken leg. Quirky too. He loves computers but won't use a cell phone."

"Sounds like someone I'd enjoy meeting. Expect him back soon?"

"Oh, no. When he left last week, he planned to drive to Nevada for another job, then take a vacation in Spain."

Gabe ended the call and exhaled in frustration. Of course, the guy wouldn't have a cell phone. Of course, he'd be on the road. A sure sign The Frikkin Comedian was awake and meddling.

In his small black notebook, Gabe started his "check into" list: Gwinn, Fortune Gold, Minken Minerals, TEG Mines.

When he researched Greta's Indiana Jones online, he discovered Gwinn had a PhD in geology. He'd written one textbook and reams of articles, including some about mining's environmental impact. A modest website promoted his services as an independent evaluator. Gwinn's picture on the home page showed a grinning, rugged, fiftyish man leaning against a yellow ATV. He didn't look one bit like Harrison Ford.

After Gabe sent a "please call" email to Gwinn's contact address, he scanned newspaper clippings posted on Gwinn's website. One highlighted Gwinn's testimony as a gold expert in a recent trial. It would be worthwhile to talk to him, Gabe thought, before closing Gwinn's website and turning his attention to the local sabotage victims.

Gabe's search revealed scant information. Minken Minerals and Fortune Gold, the first two sabotage targets, were public companies. Neither had been in trouble with the securities commission. Their websites revealed no common links. TEG Mines, the most recent bombing victim, was a cipher. No information at all.

Unbelievably, Google was letting him down. The sole link among the three companies Gabe could see was that they all had exploration drills in the Cheakamus area. He crossed the three names off his list.

Gabe sat in the recliner by the balcony slider and watched the sky above the mountains change from a jumble of puffed cotton to an extravaganza of orange swirls and pink foam. Barely five o'clock, and the sun had ducked behind the ridges to the west. Not only winter came early in the mountains.

The sane part of him wanted to leave the case to LeBlanc and the Mounties. They always got their man. Let them get this one. But the police suspected Jack had something to do with the explosions. And, the sabotage and its effect on Cheakamus gnawed at Harris. Only jerks turned their backs on family and friends.

His stomach grumbled, reminding Gabe he needed dinner. From the possibilities Harris had listed, Gabe narrowed the contenders to The Peak and Tiffany's. He tossed a coin. Despite his conviction the burgers would be inedible, it landed in favor of The Peak.

Gabe lingered in the recliner, juggling the purple rock and watching the sky trade its crimson garb for dark slate evening wear. He took stock of the day. One burned shack—arson. One overcooked corpse—probably Aldercott, the owner of TEG Mines. That thought made Gabe leap from the chair and return to the computer. Although TEG was a cipher, maybe Aldercott was not.

After fifteen minutes, Gabe added Aldercott to the list in his notebook and marveled at how parsimonious the internet could be. The information about the man was dull to the point of ho-hum. A professional geologist; graduated from the University of British Columbia in 1990; gained the expected and unimaginative nickname; played high school sports but not varsity. He was intelligent—at university he'd made the dean's list and a couple coaches praised him for tutoring college athletes. Not Gwinn smart, but no schmuck. An uneventful life. Until its ending.

A shudder rippled along Gabe's spine. Imagine being in your core shack counting rocks or doing whatever it was gold explorers did there and kaplooey, you were seeing wings and hearing harps.

Gabe pushed thoughts of death away and continued his inventory of the day: bad blood between miners (or at least Minken) and environmental groups; a newspaper guy who had serious issues with Harris; a Mountie who gave new meaning to zipper lips. While none of those surprised him, there were three things that did.

Surprise number one: Jack as a suspect. If all the RCMP had was graffiti and a history of school hijinks, their case was weak. But feeble cases could ruin a guy's life as easily as strong ones. Case in point: D. S. Gabrieli, former riding-high lawyer, now part-time bartender, part-time private eye, full-time scraping by.

Surprises two and three: the money-machine Peak being for sale and Kate raising Percherons. Gabe had no answer for the sale of the bar but suspected there was more to the story than Harris was telling. He chalked the Percherons up to Kate's genes. Her father, Seamus O'Malley, raised rodeo stock. But Percherons? When people lived in sod huts, Percherons helped pull stumps, plow fields. Today, what good were they except for hauling wagons in parades?

After another "hey, remember me?" twinge from his stomach, Gabe grabbed his jacket and headed downstairs to his truck. His mouth watered as he pictured The Peak and envisioned a pint of beer, foam gliding down its side. His choirboy self, the part of him that kept track of worthy accomplishments, reminded him of his no-booze-in-October vow. He hadn't consumed alcohol for fourteen days, fifteen hours. Give or take. "A record not to be sniffed at," Choirboy said. "You should go to Tiffany's."

As Gabe backed his truck out of the garage, his screw-it self reminded him he missed the bite of beer as it traveled down his throat.

After exactly two minutes and fourteen seconds of an energized debate between Choirboy and Screw-it, Choirboy won by pointing out the pitch of Lookout Road. "Have a beer and it's a steep hike home. One your knee will hate."

Gabe sighed. Tiffany's it would be.

Gabe parked and went inside the café. Rhonda was alone, the rush evidently over. He checked out the coffees listed on the antique mirror. It was a tough choice between Red Sea Blend—*winey, like a good red*, and Prince of Darkness—*hearty, snappy, bold*. He opted for Red Sea Blend.

"I can usually guess which coffee a customer will choose," Rhonda said, when Gabe sat at the counter. "For you, I would've bet on Prince of Darkness."

"Any other time you'd be right. I *am* your basic hearty, snappy, bold guy. But Harris Chilton dragged me around the mountains all day and beat those traits out of me."

"Are you looking for dinner?"

When Gabe nodded, she said, "Give me one reason I should feed you."

"I'm hungry?" Gabe searched Rhonda's face for her usual grin and found a frown. His inner voice said, "Uh-oh, this could be trouble."

"So, this morning, when you walked out on my cooking, *twice*, you weren't hungry?"

Yep, definitely in trouble here. "Awww, believe me, I never woulda done it except for Harris." Not really a lie. Harris had been involved both times.

Rhonda shook her head. "When my kids were little, they did that. Blamed someone else."

"All us five-year-olds do it." He clasped his hands together. "I promise to behave myself. Please feed me?"

Rhonda laughed. "I don't buy that whimper either. Kitchen's closed, but I can make you a sandwich."

"Roast beef?"

While he waited, Gabe opened the *Journal* someone had abandoned on the next stool. He read about an unfortunate soul nabbed while sneaking into the United States through a mountain pass. The fourth episode in six months, apparently. Gabe considered the money an entrepreneur could make selling fake IDs to the border-jumping crowd, and then turned to the announcements: children's horse-drawn wagon rides at the Evergold Museum open house and fundraiser from Wednesday to Saturday; free u-pick Halloween pumpkins at Findrich Ranch; elections for mayor and town council in November.

Rhonda plunked his sandwich on the counter. Brown bread, like Gabe remembered his grandmother making, cradled folds of rare roast beef, lettuce, red onion and tomato. He bit into the sandwich, and Dijon mustard bit back. Fabulous.

"Wanna marry me?" Gabe said.

"Got a husband," Rhonda said.

"Wanna adopt me?"

"Got kids already. Much as I love 'em, I'm not looking for more."

"Well, hell."

"You're visiting Harris and Kate?"

Gabe nodded around a mouthful of sandwich. "I might

buy the bar so I'll be hanging around, checking things out. And I'm gonna be godfather to their daughter next week."

"You must have known them a long time."

"Harris, since kindergarten. Kate, about nine years." Gabe tapped the election announcement in the paper. "Do you think Harris will be re-elected?"

Rhonda shrugged. "Before this trouble began, I would've said definitely. Now, he could lose."

"Why's that?"

Rhonda moved to the fridge to put away the sandwich makings. "Jacobson says a good mayor would stop the sabotage and save Cheakamus from economic ruin. Every day more people echo that view."

"Politics, eh? Go figure." Gabe snatched the opening she'd presented. "Who d'you think is responsible for the bombings?"

Rhonda closed the fridge and returned to the counter. "Dunno, but I hope the cops catch him fast."

"Is business hurting?"

She shrugged. "It's only been a week. However, now someone's dead, which could scare people away. We depend on tourism. If skiers go elsewhere...."

They talked a while longer about nothing much and then Gabe finished his sandwich, put ten dollars on the counter, and said goodnight. Outside, the air was crisp. Definitely fall and moving quickly toward winter. Laughter wafted across the street. The Peak's warm lights made promises every hurting, angry, or lonely soul wanted to hear. Gabe hesitated with his hand on his driver's door.

Chapter 13

FOR HIS COVER story to ring true, Gabe needed to spend time in Harris's bar. Something that was never a hardship. He crossed the street.

The Peak was warm, noisy, and smelled of beer and wood smoke. Tom Mitchell and two waitresses hustled to keep up with the orders. Gabe asked, "Need help?"

Tom tossed over an apron. "Thanks."

Working behind a bar in Cheakamus didn't differ from working at his sister's bar, The Diamond Lucy, in Alberta. Keeping one eye on the Yankees game on the flat-screen TV above the bar, Gabe slipped into the easy rhythm of pulling pints.

A linebacker-sized man perched on a barstool caught Gabe's eye, raised his pint in a weathered hand, and said, "Carl Dochmann. You must be Gabrieli. Tom said you might buy this place."

"Call me Gabe." He placed five Irish coffee glasses in a line along the bar and grabbed a handful of sugar cubes from the container on the shelf. He surveyed the crowd. Mostly locals, he'd bet. Tourists usually kept to themselves, their eyes traveling the room. Judging by the easy banter and table-hopping, this bunch knew each other. "If the bar's always this busy, it looks like a superb investment."

"I considered buying the Peak for a nanosecond," Carl said. "Until I remembered that all I know about bars is how to sit at one. So, I'm sticking with what I do best."

Gabe moved to a spot three feet from the glasses on the bar. "Which is?"

"Carl runs Solomon's Choice Ranch," Tom said. "Big resort outside of town."

"Oh right, the ranch near the firebombed exploration site."

Carl raised his eyebrows. "For a visitor, you know a lot about the area."

Gabe tossed a sugar cube into the first glass. Then fired four more, in rapid succession, sinking a cube in each of the four remaining glasses.

"Whoa," Carl said. "Is that luck or talent?"

"Talent," Gabe said. "I know about the ranch because I was with Harris Chilton today. I tagged along when he checked out the damage."

"Find out anything interesting?" Carl drained his pint.

Gabe shook his head. "Cops weren't sharing. Invited us to leave. That ranch is yours?"

"I wish. No, Sol Phoebus owns it. I merely manage it. We host corporate retreats, trail rides, wilderness experiences, that kind of thing." Carl pushed his empty pint forward. "Let me have another. Rickard's Red."

Gabe pulled the pint. "But it ain't no dude ranch."

Carl's laugh boomed out. "You musta had the special at Tiffany's. I don't care what people call us, so long as they book a stay."

"These explosions have me worried about buying a business here. Who do you think's behind them?"

Carl shrugged. "Best guess? Someone who hates mining. Environmentalists, maybe."

"Aren't there others who want mining gone? Businesses that depend on tourism, say?"

Carl sipped his beer. "Our resort depends on tourism, but we're okay with mining. They don't put their drill rigs or mine shafts on our riding trails. In fact, some companies have built fresh trails. Saves us doing it."

"Rhonda at Tiffany's Café is worried tourists might be afraid to visit."

"Me too. You'd think tourists would realize all three targets were exploration sites so they could stay safe by avoiding places with drill rigs sitting on them." Carl nodded hello to Bill Jacobson as he planted himself on a nearby stool.

"If I was a tourist," Carl continued, "I'd worry more if the targets were random, because then I'd never know where danger might be. But tell that to the guests who've canceled their bookings. We're almost empty—only one brave soul still renting a cabin. If our chef didn't have a catering sideline, we'd be desperate."

The rush had calmed somewhat when the street door banged open. Two young guys entered and slouched over to the bar, sliding onto barstools between Carl Dochmann and Bill Jacobson.

Gabe pitched more sugar cubes into glasses and assessed the newcomers' basic corporate-hemp image—plain flannel shirts over cargo pants, short hair, black eyeglasses à la Oliver Peoples. "Got some ID, fellas?"

The taller one chewed on a toothpick and eyed Gabe. "You're kidding, right?"

"Nope. I card everyone who appears to be under thirty. No ID, no service."

"Tom knows us. Tell him we're legal, Tom."

The young bartender pulled his eyes away from the TV and shook his head. "Gabe might buy the bar. Then he'd be my boss. I don't want to cross him."

"For Chrissake," Toothpick said. "How lame is that?" He slapped his driver's license on the bar.

Gabe studied it. "Craig Westburg. Twenty-three, from North Bay. Welcome to The Peak."

"Twenty-two. Testing me or bad at math?"

"Honest mistake." Gabe studied the second ID. "Frank Palmer. Nanton, Alberta. Hey, that's near my hometown. What'll you guys have?"

He pulled their pints of Molson Canadian and placed them on the bar, then took a moment to watch Jeter hit one into left field. "Maybe twenty million bucks a year he makes. I shoulda played more Little League."

Craig from North Bay laughed. "Dream on. Almost nobody gets to the majors from Canada."

"Yeah, slight flaw in my plan."

Gabe alternated between tossing sugar cubes and watching the ball game. When the inning ended, he said, "How does a guy from Nanton, Alberta end up in Cheakamus with a guy from North Bay, Ontario?"

"Skiing," Frank said at the same time as Craig said, "College."

"Which is it? Skiing or college?"

"Both," Craig said. "We met at UBC and used to come here to ski Blackstrap Mountain."

"You work at the ski hill now?"

Craig snorted and shook his head. "No way. I run Earth First, an environmental defense fund." Frank nodded his head and slurped his beer.

Gabe's antennae quivered. He wondered how much offense they put into their defense of the environment. "Really? What does your fund do?"

"We raise money to invest in green businesses," Craig said. Frank nodded, slurped.

To see if they were legit, Gabe said, "Got any brochures?

My sister is into environmental causes. She might want to invest."

Craig straightened on his barstool and flashed a white grin, his interest obviously heightened by the mention of money. "Tons of brochures. In fact, come visit us. Bryson Road, southeast of town. There's a big Earth First sign. Can't miss it."

"I might do that. Are you worried about the bombings?"

"Nah," Craig said. "No drills on our land."

Frank nodded his agreement.

"I heard some people think environmentalists are responsible. It could be all talk, but suppose someone strikes back?"

Frank looked at Craig, wide-eyed, and took a long swallow of his beer.

Craig folded his arms and leaned back. "I'm not worried."

Frank nodded his head, a shade slower this time.

————

It was closing in on ten o'clock, the ball game had ended, and the bar was thinning out when Harris showed up. "Thought I'd catch up on paperwork. How's business?"

"Steady," Tom said. "Gabe helped with the rush. Did you know he can plunk a sugar cube into an Irish coffee glass from five feet?"

Harris shook his head. "No. When'd you add that to your resumé, Gabe?"

Gabe lined up ten glasses, backed up, and fired sugar cubes into each of them. No misses. "About a year ago. Going for a Guinness Record."

Tom laughed. "Gotta say, Gabe's one hell of a bartender."

"Law's loss is the bar's gain."

"What? Gabe's a lawyer?"

"Once upon a time. And a skilled one," Harris said, before

pouring himself coffee and disappearing through the archway at the back of the bar. Gabe watched him go, thinking that things must really be piling up if Harris did paperwork late at night. When Kate and Harris moved to Cheakamus, it was to realize their dream of a simpler life. Yet now they had the ranch, a growing herd of horses, a busy bar, and a three-month-old daughter. Plus, Harris was mayor and still practiced law. The simpler life seemed complicated. If Harris asked him for advice, Gabe would say keep the ranch and the bar, lose the law practice and public office. Answer to no one but yourself.

"Why did you give up being a lawyer?" Tom said.

"It stopped being fun."

Gabe checked the customers to see who wanted refills. Carl Dochmann, the manager of the dude ranch, seemed happy to nurse the last of his pint. The town journalist, Bill Jacobson, stroked his B-Movie beard and regarded Gabe with a quizzical expression. "Need another?" Gabe said.

Jacobson shook his head and pushed his glass forward. "Nope, I'm done."

Gabe fought back a yawn. "Me too. Long day." He removed his apron. "Catch you all later."

"I think I'll call it a night too," Carl said, clapping Gabe on the shoulder as they walked to the door.

After he climbed into his truck, Gabe rubbed his shoulder where Carl had whacked him. The size of a linebacker, and the power too. Running a dude ranch wasn't for weaklings.

Chapter 14

IN THE APARTMENT above Greta's garage, Gabe did his nightly pushups. Fifty. Then ten more to prove he could.

When he tossed his workout gear in the closet, he noticed an orange cat hair on his suit jacket.

Doofus.

The obstinate, haughty cat, which Bethany had christened Rufus, was almost all Gabe had left from his marriage.

Eighteen months ago in Calgary, he'd had Bethany, Doofus and Tornado Callie. A ranch and a law practice. Then Drake, Bethany's relentless stalker, got himself killed. The moment the police charged Gabe with Drake's murder, Gabe's law practice slid into the trash. Clients shunned him, many immediately, others after a minimal grace period. By then he just cared about saving his own hide. When Harris worked his magic and the prosecutor stayed the charges, Gabe thought the worst was over.

He expelled his breath in disgust. How naïve was that? The worst had merely begun. Bethany looked at him with questioning, fearful eyes. Drake's murder remained unsolved. People remembered only that Gabe, and no one else, had been charged. Bethany couldn't seem to get past the suspicion that surrounded him.

Six months after Drake's death, saying she needed space, Bethany accepted a year-long assignment as her network's foreign correspondent in Europe.

And in a flash, Gabe went from having a life to barely hanging on. The next months were ones of treading water, watching dust multiply like rabbits in the corners of the bedroom. He spent more time in bars than in a house that held only one ornery cat, more time downing Scotch than grooming a lonely, gentle horse.

Harris came to the rescue, just as he'd done ever since Mean Jeanie tried to pound Gabe's four-year-old behind. He helped Gabe deal with the separation, dragged him out of bars when he threatened to take on bikers, and wound up his law practice. Finally, when the ranch and house had to go, Doofus the ornery feline stayed with Gabe. Tornado Callie got the better deal and moved to Cheakamus to live with Harris and Kate.

Gabe shook himself out of his reverie. He loaded a Dylan CD and logged onto the internet. The website for Solomon's Choice Ranch—the dude ranch that wasn't a dude ranch—revealed Solomon Phoebus opened the resort fifteen years ago and soon added Etta Clayton as chef. Carl Dochmann joined the team a decade ago, after running an outdoor adventure company for several years. Carl's bio mentioned a physical education degree in 1989 from UBC.

Gabe researched all three of the dude ranch group—Sol, Etta and Carl—and found nothing except articles from the university paper celebrating Carl's skills as a quarterback: smarts, agility, and a great arm. "Nicknamed 'The Doc' for the surgical precision of his passes," one article said, "Dochmann was expected to win a seat on the pro football train but a shoulder injury this season has derailed him."

Yawning, Gabe shut down his computer. Remembering

the cat hair, he draped his suit over the desk chair, ready for the cleaners in the morning. Perhaps he'd also visit a shoeshine joint, he decided, but when he looked for his dress shoes, he found only sneakers and cowboy boots.

He phoned Lucy, his younger sister. Lucy (two years Gabe's junior) and Jack (eighteen years his junior) were products of Gabe's mother's sole marriage, which ended when Jack was two. Technically, Lucy and Jack were Gabe's half siblings. Technically, Gabe was illegitimate. If a person cared about technicalities, which he didn't.

The background noise when Lucy answered the phone told him she was at The Diamond Lucy, her bar back home in Eau Claire. "Hey, Luce. How are things?"

"Rufus hasn't peed on my floor yet, if that's what you're asking."

"Nah. I'm not concerned. As cat-sitters go, Doofus thinks you're okay."

"Don't call him that. He'll get a complex."

"Cats don't get complexes, they give them. I found a cool purple rock for you. It'll make a great paperweight."

"It's gonna cost you more than a rock if Rufus pees on my floors."

Gabe grinned. "Doofus is way too smart for that. He knows you'll cut off his treats."

"That's the least of what I'll cut off."

Gabe winced and crossed his legs. "He's fixed."

"Details. Seen Jack yet?"

"Yep." After a pause, he said, "Now, don't fret. It will all be okay, but you know the sabotage that's been going on around here? The cops think Jack had something to do with it."

"What?" Lucy's voice rose. "You're kidding. Does Mom know?"

"Not so far. Can you call her?" Gabe then gave Lucy the high- and lowlights of the day, calmed her concerns about

Jack, and asked her to ship his dress shoes. "I need them for the christening."

"It still amazes me you're the godfather. I mean, seriously, you?" She was grinning. He could hear it in her voice.

"Harris says Devon needs an upstanding man to advise and guide her."

"And since Abraham Lincoln is dead, he opted for you?"

"Yeah. First, I'm a man. Second, I'm upstanding. Except when I'm lying down, nyuk nyuk nyuk."

"Gawd, that's terrible."

"It's the altitude. Makes me light-headed."

"How are things going, otherwise?"

"I'm unofficially looking into the case. I have no suspects and no possibles. I've discovered the best coffee in the country and a short-order cook who should be on the Food Network. I convinced a couple newbie environmental fundraisers you might invest in their cause. I'm living above the garage of a woman who's Mae West in yoga gear. And not the least of it, I'm a relief bartender in the best bar in town."

"The Peak, Harris's bar?"

"Yep. Guess what? He's selling it."

"Whaaaaat? Why?"

"Beats me. It's a license to print money. I just worked a shift there, trying to pry confessions out of the mouths of the patrons."

"And?"

"And bupkis. I'm heading to bed. Don't worry about Jack. Don't forget the shoes."

He ended the call smiling. Lucy never failed to lift his spirits. Her sarcasm hid a deep well of caring. He sat in the recliner and stared at the warm, lighted windows and street-lamps of the town below. Cheakamus resembled a greeting card picture that made him wish he could insert himself into the scene—assuming he could ignore the facts that the mountains smothered the horizon, the altitude made him giddy, and

Doofus didn't travel well. And that Tornado Callie lived here and made his soul ache.

Gabe pushed out of the chair and readied for bed. He had one foot under the covers when his phone rang, the display showing: "K. Chilton."

"Hi, Kate."

"Feel like coming for dinner tomorrow?"

"Absolutely. I'm glad you called. I wanted to ask about Jack. Does he seem his usual self to you?"

She was quiet for a moment. "I know he's had a few run-ins with my father. It isn't always easy living with Dad. *And* trying to fit in at a new school. But Jack seems okay. Why?"

"I think he was hungover this morning."

"Mmmm. Teens always experiment with booze."

"I guess. Speaking of liquor, I'm surprised you're selling The Peak."

"I don't want Harris to sell it. I hope there's another solution. More time would be good."

"He could give up the mayor's job. That would free up time."

"Huh? That won't extend the deadline."

"What deadline?"

Kate sucked in her breath. "Nothing. I was thinking about something else entirely. I hear the baby. Tomorrow, seven-ish?"

After Kate clicked off, Gabe sat staring at his phone. What deadline?

SUNDAY

Chapter 15

SUNDAY MORNING ARRIVED on the tail of a fierce storm that had roared through Cheakamus overnight, rattling windows, shearing branches, and dumping snow in the mountains and slush in the valley. When Gabe squinted at the view through the balcony slider, he regretted leaving his fleece-lined gloves at home in Eau Claire.

Harris phoned just as Gabe finished shaving.

"Hey, Harris," Gabe said. "What's up?"

"A couple things. First, Sergeant 'Too Early to Tell' LeBlanc invited me to a meeting with everyone from the exploration companies to discuss security measures. Second, Kate says you need to meet Reverend Beam when he returns. Nicole Mitchell too, the godmother."

Gabe gritted his teeth. No meeting with clergy was without an inquisition. "Why?"

"Merely passing on what Kate told me. Protocol or something."

"Protocol. Save me. Okay, whenever the minister wants to meet god-mama Nancy and me, I can spare five minutes."

"Nicole. Reverend Beam needs to meet *you*, not Nicole. He

already knows her, thinks she'll be a perfect godmother. It's Kate who wants you to meet Nicole."

"Poor Devon. Having someone a minister calls perfect as her godmother means she'll get nothing but grief. Fortunately, you have me to counterbalance Nora."

"Nicole. Stop jerking around."

"Whatever. Let me know when the reverend's inquisition is scheduled and what happens at your meeting with the cops. Meanwhile, I'm going to rent an ATV, get Jack to show me his graffiti handiwork, and tour Horace Minken's drill site out at Findrich's ranch. Then maybe you and I can hit a few trails."

"Ambitious plan. Call me when you're done with Minken, and I'll meet you at Deception Ridge Viewpoint."

———

GABE PHONED his mother in Eau Claire. "I thought I'd check in," he said, when Mercy answered. "Did Lucy tell you about Jack?"

"Yes. I'm worried sick. Unfortunately, I have to take care of a few urgent things here today. I plan to leave for Cheakamus early tomorrow morning. I should be there by mid-afternoon. Thank heaven you're there, Sunny."

"Mom."

"Yes?"

"Please. Please don't call me Sunny."

"What should I call you? Des?"

"Gabe. Just call me Gabe. Everyone else does."

"*Desert Sun Gabrieli.* Everyone else is not your mother. Everyone else did not choose your name to remind them of beautiful, serene vistas." She paused for a breath before rushing on. "Now. I've told Jack the rules. Last night was the first I heard of his extracurricular activities. Frankly, I don't mind the protests. I did a fair bit of protesting in my day too. But I'm very upset about the graffiti. It all makes him look like a good suspect. It's imperative Jack can prove his whereabouts if there are more explosions. I told him to have someone with him at all times unless he's at Seamus's ranch or at Harris and Kate's. No riding solo except within sight of someone I trust."

"Sounds like house arrest."

"Better that than the real thing. I'll text you when I arrive tomorrow, Sunny." Mercy disconnected.

Why did he even try to get her to stop with the name? Gabe pocketed his phone and decided to pick up breakfast-to-go from Tiffany's before meeting Jack. On the shelves in Greta's garage he found a well-used pair of heavy-duty garden gloves, a size too large for him. Gloves in hand, he trudged the walkway to the house. Greta opened the back door and waved before he reached midpoint. Hound stuck his nose out the door, sniffed the air, and backed away.

Today Greta wore a black jacket and tailored slacks. A fuzzy black hat hid most of her hair. The unmistakable uniform of church.

"Morning," Gabe said. "I'm going to the wilds today. I'm guessing these gloves belonged to Pierre. Could I borrow them until I buy a pair?"

"Of course. Where are you going?"

"Rimrock. Sightseeing."

She glanced at his boots. "Last night's storm was fierce. Want to borrow Pierre's snow boots?"

"Nah, I'm good."

"Got binoculars?"

Yes, Gabe thought, in the same Eau Claire closet as his winter gloves. He shook his head.

She let out a theatrical sigh. "You can't see sights without binoculars. You'll miss the details. I'll lend you mine."

When she returned with the binoculars, she said, "I have an hour before church. Stay and chat."

"Another time, Greta. I'm grabbing breakfast on the run, then heading off."

Her face fell.

Choirboy nudged Gabe. "Then again," Gabe said, "if your church is close to the café, why don't I treat you to a cup of Rhonda's coffee?"

A wide smile creased Greta's face. "Let me grab my coat."

———

AT TIFFANY's, Gabe poured their coffees and followed Greta to a booth. Rhonda dropped menus on the table. "If he's buying," she said to Greta, "I recommend the steak and eggs." To Gabe: "If Greta's buying, you can have coffee. No refills."

He pointed to the bottom of the menu. "Refills are free. But I *am* buying."

Bill Jacobson entered the café, poured a coffee, and approached their booth. Gabe kept his expression neutral.

"Morning, *Dee Ess.* Mind if I join you?" Jacobson slid into Greta's side of the booth before anyone could answer. He shouted across the café. "Help me, Rhonda. The usual."

When he focused his attention on Greta and Gabe once more, Jacobson stroked his pitch-black beard. "Imagine you two knowing each other."

Gabe blew on his coffee and took a sip, ignoring Jacobson's words. If Greta was correct about the town's grapevine, Jacobson must know Gabe had rented her suite. Unless his head was stuck far, far up his butt. Which no doubt was the case.

Greta sighed. "I might as well tell you, Bill. You'll find out soon enough. Gabe's my illegitimate son."

Gabe coughed into his napkin. Jacobson sat motionless, his mouth open. He swiveled his head from Greta, to Gabe, and back again. Gabe studied the polished wood tabletop and coughed again.

Greta reached over to pat Gabe's hand. "I'm sorry. I know you wanted this to be our little secret."

Gabe cleared his throat, took a swig of coffee, and nodded at her. The effort not to laugh made his eyes water. He wiped at them.

"Why's Gabe crying?" Rhonda said, placing Jacobson's order on the table.

"I confessed to Bill that Gabe's my illegitimate son. It upset him."

"Ahhh. That would do it."

Jacobson eyed them. He broke off a piece of toast and speared a sunny-side egg. Yellow oozed out. "If you're his mother, Greta, you can tell me what *Dee Ess* stands for."

"Dry Sack," Gabe said.

"Dip Stick," Greta said. Gabe smiled. Greta caught on fast.

"Dumb Shit," Rhonda said and walked away. Rhonda was no slouch in the catching-on department either.

Jacobson sopped up his egg and chewed. Greta and Gabe concentrated on their coffees.

"You're having me on."

Greta nodded, her eyes downcast. "I fibbed. I'm not his mother." She drank some coffee, then said, "But I do know his name. It's Dithering Sycophant. I'm deadly serious."

Gabe laughed out loud. "Damn straight."

Jacobson harrumphed and pushed his plate away. "Fine, be that way." He tossed money on the table and slid out of the booth. "All I'm doing is showing interest."

———

AFTER GRETA LEFT FOR CHURCH, Gabe poured an extra-large Mudshark to go and studied the oversized muffins in the display case.

"Not staying for breakfast?" Rhonda said.

"No time, lots to do today. Besides, if I take it with me, I might get to eat it." Gabe eyed the muffins. "Help me—" He stopped mid-sentence when he heard Rhonda's sharp intake of breath, and glanced at her.

Her hands were planted on her hips and her eyes shot daggers. "I swear if you say it, I will ban you from Tiffany's."

"What? Say what?"

"You know."

Gabe stared at her.

"Don't make me say it. That song. The one Bill uses every time he orders."

The light dawned. Gabe made a mental note—file Rhonda under "Hater, California music."

He nodded and said, "As I was saying, can you point out a good muffin? Something with more flavor than bran."

Rhonda smiled. "You bet."

By ten o'clock Gabe had a peach-cranberry muffin stashed in the truck's cab and a rented ATV strapped down in the bed. He loaded a CD, waited for Dylan's distinctive drawl, and pulled away from Findrich's Rentals.

Gabe drove under the arch welcoming him to O'Malley's Preferred Stock just as he took the last bite of Rhonda's muffin. He licked his fingers. With food like this on offer, Rhonda's husband must weigh five hundred pounds.

By the time Gabe parked in front of O'Malley's house, Jack was on the veranda, shrugging into a jacket. Gabe got out of the truck and said, "I talked to Mercy. She's coming to Cheakamus. She'll be here tomorrow."

"She's totally mad at me."

"Yep. Also afraid for you. She spent ten minutes telling me you're grounded. Just listening to her got me all worn out." Gabe tossed the key fob over. "You drive."

Jack's face lit up. He settled in the driver's seat and conducted a painstaking inspection of the controls. After watching for several minutes, Gabe said, "Tower to Jacko. Driveway niner, niner. Clear to take off."

They spent two hours touring Jack's graffiti at three sites: a closed sawmill near the US border, ancient railcars on a disused siding north of Cheakamus, and an abandoned smelter beside the Rocque River. When Gabe finished snapping pictures at the smelter, he said, "Let's sit for a minute. I need to rest my knee."

He limped to a weathered picnic table under a clump of birch trees and sat on its top, planting his boots on the wood bench. Massaging his right knee, he watched a log float down the slow-moving river that curved past the smelter and nearby slag pile. "Mom's pretty upset about the graffiti. How'd Seamus react?"

"About how you'd expect." Jack stomped in a circle, waving his arms as he spoke. "Seamus bellowed, '*Cheeez-ussss.*' Then he made three circuits of the kitchen, asked the saints to preserve us all, and in his pretending-to-be-someone-who-cares voice threatened to ground me. Which Mom had already done."

Gabe chuckled. "Sounds just like the guy."

Jack joined Gabe atop the picnic table. "What happened to your knee?"

Gabe decided his little brother should hear the brutal truth. "I was at the bar at Eau Claire Lake. I'd had a couple shots of Scotch and forgot to pay attention. Drove my truck into the lake. Slammed my knee into the steering column. One totally wrecked truck. One semi-wrecked knee."

When Jack stared at him, Gabe continued. "Legally, I wasn't over the limit. But that's the thing with booze. Doesn't take much to make you stupid. My new rule? No driving if I drink. Period."

"Can't you have one or two, you know, to be social, and be okay to drive?"

Gabe peered at the birch-tree canopy before turning his gaze back to Jack. "Maybe." He shrugged. "But the entire episode scared me. It happened at night. Suppose it had been mid-day? And the lake full of pipsqueaks?" He rubbed his knee again. "There are so many other ways a guy can ruin his life, why add booze to the list? Know what I'm saying?"

Jack hunched his shoulders as if pulling his head to safety. He stared at the ground, his cheeks pinking. Gabe elected not to push the topic. He clapped his hands on his thighs and climbed down from his perch. "I'd like your thoughts on the explosions."

Jack stammered. "Huh? Me?"

"You're smart and you live here now. So, yeah. Everyone says environmentalists are trying to scare mining types away. Think so?"

Jack shrugged. "Maybe. I hear people complaining about the noise of the drills, or the ruts the trucks leave in the fields. But that's no reason to blow something up."

"Agreed. But what sounds crazy to us could seem rational to someone else. Know anyone with a reason to want miners gone?"

"No. No one." As soon as the words were out, Jack's face changed, his mouth made an 'O.' Then he shook his head. "Maybe. No, it's dumb talk."

"I'll take dumb right now. I'll take anything."

Jumping down from the table, Jack jiggled from foot to foot, talking fast. "There's this guy. The Viking. He hangs out in the hills. Yells at us when we—we hike off the trails. My friends think he's planting the bombs and wants to keep the mountains for himself."

"He hassles you for hiking?" Gabe watched Jack's eyes.

"Yeah." Jack blinked. "If we stray off the trails." A tic flashed beside his mouth.

"Hmm. What's his name? Where can I find him?"

Jack shrugged. "I forget. Something-son. We call him The Viking. I've seen him a lot on Rimrock and once on Granite Mountain. But I don't know where he lives. He's like a hermit."

———

AFTER GABE DROPPED his kid brother back at O'Malley's ranch, he loaded Springsteen's *High Hopes* CD into the player and set off for Horace Minken's exploration site at Findrich's spread. Following Minken's directions, Gabe drove north on River Road, the road that paralleled the Rocque River and which, according to Harris, connected Cheakamus with farms and ranches to the north of town. Gabe kept a watch for Riverbank Hall, which Minken had said marked the turnoff to Findrich Ranch.

As he drove, Gabe's mind wandered back to Jack's face when he'd spoken about The Viking. The old hermit appeared to have Jack on edge. But that tic, as fleeting as it was when it appeared on Jack's face, said much more than Jack's words. He'd have to find The Viking, if only to learn the true reason he yelled at Jack and his friends.

Chapter 16

THREE CUTS into the CD and ten minutes of nothing but trees and highway got Gabe to Riverbank Hall, the designated right turn in the instructions Minken had given him. Boxy, white clapboard, deep verandah across the front, windows evenly spaced along the sides. He knew that, like every other country hall in Canada, a well-equipped kitchen and a narrow stage would bracket a hardwood dance floor. Behind the stage would be a cavernous storage room, in which, if Gabe cared to look, he would find stacks of trestle tables and folding chairs and, behind those stacks, empty beer bottles, the butts of a couple joints, and discarded condoms. Never let it be said that rural Canada didn't know how to party.

He turned onto a secondary road skirting a field of orange pumpkins, stopped at a gate beside the sign for Findrich Ranch, and checked his watch. He was twelve minutes early.

Gabe sat in the idling truck listening to Springsteen until a horn sounded, announcing a black Xterra that jounced across the field toward him. Gabe drove onto the field as the Xterra slowed. Horace Minken stuck his head out the driver's window. "Follow me."

They lurched northward along a rutted path cut into the

field by heavy vehicles to a spot on the far side of a pine windbreak. An enormous debris pile sat between the windbreak and a drill rig with a boxy engine similar to the one in Harris's pasture. The drill's tower was the height of a two-story building.

After they parked, Minken handed Gabe a hardhat, goggles, and earplugs, before striking off toward the rig which sat about fifty feet away. He said over his shoulder, "The driller's setting up. You'll need the safety gear when he starts the rig."

Gabe plunked the hardhat on his head and caught up.

Minken pointed to debris pile. "That mess is what's left of my core shack." He sounded as disgusted as he had yesterday in the bar. "It was spread all over, a total mess. I cleaned it up some."

Adios evidence.

Splintered and charred lumber sat in a heap next to a mangled metal chair. Ragged red letters spelled "No Mining" on the ground between the debris and a concrete structure no bigger than a doghouse. Its sturdy-looking door gaped open. Above the door, a sign warned, "Danger —Explosives."

"Was that your powder magazine?" Gabe said, gesturing at the concrete vault.

"Yeah. It shoulda been safe. That's a heavy-duty door. They musta used a big mother of a crowbar to pry it open."

"What type of explosives did you have?"

"Forcite. Nothing exotic. We keep it around in case the drill rod gets stuck in the hole. I've restocked. This time I'll sleep with it under my pillow."

"Hah. Don't know I'd sleep much."

"Oh, no sweat. As long as it's dry it's safe. Until you light the fuse, that is."

"And then, kaboom?"

"Not immediately. Fuse burns six feet a minute, so you

have some time to get to safety. Unless you're stupid enough to use a very short fuse."

Gabe flexed his knee. "Me, I'd want fifty, sixty feet of fuse. Have you thought about hiring a security guard?"

"The cops suggested that at this morning's meeting." Minken snorted. "No money in the budget for that."

"Did they say anything about the investigation?"

"Nah. It was all about security and some big shot Major Crimes guy planning to interview everyone." Minken moved toward a second pile of splintered wooden trays and small cylinders and shards of rock. Gabe lingered behind and took a quick picture of the graffiti.

He was barely puffing when he caught up to Minken, who appeared not to have noticed his absence and was midsentence: "... a summer's worth of core samples. Useless."

Gabe didn't understand. He selected a smooth cylinder of rock, the diameter of a police baton, and balanced it in his hand. "What's wrong with these?" Before Minken could answer, the driller shouted, raised his hand, and made a circular motion.

"Earplugs, goggles," Minken said, and hurried to the drill rig. Gabe tossed the rock cylinder aside and followed. When the driller started the rig, a flock of birds lifted off from the trees and circled away. Even with earplugs, the noise was like a freight train screeching around a curve. A metal tube rotated inside the drill tower and soon thick black liquid oozed and streamed down the side of the tube, pooling on the ground. When the drill stopped after several teeth-vibrating minutes, the silence made the air feel hollow.

"There's a diamond bit on the end of the core barrel," Minken said. "The bit cuts through the bedrock and draws a core of rock up the barrel. That black sludge is from water we pump into the core barrel to cool the bit."

The driller reversed the drill. The tube screeched upward. "Gonna grab that core sample," Minken said and moved over to the drill. He removed a wet cylinder of rock from the core barrel, placed it in a slot on a wooden rack, and jotted something on the wood beside the slot. When the drill started again, Gabe pushed the earplugs deeper into his ears. He turned away from the piercing noise and watched a white SUV bearing the RCMP insignia park next to his truck.

Sergeant LeBlanc and another Mountie got out of the SUV and headed over. LeBlanc gestured toward Gabe and said something to his companion. When Gabe tapped Minken on the shoulder and hollered, "Visitors," Horace motioned to the driller to stop the drill.

LeBlanc introduced the newcomer to Minken. "Sergeant Ambrose, Major Crimes. He's overseeing the investigation into the incident at the TEG site."

Ambrose shook Minken's hand and then looked at Gabe. "D. S. Gabrieli," Gabe said. Ambrose nodded.

"Gabrieli is a friend of Harris Chilton, the mayor of Cheakamus," LeBlanc told Ambrose.

Gabe nodded. "Good to know you all are on the case. Harris says people are anxious, especially now that there's been a death."

Ambrose stared at him.

Gabe pressed on. "It would be helpful if I could tell Harris an arrest is imminent."

Ambrose snorted. "I wouldn't tell you if it was. If the mayor wants to update the town, he can say we are pursuing several lines of inquiry. We welcome any information townspeople can give us."

Gabe folded his arms and turned to Minken. "Translated into normal English, 'The cops got bupkis.'"

Horace snorted.

Ambrose glared at Gabe. "If you'll excuse us, Mr. Gabrieli, we're here to talk to Mr. Minken."

"No problem." Smiling, Gabe stood his ground.

"Privately."

Gabe thought about arguing the point, knowing the Mounties' questions would give him an idea of their theory of the case and perhaps evidence they'd found. But Ambrose had no sense of humor. It would be stupid to antagonize him further.

Gabe shrugged and handed his safety gear to Minken. "Got errands to run. Thanks for the tour." He nodded to Ambrose and LeBlanc and walked back to his truck.

When he checked the rear-view mirror, Horace was leading the two officers to the debris and pointing at the graffiti.

After loading an Ian Tyson CD into the player, Gabe called Harris to say he was on his way to Deception Ridge Viewpoint. It was only then that he realized Minken hadn't told him why his trashed samples were useless.

Chapter 17

As JACK STEERED the ATV around the first switchback heading up Rimrock Mountain, he congratulated himself on convincing his schoolmate and fellow stable-mucker Roxanne Zalesko to leave the horses in the stables and ride with him on his ATV. True, on horseback he could admire the way her straight black hair streamed behind her as she rode. How she sat tall and easy in the saddle. The way her jeans hugged her rear. But if they'd taken the horses today, he wouldn't feel her arms around his waist nor her soft breath on the back of his neck. No contest.

The route they followed ran parallel to the western fence of Solomon's Choice Ranch on the northeast slope of Rimrock. Near the top of the trail Jack stopped his ATV, idling as Roxanne climbed off. Then he backed deep into the brush and shut off the engine.

Armed with heavy-duty flashlights, they scrambled over the split rail fence. They hiked across the dude ranch's pasture, avoiding a few patches of slush the sun hadn't yet melted. Their target was a point where the field abutted a wall of rock, and several trees partially obscured the mouth of a tunnel leading into the depths of Rimrock. Of more importance to Jack's crowd, it was the back route to Evergold Mine's storage bay they used for parties. A long walk through the tunnels—perhaps two miles from here to the storage bay—but not a big deal. The Evergold was a massive mine, with a web of tunnels running through Rimrock Mountain. A few of them, like this one, exited onto fields and pastures that once were owned by Pierre Rocque as part of the Evergold's holdings but were now owned by local ranchers.

"I told Mom I want to buy an ATV," Roxanne said.

Jack's step faltered. "What'd she say?"

"When Elvis shows up alive in Vegas."

Jack exhaled the breath he'd been holding. "Never mind. You can always ride with me."

They reached the tunnel opening and switched on their flashlights. Roxanne said, "I'll keep bugging her, and work on Dad. It's not like I'm asking them to pay for it."

Jack hoped her parents wouldn't cave. He didn't want to lose his favorite passenger.

They entered the frigid, silent tunnel, their flashlights illuminating rock walls that rose high overhead, and an uneven rock floor that had seen decades of traffic: miners' boots, ore carts, and more recently, horses.

"Cold. Smells bad," Roxanne said.

She said that every time. And every time, just like now, he said, "It's a hole in a mess of rock. Not gonna smell like flowers."

They walked side by side, separated only by the ore cart rails that ran lengthwise along the middle of the tunnel. Their voices echoed in the expanse. The tunnel was wide enough that, had they stretched their arms out to the side, their fingertips would barely brush the jagged rock walls.

When they rounded the first curve a few minutes into their trek, they stopped dead.

"Holeeeey. What happened?" Roxanne played her light

over a jumble of jagged hunks of rock that filled the width of the tunnel and rose almost to its ceiling.

"Maybe that explosion yesterday did it. The TEG exploration site's almost directly above us." Jack shuddered and looked at the rock overhead. "Let's get out of here. The Evergold Museum's closed today, so we can access the mine tunnels from there."

———

On Highway 41 Jack drove past the main access road to the museum and eventually turned right onto an old logging road that joined the highway about a hundred yards north of the Rocque River Bridge. This trail wound steeply up the eastern slope of Rimrock, eventually spitting them out by the machine shed that sat at the back of the Evergold Mine and Museum property. Chances of a vehicle entering the museum lot at 1:30 p.m. on a Sunday were slim, but still Jack parked the ATV behind the machine shed, where it would be hidden.

The two teens hurried across the empty lot, skirted behind the log building that housed the museum, and twenty feet later halted at a six-foot high chain-link enclosure, behind which sat the main portal for the Evergold Mine.

"Guess we climb it?" Roxanne said. Without waiting for an answer, she handed Jack her flashlight, scrambled up the fence, hiked first one leg over the top, then the other, and dropped neatly to the ground. "Toss me the flashlights."

Jack did so, then took a deep breath and climbed the fence, glad Roxanne's back was turned, and she couldn't see how often his feet slipped.

They stood at the mine's gloomy entrance, facing the main tunnel for the Evergold Mine. This one was slightly larger than the tunnel they had just left on Solomon's Choice Ranch. Roxanne rubbed her arms. "It's as cold as the other one." She inhaled and wrinkled her nose. "Smells as bad too."

Jack bit back his retort and shone his light down the tunnel's length. "There are overhead lights in this section, but I won't turn them on in case someone comes by. A hundred yards ahead is a ginormous door. You've walked past it every time we've been in the tunnels. On the other side of it we connect to the web of the Evergold tunnels carved out of the mountain back in the day by Pierre Rocque and his crew."

"How do you know that?"

"I was a tour guide here last summer."

They reached a slatted wooden door that spanned the width of the tunnel. "After old man Rocque died, Mrs. Rocque set up the museum and started running mine tours," Jack said. "She had guys build this barricade to separate this main tunnel from the rest of the Evergold so people on the tours don't get lost."

Roxanne's flashlight illuminated a silver padlock securing the door's hasp to a timber upright. "What now?"

Jack grinned and pulled a ring of keys from his jeans. He selected a square-headed silver one and opened the lock. "A tour-guide perk."

"You stole the key?" Roxanne stared at him.

"You could say I forgot to turn it in."

"Or you could say you stole it."

Jack pulled the door open and waved Roxanne through. "Lighten up, Roxy. It's just a key."

They stood in a small hub of rock-walled corridors. Like spokes on a wagon wheel, two branches radiated to the right, a third went left. Jack shone his light down the far right-hand tunnel, the one leading to the pasture on Solomon's Choice Ranch. "Can't see any fallen rock," he said. "But then, we can only see a small bit of the tunnel."

"Yeah," Roxanne said. "Plus, the tunnel has bends in it. Hard to see around corners, even with a flashlight. How far away do you think the rocks we saw are, from here?"

Jack scratched his head. "Maybe half a mile? We walked

about that before we saw the rocks. But the tunnel doesn't go in a straight line from here to the dude ranch. Add another quarter mile for the curves."

Jack gestured to the corridor to their left. "This is the one we want." When he shone his light down the length, the tunnel, as far as they could see, was clear of debris. Their lights bounced off massive upright timbers spaced along the jagged walls. Once more they walked on either side of the narrow-gauge rail line, careful not to stray too close to the occasional sharp protrusions of rock jutting from the side walls of the tunnel. Now and then, Roxanne flashed her light overhead. "Do you think there are bats?"

"Relax. They won't hurt us."

After passing two intersections with smaller corridors branching to the right of this major arm, they arrived at a wide wood door in the left-hand side of the rock wall. Rusted hinges creaked as Jack pulled the door open. They stepped inside a space measuring perhaps a hundred square feet and littered with wood crates, some bearing thick candles.

"Party central," Jack said. "Ever wonder if Greta Rocque realizes how many of us hang out in her tunnels and this handy storage bay?"

Jack lit four candles, sat on a crate, and pulled a baggie from his pocket. He extracted a joint and lit it, inhaling deeply. "Care to partake, mademoiselle?"

Roxanne folded her arms and shook her head. "I thought we were going to look for gold."

Jack spoke through clenched teeth, trying to hold the smoke in his lungs. "We are. This is a pit stop." He offered the joint once more.

Roxanne shook her head and picked up her flashlight. "I'm going exploring."

Jack caught sight of her face as she turned to leave. Uh-oh. She was ticked. He gave her a minute so it wouldn't look like he was sucking up to her, then extinguished the joint and pocketed the roach. He secreted the baggie in a crevice, turned on his flashlight, blew out the candles, and re-entered the tunnel, pushing the door closed behind him.

"Roxy?"

He shone his light along the tunnel and saw nothing but the rail line and rock. It was eerily still, quiet, cold. "Roxanne?"

Where had she gone in under two minutes? Should he retrace their steps to the barricade? He shook his head. Better to turn left and follow this tunnel to the end and, if she wasn't there, do an orderly search on the return trip. He asked himself, "Who says dope muddles your thinking?"

He struck off, focusing the light on the ground. He hunched his shoulders, burrowing his neck deep into his jacket, hoping the stories about bats in the tunnels were fake, praying the rock overhead was stable, and resisting an urge to whistle.

By the time he reached the spot where the tunnel exited the mountain, he was jogging. He told himself it was anxiety about Roxy that quickened his steps. He burst from the tunnel onto a remote pasture on the southeast side of Rimrock, stopped, and sighed with relief. After the gloomy tunnel, the bright sunlight blinded him.

When his eyes adjusted, he realized that, aside from a bare strip near the mountain's face, snow covered the entire plateau. White, bright, pristine. Marked by two sets of rabbit tracks and four snow angels. And at the end of the row of angels, Roxy lay flat on her back in a drift, eyes closed, a grin on her face, arms and legs scissoring to make a fifth angel.

"Roxy!"

She squinted at him. "Winter's here! I'm putting an angel bracelet around this field."

He waded through knee-deep snow to stand by her feet. "Awesome. I'll help you up." She grabbed his outstretched hands. Jack pulled. When she was almost upright, Jack still pulling, leaning back for leverage, she shifted her weight and pushed, letting go of his hands at the moment he lost his balance and fell backward. The dry snow oomphed upward and settled again, dusting his body with white. He gasped, sucking in snow. "Arrgh! Geez, that's cold."

Roxanne doubled over, laughing. "You look good in white, Ja—aahhh—"

She squealed as his feet caught her ankles in a scissor and tumbled her to the snow. Instantly, they were wrestling in the drifts, each struggling to stuff snow under the other's jacket, their laughter and shouts echoing over the field.

Soon Jack was on his back with Roxanne astride him, about to drop a handful of snow on his face. He shouted, "Give! I give up!" Roxanne rolled off and collapsed prone beside him. They rested, exhausted but grinning, their breath puffing white.

A whinny floated across the air to them.

"Horses on the trail below?" Jack got to his knees, eyes searching the expanse to the east, trying to glimpse the ATV trail to the Chilton ranch that abutted the eastern slope of this plateau. A second whinny sounded. Not from the east. Behind them, around the corner of the mountain's wedged face.

"Someone's here," Roxanne whispered, her voice shaking. "The Viking?"

Jack's heart pounded. The Viking had a temper, and probably a shotgun, and hated the bunch of them. Called them nogoodniks. A Russian Viking. A giggle of hysteria bubbled upward. Jack sucked in air and fought it down.

"The Viking doesn't have a horse," he said.

When Roxy said, "The bombers?" Jack hesitated. They had been laughing, shouting. Would bombers hang around when they heard the noise? Odds were, no. He hoped.

Then he remembered the herd he and Roxy had seen here this summer. He grabbed Roxanne's hand and helped her stand. "My bet? It's the dude ranch herd. Let's go see."

Jack stuck to the patch of bare ground next to the mountain face, with Roxanne close behind him. They skirted around the wedge to the western side of the pasture. While the eastern portion had been a benevolent snowscape, here was devastation. Last night's storm had attacked the plateau from the west with a vengeance. Along the southern tree line, severed branches and toppled trees littered the ground. To the west, snow engulfed the connecting basin, drifts mounding and abutting the field, almost obscuring the threshold where the plateau dipped into the basin. Some fifteen feet along the west side of the pasture the wind had cleared much of the snow, while toward the field's center, the snow deepened markedly, and sharply crusted drifts smothered rocky outcrops.

A cluster of horses eyed them warily from the windswept portion where green grass poked through the sparse snow. Closer to Jack and Roxanne, about twenty feet from the western edge of the pasture, what used to be the lean-to was now a snow-covered jumble of wood lying beside a downed pine. Two horses stood by the woodpile, one tentatively nudging what Jack knew had to be hay, even though his eyes registered colors more red and brown than golden.

"What's he so interested in?" Jack said.

They crept through the deep snow, lifting their knees high and planting their feet carefully in an attempt not to sink past their knees. When they neared the pair of horses—a gelding and a mare—Roxanne cooed soothing words to convey a "we come as friends" message. The horses stood calmly and allowed her to grasp their halters.

Jack leaned forward and studied the mess of pine boughs, scrap wood, hay, and snow.

"Oh Jesus, Roxy. Look."

Chapter 18

AFTER GABE and Harris unloaded their ATVs at Deception Ridge Viewpoint just before 1:30 p.m., Harris asked about Gabe's meeting with Horace Minken at his sabotaged exploration site. "Find out anything?"

Gabe shook his head. "Not much. Anti-mining graffiti was sprayed around. Some of his explosives had been stolen. Cops arrived and shooed me away."

"LeBlanc?"

"And some big kahuna from the Major Crimes Unit who sorta took over. I wonder how that sits with LeBlanc."

"Why not tell LeBlanc you're an investigator?" Harris said. "He might welcome professional help."

"Dream on. I think his antenna's vibrating because I was at both TEG's and Minken's exploration sites. Like the perp returning to the scene."

"But you weren't here when Minken's operation was sabotaged."

"LeBlanc doesn't know that." Gabe revved his ATV engine. "Let's do this."

Harris led Gabe southward. During last night's storm, snow and slush had accumulated on the exposed portions of the trail, but under cover of the trees the trail was drier and the traction better. As his ATV lurched over ruts, Gabe grinned. This was almost as much fun as off-roading.

The few times they exited tree cover, Gabe could see across the Rocque River to the range of mountains on the east side of Cheakamus. What snow the storm hadn't dumped on Rimrock and the western hills, it had deposited on those eastern peaks.

The trail became a series of wide switchbacks winding down the eastern face of Rimrock. Harris pulled into a lay-by and pointed downhill. "That red roof is Evergold Museum. Greta set it up after Pierre died. This trail connects to a logging road off Highway 41, just south of the museum."

Gabe focused his binoculars on the area—at one end sat a metal machine shed large enough to hold a fleet of thirty F150s, and at the other sat a red-roofed log building about the size of a two-bedroom bungalow. Between the machine shed and the building was a spacious, but empty, parking lot. A weathered wooden tower sat next to the log building. Behind the machine shed were several rusted ore carts and one army-green ATV. "Does that ATV belong to the museum?"

Harris shrugged. "Beats me."

Gabe scanned the slope above the museum, looking for trails that could provide access to TEG's site. "If the saboteur knows the trails well, he could avoid the main roads."

When he swept the binoculars over the property, he noticed a high chain-link enclosure around a stone archway about twenty feet behind the museum. "What's that archway?"

"That's the primary adit. The entrance to the Evergold Mine. They use it now only for the mine tours."

Next, Harris and Gabe backtracked to Deception Ridge Viewpoint, traveled along Timberline Road a few hundred yards, and finally followed the logging road to TEG's exploration site.

They skirted the edge of the clearing, gave the slush-covered debris pile a wide berth, and entered a new trail, which they followed uphill and toward the afternoon sun. When they broke out of the trees, they faced a view of ski runs and chairlifts on a neighboring peak.

"That's Blackstrap Mountain," Harris said. "Some of the best powder skiing in BC. They'll be happy about the storm."

Gabe studied the valley through the binoculars and saw a gray snake of highway. "Is that Highway 41? The one that leads out of Cheakamus?"

"Yes, it goes west and intersects the Trans-Canada. See Silver Lake in the distance? On its eastern shore is Singleton, a small town boasting of great ice wine and a so-so casino."

After another half hour riding trails and finding nothing of note, Gabe called it a day and suggested they head back to their trucks. On their way down the logging road toward Deception Ridge Viewpoint, an oncoming RCMP vehicle passed them. Gabe recognized Ambrose and LeBlanc. Ambrose glared at them. If personality were a criterion for membership, Gabe thought, the entire RCMP organization would disappear.

At the viewpoint after they loaded the ATVs, Gabe checked his phone. No bars, no service. "Doesn't this drive you crazy? Dead cell zones." He swooped his arm at the mountains. "No horizon. Rock everywhere, hemming you in."

Harris shrugged, hopped into his Jeep, gunned the engine, and threw it into gear. "Follow me to the ranch," he said.

Gabe balked. "I have a case to investigate. I can tour the ranch tonight when I show up for dinner."

"I told you the sun sets early in the mountains. It will be dark by dinner, maybe sooner. I want to show off the place in daylight. Half an hour tops and you can get back to the case."

It was a nine-minute trip from Deception Ridge View-point—down Timberline Road, south on Highway 41, and then a right turn onto the short access road leading to the cedar arch for the Lazy C Ranch. Gabe's truck bumped over the cattle guard onto a wide driveway that climbed an incline. At the top sat a log home, its gables looking east over the river, its logs gleaming caramel in the sun.

Gabe parked next to the garage and climbed out. He spent a moment looking at the grounds and listening to a chickadee's call before hustling to catch up with Harris.

Their boots landed on the wide planks of the veranda just as the front door opened and Kate emerged, a welcoming smile on her face. She held a gurgling, squirming baby with hair the color of copper.

"Saw you pull in." Kate hadn't changed much. She still wore an antique Celtic ring on her right pinky. Her hair was darker than Gabe remembered, more auburn than red. A few silver strands glinted in her long braid. A smattering of freckles still sprinkled her nose and cheeks. And dimples still bracketed that knockout smile.

"What happened to your head?" she said.

"Whacked it." He nodded at the baby. "Cutie."

"Want to hold her?"

He had misgivings but wiped his hands on his jeans and took the baby. She was warm and small. He turned on the charm. "Pleased to meet you, Devon. I'm D. S. Gabrieli. You can call me Gabe."

The baby stopped gurgling. She stiffened and stared at him with large, blue, solemn eyes. A baby-sized frown creased her forehead. Gabe recognized the frown: straight out of her mother's repertoire. It always meant trouble coming.

"She's frowning," Gabe said.

The baby looked from Kate to Gabe. Her bottom lip quivered. She opened her mouth, squinched her eyes, and wailed. So much for charm, Gabe thought, and passed Devon to Kate.

The wailing stopped. He tried not to take it personally.

"Follow me," Harris said to Gabe. He walked downhill

99

toward the barn, pointing at the nearby mountain. "To help you get your bearings, that's the southeast slope of Rimrock."

"Where's the firebombed site in relation to us?" Gabe said, limping as he hiked behind Harris.

"Northeast slope." Harris gestured at the rolling pastures. "We have just under four thousand acres. I want to show you our newest filly and see if Tornado Callie is in the paddock."

When Harris mentioned Callie, Gabe wished he were five again so he could throw a tantrum and refuse to face her. Instead, he straggled behind Harris and steeled himself for the beating he knew his conscience was about to give him.

Inside the barn, Harris removed some cookies from a small fridge. "Molasses-and-oat treats. Good and good for them."

They followed a well-traveled path from the barn's back doors to fenced paddocks in front of the stables. Three Percherons occupied the far paddock. No evidence of Tornado Callie. "Callie must be in the pasture," Harris said.

Gabe relaxed.

Harris whistled. "Blackie."

The Percheron mare ambled over, dinner-plate hooves plopping on the ground. Dark as French roast coffee except for her white socks, she stood close to seventeen hands. A nicker sounded behind her, and a small clone of the mare trotted to the fence.

Harris stroked the mare. "This beauty is Blackberry. She's four. And the filly, all 750 pounds of her, is Blackie's first baby, Hollyberry. Five months old."

Blackberry stretched her neck over the railing and nuzzled Harris's pocket. He held out a treat, which quickly disappeared. She nosed around for more.

Gabe reached through the fence rails and offered the filly a cookie. Hollyberry slobbered it from his palm, chewed, and studied his face.

Gabe whispered. "I agree. I look pretty rough." He swiped

his hand down his jeans. "You wouldn't believe how I got this shiner if I told you."

Harris pointed to the gelding slurping water from the trough. "That cool dude is Hollywood Hank. Kate bought him and three others from an outfit in Alberta that hired their horses out for films. Hank was a favourite of several commercial producers."

The gelding suited his name. Solid black with a shock of mane falling over his forehead. When he finished his drink he surveyed the paddock, fixed on a pile of hay, and sauntered toward it, his gait proclaiming, "All the paddock's a stage and I'm the star, baby."

"Shall we hike to the pasture and find Callie?" Harris said.

Before Gabe could say no, Harris's phone rang. As he listened to the caller, Harris's expression changed from neutral to interested. "Hang on, Gabe's with me."

Harris punched the speaker button and said, "It's Jack. This is about the herd we saw yesterday on Rimrock."

Jack blurted words out, his voice pinched. "Roxy and me, we were on the ledge above that plateau on the south side of Rimrock, and saw ..." He took in a breath. "The storm toppled a pine and trashed the lean-to. There's a horse trapped underneath the whole mess. Can you come?"

"Where are you now?" Harris said.

"We came off the mountain to get cell service. We're on the public ATV trail behind your ranch. Near the turnaround. We're going to hike back up to the plateau and stay with the horses. Bring axes and saws. Hurry."

After he ended the call, Harris grabbed tools and an equine first-aid kit from the barn. They rushed back to the house and while Gabe unloaded their ATVs from their trucks, Harris updated Kate. Returning outside, Harris glanced at Gabe's boots. "It might be sloppy up there. Want snow boots?"

"Nah. These are Alberta boots. They can handle winter."

"Okay. Your call. We're going to take a narrow trail through the ranch and then join one of the public ATV trails. A network of them runs from the US north to the Slocan Valley near Nelson. Some have been here for decades, cut by logging companies."

They drove their ATVs beside the fence line for a few minutes, moving west along the south end of Harris's land. Then Harris turned onto a path, just wide enough for an ATV, and headed into the trees. Soon the path intersected a wider trail that climbed uphill.

The higher they climbed, the more bite Gabe felt in the air and the more he smelled the coming snow. It was the air of harvest, the World Series, and football. He gripped the ATV handles and longed again for his fleece-lined leather gloves, sitting in his closet in Eau Claire.

After five minutes of switchbacks and popping ears, the trail ended at a steep rocky slope that rose several feet from the trail to flatter ground. They parked next to a dull-green ATV.

Gabe juggled the ax and studied the slope. "Let me guess," he said. "Now we're gonna climb a mountain."

Harris laughed. "Any sure-footed person can make it up this little hill. We simply pick our way from one rock to another."

Flexing his knee and not feeling any twinges, Gabe climbed, doing as Harris suggested, zigzagging from rock to rock. Harris followed close behind.

Gabe had reached a relatively level spot almost at the top of the slope when his right foot skidded backward on slush. He went down, planting his right knee onto the rock. It felt like a branding iron had been stuck into his kneecap. He yelped.

"You okay?" Harris said.

Gabe fought down nausea, used the ax for leverage and

hauled himself upright. "It could be worse. I coulda smashed my good knee."

He limped up the remainder of the slope and finally gained level ground. Once there, he studied the field and tried to ignore the sensation his jeans were shrinking around his knee. The ground along the northern perimeter of the plateau, where it met the ship's prow of Rimrock's south face, was bare of snow. Deep snow covered the rest of the area, including about fifty feet between Gabe and the bare strip. A path of sorts, presumably blazed by Jack and Roxanne, formed a ragged line between Gabe and the northern perimeter. Gabe gazed at Rimrock's face and picked out the ledge on which he and Harris had stood yesterday. Almost directly below it was an opening in the rock face.

Harris hollered for the two teens. Jack appeared from the backside of the wedged rockface and waved. "Over here."

Harris and Gabe hiked toward the perimeter, following the ragged path. Almost immediately Gabe sank to his boot tops. "Aaarrgh. Hard slogging."

Harris grinned. "Hope your Alberta boots are weather-proofed."

Gabe lost count of how often he fell. His jeans pushed above the tops of his boots, allowing snow to seep inside. His feet were cold. His bum knee ached, a hot, throbbing pain. He was breathing hard and wishing for a beer and a sauna by the time they reached Jack, who waited for them by a pile of weathered planks near the opening in the mountain face Gabe had noticed. "They're around the corner," Jack said.

Gabe bent over, sucking in air. "Hang on." His chilled, oxygen-starved brain briefly registered a few snow angels in the drifts near the opening and a section of churned snow where someone had taken a tumble. He gestured at the opening. "What this?"

"I'm guessing another adit for the Evergold mine," Harris said.

Gabe peered into the gloom and shivered. He made out several yards of timbered walls and overhead beams, then blackness. "Need a light."

"Why?" Jack said. "It's just a tunnel."

"Is it a dead end? Or does it connect with the main entrance at the museum?"

Jack turned away. "Who knows? A guy's gotta be nuts to explore old mine tunnels."

Gabe silently agreed with Jack. An involuntary shiver worked its way along his spine at the thought of rock crashing down.

"C'mon," Jack said. "We've moved some of the wood from on top of the horse, but she's still pinned by branches and can't stand up." He nodded at the first-aid kit in Harris's hand. "She's bleeding. We're gonna need that."

They hiked along the perimeter and around the corner to the western side of the field where a confused scene greeted them: sculpted drifts, downed trees, and scattered branches. Yet, fifty feet away several horses stood in sunshine, placidly pawing and nudging light snow cover away from the pasture grass. Then, chaos again closer to Gabe: a mess of lumber tossed haphazardly into trampled ankle-deep snow; a jumble of hay bales and more wood; two horses standing guard near a toppled pine tree; and at the edge of its overhanging branches, a black-haired girl wearing only a sweater and jeans, kneeling with her back to them, obscuring their view of a third animal.

Gabe studied the guard horses. The gelding was chestnut brown with white socks and a long, white streak on his forehead. The mare was a black-and-white pinto. Both appeared tense.

When Jack shouted, "Roxy, I'm back," the girl rose and turned, giving Gabe a view of the horse lying on red-stained hay and partially hidden by pine boughs.

His heart sank.

Chapter 19

GABE CHARGED through the snow to the injured horse, lurching and stumbling as his fireball of a knee fought against both the terrain and his insistence that it move. The mare and gelding shied and snorted, bringing him to a halt a few feet away.

"Careful," Roxanne said. "I just got her calmed down."

Gabe took a closer look at the injured horse.

His heart rate slowed. He felt lighter.

He nodded at Roxanne. "I'm Gabe, Harris's friend. I thought she was my ... one of Harris's."

He approached slowly and studied the horse. Her mane was dark blond, like Callie's. Her coat, at least the part not covered by Roxanne's blue ski jacket, was a glossy, rich brown. Again, like Callie. But not Tornado Callie. This horse was at most a two-year-old. Still, so close in coloring and features she could be Callie's sister.

Roxanne lifted her jacket from the filly's back to reveal red stains running down her side from a long gash on her withers. "It's mostly stopped bleeding," Roxanne said. "But see all the blood in the hay? Will she be okay?"

Harris opened the first-aid kit and handed a thick wad of

bandages to Roxanne. "Press this on the cut. Firmly." To Jack he said, "Help us cut the boughs away."

After ten minutes of furious hacking and sawing, they had removed the branches that overhung the horse and impeded her ability to stand. Gabe put down the ax and hiked to the western edge of the plateau. The shallow basin he'd seen yesterday now contained heaps and mounds of snow that rose almost level with the edge he stood on. When Jack appeared beside him, Gabe said, "Good thing you two spotted this mess. Now all we gotta do is figure out who the herd belongs to. And then the owners will need to get their horses off the mountain."

Jack said, "The horses are hemmed in by the drifts. I can't see any route off this plateau, now that the basin's all drifted over. Maybe they could cut a path east to the top of the ATV trail? Maybe build a ramp down that rock slope to the trail, walk them along the ATV trail and load them into trailers at Harris's ranch."

Gabe clapped Jack's back. "Good thinking."

Jack grinned.

Harris and Roxanne joined them then. "The bleeding's stopped, but the filly can't stand on her own for long," Harris said. "We need a vet." He checked his cell phone and frowned. "No bars. I'll have to call Nicole Mitchell from home."

Gabe wondered why Harris would need to call the woman Reverend Beam wanted to nominate as a saint of godmothers. "Why Nicole?"

"She's the local vet."

"Ahh, okay," Gabe said, "So whose herd is this?"

"Dunno," Harris said. "Nicole might know. I should get back to the ranch and call her."

Jack said, "Roxy and I can stay here and watch over the filly, until Dr. Mitchell gets out here." He looked at Roxanne. "Is that okay? She probably won't be long."

Roxanne stared at Jack for a long moment, her face grim. Finally, she nodded. "Sure."

Promising to come back, with or without Nicole, Gabe and Harris struck out single file along the path toward the trailhead. Gabe's knee began complaining with the first step he took onto the uneven path.

On the return trip to Harris's ranch, Gabe's wet jeans stiffened in the air rushing past him, his toes numbed inside his sodden boots, and his fingers fought to grip the ATV's handlebars. To convince himself he was warm, he imagined saunas, blast furnaces, and Santa Ana winds.

As soon as they reached Harris's ranch, Harris filled Kate in. "The horses have grass and hay. There's snow too, but we could take them some water. A filly's been gashed and can't, or won't, stand on her own for more than a minute. We don't know how long she was down. Can you call Nicole while we dry off? Tell her Jack and Roxanne are horse-sitting."

Gabe pried off his boots. His socks made wet prints on the tile floor. When Harris tossed him a towel, Gabe removed his socks and dried his feet.

"Fireplace in the great room," was all Harris needed to say to make Gabe trudge barefooted down the hall, aiming for heat. The more, the better. He was calculating the optimal distance from the flames to place his feet when Kate returned.

"Nicole's on the road and won't be back until just before dinner. I volunteered to have a look at the horse in the meantime."

"Why don't we call another vet?" Gabe asked.

"Unless you want to call one in from Trail, Nicole is the only vet in the area," Harris said. "Plus, I trust her. If she doesn't know who owns the horses, then she'll probably alert the SPCA so someone can make decisions about the herd."

Gabe wriggled his toes. "Ah, okay. That makes sense."

Kate turned to Gabe and fiddled with her Celtic pinky

ring. "Can you take me to the site while Harris stays here? Or would you prefer to babysit?"

Chivalry required Gabe to escort Kate. But he was in front of a warm fire, his feet were thawing, his eyelids feeling heavy. His knee had stopped throbbing. It was cold out there with the horses.

But, if he stayed, he'd be alone with a baby. Who would cry. Or need changing. Or both.

"Horses, it is." His choice had everything to do with fear and nothing to do with chivalry.

Harris said, "Let me get you dry clothes and some snow boots."

When Harris returned with an armful of clothing, Gabe heaved himself from the chair, cast a forlorn look at the fire, and limped to the bathroom. He peeled off his jeans and inspected his knee. It was a melon-sized sausage, with a purplish-red splotch dead center, where his kneecap normally resided. After struggling into the dry clothes and boots, he rooted through the medicine cabinet until he found a bottle of painkillers. He popped a couple, hoping they'd keep the swelling down and allow him to walk without screaming.

He found Kate and Harris outside loading an old toboggan with supplies: a huge stack of horse blankets, two pairs of snowshoes, a canvas sling and pulley, two heavy-duty flashlights, the first-aid kit, a box of kindling, four plastic buckets, two metal pails, and six large thermoses.

Harris tied down the load, attached the sled to the ATV, and kissed Kate. "Drive slowly. The trail's rutted and that toboggan's old."

Kate reached inside the mudroom and brought out a rifle. "Just in case we run into things that do more than go bump in the night."

Chapter 20

AT THE TURNAROUND on the ATV trail, they untied the toboggan from the ATV. Gabe carefully climbed the rocky slope, dragging the toboggan behind him. Kate followed behind, pushing on the toboggan to help guide it. When they reached the field at the top of the slope, he and Kate clipped on snowshoes and trekked across the snow. Once they reached the bare perimeter path, they removed the snowshoes and hurried on. The hike pushed Gabe's heart rate into the fat-burning zone and made his knee screaming hot.

"You two can take off," Gabe said to Jack and Roxanne.

"I'll be back," Jack said. "Gonna take Roxy home and then grab sleeping gear, just in case Doc Mitchell says someone needs to watch over the horses tonight."

After Jack and Roxanne left, the filly rose and stood, trembling, and favoring her right front leg. Her ever-present guards, the mare and gelding, moved closer to her. Within thirty seconds, the filly sank to the ground.

"Could you take some water to the rest of the herd while I check over this little darling?" Kate said. "Pour it from the thermoses into the plastic buckets. They have battery-operated heaters."

Gabe chased a few of the herd around their small island in the sea of snow, limping and losing the contest until he bribed them by dragging over a hay bale from the trashed lean-to. He loosened the bale and placed two pails of water nearby. "Horsey, horsey, horsey. Get your vittles here. C'mon by, don't be shy." Soon he had five horses happily chowing down on hay and slurping water.

"I oughta be a horse whisperer," he said, when he rejoined Kate. "How's our patient?"

"I cleaned and sutured her cut. Nicole may want to redo the sutures and give her a tetanus shot and antibiotics. The poor thing must have been standing under the shelter when it collapsed. She has a nasty bruise on the back of her head. Another on her right shoulder, which may be why she's favoring that leg."

"There was a lot of blood in the hay."

"You'd be surprised how much blood a horse has: about seven gallons when full grown. However, I am concerned that she can't stand for long and is so shaky. That could be from blood loss, or perhaps fright. Or worst case, she was down too long and there's organ damage, which can be deadly."

Kate watched the filly for a long moment, then faced her head on and stared at her eyes. Gabe remembered Kate studying him like that not long after Bethany moved out.

Kate nodded, as if making a decision.

"What are you doing?" Gabe said.

"Seeing what's in her eyes."

"Huh?"

"If she's a fighter or has given up."

"You can tell that by looking at her eyes?"

"Not *at* her eyes so much. It's more what's inside her head and heart. The eyes are just the way in."

"What's the verdict?"

"I think she's a fighter." Kate grinned. She gestured at her rifle where it sat atop the toboggan. "Assuming we find the owners, they won't need a rifle."

Gabe thought about what would have happened if Kate had a rifle handy the last time she stared in his eyes.

"Help me prepare the sling?" Kate said, breaking his reverie. When Gabe looked at her quizzically, she pointed to a sturdy pine ten feet away. "We guide her to that tree. The canvas goes around her body, the ropes and pulley go over a branch and voilà, we relieve the pressure on her legs, and she'll stay upright. With luck, she won't need it after a few hours."

Gabe climbed the pine and looped the pulley end of the sling snugly over a thick branch while Kate coaxed the filly to stand and guided her over. She wrapped the sling under the filly's torso and hooked it to the pulley. Together Kate and Gabe tightened the pulley to secure the sling around the horse. "Good," Kate said as she checked the sling. "Not too tight, but she won't collapse. Now, if you can pull over more hay, I'll collect snow to melt."

Gabe cast his eyes to the mess of wood and hay fifteen feet away. He'd been flailing around in snow, falling up and down rocky trails for most of the afternoon. He'd made firewood out of a toppled pine. He'd dragged a bale halfway across this freezing field and played catch-me-if-you-can with a bunch of juvie delinquent horses. His knee was a pulsing, aching football. He wanted to collapse like a cheap deck chair. He trudged over to the bales.

"A clean one," Kate said. "No blood."

He wrestled a clean bale from the chaos.

"And the kindling," Kate said. "I need to make a fire so we can melt snow to top up the buckets."

Gabe dragged the bale over, slogged to the toboggan, collected kindling, and dropped it near Kate. Last, he searched the debris for dry lumber and shuffled back, his knee throbbing with each step.

After they loosened more hay from the bale, Kate built a small fire, grabbed one of the metal pails she had filled with snow and set it on top of the fire. While Kate stood by the fire, watching the snow melt in the pail, Gabe sat on the remains of the bale and massaged his knee. "Harris mentioned things were piling up. Anything I can do?"

Kate's cheeks flushed in the firelight. "Your being here is helping him, relieving anxiety over the bombings."

"Except I haven't figured it out."

"Yet. You will. He knows that." She swiped at her eyes and then turned toward him. "Thanks for agreeing to be godfather."

He studied her face, searching for the sign that would tell him she was blowing smoke.

Her brow wrinkled. "You think I don't mean it?"

Kate frowning equals trouble, Gabe told himself. And she had that rifle. Luckily, it was on the toboggan a fair distance away. And the sun had dipped behind the mountains thirty minutes ago. By the time she got to the rifle, he could dive into the drifts in the basin. She'd never find him in the fading light.

"I figured you'd veto Harris."

Her jaw dropped. "Why?"

He shrugged. "I might not be the right choice 'cause I don't live here." He cleared his throat. "And, you know—I have an issue or two."

"That's true. You're stubborn, cynical, hot headed, and get into situations that defy comprehension."

"Yeah."

"You've got some pluses too. I'd tell you, but it will go to your head." She paused for an instant. "Harris and I want someone who can talk to Devon about the reality of life, how to survive when things are tough, how to enjoy it when things are good. And that's you." Her eyes glistened in the firelight. "We both chose you."

Any more of this and Gabe would be tearing up along

with Kate. "She'll cry through the entire christening. You'll be sorry yet."

Kate laughed.

He touched the small bandage on his forehead. "She cried when I held her. You think my bandage and shiner scare her?"

"No. She's making strange. But now that you mention it, what happened to your head?"

"I walked into a door."

"Right. What really happened?"

Gabe sighed. "A waterslide."

"I've always wanted to try that."

"Don't, unless you want to spend three hours in emergency. Adding insult to injury, your baby hates me."

"You could try singing to her. She likes Ian Tyson."

He said, "Or I could adopt the approach Italian pedestrians take with Rome drivers. 'Never let them see your fear,' they say. If it works crossing Rome's streets, it should work with babies."

He watched the horses dip their heads for hay and noticed that the gelding and mare had taken up stations on either side of the filly in her sling. "So, the herd. What now?"

"Well, we have to find the owners. If we can't, then the SPCA will step in. Meanwhile, the weather forecast is good. Nicole can assess the filly later tonight. Maybe the sling can come off. If not, with Jack standing guard, the filly should be fine overnight."

"Good."

Kate sighed. "Since Nicole needs to tend to the horse, I'm going to postpone our dinner. You can meet her another time."

"What?"

"She was supposed to drop by the house after dinner. But now, with this filly…."

"What's going on? Were you trying to fix me up?"

Kate laughed. "That's what Nicole asked when I invited

her. I had to talk long and hard before she agreed to stop by. Technically you're still a married man. So, the answer's no, I wouldn't try to fix you up. But if I did, it wouldn't be with Nicole. I don't think you're right for her."

Gabe relaxed. Yet Kate's comment niggled him. What'd she mean, he wasn't right?

"You'll come for dinner another night? Meet her then?"

Gabe hung his head. He wasn't a chitchatter. Meeting Nicole, the godmother, meant he would be expected to make chitchat. The screw-it side of him wanted to say he could meet Nicole at the front of the church just before the christening. Choirboy said, "That tactic is not godfatherly."

And Gabe knew Kate. She would never give up until he agreed to have dinner and meet the sainted, perfect godmother.

He gritted his teeth. "Wouldn't miss it. Just tell me when."

Chapter 21

IT WAS ALMOST six o'clock when Gabe returned to Cheakamus, cold, sore, and weary. Dealing with the horses had consumed time he couldn't afford to lose. Intuition told him the bomber wasn't finished with Cheakamus. He wanted to catch the saboteur before the next explosion. The problem: only the bomber knew when that would happen.

On the upside, now that Kate had canceled dinner at the Lazy C, he could do some online research. Still, he needed to eat, so on his way to Greta's guesthouse, he stopped at Tiffany's and found the café two-thirds full.

Rhonda approached him as he lingered by the cash register. "Staying for dinner?"

Gabe shook his head. "Looking for takeout. What's good tonight?" When he saw the fire come into her eyes, he added, "Scratch that. I mean, out of all your Michelin-rated offerings, what do you recommend to a guy who's been beaten into submission by snow drifts and has the scars to prove it?"

"Seven out of ten for that recovery," Rhonda said. "It woulda scored nine but I deducted two for the 'poor, poor pitiful me' ploy."

"So you'll feed me then?"

"The spaghetti and meatballs is good as a takeout. Partner it with a caesar salad. That takes it up to great. And healthy. Especially for out-of-shape Italians."

"That would be me. Can you give me extra sauce on the spaghetti? Thanks Rhonda." He noticed Ches Ubrowski, the fire chief, talking with Horace Minken in a booth midway down the row. "Shout at me when it's ready."

Gabe nodded at Bill Jacobson, who sat halfway down the counter eating apple pie, before limping to Ubrowski's booth. Gabe gingerly lowered himself to the edge of the seat, with his leg stretched out into the aisle. He told the two men about the stranded horses and the injured filly. "Any idea whose herd might be up there? South side of Rimrock. A plateau where one of the old Evergold mine tunnels exits."

Ches and Horace shook their heads. "Greta Rocque might know," Ches said.

Gabe smiled. "You're right. She knows almost everything about this town."

"True," Ches said. "But I was thinking more about the fact she owns that land. My father worked at the Evergold. They held picnics for the miners and their families on that field. I remember playing softball up there."

That surprised Gabe. "How'd everyone get there? I damn near crushed my kneecap trying to climb the slope at the end of the public ATV trail."

"We used a mine tunnel. Pierre Rocque had put lights along a few of the main tunnels to make the miners' jobs easier, so it was almost like walking in daylight. I think my mother worried about bats but all us kids loved pretending we were explorers looking for pirate treasure."

Gabe glanced over at the counter and spotted Rhonda exiting the kitchen, carrying two takeout containers. He pushed himself upright and when he put his weight on his right leg, his knee protested. "Oof. I shoulda remembered bartending is way less painful than mountaineering."

He limped over to the cash register and stood with most of his weight on his good leg while he paid Rhonda for the meal. He'd pocketed his change and picked up his takeout containers when the café door opened. Sergeant Ambrose strode in and approached Gabe. "Fancy you being here, Gabrieli."

"Nice to see you again too," Gabe said.

"What were you doing at the TEG scene today?"

Gabe's knee throbbed. He took advantage of an empty counter stool and sat down with his back to the counter. He placed his containers on the counter, stretched his right leg in front of him and massaged his knee. "Not that it's any of your business, since you released the scene, but Harris Chilton and I drove across the field to get to a trail on the back side of Rimrock."

"Sure. So, you're out there this morning." Ambrose then jutted his jaw toward Minken. "And when I was parking, I spotted you cozying up to a witness. Are you pumping him for information about my investigation?"

"Again, none of your business," Gabe said. "But we were talking about horses." Gabe caught sight of Jacobsen pulling out his phone. Recording the conversation, he'd bet.

"That's what you say, Gabrieli. But I checked you out, so I have my doubts. You're a private investigator. And if you interfere in my case, it definitely *will* be my business."

Gabe sighed. So much for his cover.

At that moment Sergeant LeBlanc entered Tiffany's and called to Ambrose. "Sergeant Ambrose, join me for dinner?"

Ambrose turned away from Gabe and walked toward LeBlanc. Gabe pushed up from his stool, wincing as his knee locked, almost giving out, and picked up his takeout containers. The instant he put his weight on his right leg, his knee spasmed. "Whoa!" Before Gabe could stop himself, he pitched forward. In the process of reaching out to break his fall he let go of his containers of spaghetti and salad.

LeBlanc, who was lucky enough to see the live action unfold, leapt backward. Ambrose, on the other hand, stopped and turned around when Gabe shouted.

The next instant Gabe was on his hands and knees on Tiffany's floor. The food containers landed a couple feet in front of him, their lids bursting open on impact. Gabe watched green romaine leaves, and spaghetti noodles with their extra sauce, explode upward from their cartons and attach themselves to Ambrose's jacket and shoes. Two glistening meatballs rolled lazily along the floor and came to rest between Ambrose and LeBlanc.

Rhonda and most of the diners gasped out loud.

"What the hell?" Ambrose said.

Thinking Ambrose would never understand, or believe, his relationship with The Frikkin Comedian, Gabe offered a wry smile from his spot on the floor. "Geez, Sergeant, I slipped. Sorry."

Ambrose brushed at the noodles on his sleeve. "The old 'I slipped' excuse might work in Alberta, Gabrieli. But not here, not with me." He held his thumb and forefinger an inch apart. "You are *this* close to an assault charge."

Several diners said, "Whaaaaaat?"

Jacobson's camera clicked rapidly.

Ambrose waved LeBlanc over. "Sergeant, take Gabrieli to your vehicle."

LeBlanc hauled him up. As the three of them exited the café, LeBlanc muttered under his breath, "Jesus, Gabrieli, what is it with you?"

On the sidewalk outside Tiffany's Gabe said, "Look Ambrose, I have a bum knee and it gave out in there. I'm sorry about the mess on your clothes. I'll pay for the dry-cleaning."

Ambrose whirled around. "A cleaning bill might be the least of your worries if you insist on making my job difficult."

Gabe raised his hands, palms out. "Hang on a minute. I'm

here visiting friends, waiting for the christening of their baby. For sure I'm not in the business of making anyone's job difficult." He paused and then smiled. "You know, I'm a good investigator. Great, even. I could actually make your job easier. Work with you and Sergeant LeBlanc here."

They stared at him.

"Gratis," Gabe said. "I'd be doing my bit for society."

"We don't work with private investigators," Ambrose said. "Especially ones who were drummed out of the legal profession, like you were."

Gabe's chest tightened and his heartbeat quickened. To calm himself, he breathed in slowly and visualized a field of grain swaying in soft prairie breezes. "You're mistaken, Ambrose. I'm retired from practice."

"But what prompted your retirement? According to my sources, it was a slight problem with the law. If you can call a murder charge a slight problem."

"My problem with the law had everything to do with cops being too lazy to do their job and fixing on a convenient fall guy. Namely, me."

"Sure, yeah, blame it on the police. Let me assure you, we are doing our job here, and I don't need civilians poking around and interfering with my witnesses."

Gabe blew out a long breath. "Look, I wasn't interfering with your witnesses. I honestly was talking about horses with Horace Minken. This whole thing is bullshit. If you think I assaulted you, I'm happy to sign a promise to appear. Either that, or let me call my lawyer."

LeBlanc said, "Why don't you take a seat in the SUV for a bit, Gabrieli?" He guided Gabe to the vehicle and opened the back door. Gabe balked for a moment, then said, "Oh, what the hell," and slid inside. LeBlanc shut the door and returned to the sidewalk where Ambrose waited.

Gabe watched the two cops talk for a few minutes. Finally, Ambrose shrugged, and they both returned to the SUV.

Gabe's phone began ringing just as Ambrose opened the back door.

"Okay, Gabrieli, it's your lucky night. I'm not charging you with assault—yet. Keep your nose clean and it will stay that way." He nodded at LeBlanc, walked a few steps away, and then said over his shoulder. "And I'll send you the cleaning bill. Count on it."

Gabe hauled himself from the SUV and said, "I'm guessing you talked sense into him, LeBlanc. So, thanks."

LeBlanc said, "Try to stay out of trouble, Gabrieli? At least until I've finished my dinner?" He moved toward Tiffany's door, halted, and turned back to Gabe. "I checked you out too, Gabrieli. Interesting name, Desert Sun."

Gabe winced and shrugged. "Yeah. What can I say? My mother's an artist who was in love with the desert."

LeBlanc worked hard at suppressing a smile. "Ever thought of changing it?"

"You gotta put a notice in a paper. Small towns, everyone reads the ads."

LeBlanc nodded. His lips moved slightly upward at the corners. Gabe sensed he was thawing. "Using initials works," LeBlanc said, and then entered the café.

Gabe had taken a couple steps toward his truck when Rhonda stuck her head out the café's door and called him over. "Are you okay?" she said. When Gabe nodded, she said, "Wait there."

Rhonda reappeared a minute later, bearing two takeout containers, which she handed to Gabe. He dug in his pocket for his wallet, but Rhonda stopped him. "On the house," she said. "It's not often Tiffany's can brag about live entertainment."

Gabe drove back to Greta's guesthouse slowly. Almost getting arrested was a less-than-perfect way to end the day. Then again, it was a long shot better than sitting around with not-right-for-you-Nicole-the-godmother making chitchat.

MONDAY

Chapter 22

If Rocky oversaw the Nobel Prize, he'd create a new category and call it the Butt Saver Award. He'd give it to the dude who invented heated seats. Because when you're freezing your keister off driving a pickup with a clunky heater and vinyl seats on your way to the top of Rimrock Mountain, nothing's better than knowing the return trip will be in a top-of-the-line vehicle. With top-of-the-line heated leather seats.

Twelve-thirty Monday morning and Rocky was midway through the latest task on Doc's master plan: get rid of the dead guy's truck and ATV. A simple thing, if he wanted to follow that directive to the letter. Drive the outfit to the coast, Doc had said. Park on a side street in one of Vancouver's burbs and everything would vanish in two minutes flat. End of story.

Doc was smart about making things disappear, one reason Rocky valued his partner. Rocky knew he should follow the plan.

The problem? A trip to Vancouver was an expedition. Especially in this piece-o-crap ancient Ranger. Freeze his patootie off for twelve hours? Get serious.

Rocky had asked himself, "Why not get rid of the outfit in

Cheakamus?" A complicated feat, because in this two-bit excuse for a metropolis, every guy and his mother had a truck and ATV. The chances of someone stealing the dead guy's outfit and spiriting it away were zilch.

On Sunday, while others enjoyed their day of rest, communing with the heavens or watching Drew Brees and his Saints come marching in, Rocky was hard at work thinking, figuring out a plan. In the end, it was simple. The answer was in the fact that everyone had a truck and ATV. The mountains were full of them: parked on trails, idling in viewpoints, rusting in the bush. No one paid any attention. Just another piece of the scenery.

When most people were enjoying Sunday dinner and prime-time television, Rocky had loaded his Arctic Cat ATV into his Sierra. He drove up Timberline Road well past the turnoff for TEG's site until he spotted a narrow, rutted track, which he followed as it snaked through the bush. When the trail ended in a small turnaround, he parked and unloaded his ATV. The return trip on his Arctic Cat was chilly but uneventful. Back in his cabin, he had opened a beer and congratulated himself. Stage One accomplished. Brilliant.

Stage Two began about half an hour ago, just after midnight, when Rocky backed the dead guy's old Ranger out of the even older barn where they'd stashed it.

Now, sitting on the frigid driver's seat reminded him of hemorrhoids and the bags of frozen peas he sat on to shrink them. The difference was, with hemorrhoids he froze his nethers for ten minutes max. In this gutless pickup, the trip to the drop site would take at least thirty butt-freezing minutes.

Cursing the cold, cursing Cheakamus, cursing corpses who owned trucks without heated seats, and thinking about the Nobel Prize, Rocky retraced his route along Timberline Road and onto the track to the turnaround where his Sierra waited. Before he abandoned the pickup and the ATV in its bed, he removed the truck's license plates and registration.

Why make it easy? He found the ATV keys in the glove box, thought about taking them, and decided no. He stashed the Ranger's keys under the driver's seat. Damn near everyone left keys in their vehicles. And if someone stumbled by and stole the outfit, welcome to it.

By two in the morning Rocky was driving back down Timberline Road in his loaded Sierra—heated seats on high, singing along with Tim McGraw, and congratulating himself on accomplishing Stage Two.

Soon, one week max, the investors' money would be in the bank. Not all of it. He'd likely blown one contribution. But still, thirty million would be there. And Rocky could execute his end game—head for Grand Cayman. Sun. Sea turtles. White sand. Conch fritters. Babes to share it all with.

Did yachts come with heated seats for the captain? Like that would matter in the Caribbean.

Chapter 23

JACK READ the text from one of his Green Dude buddies: "Dad's up for lending us livestock waterers."

"Rockin'," Jack responded. It was only seven-thirty in the morning and already things were coming together for the rescue of the trapped horses. Last night, when Kate came out to the site with the vet, Nicole Mitchell, Jack had talked to them about his plans to rescue the horses. Kate had offered up the Lazy C as a base for the operation. Doc Mitchell said if she didn't identify the herd's owners by the morning, she would call the SPCA and get approval to deal with the herd. "I'll let you know," she said.

Jack could have told Kate and the vet exactly who owned the herd. But he and his crowd spent their spare time hanging out and toking up in the Evergold tunnels and if Jack revealed what he knew about the horses and how they got to the plateau, it wouldn't take long for Greta Rocque to seal up the tunnels again. Goodbye party central. Better to hope Doc Mitchell called the SPCA and that they got the horses off the mountain before anyone found out the truth.

When they had removed the sling from the injured filly, the horse had no problem standing on her own. After an hour of observation, Doc Mitchell had said, "I think she's fine without the sling, Jack, so you won't have to guard her overnight."

It was close to midnight by the time Jack returned to O'Malley's ranch. Seamus, who was on his computer, asked about the horses. When Jack updated him, Seamus had stopped being his usual annoying self and helped Jack make a list of things they would need for the rescue plan if it went ahead. Before Jack hit the sack, he texted the Green Dudes and by this morning they had scored most of it: generators, heaters, plywood, lumber, shovels, feed and water, sleds. And now, heated waterers.

It didn't bother Jack that Doc Mitchell hadn't yet okayed the rescue plan. If things got delayed, he'd just wing it. Tell the Green Dudes some story. Blame it on the vet. Whatever.

He'd yet to hear back from Roxy about food. Her mom owned Tiffany's and made awesome sandwiches. Rather than text Roxy, he picked up his phone.

"Mind reader," Roxanne said. "I was just gonna phone. Did you hear about the kerfuffle at the café?" She didn't give Jack a chance to answer. "That Gabe guy, Harris's friend? They say he threw some spaghetti at a cop, but Mom says he slipped and fell. Whatever, they hustled him outside the café and had him in a cop car for ages."

Jack sucked in his breath. "When?"

"Last night around dinner time. Mom heard the cops say Gabe's a private investigator. Do you believe that?"

"Yeah, he is. An excellent one."

"How do you know that?"

Jack smacked his thigh. Had he blown Gabe's cover? No, Roxy was cool. "I'll tell you, but you're sworn. He's my brother, working undercover, investigating the explosions."

"Sure. And I'm Lady Gaga hiding out in Cheakamus to avoid crazed fans."

"You're more Katy Perry but if you say you're Lady Gaga, I believe you."

"Are you being straight with me?"

"For sure. He's actually my half-brother. Lives in Alberta."

"And he's a detective? For real?"

"For sure. He used to be a rich lawyer until things got screwed up. Now he's a bartender and private eye."

"What got screwed up?"

"Some dude who hassled Gabe's wife ended up dead. They thought Gabe did it, but Harris saved him. Then Gabe stopped being a lawyer." Jack could have told her the complete story but needed to get off the phone before Christmas. "What did your mom say about the food?"

"She's kicking in sandwiches. You owe me big time. I got up at six to make them."

"Rockin'. Can you bring the food to Harris's around noon?"

"No. I have classes all day."

"Cut school. Aren't you helping with the rescue?"

"Yeah, but after school. Mom won't let me miss classes."

"You're exactly like the others. Afraid to cut school. Tell her you don't have classes today. That's what I tell O'Malley. Works every time."

Roxanne's voice cooled. "You're always lying or not telling the whole story. Like when you didn't admit you know who owns those horses.

"They're not actual lies." He laughed. "They're omissions. Or truth adjustments."

"But you *know* how those horses got there. Solomon's Choice ranch moves them to pasture through the tunnels. Why not tell Harris and Gabe? They could move the horses back to the ranch that way."

"Two reasons. One, the tunnel to the dude ranch is blocked. You know that because we saw it. Two, we'll blow party central for everyone."

Roxanne fell silent. When she spoke again, her voice had a heated edge. "You want to *omit or adjust the truth*, Jack Diamond, go ahead. But don't involve me."

"Aw, c'mon. What's the big deal? I don't lie to you. You're different."

"The sandwiches are ready. Pick them up at the café."

Jack knew by the hollowness of the line she'd hung up. Straight. Ramrod. That was Roxanne.

He considered calling her back. And watching his phone melt as the firestorm of her anger blasted through. He'd been there, done that, got the scorch marks on his ear to prove it. Tomorrow. Tomorrow a person could maybe approach Roxanne and survive.

Chapter 24

GABE STEPPED onto the balcony of his suite and glanced across the yard to Greta's house. When he spotted lights on in her kitchen, he grabbed his phone and called her.

"Morning," he said, when Greta answered the phone. "Ches Ubrowski tells me you own that plateau on the south side of Rimrock. Says you used to have summer parties there for all the mine crew."

"Yes. Why?"

"Harris and I spotted a herd of horses grazing there. After the storm hit, the horses seem to be trapped by snow drifts, and one of them is injured. We're wondering who owns the herd."

"Good grief! There shouldn't be any livestock up there. I leased that land out years ago to a farmer who had a place nearby. He cut a trail through the bush and pastured his herd there. But when he died, his children sold off the herd and terminated the lease of the pasture. That was at least five years ago."

After Gabe ended the call with Greta, he phoned Harris and relayed Greta's information. "She says she has no idea who might be pasturing their herd on her plateau."

"Interesting," Harris said. "I'll pass that on to Nicole."

"Anything new on the injured filly?"

"Nicole planned to assess her this morning, but Kate says the filly's a fighter. Jack's waiting to get Nicole's go-ahead for his rescue plan. My bet is, with Greta's information, Nicole will call in the SPCA and get their okay to move the horses."

Gabe remembered Kate staring into the filly's eyes when they had been on the plateau. "Do you think Kate can really see inside a horse's head?"

"Horses aren't the only animals whose minds she can read." Harris paused, then said, "Hear you had quite a night last night."

"Uh, yeah, I was going to tell you. But it sounds like you already know the basics."

"Yep. Rhonda phoned me and gave me the play-by-play. I think she's betting on the whole thing to increase the number of people frequenting the café. 'Dinner and a show' is what she mentioned."

"It was an accident," Gabe said. "But still, miserable Milton Ambrose is threatening assault charges unless I'm a good little boy. You're the trial lawyer, not me. What are the odds an assault charge would stick?"

"Fifty-fifty."

"Fifty-fifty! Geez, Harris, the last time my doctor checked my blood pressure he made me promise to avoid courtrooms."

"Relax. Ambrose has much more to worry about than you. Let's meet at Tiffany's for lunch today. You can tell me all about how you got the shiner and stitches."

"Yes, to lunch. No, to the rest."

Harris laughed. "Don't you think Kate and I talk? She told me. What the hell were you doing on a waterslide?"

Gabe let out a long sigh. "You know, hanging out with Lucy and her crowd. They told me it was completely safe. So, I tried it. But they also said it was 'easier' if I lay down—do you know how fast you go if you lie down? Too fast. I came screaming around one of the bends and tried to sit up and whammo! Planted my face into the side of the tube."

Harris chuckled. "If you'd told Ambrose that story last night, he would have been too busy laughing to even think of assault charges. By the way, I called him yesterday and asked how the case was coming along."

"Huh. Did he share anything?"

"Nothing, except Jack is on their list of suspects."

"We need to change that," Gabe said. "If we prove he was elsewhere, even for one explosion, it will help. I'll ask Jack again where he was at the relevant times. And I'll try to add more suspects to the Mounties' list."

"Who have you got so far?"

Gabe huffed out an exasperated breath. "Slim pickings. There are a couple young enviro-types. And Jack mentioned a hermit—The Viking—who hangs around the area. Apparently, his name is something-son. Any guesses?"

"Could be Anders Thorvaldsen. He's an old-style prospector. A loner."

"Is he mentally stable?"

"It upsets him if people get too close to his mining claims. But I doubt he's violent."

"Hmm. I guess I'll hike a few hills and try to flush him out." Gabe rubbed his knee and groaned. "If my knee holds out, that is. I've been speculating about how the bomber accesses the sites. The miners don't seem big on security. Late at night the saboteur could waltz right in. In daylight, however, he must look like he belongs."

"Yeah. So many mountain bikers and hikers use the trails, you could put your explosives in a backpack and blend in."

Gabe laughed. "Wow, when did you become a terror strategist?"

"When Jacobson wrote his first article about how a good mayor could stop the sabotage."

"Will people believe that?"

"Hope not."

"Why not give up the mayor's job? It would free some time for the ranch."

"No one else wants it."

"Jacobson does."

Harris laughed. "That's how it started. When my predecessor retired midterm, no one but Bill wanted the job. George Findrich and Rhonda Zalesko asked me to step in, saying I could deliver what the town needed."

"Which was?"

"Leadership. Before you say it, I know. I'm a sucker for flattery. The time commitment wasn't huge—a day a week— so I agreed. I planned to finish the term while we recruited a replacement. But now it's election time and no one else wants to be mayor."

"Except Jacobson."

"Right."

"And for some reason I don't understand, you."

"Yeah. The job grew on me. At first, it felt good to do something for my neighbors. Then—" He cleared his throat. "It's gonna sound soppy, but then Devon arrived. I want to shape the town where she grows up, make it safe and wonderful for her. I can't do that if voters don't trust me to protect their interests."

"When's the election again?"

"Three weeks."

"Plenty of time. We'll solve the case; you'll be a hero and be re-elected. Live happily ever after."

"That would be good."

Chapter 25

AFTER HE ENDED the call with Harris, Gabe uploaded his pictures of the graffiti at Minken's site and the ones he'd taken of Jack's handiwork at the smelter. He studied them. His stomach lurched. The graffiti at Minken's was all uppercase, with a dot over the letter *i*. It looked exactly like Jack's graffiti. Had Jack lied again?

He squinted at the lettering on the pictures of Jack's graffiti. The dot over the *i* was a distinct diamond. On the pictures of Minken's site, the dot was a sloppy starburst. Not absolute proof that Jack was innocent, but a start. Would the cops bother to do the comparison? LeBlanc, yes. Ambrose, doubtful.

Gabe googled Ambrose and found a well-managed bio: Sergeant Milton Ambrose, twenty years with the RCMP; five of those with the Major Crimes Unit; responsible for solving several high-profile crimes in British Columbia. A paucity of personal details. Nothing that said, "This man does not look past the surface."

There were several images of Ambrose online, mostly crowd shots of official functions. Gabe scrolled through them quickly. Ambrose looked bored and stiff in all of them, until the second to last image, from a 2002 issue of the *Kootenay Register*. The caption below the picture of Ambrose shaking the hand of a young police officer read, "Corporal Milton Ambrose congratulates nephew on joining Calgary Police Service."

Gabe studied the picture. The nephew looked familiar. Or perhaps Gabe was merely reacting to a family resemblance between Ambrose and his nephew. Rather than depicting a stiff, uptight man, this picture showed Ambrose as, if not happy, at ease with the world. Was it aging or advancement in the ranks that resulted in the sourpuss Gabe had met in Cheakamus?

When he turned to researching LeBlanc, the results were more fruitful, revealing that Sergeant Paul Luc LeBlanc had held varied positions within the RCMP, from Major Crimes to Homicide, before his assignment to head up the Trail Detachment. Gabe also found pictures of the officer at the finish line of the Cops Ride for Kids bike race, at a podium delivering information about substance abuse to a group of teens, and in the Valleyboys players' box at a charity hockey game against NHL old-timers.

Hungry, and noticing it was approaching noon, Gabe headed for Tiffany's and found Harris in a booth toward the back of the café, engrossed in the *Journal*. Gabe grabbed a mug of Mudshark, waved at Minken on a counter stool, and slid into the booth. Harris glanced up and tapped the paper. "You're famous."

The headline "Mayor's Close Associate in Food Fight with Cops" sat above a picture of a spaghetti-splattered Ambrose staring stonily down at Gabe who knelt on Tiffany's floor.

He read the article.

"Peaceful Sunday dining was disrupted as Mayor Chilton's close associate D.S. Gabrieli tossed his

takeout meal at an RCMP officer from the Major
Crimes Unit. Sources say assault charges are possible.

"Gabrieli arrived in Cheakamus claiming to be interested in buying The Peak Bar. In reality, he is a private
investigator from Alberta, a former lawyer, and a
onetime murder suspect."

The article then summarized several old Calgary newspaper stories outlining Drake-the-stalker's death and subse-
quent murder charges against Gabe. The article concluded:

"Charges in the Drake case were stayed by the Crown.
Drake's murder remains unsolved."

Gabe lowered the paper and twirled his coffee mug on the
table. "Not very favorable, is it? Yet all true."

Harris said, "In his editorial, Jacobson rants about a
rumor I funneled town money to you for an investigation.
Then he suggests rational voters will boot me out rather than
have the town run by crooks, meaning me, who hang out with
hoods, meaning you."

"What rumor? You haven't given me any money."

Harris shrugged. "Politics. You get used to lies and cheap
shots."

Rhonda appeared tableside, menus clutched to her chest.
"I dunno if I should let you have a menu, Gabe. A couple
days ago you ordered and walked out before I could get the
food up. Now you have moved on to ordering, picking up, and
throwing your food around the café." She grinned to take the
bite out of her words.

"Turns out that last plan was a bad one." Gabe studied
her for a second, and then said, "How about I sing in
exchange for a menu?" He hummed a few notes of *Help me,
Rhonda.*

Rhonda raised her hand. "Stop that." She handed over the menus, and after they ordered, she turned toward the kitchen. Gabe touched her arm and stopped her. "Listen, Rhonda, I didn't kill anyone."

"I believe you. Don't sweat that article. We all read the *Journal* with a jaundiced eye."

———

PARTWAY THROUGH LUNCH, Jack entered the café and spoke with Rhonda, before joining Harris and Gabe in the booth.

"I'm real glad to see you," he said to Gabe. "Are you okay? Roxy told me what happened last night."

"Thanks, Jacko," Gabe said around a mouthful of burger. "Things are copacetic. Shouldn't you be in school?"

"No classes for me today," Jack said in a rush. He flicked his eyes around the café. "Doc Mitchell just called me. She spoke to the SPCA about the herd and the fact no one knows who owns it. They told her to go ahead with the rescue."

"Yeah." Gabe watched Jack carefully.

"The Green Dudes can help after school. We've got supplies. I came to pick up sandwiches."

Minken slid off his counter stool and approached the booth, yanking on his wide red suspenders. He turned to Jack. "You're the kid who found those horses. How're you getting them off the mountain?"

"A ramp down to the ATV trail."

Minken smacked Jack on the shoulder. "That makes complete sense. Good to see a young man with initiative."

Jack blushed. "Thanks."

With a tug on his suspenders, Minken reclaimed his counter seat. Jack turned to Gabe, a hopeful smile on his face. "Can you help?"

Gabe ranked manual labor far, far down his list of favorite pastimes. Especially with a wonky, swollen knee. And a series of explosions to investigate. But Jack was looking at him the way he used to when he was eight, with a new baseball, hoping to play catch with his grown-up brother. "Gotta find the bombers, so I can't give you much time, Jacko. I'll try to hammer a few nails with you, but first I'm buying some snow boots."

Jack jumped out of the booth. "Rockin'. See you out at the Valley of Horses. Cool name, hey? I dreamed it up."

"Jacko, hang tight. I have some questions."

Jack stopped, his expression neutral.

Gabe lowered his voice. "Were you at the Evergold Museum yesterday?"

Jack brushed at his jeans. "Nope. I told you. Roxy and I were on the Rimrock trails. That's how we spotted the herd."

"Huh. We were on the trails too. It's strange we didn't run into you. I saw an ATV that looked a lot like yours parked at the museum."

"Lots of ATVs like mine, I guess."

"I guess." Gabe studied Jack's face. "Help us take you off the suspect list. Wednesday afternoon, when the Fortune Gold explosion happened—were you at school?"

Jack's face tightened. "I don't memorize where I am every minute of every day. I said I didn't do anything. Isn't that enough?"

"In a perfect world, sure. It's a simple question. Did you have classes Wednesday afternoon?"

Jack stared at the ceiling. "I can't remember. Gotta go." He hurried to the front counter, collected three large trays of sandwiches, and left.

Gabe watched Jack leave and then grimaced at Harris. "He's hiding something. I hope it's a girl and not explosives. Perhaps the school will tell me his class schedule."

Harris shook his head. "Maybe they'd tell Mercy cause she's his mother. But you, not a chance. Privacy issues."

Privacy sometimes sucked.

Chapter 26

NOT LONG AFTER Jack left Tiffany's, a trim, middle-aged man walked into the café. He wore hiking boots, jeans and a black down coat that reached his knees. All conversation and clatter stopped. The man nodded at the people gawking at him and made his way to the rack of thermoses where he poured a coffee to go.

"You're supposed to be dead," Minken said to the man.

"So I hear."

Gabe leaned forward and whispered, "Aldercott?" Harris nodded.

"Where've you been?" Minken continued. "People have been trying to reach you since Saturday. Don't you answer your phone?"

"I was fishing at River's End Resort up the coast. No cell coverage. When I received the messages last night, I checked in with the Mounties and they filled me in. I got back to town an hour ago and saw the mess at my site. The vandals even blew up drill holes. Those idiots know nothing about mining if they think blowing up old holes will shut down an operation. However, by design or sheer luck, their explosives also wrecked my drill rig. And if anything will stop exploration dead, that will do it. I gotta start all my drilling over. It's gonna cost me big bucks."

"Better than costing your life." Minken said. "Who d'you think the dead guy is?"

"Well, not my driller 'cause I spoke to him last night. Maybe that old coot Thorvaldsen. I found him sleeping in my core shack a couple times. Could have been looking for shelter." Aldercott sighed as he put a lid on his coffee. "The police will figure it out. Meanwhile, I'm gonna celebrate being alive and call my insurance company." He headed out the door.

"Hell," Gabe said to Harris in a low voice. "I barely got the Viking *on* my suspect list and now he might be dead." He struggled out of the booth. "Catch you later."

Gabe limped down the sidewalk, catching up to Aldercott midblock. "Got a minute?"

Aldercott stopped, looked up and focused on Gabe's shiner. "That musta hurt."

"It looks worse than it is. My name's Gabrieli. I heard the talk in the café. I'm staying at Greta Rocque's place. She said Ed Gwinn had been working at your site."

Aldercott's eyes narrowed. "Yeah?"

"Any chance he could be the victim?"

Surprise flickered in Aldercott's eyes. "Never thought of that." He paused for a moment. "No. Ed finished up last week, Friday or Saturday, and took off right away." Aldercott sipped his coffee. "Why d'you ask?"

"Greta seems fond of him. Just worried for her sake. Thanks for your time." Gabe nodded goodbye and limped his way further along the sidewalk to Findrich's Gear. Inside the otherwise empty store, a wiry man greeted him with a firm handshake. "George Findrich. What can I do for you?"

"Gabe Gabrieli. We're going to Rimrock to help move some horses that are stranded there, and I need something warmer and dryer than these boots. Also, weatherproof pants and gloves."

"You're Harris's friend. Heard about you. And the horses. I plan to go out there this afternoon."

Gabe purchased thermal pants, two turtlenecks, gloves, and extreme-duty boots. After he rang up the sale, Findrich said, "If you need an ATV, I have a rental place. Great rates."

"Been there. Rented a Polaris. You're a phenomenon, George—this store, vehicle rentals, and Harris says you're on the council. Don't you have a ranch too?"

Findrich nodded and bagged Gabe's purchases. "The reality of small towns is you need several things on the go to make a living. Especially if you want to live on a few acres and raise some horses. Still, I'm not as busy now as when I was the town's only doctor."

"How big a load is the council?"

"A meeting or two a month. Plus, about a hundred hours on the phone with disgruntled citizens."

"I thought I'd check out tonight's meeting."

"It will be spirited. This sabotage has everyone on edge. New town versus old town kind of thing."

"How so?"

Findrich tidied a display of sweaters. "One side wants the extra business mining could bring. The other side thinks open pit mines will ruin tourism."

"Any thoughts on who's sabotaging the exploration sites?"

Findrich studied Gabe and cleared his throat. "I'm guessing Harris asked you to look into it, right?"

"Yeah, but please keep it to yourself."

Findrich nodded.

"And Jacobson's editorial is hooey," Gabe said. "Harris hasn't given me any money."

"Never doubted that," Findrich said. "Jacobson wants to discredit Harris, either directly or through his friends. I read about your troubles in Calgary. Seems to me the police had no reason to charge you."

"Correct, they didn't. So, got any thoughts about who's responsible?"

Findrich hesitated and then resumed folding sweaters. "Not really."

The look on Findrich's face told Gabe otherwise. "I think the explosions are more than a fight about business choices," Gabe said. "Like, maybe someone has a grudge."

"I suppose," Findrich said.

"Anything like that around town?"

"Well. A few people detest mining."

"Anyone in particular?" Gabe said.

Findrich looked around the store. Gabe's interest heightened.

"This is just for example, okay? I don't think he'd do anything."

Gabe waited.

"Wally Mitchell. Nicole and Tom's father. Someone like him might want to get even."

"Why's that?"

Just as Findrich opened his mouth to continue, three women entered the store and made a beeline for Findrich.

Findrich smiled an apology at Gabe. "Maybe we can talk after the meeting?"

Chapter 27

CLOSE TO MIDAFTERNOON Gabe pulled into Harris's yard and parked at the end of an orderly row of pickups near the garage. "Look at that, Three. All your friends are here."

Through an open garage door, Gabe saw what Jack and his Green Dudes had accomplished today. Trestle tables held water jugs, thermoses and food. Shovels, and stacks of lumber and plywood, lined the wall. Jacko would make a great fundraiser.

Gabe lowered his truck's tailgate, ready to unload his ATV. A woman's voice said, "You *must* be the infamous Gabrieli. To hear my brother and Harris tell it, you walk on water. But to the police and the *Journal*, you're a hood. Which is it, messiah or thug?"

The hair on the back of Gabe's neck took offense and rose. He turned to face a woman wearing a bulky black jacket over tight jeans. Short black curls, a wide smile, eyes hidden behind white-framed sunglasses that reflected Gabe's unsmiling face.

"Nicole Mitchell," she said. "I recognize you from the paper, D. S. Gabrieli."

She removed her sunglasses, squinted at him, and waggled

her eyebrows. "I gotta say the picture doesn't do you justice." A pause. Then, "You look rougher in the flesh."

Ordinarily, it took a few minutes for people to irritate Gabe. This woman did it in thirty seconds. He filed her under "Work, piece of."

She moved to climb into the bed of the truck. "Want help with your ATV?"

"No."

He pulled down the ATV ramps, letting the bottom edges slam on the ground. He climbed the ramp, metal clanging with each step, matching the pounding of his pulse. At the top, he turned and saw her watching him, sunglasses back in place, her grin revealing a tiny gap between her front teeth.

"We're going to be godparents." She said it as she would if they were a couple, and she were announcing a pregnancy.

Gabe clenched his jaw and glared at her. "I'm gonna stand at the front of a church for five minutes. You might be there too. But that doesn't mean we're gonna have a relationship, if that's what you're getting at."

Nicole's mouth dropped open. Her cheeks flamed. She clamped her lips together. "Not a chance. I was just making polite conversation."

"Calling someone a common thug when you know squat about diddly is not polite conversation."

She stood wide-legged, arms akimbo. "Ooh, no sense of humor. Are all Albertans as prickly as you? Hold it. I forgot. Harris is an Albertan, and he's laid back. So, it must be just you who's an asshole."

She spun on her heel and stalked off, tossing her last words over her shoulder. "See you in church, bucko."

Gabe turned his attention to the Polaris, wrenching at the tie-down straps and muttering to himself as he guided the vehicle down the ramp.

He flung the ramps back into the truck bed and slammed

the tailgate. "Bucko. Give me a break. Ms. Perfect Godmother."

———

HALF AN HOUR LATER, Harris and Gabe parked at the trailhead near Jack's Valley of Horses. ATVs and piles of lumber crowded the turnaround, where Jack and a collection of teens and men studied a diagram.

"Hey, Jacko, what's up?"

Jack grinned at Gabe. "A Dude's father designed a plan for the ramp and we're divvying up the work."

"What can we do?"

"Some guys are with the horses, digging a path to connect to the ramp here. Maybe help them?"

Harris and Gabe climbed the slope, Gabe planting his feet carefully to avoid slipping on the rocks once again. When they reached the plateau, they trekked the now well-traveled path through the snow to the bare route beside the mountain face and from there to the Valley of Horses.

Yesterday's quiet but anxious field now buzzed with purposeful noises. Gabe spotted Tom Mitchell hauling water to the small herd in their still-green oasis. Several feet from the original site of the lean-to, at a spot perhaps ten feet from the western perimeter of the pasture, George Findrich worked alongside Horace Minken digging a trench through the drifts. Helping them was a tall, thin man with dreadlocks spilling from the bottom of his ski hat.

Gabe spotted the filly and her buddies standing nearby, a three-inch cushion of clean straw beneath their hooves. Horse blankets, along with a bulging bag of alfalfa and a plastic water trough, sat nearby. The young horse, a clean white bandage on her withers, stood between the gelding and mare. Gabe doubted he could slide an onionskin between their bodies.

He inched over to the filly sandwich. Although the filly's legs trembled, the horses stood their ground. He grabbed a fistful of alfalfa from the sack, held the offering beneath the filly's mouth, and stroked her left ear with his free hand. "Looking good today, sweetie. Got your buddies keeping you warm and safe. And good food to stoke your furnace. Wanna try some?"

She snorted out a breath and tossed her head aside. "Hah. I get it. Next time, cookies." Gabe stroked her forehead, and then joined Findrich and Minken. He introduced himself to the fellow in dreadlocks, who said his name was Phil Livesay.

"Can I help?" Gabe said.

Dreadlocks Phil gestured at the pile of shovels nearby. "Grab one and dig in."

"What's the plan?"

"The snow's about a meter deep here. We're dumping it over the edge to clear a path."

Gabe peered over the lip to the small mounds of snow heaped on the bench of soil, bushes, and brambles below.

Minken and Dreadlocks Phil moved down the line, Minken talking animatedly and Phil grinning and nodding in response. Taking a spot near Findrich, Gabe dug, scooped a shovel-full of snow, and tossed it over the edge into the basin below the plateau. His arms protested immediately. Dig, scoop, toss. Over and over, the ache in his arms increasing with each effort.

He glanced at Findrich, bit back a wince, and said, "So, George, finish your story about Wally Mitchell, the guy who might hate miners."

Findrich shoveled and talked at the same time. Hardly gasped at all. "Wally was a high school teacher in town. Invested big in a mining company, a sure thing. Guess what happened? Wally lost everything—their retirement savings, funds set aside for Tom's college. The trauma affected his teaching. Eventually they fired him. He vowed to get even with scumbag miners if it killed him."

Gabe tossed a load of snow over the edge. "When was this?"

"Three, four years ago. Nicole had finished vet school a couple years earlier. Tom had just started high school." Findrich stopped shovelling. "Let's take a breather."

Gabe offered a silent prayer of thanks, leaned on his shovel, and sucked in air. "Where can I find Wally?"

"Singleton. Blackjack dealer at Lakesedge Casino."

"What's the name of the company he invested in?"

Findrich shrugged. "Can't remember."

"Anyone else in town who invested?"

"Sure. But they never threatened to get even."

Gabe tucked the information away and put visiting the casino on his to-do list. Took trench digger off his list of future careers.

Chapter 28

GABE LIMPED along the garden path to Greta's house, expecting that by now she'd read the morning's *Journal*. Expecting an eviction.

"I'm sorry," Greta said, when she opened the back door. Today's tunic was pale blue, and her leggings sported yellow lightning bolts.

Gabe proffered the apartment keys. "I'm not a murderer, but I understand you'd want me to move out."

"Good grief, what are you talking about?"

"The story in the paper."

"Oh, that. You couldn't have killed anyone, or they'd never ask you to be Devon's godfather." She waved him into the kitchen and pushed the door closed. "Will they charge you with assault? Will there be a trial?"

"I hope not on both counts. Maybe. But it's all bogus, and Harris is a talented lawyer. I'm not worried." Greta looked unconvinced. Perhaps Kate wasn't the only mind reader in town.

"When you opened the door just now," Gabe said, "you said you were sorry. I thought you were leading up to evicting me. If not that, then what?"

147

"I'm sorry Bill wrote about your history."

"No big deal." Gabe relaxed against the counter and grinned down at her. "He's getting payback for the fun we had with him over my name."

Greta toyed with one of the gold studs in her left earlobe and studied his face, her gaze moving from his eyes to his mouth and back to his eyes. "Daniel."

"Huh?"

"Your name. You look like a Daniel."

Gabe shook his head. "Promise never to tell?" When Greta nodded, he said, "Desert Sun."

Greta's face was momentarily still, then a smile started in her eyes. By the time it hit her lips, it was a full-out grin. "It definitely fits. Your mother must be prescient."

Gabe had no idea what she meant. He pushed away from the counter. "Do you have a map of the Evergold mine tunnels?"

"Somewhere. Why?"

"There's a tunnel opening on that plateau you own on Rimrock, where the stranded horses are. I want to see where it goes."

Greta said, "It will take me some time to dig through the old mine records."

Gabe pushed himself away from her counter. "I'm going to get ready for the town meeting. Will that give you time to find it?"

"Plenty. I was about to make dinner. Why not join me? We can look at the map together."

It took Gabe twenty-two minutes to shower, shave, and change into clean jeans and one of his new sweaters. Ten seconds to pick up his mother's text message that she'd arrived at O'Malley's. Two minutes to pull on boots, grab a jacket, and return to Greta's. This time he managed to knock before she opened the door. He smelled bacon.

"Perfect timing," she said. "I hope you like breakfast for dinner."

"Who doesn't?"

———

AFTER THEY WASHED the dinner dishes, Greta extracted a yellowed map from a drawer by the sink and unfolded it on the table. She put her index finger on the center of the map. "This is a bird's-eye view of the mine. The numbers beside the tunnels show the elevation."

"Does the tunnel exiting onto the plateau connect to the main entrance to the mine?" Gabe asked.

"They all do. Some just take longer to get there." She stabbed her finger on a spot just off center of the map. "Here's the largest portal, by the museum, which is the entrance to the main tunnel. It's where we moved most of the equipment in and out of the mine."

Her finger then drew a line along the main tunnel to a spot that reminded Gabe of half a wagon wheel—a hub of sorts—from which three spokes radiated outward and snaked their way farther into the mine. His eyes followed the branches as they curved and meandered along, and noticed that eventually they ended abruptly.

"Do all these come to a dead-end?" he said, jabbing his finger on the end of one of the branches.

"Those are the main secondary tunnels. See how they have a couple offshoots? Each offshoot allowed the miners to follow the veins of gold. The dead end you think you see is actually an opening, some onto pastures, or the plateau you discovered. They were emergency exits for workers. There's one on Solomon's Choice Ranch, another on the west side of Rimrock, and the third on your plateau."

Her finger moved along the farthest left of the three spokes. "This would be your tunnel. It heads south and is the correct elevation. As I said, the other tunnels go west, or north toward Solomon's Choice."

"What's the distance, from the tunnel exit on the plateau to the main portal back at the Museum?"

Greta studied the map. "Less than a mile, more than a half. Why?"

"Could we move horses through the tunnel, rather than taking them along the ATV trail behind Harris's ranch?"

She mulled it over. "You'd need to remove the boards sealing the tunnel."

Gabe shook his head. "No, this one isn't sealed. It's wide open."

She stared at him, slack jawed. "Damn kids. They're always trying to access the tunnels. I'll have the tunnel resealed."

"Would it work—with the horses?"

"You'd need the tunnel lights. The whole mine has electricity, but I shut it all down once the mine closed. However, I can activate them for you. Then, assuming you can coax the horses into the tunnel, you could put horse trailers at the museum portal, load them up, and transport them somewhere safe and warm." She grinned. "You're a genius. I love geniuses."

Gabe loved women with a penchant for wild prints and multiple earrings.

———

HALF AN HOUR before the town meeting, Gabe squeezed his truck into a spot in the lot behind the municipal building, next to a familiar orange Vanagon. He saw Harris through the office window that faced the lot, sitting at the desk, back to the window, flicking through a stack of papers. Gabe rapped on the window on his way past and opened the back door. "I parked beside that shaggin' wagon. It's the same van we saw the other day, correct?"

Harris swiveled in his chair and peered out the window, fingering tonight's bolo tie: a turquoise triangle encased in silver. "Yeah." He waved at George Findrich, just getting out of his car.

Findrich entered from the parking lot. "Harris, I have an idea." He turned to Gabe. "Suppose the town hires you? What kind of money would you want?"

Gabe glanced at Harris, who sat motionless. "I'm already digging around on the QT."

"Everyone knows you're a P. I.," Findrich said. "They'll assume you're investigating. You might as well earn some money."

Gabe thought about his bank balance. "What do you think, Harris?"

"If council approves it, I'm all for it."

"Okay. My daily rate's four hundred, but I'll cut a deal. How's two-fifty, plus expenses?"

Findrich said, "Sounds fair. I'll personally throw in ten grand if you solve the case in under a week. How about a three-liner bio for the meeting?"

"Sure. Been in business a year. Don't do divorces. Solved a missing teenager case just before I came here. I've also done some white-collar stuff. I work well with the police."

Gabe reconsidered. "After yesterday, scratch that last line."

Chapter 29

CONVERSATION AND LAUGHTER echoed and swirled through the municipal building's cavernous lobby. Drawn by the aroma of coffee, Gabe approached two long tables flanking the double doors to the council chamber. In front of trays of pastries and large thermoses of coffee and tea, a small sign stated, "Compliments of Etta's Edibles and Tiffany's Café."

Nicole Mitchell, the vet and godmother, stood talking to Carl Dochmann from the dude ranch, and a rangy man who Gabe guessed was in his late forties. On second look, he realized Nicole was doing the listening and Rangy was doing the talking. She stood against the wall, the two men blocking any escape. The set of her jaw and the flaming red on her cheeks told Gabe more about her mood than the smile she offered the men as they loomed over her. If there was one thing he'd learned earlier today, it was how to recognize anger in Nicole Mitchell.

Choirboy muscled his way into Gabe's head: "Nicole's outnumbered." Gabe shook his head. His screw-it self said, "Odds are she instigated the confrontation by calling Rangy a thug."

Gabe selected a Nanaimo bar from the tray of pastries,

poured a small coffee, and strolled over to the trio. When Nicole's eyes flicked Gabe's way, Carl tracked her glance and raised his hand, cutting Rangy off midsentence.

"Hey, Nicole," Gabe said. "I heard you checked out the injured filly." He nodded at Carl and smiled at Rangy. "Name's Gabe."

Rangy lifted a hand in greeting. "Solomon Phoebus. New in town?"

"Gabe says he's thinking of buying The Peak Bar," Carl said. "The *Journal* says he's a private investigator."

"Neither one's a lie," Gabe said. "Solomon Phoebus. You own Solomon's Choice Ranch. Quite the spread, I hear."

"We're doing okay. If my staff stopped leaving horses out in snowstorms we'd do even better."

Gabe turned to Nicole. "You've discovered who owns the herd?"

Nicole nodded and said, "The story is an employee forgot to round up the herd."

"Not only did Nestor forget," Phoebus said, "but when he remembered, he never told us. We just learned about it today from Manny."

"Manny?" Gabe said.

"Manfred Aldercott," Carl said. "A guest at our resort. He was in Tiffany's and heard everyone talking about the horses. I'd fire Nestor, but he's Etta's brother and if he goes, she'll quit. And we can't lose our chef."

"That plateau's a fair distance from the resort," Gabe said. "How did your herd get there to begin with?"

"We move them via the trails," Carl said.

Gabe turned to Nicole. "Speaking of trails, can the filly handle the ATV trail?"

She shrugged. "Hope so. It seems to be the sole choice."

Phoebus chimed in. "When we learned our herd was stuck up there and that Nicole was tending to Junebug, our filly, I called Nicole. She said she'd been in touch with the SPCA, so

I contacted them. We were just about to make arrangements with Nicole for the horses. Carl will help with the work, and of course, as I told the SPCA, we'll pay all costs."

It sounded reasonable to Gabe. But Nicole's cheeks were flushed again.

She said, "As you know Mr. Phoebus, the SPCA is now in control of the situation. I'm sure they told you this, but just to be clear: you can collect five of the horses once you get them off the mountain. But Junebug must stay at the Chilton ranch until she's recovered. And her buddies, Streak and Twyla, should stay with her. The SPCA also wants me to check your full herd and your facilities."

Phoebus reddened. He sputtered. "This is outrageous. We had no idea those horses were out there. Nestor was stupid and deceived us."

Nicole shrugged. Folded her arms. "It's out of my hands. Tell it to the SPCA."

"Yeah, and the reason we have to do that is because you butted in and called them," Carl said, stepping forward.

When Carl moved toward Nicole, Gabe stiffened and moved closer to her.

Carl stopped. He smiled, his eyes crinkling, and spoke to Phoebus but kept his eyes on Nicole. "Sol, our facilities are top notch. We know our herd's healthy and as soon as our little lady vet here sees our operation, the SPCA will know it too."

He put his hand on Nicole's shoulder. "How's tomorrow sound, Doc? Got time in your busy schedule to fit us in?"

Nicole jerked her shoulder away. "I'll phone Mr. Phoebus to schedule a visit." She stepped past them and marched into the council chamber.

Carl watched her leave. He grinned and scratched his head. "Looks, brains and spirit. Gonna get her in trouble one of these days."

CLUTCHING HIS COFFEE AND DESSERT, Gabe slipped into the chamber, wondering which of Nicole's three qualities Carl thought were troublesome. To Gabe, they were all pluses.

He sipped his coffee and surveyed the crowded room, searching for Greta. She waved from her spot in the third row on the left side and shimmied over to make space.

"The entire town seems interested in tonight's agenda," he said, easing onto the bench and straightening his right leg as far as possible. He bit into his Nanaimo bar.

"It's more likely they're here to check you out," she said.

That stopped him mid-chew. "Huh?"

Greta laughed. "Good grief, don't look so surprised. Gossiping is a tradition here. You think everyone came to listen to town business? Hah. Trust me, you're a hot topic and everyone wants to see for themselves."

She gave him the once-over. "Even with stitches, you clean up pretty good. That will please the women, for sure. They're all sizing you up."

Gone was the worried Greta of earlier. Back was Mae West. Her words struck a chord with Gabe. It had been a long time since any woman had been pleased with him.

He scanned the room. A few men glanced his way, including Carl and Phoebus, who occupied a bench across the room behind Jacobson. There were about forty women in the room, but none were looking at Gabe. Perhaps the sizing up was over. Perhaps Greta was having him on.

The door behind the council table opened. Harris entered, followed by George Findrich, Rhonda Zalesko from Tiffany's, and Cheryl McMillan, the realtor.

"Good evening," Harris said. "Let's get started."

Harris ran a quick, efficient meeting. The agenda dealt with renewal of a street-cleaning contract, approval of a poop-and-scoop bylaw, and a report on the need for two additional traffic lights. Twenty minutes after calling the meeting to order, Harris said, "That concludes the general business. Now, George Findrich has a proposal he'd like to raise."

Findrich stood. "Mayor Chilton was not aware of my item of business until this evening. It's about the bombings. I propose the town engage Mr. Gabrieli to look into them."

Jacobson jumped up. "How can you even consider hiring an accused murderer?" He gave Gabe a small salute. "Nothing personal. It's just the facts."

Gabe called up every shred of acting ability and offered a serene smile.

"Your own article said the charges were stayed, Bill," Rhonda said. "So, not relevant."

"Well, what does that say about the mayor that he has thugs for friends?" Bill said.

"Why hire anyone?" Cheryl McMillan said. "Especially someone who doesn't live here."

She sent an icy smile in Gabe's direction. Okay, he thought, Cheryl's figured out I'm not buying The Peak.

"No offense to Mr. Gabrieli," Cheryl said, "and yes, I want this sabotage stopped, but why not let the RCMP handle this? They're trained for it."

Findrich said, "It can't hurt. The cost is reasonable. Two hundred and fifty a day, plus expenses, and a bonus for a quick solve."

Jacobson leaped up again. "That's ridiculous. He'll waste time, do nothing, and we still have to pay him."

"That's the point of a bonus," Findrich said. "An incentive to work hard. And don't ask what it is, because I'm paying the bonus, not the town."

"What's stopping him racking up unreasonable expenses, living large while he's here?"

Findrich's smile reminded Gabe of a timber wolf with prey in its sights. "Mr. Gabrieli is staying at the Rocque & Hound and eats most meals at Tiffany's. Are you suggesting those businesses charge unreasonable amounts?"

Greta squirmed in her seat and said, "I hope not. Come election day, I'm not voting for anyone who says my rates are too high." The room erupted in laughter.

"Mayor Chilton," Findrich said. "I move we hire D. S. Gabrieli. Let's vote."

Harris said, "I'll abstain since Gabe is my friend. All in favor?"

Findrich and Rhonda raised their hands. Cheryl McMillan sat, arms folded. The others stared at her. She sighed, raised her hand, and said, "Fine. Yes."

"Approved," Harris said. "If there's nothing else—"

Horace Minken interrupted. "A comment. Thanks for hiring Gabe. We miners are worried about the risk of more explosions. We want the madman caught."

Phil Livesay stood, his dreadlocks swinging. "Here's a solution. A moratorium on exploration. The bomber won't have any targets. We'll be safe."

A man seated beside Minken jumped up. Red hair, redder face. He pointed a finger at Livesay. "There's your suspect right there. Goddamn tree huggers like nothing better than stopping progress. They've been against mining from the get-go." He shook his finger at the crowd, and spittle appeared at the side of his mouth. "Mark my words. They'll come for you next. Backpackers, trail riders, Blackstrap Mountain—you'll all be accused of messing with ecology."

"Get serious," Dreadlocks Phil said. "We're pacifists. Miners have upset other people too. How about the ranchers whose animals step into your drill holes and break legs?"

"It's not my holes, you fool," Redhead said. "The drillers leave the holes open. They're supposed to fill 'em. And the drillers are from right here, local guys. They're the ones messing up. Go piss on them if you got a complaint."

Harris tapped his gavel on the desk. Jacobson raised his camera.

A voice boomed from two rows behind Redhead. A

middle-aged bald man stood. "I'm a local driller and I resent the hell out of what this know-nothing just said." Baldy jabbed his finger at Redhead as he spoke. His voice drowned out Harris's gavel. "You get what you pay for and you, my friend, are too cheap to pay the going rate for local drillers. Instead, you hire some brainless screw-up from who knows where to drill your holes." Baldy sat down, his chest heaving.

Harris's gavel pounded the desk. "Calm down, everyone. Gabe will look into things. We'll work with the police to put things on an even keel."

Easier said than done, Gabe thought, studying the restless crowd.

Chapter 30

ROCKY'S MOOD was upbeat tonight. Bright moonlight and a deserted trail. Everyone would be at the town meeting, arguing about mining and dynamite.

Doc's plan called for a loud, daylight explosion to flatten Minken's second drill. Fine. Except the sole access to Chilton's pasture where Minken's drill sat was this public trail, which the do-gooders were using for their horse-rescue mission. Plus, the drill was visible from the trail. Even though Minken's driller was away for a week, Rocky knew better than to spend hours rigging explosives in full view, in a daylit pasture, with all the horse-lovers traipsing by.

Rocky was somewhat concerned about ignoring instructions again. He could do without a repeat of the shouting match that erupted when Rocky admitted he'd stashed the Ranger on Rimrock. Doc had been apoplectic.

Mountains from molehills was what Rocky had thought. Who cared if the dead guy's truck was discovered? People would think the driver had gone hiking. Okay yeah, the lack of license plates could make people suspicious. Round and round they went, until Rocky said he'd fix it. Which he did. One call and a couple hundred bucks later got him truck jockeys who were ecstatic about driving the rig to Vancouver and enjoying a night in the big city.

Perhaps Doc was right about the Ranger. But planting and setting off explosives in daylight was another story. Although Rocky had pulled it off at Fortune Gold, that site was far from public trails and work had finished for the day.

Rocky had decided to prepare things tonight, when everyone was off the mountain. Tomorrow, he'd merely need to visit the pasture long enough to light the fuse. Three minutes tops. A risk, but minimal.

He worked methodically when he got to the drill, concentrating on making the setup look amateurish. Three times his usual amount of Forcite went on the metal tower. Doc wanted it loud. Loud it would be. More Forcite went under the core racks. When the explosion hit, pieces of core would whiz past the Space Station.

Their plan was coming together. The cops and townspeople believed the sabotage was the work of angry environmentalists. And the tree huggers in Cheakamus were young and mouthy, like that Diamond kid. They made excellent suspects.

After Rocky finished securing the explosives, he laid out fuse in a Y, one arm from the drill, the other from the core shack, and the tail extending toward the trees. It would burn in about seven minutes—ample time for him to be far away when things got busy.

He shook the aerosol can. Sprayed "No Mining" in ragged red letters over the ground by the core shack. He collected his supplies, got on his ATV, and left.

Chapter 31

After the meeting Gabe offered Greta a ride home and escorted her to the parking lot, where a blonde was busy organizing the contents of the orange Vanagon and a goliath leaned against the front fender of the Truck Named Three.

Gabe would have told the hulk to get his rear with its collection of wallet chains and jean studs off Three's pristine paint, but the closer he got, the bigger and more fit the guy appeared. He wore a denim jacket and down vest, serious boots, and a frown. Gabe filed him under "Huge, trouble variety."

Gabe could do many stupid things, but given a chance, he favored avoiding poundings. Especially by a colossus in steel-toed boots. He hit the unlock button on his key fob and his truck chirped twice. Huge jumped in response and moved away.

"Evening," Gabe said, as he and Greta passed.

"Hi, Maggie. Hi, Nestor," Greta said.

The blonde flashed a warm smile their way. The giant inclined his head a smidgeon.

Gabe helped Greta into the passenger seat, resisted the

urge to check the paintjob, and drove away. "Who's that mammoth?"

"Nestor Clayton," Greta said. "He works at Solomon's Choice Ranch. His sister Etta is their chef. And the woman with him is Maggie Samuels, one of their staff."

Greta sounded almost fond of Nestor. Gabe admitted to himself he might be paranoid. Massive, mean-looking guys brought that out in him. "So *that's* the guy who can't manage horses."

"What?" Greta said.

"Turns out those horses on your plateau belong to Solomon's Choice Ranch. Sol Phoebus, the guy who owns the ranch, said Nestor forgot about the herd and never fessed up."

"That doesn't sound like Nestor." Greta paused, and then said, "I'm disappointed in Sol. I'm sure he knows I own that land. I'll have to give him a call."

Gabe escorted Greta to her front door and said good night. Before he drove back to The Peak Bar, he took a chamois from the console and rubbed the front fender, checking it under the streetlight. Not a scratch. He wouldn't have to go to Solomon's Choice to seek redress after all. Good thing. He had neither the time nor inclination to visit any more emergency rooms.

———

AT THE PEAK, Gabe found Harris, Rhonda, and Cheryl lining the bar. He poured a club soda, added a twist of lime, and looked around for a bartender's apron.

"No need to work," Harris said.

"Especially now we know you're not a potential buyer," Cheryl said.

"I'd love to own it," Gabe said. "If things were different—"

Cheryl flicked her blond hair over her shoulder. "It doesn't matter. I'm in discussions with another interested party. One who's serious."

"Welcome news." Turning to Harris, Gabe said, "I met Nestor Clayton in the municipal lot. He was driving the shaggin' wagon. I thought the owner of Solomon's Choice drove it."

"Hah! No. That van is the only junker at the dude ranch. The rest of their vehicles are high end." Harris slid off his barstool. "Heading out. I need my rest in case we move the horses tomorrow."

Gabe said, "I'll see you there. I promised Junebug cookies."

"No need," Harris said. "I'll take her treats."

"Let us worry about the horses," Rhonda said. "You solve the bombings. Got a plan?"

"Originally, I was gonna find Thorvaldsen. But since Aldercott turned up alive, Thorvaldsen seems to be everybody's choice as victim. So rather than waste time, I'll do what I always do. Talk to people, see what shakes out." Gabe chuckled. "From tonight's meeting, it seems some locals are more than ready to accuse others of being bombers."

Cheryl said, "I wish they'd identify the dead guy. Can't they test his DNA?"

"The thing with DNA," Harris said, "is you need something to compare it to. Unless the victim's DNA is in a database somewhere, it's difficult."

Gabe said, "Getting back to the sabotage, is there any merit in the suggestion Dreadlock Phil's group is responsible?"

Harris shook his head and shrugged into his jacket. "No more than the Green Dudes. Phil got hot tonight because people lumped his group with radicals."

Rhonda chimed in. "Phil's bunch and Green Dudes are kindergarten classes compared to BAM."

"BAM?" Gabe said.

"Acronym for By Any Means," Harris said. "The group's

formal name is Earth First. They tag BAM on the end for effect."

"Young guys? Craig Westburg?"

Harris nodded.

"Huh. Craig omitted the BAM part when we talked the other night," Gabe said. He remembered Craig's invitation to pay them a visit. He opened his notebook and added BAM to his list.

TUESDAY

Chapter 32

ANY DOUBT GABE had that he wasn't eighteen anymore vanished when he stood in the shower Tuesday morning. Who'da thought shoveling snow would make him whimper with the effort of shampooing his hair?

Still, he was feeling positive. That was primarily because he hadn't had a run-in with Ambrose in more than twenty-four hours, a sign The Frikkin Comedian was occupied elsewhere.

He had a lengthy to-do list today: return to TEG's site; check out Wally Mitchell, the swindled investor Findrich had mentioned; and visit the BAM group.

And despite Rhonda's admonition not to worry about the horses, the injured filly pulled at Gabe, triggered his need to prove to Tornado Callie, or perhaps himself, that he wasn't beyond redemption. That meant investigating whether the tunnel offered a shorter route off the mountain, for which he needed his favorite landlady.

"How about a tour of the mine today?" he said, when Greta answered his phone call.

"Gee. Hang out with a bust-up gumshoe or do another load of washing? No contest, I'll take the gumshoe."

He felt like the first pick for the schoolyard red-rover team. Winning a popularity contest with laundry might not be something to cheer about, but life had a way of humbling a person. "Name a time."

"Eight thirty."

Gabe looked at his watch: a half hour to take care of remaining business. In Cheakamus, that was six times what he needed. He called Lakesedge Casino in Singleton and asked for Wally Mitchell. The receptionist said, "Due in at ten. Can I take a message?"

"Nope, thanks."

Grabbing his jacket and gloves, Gabe hurried to his truck. When he backed out of the garage, he noticed a skiff of snow on the lane. Flakes floated down. At this rate the town's kids would need snowshoes to make the rounds at Hallowe'en.

He patted the truck's dashboard. "Morning, Three. Busy day. We're heading down the highway, looking for adventure. Gonna check out a tunnel, play a little blackjack, visit those BAM guys and a gorgeous filly. I'm tired just talking about it. Do what you can to help a guy out."

At the service station near the Parkview Motel, he gave his truck a breakfast treat of premium, cleaned the windshield, and wiped crud off the plate. His sister Lucy had laughed when he'd bought a vanity plate, but a fine-looking truck deserved more than the basics. "Three's proud of his name," he'd said. "At least I can let him announce himself to the world."

Gabe collected Greta at precisely eight-thirty. She wore a down jacket and well-used hiking boots, and carried a bulging brown paper bag and a heavy-duty flashlight.

Once Greta settled in the truck, he loaded Ian Tyson's *All the Good 'Uns* CD, wanting some down-home music from a down-home boy. They moseyed along Lookout Road and turned onto Main Street, heading for the highway.

"Our adventure awaits, Three," Gabe said, tapping the console. "Onward."

"Do you always talk to your truck?" Greta said.

"Why not? He listens."

Soon after Gabe turned north onto the highway, Greta gestured at an overgrown track into the bush. "Once upon a time, that trail was our sole route to the Evergold." Gabe recognized the trail as the logging road Harris pointed out Sunday when they were on their ATVs above the museum.

"Any news about the body in the fire?" Greta asked. "I know it's not Manfred Aldercott."

"I'm surprised you haven't heard. People think it's someone called Thorvaldsen."

Greta jerked in her seat and gasped. "Oh no! Not Anders?" Tears welled in her eyes.

"Do you know him?"

She dug a tissue from her pocket and wiped her eyes. "Good grief, yes. A prospector, eccentric as anything, but then all geniuses are a bit that way. He rarely comes into town. I hope you're wrong."

Gabe squeezed her hand. "People could be mistaken. Meanwhile, Aldercott says he has to re-do all his drilling."

"So much for the end game," she said.

"Huh?"

"TEG Mines, Aldercott's company. T-E-G, for The End Game. I heard Aldercott coined the name because the gold deposit he discovered was his path to retirement." Her lips turned down, like she had a bad taste in her mouth.

"What do you think of him?" Gabe said.

"I don't trust him. Pierre always said, 'The more a fellow talks things up, the more reason to be warned.' Aldercott talks up a storm."

If Greta's assessment was correct, and Aldercott was shady, was that motive for the bombings? Perhaps, but there'd been two earlier explosions, one of them at Horace Minken's site. Gabe assessed Minken as a straight arrow. Whoever was flinging dynamite around seemed to toss it indiscriminately at drill sites without regard to whether or not the company exploring for gold was legit. It was Aldercott's terrible luck his operation was one of the targets. And the victim's even worse luck that he was in Aldercott's core shack at the time.

Tyson's second song on the CD ended just as Greta motioned toward the highway sign for the Evergold Museum. The access road was white with snow. "At the top of this rise, the road curves to the left. Then a couple switchbacks and you'll reach a flat table where the museum is."

Gabe shifted into four-wheel drive to negotiate the steep incline. When they rounded the second turn and entered a wide parking lot, Greta pointed at the machine shed behind the compact, red-roofed museum. "Can you park over there?"

Clutching the paper bag, she disappeared inside the shed. When she rejoined Gabe, her hands were empty.

"Ever seen a headframe?" Greta's breath puffed white as they walked through fresh snow toward the museum.

When Gabe shook his head, she pointed at the four-sided wooden tower beside the museum. "This is a mock-up. They use headframes at mines where shafts access the tunnels. It's like a freight elevator—moves miners down the shaft and lifts out the ore."

Gabe took in the cage-and-pulley system. He pictured being lowered into a narrow, dark shaft. Working far below the surface. Knowing the cage was the sole way out. Trusting the pulleys, trusting the cables. Trusting the rock overhead to stay where it belonged. He gritted his teeth and pushed the images away, taking a moment to study the layout of the museum grounds.

"Does the museum own an ATV?" he said.

"Nope, no need for one."

Greta led Gabe behind the museum to a heavy-gauge wire enclosure in front of a timbered archway in the mountain face. She flicked through a fistful of keys and unlocked the gate. "The staff opens the gate for tours between ten and three. The rest of the time it's locked."

She motioned Gabe through. "As I mentioned the other night, this portal is the primary access for the mine."

Empty ore carts sat on narrow tracks leading into the tunnel. In the tunnel's gloom, Gabe picked out timber braces spaced along its walls. Enormous wood beams and thick planking ran overhead. They had held the mountain at bay for decades, but when Gabe studied the massive load of rock they supported, he thought of Popsicle sticks and balsa. A prickling numbness attacked his cheeks and crept downward.

His ears were straining to pick up hints of beams groaning under the mountain's unrelenting pressure when Greta reached inside the timbered opening and switched on overhead lights. "Not many mines have lights in the tunnels, but Pierre installed them in the Evergold twenty years ago. This is the only section where I didn't disconnect the power. It helps us run the mine tours." She entered the tunnel.

Cold air wafted past Gabe where he stood rooted to the ground at the portal. Frigid, ancient air, carrying images of deep, still tombs. "Are we going down a shaft?"

Greta turned, a bright smile on her face. "No. All the tunnels were cut on inclines through the mountain. Lots of walking. No shafts."

Gabe's blood flowed again, the prickling eased, and the timbers and planking took on a reassuring heft. He exhaled a shaky breath and entered the tunnel. It was wider and higher than his F-150. Ore cart tracks ran down the center, leaving a bare rock, uneven walkway on either side, the surface reflecting the overhead lights.

"We'll follow this main tunnel about a hundred yards to the closed sections," Greta said. "Then we'll pass through a barricade and should be near your tunnel."

She marched ahead, sure-footed on the walkway. Gabe

limped behind, alternating between watching his step and studying the ceiling, searching for chunks fixing to fall on their heads. Each time his feet connected with a loose rock on the walkway, he checked the ceiling. "Did these rocks fall from overhead?"

"Maybe. Might have been here forever. Could have tumbled out of ore carts."

If Gabe had his druthers, Greta would be less wishy-washy and say, "Nothing to worry about, this mountain isn't coming down, ever."

When they reached a slatted wooden door that spanned the tunnel's width, Greta flicked through her keys again, selected a square-headed silver one, and turned to the door. The hasp hung open.

"Good grief! Kids. Continually unlocking the padlock. Where do they get the keys?"

"All you need is a nail file." Gabe pulled the door ajar to reveal a semi-circular cavern. Still, gloomy, stale. Waiting.

Greta eyed him. "How do you know about picking locks? Do they teach that in P.I. school?"

Gabe's quick laugh bounced off the jagged rock walls. "In our teens Harris and I were always looking for party places far away from parents and cops. Padlocks never stopped us."

Greta stepped through the doorway, switched on her flashlight, and illuminated three tunnels radiating from the circular hub, two angling to the right, one to the left.

She pointed the flashlight toward the far right-hand tunnel. It illuminated several feet of jagged rock walls and a narrow-gauge rail line. "If I remember correctly that tunnel heads in the general area of the logging road near TEG's site."

Gabe thought of the explosion at Aldercott's exploration site. His skin crawled. "What are the odds the explosion out at TEG loosened rocks in the tunnels?"

Greta thought for a moment. "Well, I can't see any rockfall

along that tunnel. But then, by my reckoning, we are a long distance away from where the TEG site is, so we wouldn't necessarily see a collapse."

Gabe asked himself if that was good news or not.

"Fortunately," Greta went on, "no one's drilling above your tunnel. It would take a massive amount of explosives to weaken all the tunnels in the Evergold. Much more than they apparently used at TEG Mines' site. We should be okay."

There was that wishy-washiness again.

Greta moved past him. Her flashlight beam flickered in the gloom, illuminating perhaps six feet of tunnel. The blackness closed around Greta, enveloping her until he could see only the beam of light. Trying to beat back clammy numbness, Gabe closed his eyes and drew in a deep breath. When images of concrete rubble leaped behind his eyelids, Gabe snapped his eyes open, but too late. Too late to turn away from memories of a confining space beneath broken concrete —rubble that grated and groaned as it teetered above and beside him—and the still, stale darkness that surrounded him as he waited, seven years old and petrified.

"Are you coming?" Greta said.

Gabe focused on her light bouncing toward him and allowed it to pull him to the surface. He worked some saliva into his mouth and cleared his throat.

"I'm running late, Greta. I have to meet a guy at the casino. I've seen enough to understand the general layout. The rest I can get from your maps, right?"

She came into view, her head cocked to the side, studying him. She stared at him for a moment and then nodded, her eyes warm. "Of course. Let's get out of here."

Nothing wishy-washy about that. Gabe turned toward the main tunnel and its welcoming bright lights.

WHEN THEY ONCE MORE STOOD IN the enclosure outside the archway, Gabe lifted his face to the blue sky, raised his arms, and grinned. He opened his eyes to see Kate's Escape, towing a horse trailer, crossing the museum's lot toward the machine shed.

"Good," Greta said. "They've brought the horses."

"Pardon?"

"Children's wagon rides. The Museum open house. It's an annual fundraiser. We've borrowed two of Kate's Percherons to pull the wagons."

They walked to meet Harris and Kate. While Greta cooed at Devon in her baby carrier, Gabe helped Harris ready the trailer's ramp.

"We brought Blackie and Hank for the wagons," Kate said. "And Holly tagged along."

Kate backed the horses down the ramp one by one. She grabbed Hank's lead, clucked, and moved toward the machine shed. Hank ambled his "I'm too sexy for my harness" walk behind Kate, now and then reaching his head over her shoulder and batting her with his mouth. Blackberry and Holly plodded behind like enormous, well-trained heelers.

The machine shed held a newly constructed, spacious horse stall. The building was warm; daylight streamed through large windows. While Kate tended to the Percherons in their luxurious digs, Greta told Harris about the tunnel. "I'll double-check the maps, but I'm sure the tunnel connects to Jack's Valley of Horses. If Horace Minken says it's safe, you can walk the horses through it. You'll need horse trailers at this end. As for light, the switch is over there on the wall. I'll make sure the power is on, so all you need to do is flick the switch."

"Got it," Harris said.

"I have an appointment in an hour," Gabe said to Greta. "Can I drop you home before I hit the road?"

She joggled Devon in her carrier. The baby gurgled and

waved her fists. "No need. I'm going to spend some quality time with Devon."

Devon moved her eyes away from Greta and spotted Gabe. A tiny frown creased her forehead. Gabe stared her down. She looked back at Greta and gurgled again. Gabe congratulated himself. No tears. Never let them see your fear.

Chapter 33

SINGLETON WAS HALF an hour west of Cheakamus. An hour, if a guy ignored the cops' demand to stop meddling and instead took a side trip up Timberline Road, past Deception Ridge Viewpoint, to the rutted access road for TEG's site.

Grabbing his phone, Gabe hustled along the trail and stopped at the edge of the clearing. When he was certain he was alone, he snapped pictures of the site and the surrounding treed inclines.

Had he taken pictures Saturday, he admitted as he drove back to the highway, it would have saved him half an hour. However, Springsteen was singing, the sun was shining, and Highway 41 was wide, with enough tight curves to keep it interesting. A brief delay was nothing.

The highway crossed a small bridge and followed the riverbank before climbing toward a pass between low mountains. When Gabe checked his rear-view mirror at the crest of the pass, he noticed an orange-and-white van on the bridge.

On the west side of the pass, the road declined gently and he spotted Singleton hugging the eastern edge of an immense lake. Beyond the town the land opened to rolling hills.

According to Harris, vineyards and fruit orchards made

Singleton a popular tourist destination in the summer. Winter was a different story, so the town had opened the casino to increase winter tourism. Perhaps a dozen cars and trucks dotted the casino parking lot. Gabe filed the casino under "Tourists, busy elsewhere."

He parked near the casino entrance, turned off the engine, and waited. In a few minutes, the van entered the lot and stopped by the casino's loading dock. Nestor Clayton, the behemoth ranch hand, and his blond friend Maggie unloaded cartons and plastic crates.

Gabe shook off his paranoia and entered the casino. It was the size of a school gymnasium. Ten Lakesedge Casinos would fit inside the Bellagio Resort in Vegas with room to spare. Still, this place had the same bright lights overhead, busy carpet underfoot and shiny metal bars around the cashier's cage.

Four poker tables sat to the left of the entrance, but only one hosted a game. The five men and one woman clicking their poker chips and staring each other down as the dealer fed them a new hand accounted for a quarter of the casino patrons. The others were sprinkled among the slot machines and blackjack tables that bracketed the two craps tables and their lonely croupiers.

Gabe strolled along the row of blackjack tables, reading nametags on the dealers' shirts until he found a dealer wearing "Wally." His table was empty, ideal for a conversation. The table sign advised: "Single-deck blackjack, $10 minimum." Not so ideal. At those rates, Gabe needed to get him talking fast.

Gabe bought fifty dollars' worth of chips. His first ten-dollar bet gave him a queen and a ten. Wally had an eight showing. Gabe waved off more cards. The dealer's hole card was a seven, giving him fifteen. Gabe held his breath as Wally dealt himself another card.

A seven, for twenty-two. A bust. Gabe nodded, smiled at Wally, and pulled his profit off the table.

"Haven't seen you in here before," the dealer said. "Just visiting?"

"Yeah. Name's Gabrieli. I'm helping the folks in Cheakamus, trying to find out who's blowing up drill rigs and core shacks."

"Ahhh. I'm Wally Mitchell. 'Course, you know that."

He dealt Gabe blackjack. Things were picking up. Wally smiled and waited until Gabe put down a chip for the next hand. "I figured you'd come by sooner or later. You phoned this morning looking for me, right?"

Wally dealt. Gabe busted, Wally pulled the bet away, and Gabe pushed another chip forward. Of course, the receptionist would mention the call. What surprised Gabe was that Wally had put it together. Not a dumb man. "Yeah. I thought it would be good to talk to you. I heard you might have a reason to dislike mining."

Wally dealt Gabe two face cards. Wally had a six showing. Gabe waved off more cards.

"Not enough to blow up stuff." Wally's hole card was eight, giving him fourteen. He dealt himself another card, a ten. Busted. Wally shuffled the deck. He had smooth hands, long fingers, well cared for. "I didn't do it, so you came out here for nothing."

Gabe stretched his arms over his head. "Well, I don't know. It was a pleasant drive, and I enjoy blackjack. Do you always work the day shift?"

Wally eyed Gabe. "Mostly. For the record, I've been away four days, since Thursday. Got back Sunday."

"Where?"

"Just away. You gonna play some more?" He placed the deck on the table. Gabe cut the deck, pushed a chip forward, and Wally dealt. They played three hands in silence, Gabe winning two of them.

"It would help if you told me where you were," Gabe said. "I could take you off my list and go find the real bad guy."

Wally said, "Look. I got burned investing in a company run by crooks. Lost everything. I hate those scumbags. I'd like to get even, but with *them*, not every mining company."

"Any idea who might want to blow up exploration sites?"

"Some loony tunes." He dealt Gabe another blackjack. "I know what you're thinking. I went a little bonkers when it happened. But I want the crooks broke and in jail, not dead. Dead's too easy."

Wally's hands didn't look like they had been messing around with crowbars and dynamite. Gabe's intuition said Wally was giving him the straight goods. He put Wally low on his list of possible suspects. "What was the company you invested in?" Gabe said.

"High Yield. What a laugh. High yield, my ass."

Gabe pushed a tip forward and stood. "Any idea who the dead guy at TEG's site is?"

Wally shook his head. "Not a clue."

"Any idea why someone would target Minken Minerals, Fortune Gold, or TEG Mines?"

Wally had a superb poker face. Not a flicker in his eyes, not a tic anywhere. "Not a clue."

Gabe turned to leave, coming face to chest with Nestor Clayton. Nestor stepped around Gabe like a piece of furniture, put a chip on the felt and took a seat.

Chapter 34

GABE HUNG out by a slot machine and watched Nestor and Wally for a spell. Nestor bet, Wally dealt. Nestor won a hand, lost two hands, won another. Wally smiled and talked. Nestor nodded. Wally appeared to enjoy the one-sided conversation.

As Gabe drove away from the casino, he wondered how long Nestor had stood behind him. Nothing in Wally's behavior indicated anyone had been nearby, but Wally's poker face was formidable. He wouldn't react to a naked, machete-wielding woman. Suppose Nestor wasn't there to play black-jack but was in cahoots with Wally, the grudge-bearing investor?

A short distance past O'Malley's ranch, Gabe turned onto Bryson's Road. He slowed when he spotted a hand-painted wood sign announcing BAM's headquarters in lopsided green letters on a blue background: "Earth First, B.A.M. Not Far Ahead."

A few hundred yards farther a smaller version of the sign was nailed to a gate dangling from a rusted hinge: "Friends of the planet welcome. Others stay out."

Gabe tapped his dash. "Friends of Earth. That's us, Three."

The access road bumped through poplar, fir, and birch trees. It was a slow, jerky trip over bone-jarring potholes connected by ruts that lifted the truck and threatened to spin it sideways into the bush.

After six teeth-clenching moments, the trail ended at a somewhat smoother circular clearing. A large A-frame held center stage across the clearing. Nearby, a weathered barn leaned drunkenly. Butted up to it was a chicken-wire enclosure that held rusted appliances, bed frames, and metal fencing. Gabe noted two gas canisters and a wooden box bearing a yellow explosives symbol tucked beside an old washtub.

The chickens enjoyed a much classier residence on the other side of the barn—a well-constructed coop surrounded by a wire enclosure—far enough away that when the barn collapsed, it wouldn't kill them.

Gabe parked by two mud-covered trucks nosed in beside the coop, nodded hello to the girl feeding chickens, and headed to the A-frame. Two mangy hounds sprawled on a bench-style car seat on the porch. The door opened before Gabe reached the first step. Not only Greta kept an eagle eye.

Craig appeared, chewing his toothpick and toting a rifle. "It's the Gabester, bartender slash private eye."

"Nice rifle."

"I got a right to have this." Craig looked ready to call Gabe out to the OK Corral.

Gabe shrugged. "I'm sure you do."

Craig's shoulders relaxed.

"The town hired me to look into the explosions. I wanted to talk to you all."

Craig nodded. He tossed his toothpick onto the dirt and motioned Gabe inside.

The neat, warm interior was large, with an overhead loft. The main level contained an open kitchen with a long wood table, two couches, and several deep-seated chairs clustered around a river-rock fireplace. In a corner, a desk and filing cabinets sat beneath a poster Gabe recognized.

Frank Palmer, Craig's sidekick from the bar, raised a hand at Gabe. In addition to Craig and Frank, the room held four young men sporting various beards, tattoos and piercings, and two petite women, each with a shock of bright color in her bangs.

"Everyone, meet Gabe," Craig said. "He's here about the bombings."

No one seemed agitated by the announcement. Gabe had no doubt they'd spotted his truck well before it disengaged from the clutches of the trail. The guys nodded at Gabe, then stared at the fire or their navels. The women focused on a large stockpot on the stove.

"Smell's great," Gabe said. "Something Italian?"

"Minestrone," Craig said. "Hey, want some?"

"Thought you'd never ask." Gabe doffed his jacket. "I'm starved."

The group of them, ten counting the chicken feeder, gathered around the table that had room for a dozen chairs. The food would have fed another twelve ravenous people. Fresh, homemade rolls. Minestrone like that of Gabe's Italian neighbor in Eau Claire: full of pasta, tomatoes, shredded cabbage, and beans; thick like a stew and topped with freshly grated Parmesan.

"Fantastic," he said. The chef with fluorescent pink bangs smiled and ducked her head.

"Pinky and Green Goddess are super cooks," Craig said.

Gabe studied Craig across the table. "I'm trying to sort out these explosions. Do you know anything about them?"

"Just what we see on TV or read in the papers. Interesting stuff in the *Journal* about you being a murderer."

Gabe blew on a spoonful of soup and then cricked up the left side of his mouth. "The way I hear it, the *Journal* inflates, obscures, and massages the truth. Or, as in my case, avoids it completely. My hands are clean."

Craig leaned back in his chair and raised a palm. "Hey, no sweat. Just proves you never know the whole story."

"Any idea who died in the TEG explosion?" Gabe said.

Craig shrugged. "My guess? The old hermit, or some unknown draft dodger who never came out of hiding."

"Tell me about Earth First. I heard your group has activist leanings. I noticed the poster by your desk. Is that your general philosophy?"

Craig glanced at Malcolm X's infamous By Any Means poster—Malcolm X, in a suit and tie, holding a carbine, and peeking out a window. In the original version of the poster, the text beneath the image stated, "Liberate our minds by any means necessary."

The poster stirred Gabe's memories of his undergrad liberal arts courses, which he'd selected based on the proportion of women in the class. One semester, he and thirty-five sophomore women studied Jean-Paul Sartre. To Gabe's surprise, he learned a thing or two, including that Malcolm X had borrowed the sentiment for his catchphrase from a Sartre play in which the lead character advocated eradicating class by any means necessary. Gabe's professor said the word "necessary" softened the threat. If violence was unnecessary to achieve an end, Sartre's character, and presumably Malcolm X, would refrain from violence.

Someone had altered this copy of the poster to read "Protect our planet by any means."

Craig pulled his eyes back to Gabe and smiled. "We believe in being assertive, but we keep our hands clean too. We pursue legal means to protect the environment."

"What's the box of explosives out by your barn for?" Gabe said.

Craig's smile died. "Removing stumps. What else?" His face became a study in earnestness. "We're into recycling. We oppose anything that hurts the planet. Refineries, pulp mills, chemical plants. And yes, mining. It puts big scars in the earth, rips up forests. They use cyanide to remove gold from the ore. Smelters spew fumes and make ugly slag piles. But we're total pacifists."

"You ever hear of a company called High Yield something?"

Craig looked confused at the shift in direction, and then shook his head, no. Eight other heads shook in tandem.

"How about Manfred Aldercott or Horace Minken—know either of them?"

Craig shook his head. "Nope." Again, a uniform shaking of heads around the table.

"What does your group do besides recycle?"

Craig buttered a roll. "We try to attract sponsors. You said your sister invests in causes. Still want that brochure for her?"

"Sure."

"We go to protests. Chain ourselves to old-growth trees, raise money to buy land so developers can't have it, campaign and vote for the green ticket, throw punches to defend ourselves. But no bombs." He raised his palms outward. "Like I said—"

"I know. Clean hands." Gabe pushed away from the table. "How about a tour of the spread?"

Craig selected a toothpick from the holder on the table and stuck it between his lips. He leaned back in his chair, crossed his arms, and smirked at Gabe. "Not a chance."

Gabe collected his jacket, thanked them for the soup and moved to the door. Craig handed him a brochure. When Gabe stepped onto the porch, one of the mangy dogs thumped his tail on the bench seat.

"Interesting thing about that poster," Gabe said. "Did you know Malcolm X adopted the slogan 'by any means necessary' from a Sartre play?"

"So?"

"So the name of the play was *Dirty Hands*." Gabe waved the brochure. "Catch you later, Craig."

As he drove away, Gabe said to himself, "Or sooner, Craig. Maybe we'll catch you sooner."

Chapter 35

SHORTLY AFTER TWO-THIRTY Gabe reached the Valley of Horses, feeling pleased he'd checked today's items off his to-do list.

He noticed Carl Dochmann from Solomon's Choice Ranch, along with Horace Minken and Dreadlocks Phil, hauling hay. All eight horses now hung out in a clump by the bales: some with their noses stuck in the hay. Streak, Twyla, and Junebug were in their usual sandwich formation beside the trashed shelter, near the threshold with the snow-covered basin.

Gabe approached Harris, who was working by himself, loading supplies onto sleds. "Got any horse treats?"

Harris dug several from his pocket and handed them over. "Shouldn't you be off finding saboteurs?"

"Using my brain all morning wore me out," Gabe said, "so for a break, I'm gonna use my brawn."

"Nicole thinks the filly might be good to go today. Greta had Minken check out the tunnel, just to make sure it's safe. And he says it is, so I'm optimistic we can move the horses in a bit."

Gabe glanced at Junebug. She looked brighter today but still favored her leg. "D'you think they'll balk at the tunnel?"

"Dunno. But Greta has reconnected the power so we'll have lights, which should help."

When Gabe pictured the tunnel, his stomach clenched. If the horses were skittish, they wouldn't be alone. "Where's everyone else?" he said.

"Jack was due earlier but hasn't shown up. Nicole should arrive soon to check Junebug again."

Gabe glanced around, ensuring no one was within earshot, and then brought Harris up to speed on his day. "Wally Mitchell seems to be a straight shooter. Those kids at BAM have Malcolm X and his carbine on their wall and a box of explosives by their barn. Nestor Clayton pops up wherever I go. What's new at your end?"

"Kate's stressed. She's running back and forth between the ranch and the museum."

"You should hire someone to help out at the ranch."

"We have Jack, and Rhonda's kids."

"I mean a herd manager or a cook and housekeeper."

"Yeah, no. Money's tight."

"I thought The Peak was doing well?"

"It is." Harris stared at the trees for a moment, then brought his gaze back to Gabe. "The ranch sucks money like a vacuum. Plus, we have a balloon payment due on a loan. I'm not sure we can meet it."

"Renegotiate the terms."

"Impossible."

Gabe had spent his legal career negotiating business arrangements. Everything was possible, a matter of balancing costs and benefits. Before he could remind Harris of that, Phil Livesay loped over, grinning, his dreadlocks bouncing. "We've finished the path to the tunnel. Now let's move horseflesh."

"Lordy," Horace Minken said, when he and Carl Dochmann joined the group. "Who'da thought snow could weigh so much? I deserve a vacation. I'm gonna call that fishing lodge Aldercott went to last weekend and book a spot."

"For an old guy, you did good," Phil said.

Carl guffawed, a booming sound that made Junebug jump and skitter back.

Minken narrowed his eyes. "I told Gabe if my daughter brought home a man with a rat's nest for hair, I'd shoot myself. But if she brought you home, it'd be different."

"You'd shoot me?" Phil said.

Minken gave a tight smile. "Nah, you're okay, kid. I'd just wait till you were asleep and give you a buzz cut."

When Phil's laughter died down, Harris said, "I'm confident Nicole will give Junebug the all-clear. Let's move the horses to the tunnel mouth. We'll take the filly and her buddies last and then wait for Nicole's okay."

Gabe and Minken stayed with the filly sandwich, feeding them treats, while the others moved the remaining horses along the cleared path around the wedge-shaped rock face to the tunnel opening. Harris then asked Gabe, Minken and Phil to move Junebug and her buddies while he and Carl returned to the main mine entrance via the tunnel so they could ready the horse trailers that waited in the museum lot.

Phil grabbed Twyla's lead and followed Carl and Harris along the perimeter of the pasture and onto the path to the tunnel. Junebug watched Twyla leave, whinnied, and began trembling. "She's skittish," Gabe told Minken. "But she dotes on Streak. If you lead him ahead, she should follow along."

Streak was mellow, happy to walk with Minken. Gabe allowed them a short head start and then tugged on Junebug's lead rope. She snorted once, looked past him, and spotted her buddy. She moved forward, stopped, and whinnied. Gabe faced her, speaking softly. "Come on, Junebug. A warm barn's waiting."

Her legs trembled; her sides heaved as she sucked in air. Gabe backed a few steps toward the pasture's threshold with the basin and tugged on her lead. "It will be fine, sweetie. Nothing bad can happen to you now."

Junebug moved forward, trembling but determined to follow Streak. Gabe walked backward, coaxing her along. They made their way along the threshold between the pasture and the basin, aiming for the path to the tunnel. Things were looking good. They'd be at the tunnel opening in no time.

Chapter 36

FROM HIS HIDEOUT in the trees at the south end of Harris's far pasture, Jack had watched Gabe's ATV roar up the trail toward the Valley of Horses.

He'd intended to be up there with everyone. But he'd brought a couple vodka bottles that needed stashing. That was the trouble with living at O'Malley's. A dude couldn't just toss stuff in the garbage. Seamus would do the math eventually and realize the number of empty liquor bottles going out exceeded the full ones Seamus brought in.

It should have cost Jack a mere five minutes. However, one bottle still contained a couple inches of booze, so he sat unseen in his safe spot and sipped, emptying the bottle.

When he saw Gabe go by, he wanted to follow. To join Gabe and Harris, to help move the horses off the mountain, to finish the rescue he, Jack, had planned, and to hear Gabe tell him, "We need more guys like you, Jacko."

However, he was a touch unsteady on his feet. His cheeks tingled. Only an idiot would charge up the mountain right then. For sure Gabe would go apeshit. Jack stayed in his lair, leaning on a sturdy birch beside his ATV, tossing its keys in the air, waiting for the tingling to go away.

Twenty minutes passed. Jack was bored and cold when he saw the freakiest old dude squirt out of the trees on the east side of the pasture, perhaps half a football field away. He wore black, from his boots to the long coat that flapped behind him, to the watch cap pulled low over his sunglasses. Jack ducked, wiped his eyes, and squinted. Not really sunglasses. Tight fitting, with small, black lenses that reflected the sun. The guy belonged in a swim meet or a cockpit of an old plane.

Freako stood at the edge of the pasture, his head jerking from side to side. Twice the spooky goggles swung to the south and Jack's hideout in the trees. Twice Jack held his breath and froze in place. Twice the goggles moved past.

Finally, Freako scurried to the drill tower in the pasture and inspected its struts. Had Jack seen him before? Nah, he'd remember those weird sunglasses. The guy sidled to the core shack and disappeared inside for a few seconds. When he reappeared, he raced to a spot near the drill tower, stooped, grabbed a thin green rope, fumbled with it, then dropped it and hurried into the trees and out of sight.

Jack crouched in his hideout clutching the ATV keys, watching the tree line until he was sure Freako was gone. Who was he? Maybe the driller, worrying about the explosions and checking his equipment? No, the way Freako skulked around told Jack he didn't belong there.

Jack pocketed his keys, crept from his lair, and approached the drill tower. About twenty feet away, he noticed something glinting on the ground midway between the tower and the shack. Sparks. Coming from a thin green cord. He walked faster and reached the sparks just as the cord separated into two hissing sections, one running to the tower, the other to the shack.

A fuse. Burning.

Jack stared at the tower, his eyes tracking the fuse up the nearest strut. He spotted a bundle of dynamite attached to the strut maybe six feet from the ground. Another one on a cross-beam. Perhaps a third on the far strut.

He followed the other fuse as it crossed over red spray paint on the ground and snaked to the core shack. He peered inside the shack and saw more explosives under the core racks.

Holy shit! Freako was the bomber. Jack could solve the sabotage case. And if he extinguished the fuse, he'd be a hero. Yes! The world did need more guys like him.

Jack ran back to the hissing, sparking fuses. He stomped on the burning end of the one nearest the shack, fumbling in his jacket pocket at the same time for his phone. The fuse kept burning. He stomped harder. It burned on. He ground it under his boot. It burned on.

He checked his phone. No service. Shit, phones never worked up here.

Jack stared at the fuse. How fast would it burn? The burning end had moved almost ten feet since he first saw it. Another ten and it would be inside the core shack. The second fuse worked its way to the drill tower, its sparks a couple feet from the bottom of the strut.

Jack didn't understand why he couldn't smother the sparks, but he had no time to waste. It'd be faster to rip the fuse from the bundles. He ran inside the shack, dove under the racks, and grabbed the nearest bunch of explosives. The cord was crimped into a small spike inserted in one of the sticks of dynamite. He wrenched at it. Nothing happened. He wrestled with the bundle, pulling, twisting, trying to sever the connection. Nothing budged.

There were two bunches of dynamite in the shack. He'd seen two, maybe three, on the drill tower. He couldn't remove even one spike. How could he handle four or five?

When he crawled from under the rack, he heard sparking. The fuse had burned its way to the shack; the hissing end was at the entrance, three feet away. Suddenly, finally, he realized the danger he faced. He spun and sprinted for his hideout.

Get on the ATV, he thought, and split. He pulled out his keys and raced full out.

As he passed the drill tower, his eyes were drawn to sparks less than two feet below the first bundle of dynamite. He stumbled on the uneven ground, fell and skidded along the wet grass. When he scrambled to his feet, a sharp pain pierced his ankle. It hurt like hell, but he kept going.

He was nearly there—the first white birch trunk twenty feet away, his ATV another ten, when he fell again, ramming both hands and a knee against the hard ground. This time he was slower to rise, his breath ragged, his eyes tearing.

His knee throbbed. His ankle burned. His palms were scraped and bleeding. His empty palms. Where were the ATV keys? He swung his head from side to side, searching, but saw nothing. "Go," he told himself. "Just go."

Jack hopped and limped forward. He reached the first of the birches edging the pasture when he heard the rapid-fire cracking of the explosion, followed by a high-pitched pinging, and in spite of himself, stopped and looked back.

Chapter 37

THE EXPLOSIONS HIT Gabe's eardrums with a percussive whump. For a second, things were still. Then the air was full of horses shrieking, men shouting, and snow spraying up and around.

Something hard and sharp smacked him in the shoulder and cheek. Then he was on his back staring at an undulating sky. Things spun, moved in waves, made his stomach churn. Off to the side, he had a foggy view of Horace Minken holding Streak's halter.

"You okay?" someone said through an echo chamber.

Gabe sat up. The world tilted, then jerked back into plumb.

Harris said, "Christ, what happened? We were halfway to the tunnel when we heard the blasts." He leaned over and gulped in air.

"Explosions," Minken said. "Downhill. My drill site, I bet. Damn."

Junebug was off the path, caught up in the mounds of snow in the basin. She lay partly on her back, partly on her side, in a trough between mounds of snow. Her legs were elevated and rested on the upside of the trough. She squealed in fright, pawed her legs, and struggled to right herself.

Carl and Phil scrambled into the basin. Carl threw his jacket over Junebug's head, covering her eyes. When she quieted, he said, "We can't risk her standing. She'll sink in the snow, and we'll never get her out."

Phil tossed his jacket at Carl. "Use this to hobble her." He kneeled and held Junebug's head in his lap, cooing, stroking her forehead. She rocked back and forth, struggling to move in the snow. Harris removed his jacket as well and helped Carl hobble Junebug.

Horace Minken and the gelding stood on the pasture near a patch of churned snow. Streak appeared jittery. Minken was pale and leaned into the horse. Gabe wasn't sure who supported whom. "How're you two doing, Horace?"

"Streak shied. Almost knocked me over, but I managed to hang on. I think he's okay."

Gabe rose to his knees, waited for the world to settle again, and then stood. His left shoulder and arm throbbed. Warmth trickled down his cheek. When he swiped at it, his hand came away red.

"She kicked you," Minken said. "That explosion hit and Junebug reared up and smacked you, and you went down. Then she lost her footing and toppled off the edge into the snow and flipped over, her legs ending up in the air."

Streak whinnied, and Junebug responded by kicking her hind legs, and trying to lift herself out of the snow. The jackets they had used as makeshift hobbles held firm. As Junebug struggled, she sank deeper into the snow. Her belly heaved. Her breath came in staccato puffs. Phil cooed and stroked her neck. She stopped moving at last and lay still, breath spurting from her nostrils.

"What the hell do we do now?" Minken said.

Chapter 38

GABE STRUGGLED upright and joined Minken on the pasture. "The other day, you mentioned your driller at Harris's pasture would be away this week. Who else knew?"

Minken wrinkled his brow in concentration. "I mentioned it in Tiffany's. Anyone could have overheard."

Gabe nodded. A café full of suspects.

"And I might have mentioned it at the town meeting Monday night. It wasn't a secret."

Gabe sighed. Make that a town full of suspects.

Junebug snorted and struggled.

"We have to get her back onto the field," Gabe said.

"That means lifting her over the lip," Phil said. "How much does your average filly weigh? Six, seven hundred pounds?"

"Yeah, we'll need help."

"It better come soon," Harris said. "The trough she's lying in is a problem. Even if we let her try, she won't be able to roll over and stand. And if we leave her down too long, her organs could fail. She could die."

Junebug struggled again, pawing at the snow. Gabe said,

"The struggling may aggravate the cut on her withers. Those jackets won't hold her legs forever."

"I'll get some ropes from the sleds," Minken said.

Ten minutes after they had hobbled Junebug properly, Gabe heard loud voices on the path. "Cavalry's coming."

Nicole Mitchell, the vet, and her brother Tom, the bartender, sprinted around the corner, red-faced and panting. "Omigod, what happened?" Nicole said.

"Explosions, plus freaked horses, equals one effing mess," Carl said.

"We were on the trail near Harris's pasture when it happened," Tom said. "From what we could see through the trees, the drill rig is mangled. The core shack's flattened."

Minken hung his head. "Shit, I knew it."

Nicole kneeled by Junebug and inspected her cut. "Looks like the sutures held. She's not bleeding." She looked at Gabe and winced. "But you are."

"Can we haul Junebug out?" Tom said.

Nicole thought for a moment. "The sooner, the better. Is the sling Kate used still here? Mine's at the clinic in town."

"No, it's back in our barn," Harris said.

Tom volunteered to collect the sling and extra ropes and ran off.

Nicole gauged the snow level where the basin abutted the plateau. "We'll need to build up the snow between Junebug and the threshold, so she doesn't get more scrapes."

Gabe hung his head. Shoveling. Great.

"I think I have some butterflies for that cut," Nicole said to him. While the others began moving snow, she led Gabe to the hay bales and dug through her backpack. "You're pale. Sit, before you pass out."

He sat, silent and wondering who had switched the concerned woman facing him for the angry spitfire he was used to.

"How did it happen?" Nicole said.

Gabe rubbed his shoulder. "She kicked my shoulder. I think her hoof grazed my cheek."

"Sit still." Nicole poured astringent on gauze. Gabe pulled his head back when she raised it toward him.

"This won't hurt." She wiped the area below his left eye and patted it dry, then closed the cut with three butterfly bandages. She was right. It didn't hurt. Unlike the cramping in his shoulder.

"You're lucky she missed your eye. I don't think you'll have another shiner, but it will be puffy for a while. Ice will help. Let me see how your other injury's doing." She removed the small bandage from his forehead and studied the stitches. Gabe grabbed a fistful of snow and held it to his cheek.

Nicole said, "I think those sutures can come out. Shall I do that?"

"Anytime I don't have to go to a hospital, I'm all for it." Gabe watched her warily. Where had the real Nicole Mitchell gone?

She had a gentle touch. It took less than a minute. She ran her fingers over the area when she was done, smoothing the skin. It felt nice. Warm. "Tiny scar," she said. "But it adds character, I think."

"Good. That's something I lack."

She flushed. "I didn't mean it that way."

"I know. Thanks for fixing me up."

"Thank *you* for rescuing me at the meeting."

"Huh?"

"Phoebus was giving me grief about his herd and the SPCA. You defused things."

"Actually, I was trying to save *him* from *you.*"

Nicole jerked, and then squinted her eyes at Gabe. "Are you kidding me?"

He shrugged.

She laughed. A clear, musical sound. "Almost had me going."

Nicole crooned to Junebug while Gabe helped the others shovel snow near the threshold, packing it down. Snow seeped over the tops of his boots and up his sleeves. He allowed the cold wetness to divert his attention from the burn in his shoulder and numbness in his arm.

They were almost finished when Junebug began struggling again. Streak snorted, and Junebug craned her neck and snorted in response.

"Maybe if she knows Streak is here, it will calm her," Gabe said.

Minken led Streak to a spot on the plateau near the filly's head. The gelding lowered his head toward Junebug and blew out a breath. The filly craned her neck again. Nicole removed Phil's jacket from Junebug's head, uncovering her eyes. When she looked toward Streak, he blew another noisy breath into her face. She blew back and stopped struggling.

"Far out, the power of friendship," Phil said.

"In horse language, those big breaths mean everything's fine," Nicole said.

Phil and Gabe traded a look. Phil shook his dreadlocks and raised his eyebrows.

"It's true," Nicole said. "Look it up if you don't believe me."

They settled in to wait for Tom to return with the sling and ropes. Gabe grabbed another fistful of snow, held it to his cheek, and plopped down in the snow. The heavy-duty clothing he'd bought at Findrich's Gear did its job and kept him warm and dry. He closed his eyes and thought about talking horses. Minestrone soup. Boxes of explosives. And the other things LeBlanc might find if he showed up at BAM headquarters with a search warrant.

Gabe had called LeBlanc not long after leaving BAM's headquarters. "It's D. S. Gabrieli," he'd said. "Cheakamus hired me to look into the sabotage."

"I know." LeBlanc's tone gave Gabe a vivid picture of him

—peering down the length of his French nose, his arms folded across his chest. "Nice to hear you're gainfully employed."

"Why thanks. Can we work together on the investigation?"

"Impossible." LeBlanc's tone remained snotty.

"Okay, how about trading information?"

"Tell me everything you find out, Gabrieli. Like a good citizen. But I'm telling you *rien*. Nothing. It's not my investigation."

Gabe saw the button. He pushed it.

"You're letting Ambrose call the shots? A well-respected fellow like you, someone who spent years with Major Crimes himself, letting Ambrose make you look like a goofball in your own town?"

"Sergeant Ambrose returned to his homebase to deal with other pressing matters."

"That figures. Leaving you to do the heavy lifting, right?"

LeBlanc was silent.

Gabe went on. "But that's not why I called. Today I visited a group called Earth First By Any Means. BAM for short. Interesting bunch. They store gas cans and explosives by the barn. The head kid, Craig Westburg, refused to give me a tour of their outbuildings."

"Hmmm."

"If you visit Craig, this good citizen would be happy to tag along."

"Impossible. The RCMP does not offer tag-alongs. Keep your nose clean, Gabrieli." Without so much as a "see ya," Leblanc had ended the call.

Now, Gabe rested in the snow as the sun warmed and eased his throbbing shoulder. He pictured BAM's headquarters. A rutted excuse of a driveway. Graying, slapdash outbuildings, ramshackle cabins. The chicken coop was the lone building not held together with duct tape, and BAM's trucks hadn't seen a showroom in decades. It didn't look like Craig made a wad of dough with his environmental defense fund—perhaps it was merely a cover for more incendiary activities. Then again, maybe Craig followed the first rule of being safely rich: never flaunt it.

What Gabe did know: Craig was definitely in charge of BAM. If he wanted lunch, Pinky and Green Goddess made prize-winning minestrone. If he wanted to blow up core shacks, Frank and the boys would nod their heads, learn how to rig explosives, and get to it. And they had the supplies at the ready. Gabe moved BAM to the top of his suspect list.

Tom hollered from the path. Gabe checked his watch. Thirty minutes—noteworthy time for a trip to Harris's ranch and back.

"I filled Kate in," Tom said as he tossed the sling and ropes on the ground. "That pasture's so far from the house she hadn't heard the blast. She's driving to the museum to prepare the horse trailers."

Following Nicole's instructions, the men lifted Junebug's head and shoulder and slid part of the canvas sling under her body. Then they wriggled, pushed, and pulled until half the sling was centered underneath her. They wrapped the rest of the sling over her belly, encasing her in a canvas envelope. Last, they attached the ropes to rings on the sling.

Nicole kneeled beside the filly, holding her head and crooning. "Everything's fine, sweetie pie." Junebug's legs twitched; her sides heaved.

"On three," Harris said. The six men pulled. The ropes became taut, and Junebug slid backward across the packed snow while Nicole crawled along, murmuring to her. Every pull on the ropes pushed a spear of pain through Gabe's shoulder. Sweat popped out on his brow.

The filly barely struggled as they pulled. Either she was exhausted, or she trusted them. Gabe's guess was exhaustion.

After several minutes of alternating between pulling and resting, they had hauled Junebug back onto the plateau. Gabe sat on the ground, wanting nothing more than to be off the mountain. And prone, under a down comforter.

Junebug rolled herself partially upright. Nicole sat with her and stroked her head while Carl and Phil untied the hobbles. Then Nicole stood and tugged on the halter. When the filly spotted Streak standing nearby, she scrabbled to her feet.

"Hallelujah!" Phil said. "We're losing daylight. Let's get them outta here."

Gabe struggled to his feet. "Is Junebug strong enough to make it through the tunnel?"

"So long as nothing else explodes, she should be okay," Nicole said. "Someone checked the tunnel, right?"

"Yep," Minken said. "All's good. No explosives, no cracks in the rock."

Gabe pictured the tunnel and hugged himself. As a chill overtook him, he rubbed his upper arms to get blood flowing, but stopped abruptly when his shoulder spasmed in protest.

"We don't need you in the tunnel, Gabe," Harris said. "Nicole and I will lead the horses, if the rest of you can clean up the equipment."

Gabe acknowledged Harris's gesture with a quick tilt of his head. "I need to check out the explosion."

"I'll join you," Minken said.

The five men watched Nicole and Harris lead Junebug and Streak along the path. Then they finished tidying the site and loading shovels and other equipment onto the sleds. By the time they hauled everything to the ramp at the ATV trailhead, daylight had almost leached from the sky.

When Gabe started his ATV, he wondered if the filly was now in Kate's horse trailer, on her way to the warm stables at the Lazy C ranch. His cheeks burned. Even if Harris had needed help to manage the horses, Gabe knew he'd insist he had it covered, giving Gabe a reason not to enter the tunnel.

Nothing had changed since kindergarten. Harris still protected Gabe's flanks.

Gabe was grateful, yet part of him wanted to punch his friend for recognizing his weakness. Someday Gabe would need to deal with his bugaboo.

Someday.

Chapter 39

It was late afternoon by the time Horace Minken and Gabe veered off the ATV trail through a gap in the trees and traveled cross-country over Harris's pasture, heading toward a twisted heap of black metal. They parked nearby in the fading light, leaving their ATVs idling, lights on.

The core shack was flattened, its pillars collapsed, its roof shredded. The words "No Mining" were sprayed on the ground in red. Each *i* had a starburst for a dot. Shattered core samples littered the site.

A portion of the drill tower was folded in on itself. Ragged, twisted pieces of its metal rails and struts lay in the pasture. The drill itself had fared slightly better—the drill rod was in one piece, but the lower third bore jagged rips along its length. Although the sky was darkening Gabe snapped pictures, relying on illumination from their ATVs' lights. His cheek had swollen, almost pushing his left eye closed, which made focusing difficult. He hoped the pictures would record details he couldn't see.

"I'll call the cops," Minken said. "And tell my driller his rig's wrecked. I can't believe this. If they don't catch the bomber soon, my insurer's gonna cancel my policy."

Turning in a slow circle, Gabe checked out the site one last time. Something niggled, a difference between this and TEG's site. It was after five o'clock now and there was so little daylight, he couldn't pick out details. The bank of trees about forty yards away was merely a spiky line of black against a charcoal sky. Perhaps the pictures he took earlier today at TEG would help him identify the inconsistency.

———

GABE'S ACHING shoulder and blurring vision made the fifteen-minute trip to Harris's ranch an eternity. When he arrived, Jacobson's Ram 1500 sat in the yard and a horse trailer abutted the barn, its ramp down. Lights shone in the outbuildings.

Gabe found everyone in the stable. Streak, Twyla, and Junebug shared an oversized stall near the entrance. Come daybreak, they would have a premium view across the paddocks to the fields and the trees at the base of Rimrock. At the moment, they munched fresh hay, stoking their furnaces.

He walked through the stable and spotted Tornado Callie in the third stall from the end. His heart rate quickened. She had her nose stuck in a feed bag. She was trim and her coat gleamed with health. Gabe took a deep breath and debated approaching her. If Tornado Callie remembered the months of loneliness after Bethany left, he expected she'd kick him in the head.

He turned on his heel.

Hurrying, afraid he would wimp out, Gabe went to the fridge in the barn where he found the molasses-and-oat treats. He grabbed two and returned to the stable.

At Tornado Callie's stall, he whistled softly. She abandoned the bag and looked over. Her ears pricked forward. "Hey, Callie," he said.

She nickered and tossed her head. He offered a cookie.

She approached the stall door and checked him out. Gabe stood still, his eyes on hers.

Tornado Callie stretched her neck over the stall door and blew through her nostrils. He reached up and stroked her ear. She dipped her head to take the cookie from his palm, raised her head, chewed, and then put her muzzle against the side of his head. He ran his hand along her neck, and she blew out again—a long, relaxed shudder of a blow—and rested her head on his shoulder. He felt her mouth move as she chewed. "Looking good, Callie."

She pulled back and nosed his jacket pocket. She'd had enough small talk. Gabe laughed and pulled out the second cookie.

"She remembers you," Kate said, coming up beside him.

"Maybe," Gabe said, trying to sound nonchalant. "Or maybe it's these treats." Tornado Callie snagged the second cookie.

Kate sucked in her breath when she saw Gabe's face. "Oh, wow."

"It's just a little nick. Nicole says there's not even a shiner coming. Once I have dinner and coffee, I'll be a hundred percent." Gabe stroked Tornado Callie's nose. "She looks great, Kate."

"She's a special horse and we love her." Kate put her hand on Gabe's arm and smiled up at him. "Thank you for sharing her with us."

Gabe heard the whir and click of a camera just before Kate squeezed his arm and turned to leave. Jacobson lowered his camera, gave a small salute, and left the stable.

Five minutes later Gabe found Nicole rubbing Streak down. "No problems getting the horses through the mine?"

"Surprisingly, none. They went through the tunnel like old hands."

"I wanted to thank you for patching me up. How about dinner?"

She hesitated before saying, "Okay, I'll get the horses settled and meet you. How about Tiffany's in an hour?"

Gabe drove back to Cheakamus, singing along with Dylan. It had been a grueling afternoon, but a rewarding one. The horses were warm and safe. Sure, Junebug's hoof had clipped him, but on the upside Tornado Callie had recognized him. And, she hadn't kicked him.

———

IN HIS APARTMENT, Gabe held a baggie of ice cubes to his cheek and placed a call to Jack. It was odd he hadn't shown up on Rimrock. Most of the rescue plan was his, and Gabe had thought Jack was invested in it. He mentally shrugged. When he'd been Jack's age, it hadn't taken much to distract him.

His call connected to voice mail. "Hey, Jacko," he said. "We got the horses off the mountain. They're safe at Harris and Kate's. Wondering where you are. Phone me."

Still holding the ice to his face, he compared the photos he'd shot at Harris's pasture and at TEG. The drill rigs at both sites looked similar—twisted and beyond salvage. The two shots of the hillside around TEG's site showed nothing but trees, trails, and what could be a trail rider's vehicle high on the hill. The ground shots at TEG also showed nothing, which intrigued him. Harris's pasture, the scene of the latest explosion, was a mess—red graffiti, rock shards strewn over a vast area—while the TEG site looked like someone had vacuumed it. Gabe expanded the TEG shots and studied them. No visible rock shards. The other thing missing was graffiti. He checked all twenty photos. No graffiti.

Certain the cops would have better pictures or notes about the scene, Gabe called LeBlanc, got voice mail, left a message, and then headed to the shower.

Under the hot spray, Gabe massaged his shoulder and thought about core samples. Where were TEG's? He'd showered, shaved, and dressed in jeans and a clean denim shirt when the answer came to him. The TEG core shack had burned, not exploded. The core samples would be in the debris from the fire.

Satisfied he'd solved part of the puzzle, he spent ten minutes searching the internet for information about how horses communicate before checking in with Lucy. He heard whistling and shouting when Lucy answered the call. "Who scored?" he said.

"My favorite team. Anyone but the Yankees. Sorry I haven't returned your calls. Time got away on me. How're things?"

"Since we last talked, I moved an injured filly off a mountain, had my cover blown, and was hired by the town to investigate the explosions. I learned horses blow through their noses to say, 'everything's cool' and nicker to say, 'good to see you.' I played a few hands of blackjack with a suspect and had lunch with a pack of junior eco-activists. I'm taking a vet to dinner, Harris's realtor isn't happy with me, and another drill rig is toast."

"A slow couple days for you."

"Yeah, age is slowing me down. Funny thing about those horses we moved off Rimrock—according to the vet they walked through a tunnel without balking, like old hands."

"Maybe it was familiar to them. Who's the vet?"

"That doesn't mesh with what Carl from the dude ranch said. Did you ship my shoes?"

"I'm having them resoled. Who's the vet?"

"Geez Luce, what do you mean, resoled? Time's passing."

"Calm down, they'll be there in time. Who's the vet?"

"I think Harris is selling The Peak so he can pay off a loan. The realtor says someone else is interested in buying, but she could be blowing smoke."

"I thought the bar was making money?"

"Yeah, but according to Harris, the ranch isn't. Seems

crazy to sell the business. Perhaps I can talk him into renegotiating the loan. Gotta go to dinner."

"Who's the vet?"

"Say hi to Doofus." Gabe ended the call.

He grinned as he backed his truck out of the garage. Lucy would be sending a text about now: "WHO'S THE VET?"

Chapter 40

WHEN HE ARRIVED at Tiffany's just before 6:30 p.m., Gabe was thinking about *Cheers*, one of Mercy's favorite golden-oldie TV series. How, whenever a particular character entered the bar, the patrons would call his name—"Norm!"—with gusto.

Tiffany's had that kind of feel. Like everybody knew you. Like they all knew the hellish afternoon you spent rolling around in drifts with several hundred pounds of frightened horse. Like they knew the incredible feat you helped accomplish.

Gabe had a bloodshot eye threatening to close, three butterfly bandages on his cheek that pinched when he moved his mouth, a throbbing shoulder, and a numb arm, but he felt upbeat. Optimistic. Heroic. He swung open the door and strode into Tiffany's the way Norm always walked into Cheers.

And, nothing.

People ate their meals, read their magazines, talked to their neighbors. A fellow at a table near the door greeted him with, "Cold, man, shut the door."

Life is not a TV show, Gabe told himself. He poured a

mug of Wussy, the café's decaf, limped to his favorite isolated booth at the back, and sagged into it.

Rhonda dropped a menu on the table. "Kee-ryste, do you feel as bad as you look?"

And he had his best shirt on too. "I do now."

"Prime rib tonight, Alberta beef. That'll make you feel better." Rhonda left him to his misery.

Nicole arrived and people called out, "Nicole!" With gusto.

She slid into the booth, looking like she'd spent the last five hours some place expensive instead of crawling around drifts talking to horses. She set down a pill bottle.

"Good for what ails you. No more than two in four hours. And don't drink or they'll knock you flat."

He squinted at the label. Something he didn't recognize.

"Horse painkillers," she said.

"You kidding me?"

She laughed. "Yeah. So, what's good tonight?"

After they placed their orders for prime rib, Nicole said, "Okay. Spill."

When Gabe stared blankly, she said, "Full disclosure. Your name. And who you've fingered for the sabotage."

"Hasn't Kate told you my name?"

Nicole shook her head, her black curls bouncing, glimmering in the light from the lamp above their booth. "Nope. All Kate said was your name was evocative."

"Of what?"

She shrugged.

"Okay," he said. "Dire Straits."

"Get real."

"Dim Sum."

She shook her head. "No way."

"Desert Sun."

Nicole smiled. "Better, certainly evocative. Nah. Too poetic for a beat-up guy like you."

"Care to wager?"

She studied him for a moment and when Rhonda arrived with their prime ribs, Nicole said, "Loser buys dessert."

Gabe plunked his driver's license on the table. "Desert Sun."

Nicole and Rhonda looked at the license. "Works for me," Rhonda said. "Hot."

"What?" Gabe said.

"The sun in the desert. Hot. Enjoy your meal."

By the time Nicole and Gabe finished eating, the café was almost empty. When Nicole asked again about his investigation, Gabe paused, calculating how much to tell her.

"I visited the BAM group," he said. "Interesting bunch. Fed me lunch, denied involvement with anything explosive. They appear to like Malcolm X, or his slogan, at least."

"Hmmm."

"Besides lunch, they fed me the environmentalists' reasons for hating mining."

"I sympathize with that position. This town's changed from the days when mining was the only business around. Lots of people don't want it to open up again."

"Like who?" Gabe said.

"The tourism businesses—the ski hill, the adventure shops, back-country tours. They don't want the scenery spoiled. Some farmers aren't happy either. I've put down animals that have stepped into drill holes." She shook her head and snorted in disgust. "Plenty of reasons not to want mining here."

"Including poor investments and mining scams," Gabe said. She raised her head and stared at him.

"I went to Lakesedge Casino today," he said. "Met your father."

She sat erect. Gabe could see prickles coming to the surface and the warmth leaving her face.

"Why? You think he's a suspect?"

He shrugged. "I'm looking at everything."

She shifted in the seat. Glared. "That's as ridiculous as saying I might have done it."

Up to this point, Gabe hadn't considered that possibility. "Well, now that you mention it," he said, trying to lighten things up but interested in the answer.

Her face flamed; her black curls jumped. "You are a real piece of crap." She grabbed her jacket, stood, turned on her heel, and marched out. The three remaining diners watched her leave.

Rhonda came over and removed the plates from the table. When Gabe's eyes met hers, she raised her eyebrows.

"That went swimmingly," he said, and shrugged into his jacket. He left forty dollars on the table and walked out of Tiffany's into frigid night air, the kind that made him appreciate a hot Irish coffee.

He settled into the driver's seat and started the truck. "Is it just me, Three, or could Nicole use a sense of humor?"

When his phone rang, he considered letting it go to voice mail. It was late, a horse had kicked him, dinner had been a bust, his knee, shoulder, and cheek hurt, and it was still the Dreaded Month of Abstinence. He did not feel sociable.

"H. Chilton" appeared on the call display.

Harris, he could handle. Harris didn't ask for more than Gabe could muster.

"Yeah, Harris."

"Gabe." Harris's voice was subdued. "It's about Jack."

WEDNESDAY

Chapter 41

NICOLE HAD TOLD Gabe not to drink if he took the painkillers. He'd listened.

Wednesday morning when he cracked open one eye, all twenty pills remained inside their bottle, sitting on the table beside the purple rock and his laptop. Unlike the Glenfiddich. A good portion of it was no longer in the bottle, having made its way to a glass and from there down Gabe's throat and into his veins.

The laptop's screensaver marquee trailed across its face. Trying to focus on it made Gabe's eyes hurt. He rolled onto his back and watched the ceiling descend and rise, descend and rise, keeping time with the throbbing in his head.

However, he had Nicole's pills. As soon as he could get off the floor, he intended to take a couple. If they stayed down, he figured he might survive. Using the arm of the sofa as a crutch, he struggled upright. "I shoulda stuck to coffee," he said out loud. Choirboy said, "Told ya so."

After two painkillers, four glasses of water, and a twenty-minute hot shower, Gabe's head still pounded but he felt he might be able to face the day. So long as no one spoke to him out loud.

He squinted out the window. The morning sky was clear and blue. The sun bounced off the fresh snow in Greta's yard and picked at his eyeballs like a woodpecker after a bug. His phone rang, setting off a tuning fork in his head that made the floor sway.

"Gabrieli."

"It's Greta, I need a favor."

His heart did a stutter step. Please, not shoveling her walk. "Uh-huh."

"You sound weird. Are you alright? I need a lift downtown this morning. I have a doctor's appointment at nine."

"Sure thing." He forced his voice into an upbeat tone.

The screensaver flickered. "Things are looking up" scrolled across the screen. Gabe had selected that sentiment a while back, right after he'd put the Truck Named Two into Eau Claire Lake. At the time he was feeling fortunate he hadn't killed anyone.

Today he'd pick a different screensaver. Like, "Are you kidding me?" What else could he say after last night?

When Harris had phoned with the news about Jack last night, Gabe had raced to the town's modest hospital. He knew only that the explosion in Harris's pasture had injured Jack, who'd appeared on Harris's veranda, glassy-eyed, disoriented, and bleeding.

When Gabe had burst through the hospital's emergency doors, he scanned the crowded and too-warm waiting room and saw Mercy standing in a tight cluster with Seamus O'Malley and a woman wearing pale-blue scrubs. O'Malley's right arm encircled Mercy, his hand moving rhythmically up and down her arm. Gabe had seen his mother's face this color —almost gray—once before, when he was seven. She leaned into Seamus, seeming to use his hefty frame to steady herself. As Gabe walked toward them, the blue-scrubbed woman nodded at O'Malley, squeezed Mercy's hand, and disappeared through swinging doors. Mercy covered her face with her hands. Her shoulders jerked, and Gabe's heart slid into a dark, frightening place.

"Mom?" He touched her shoulder. He caught O'Malley's eyes over Mercy's bowed head and saw fury. "Mom?"

When Mercy raised her head, her skin had regained some life. She hugged Gabe with a fierce grip. "Oh, Sunny, we could have lost him. It was like…just like you." She released her grip, wiped tears from her cheeks, and blew her nose.

"What's up with Jack?" Gabe said. "Harris mentioned the explosion in his pasture. What was Jack doing there?"

O'Malley exploded. "Cheeez-ussss. *You're* the reason he's hurt. Yet you ask, 'What was Jack doing there?' Typical."

Nearby conversations ceased; heads turned their way. O'Malley was oblivious and raged on. "As if you don't know. It's all your fault."

The force of O'Malley's words pushed Gabe a step back. He raised his hands. Mercy touched O'Malley's forearm and said, "Seamus. Calm down."

"Yeah, Seamus, calm down," Gabe said. "I have no clue what you're talking about."

O'Malley's face purpled, and he leaned toward Gabe. "No clue? You irresponsible jerk. Your brother, *your little brother*, was doing your job. He almost *died*. Helping you, he said. So don't act innocent and pretend you had nothing to do with it."

Gabe ignored the blast from O'Malley. He rubbed a hand across his brow and sighed.

Mercy focused on his face then and gasped. "Oh Sunny, you're cut. Did you get hit by the fly rock too?"

"What fly rock?"

Mercy fumbled in her handbag and extracted a tissue. She teared up, dabbed at her eyes, and inhaled a shaky breath. "Jack remembers the explosion and hearing pings, but that's all until he got to Harris and Kate's. The doctor found rock chips in the gash, which made her think of fly rock. He's very, very lucky. It must have ricocheted somehow. The doctor said if it had hit him straight on, he'd be dead. As it is, Jack has a gash on his head, concussion, and hypothermia. They're keeping him overnight."

Mercy's bottom lip quivered. She blinked rapidly. "Jack said he was helping you solve the case. That's why he was in the pasture."

"I'm gonna see how he is. Where is he?"

Mercy said, "Second—" but O'Malley boomed, "No!" and grabbed Gabe's arm in a vicious grip that shot a stab of pain through Gabe's shoulder. "You stay the hell *away* from Jack. And look at what it's done to Mercy. You can thank yourself for that too."

"Shh," Mercy said. "I'm fine."

Gabe's fists clenched. He shook off O'Malley's hand and fantasized about pasting him right between his brows. Then he saw the fear on Mercy's face, relaxed his hands and forced himself to smile. "Good night."

Gabe exited the hospital through the ER doors, turned right, walked around the building and re-entered through another door. He found the stairway and climbed one flight, gasping from the effort of bending his right knee. He found Jack in the sixth room along the second-floor hallway— bandaged and pale beneath the sheets, eyes closed, and an arm hooked to an IV pole and monitor. Lying much, much too still. Despite the monitor that told him Jack was alive, Gabe stood at the foot of the bed and watched until he saw Jack's chest rise and fall.

Gabe hadn't asked Jack to help him investigate, would never ask him to do something remotely dangerous. Yet Jack went to the pasture, and now he was here, lucky to be alive. Gabe remembered Harris speculating that Jack wanted to be like Gabe. "But not this way, Jack. If you're gonna be like me, be like the smart me, not the screw-up me."

Gabe had watched Jack sleep for several minutes and then took the long way home, via Findrich's Fine Spirits, where to his delight he had discovered an extensive selection of Scotch.

———

Now, he carried the Glenfiddich to the kitchen sink, feeling the weight of guilt—about the unceremonious end to The Dreaded Month of Abstinence, about Jack's injuries, about arguing with Seamus in front of Mercy. The minute he thought of Seamus, anger replaced the guilt. O'Malley was a piece of work, trying to blame Gabe for Jack's accident, assuming that Gabe would encourage his kid brother to do something dangerous. If O'Malley had his way, Gabe would turn tail and run back to Alberta. "Too bad, Seamus. I'm staying. If only to piss you off."

He was debating whether to pour the dregs of the Scotch down the drain when his phone rang. Again, the tuning fork reverberated. He held on to the counter until the floor stopped swaying and then answered the phone.

"Morning," Kate said with an energetic bounce in her voice. "We heard Jack will be okay. Seems to be a run on injuries these days. At least in the Gabrieli family. How're you doing?"

"I'm afraid I'll live. What's up?"

"You and I have an appointment to meet Reverend Beam Friday at the church. One o'clock."

"Do I have to shave?" Gabe sat in the recliner and closed his eyes. The room spun. He opened his eyes and cradled his head in his hand.

She was silent.

"Joking, Kate, I'm joking. Friday at one, you got it."

"Geez, you can't resist pushing buttons, can you?" He sensed her shaking her head, flipping her dark red hair.

"Gotta run," he said. "See you later."

After ending Kate's call, he phoned Greta. She said, "Where are you? I have to be there by nine."

"Coming." He grabbed his jacket and sunglasses, pocketed his phone and purple rock, replaced the cap on the Scotch and left the apartment.

"Morning, Three," Gabe said, as he backed out of the garage. "Try not to hit any potholes today."

When he stopped in front of Greta's house, she hurried out the door, buttoning her jacket as she hustled down the walk. As he climbed out to help Greta into the passenger seat, his phone rang. "Sunny," Mercy said when he answered, "be a dear and pick Jack up from hospital. The doctor says he can leave after eleven."

Gabe had planned to be at the TEG bombsite about that time. "Uh …"

"I'd do it myself, but Seamus has the car."

He almost suggested that O'Malley collect Jack. But then Gabe realized this would give him a perfect opportunity to talk to Jack, while saving Jack from a Seamus lecture. He mentally revised his to-do list, pushing his planned visit to the TEG site off to the afternoon. "No problem."

He gave Greta a hand up into the passenger seat.

"Not that I'm afraid of the old bastard," Gabe said to his mother, "but Seamus told me to stay away from the kid. Is he gonna shoot me if I collect Jack?"

"You know he's mostly bluster, dear."

His mother could call it what she wanted, but Gabe recognized a bully when he met one. Still, he'd never convince Mercy of that. She and Seamus had carried on a long-distance romance for over a decade now, ever since they met as members of the planning committee for the Foothills Roundup. The fact Mercy lived in Alberta and Seamus in B.C. didn't concern her at all. When Gabe had broached the subject a few years ago, Mercy had said, "We each have our own lives and then we have our relationship. The distance between us only adds anticipation to the mix."

When Gabe pulled away from the curb and pointed the truck toward downtown Cheakamus, Greta patted his hand. "You're a hero."

He glanced at her. "What?"

She grinned like a proud mother. "Got yourself clobbered by a horse and lived to talk about it. Hauled her out of the snow all by yourself, I hear."

"Not quite. There were six of us pulling and praying." He turned from Lookout Road onto Main Street. "And I'm more goat than hero. Jack got injured. Trying to help me solve the case, he says."

Greta *tched*. "How could you know he'd wander around drill sites and find a burning fuse? Lucky boy. Fly rock can kill. Just ask whoever died at TEG."

"Sorry, what?"

"I hope it's not Anders. Anyway, they say the fellow died from head trauma. When the explosion happened, rock or pieces of core flew up and hit him."

"Where did you hear that?"

"Rhonda got it from someone who got it from someone. Is it true Jack is your brother?"

Cheakamus. Bill Jacobson should worry about his future. Why did the town need a newspaper when it had Greta and her sources?

"Half-brother. And you got that—?"

"Rhonda. Someone overheard the commotion between you and Seamus O'Malley last night."

"I'm surprised the entire province didn't hear O'Malley bellowing." Gabe stopped near the medical clinic. "He blames me for Jack's injuries. He thinks I encouraged Jack to poke around. I didn't, but there's no convincing O'Malley."

"Never mind. You have heart. You're fitting right in here. You could stay awhile, and we wouldn't mind."

Where was Greta last night when he could have used a pat on the back? He smiled at her. It made his skin hurt.

"But I have to say," she said, "you look like you've lived five hard years in the few days you've been here."

"Really?" He patted his cheek. "Gee, just this morning I told myself the mountain air was doing wonders for my skin."

Greta *tched*.

He let the truck idle at the curb for a moment after dropping Greta off, thinking about Jack discovering burning fuses. And how, for a fuse to burn, someone had to light it. How much had Jack seen? Who might have seen him?

Chapter 42

It was bright inside Tiffany's. When he squinted, the cut below his eye protested. Gabe patted the butterflies Nicole had applied.

The café was half full. Bill Jacobson occupied a booth near the back. Horace Minken and Dreadlocks Phil were deep in conversation at a nearby table. The sign over the coffee thermoses announced today's Oso Negro selections. Gabe poured a mug of Messy Room to match the state of his head and slid onto a counter stool. He told Rhonda's son David to bring him the Ain't No Dude Ranch Special with hot sauce, counting on the extra kick it delivered to clear his head and get him right with the world again.

He asked David, "Are you the entire morning shift?"

"Mom was here for the breakfast rush. She's running a couple errands."

"Shouldn't you be in school or something?"

"No classes for me today."

"Lot of that going around. Your mother actually buys it?"

The kid should be on stage, Gabe thought, as David raised his hands and arranged his face to project the innocence of a three-year-old. "Straight goods, Mr. Gabrieli."

Gabe shook his head. When a teen calls you mister, you're eighty, or he's conning you.

While Gabe waited for his breakfast, he consulted his to-do list in his notebook. Gwinn, TEG, and Aldercott. He added LeBlanc and High Yield. He used the purple rock as a paperweight on the notebook's pages and phoned LeBlanc.

"It's Gabrieli," he said, when LeBlanc answered. "I guess you missed my voice mail. There was another explosion yesterday."

"I know."

"The scene got me thinking about TEG. How about lending me your photos and notes of what your crime scene guys found under the debris?"

"We're the RCMP, not a lending library. The answer's no. What do you think should be under the debris?"

"Core samples. Did you see any graffiti at TEG?"

"I'm not here to answer your questions."

Gabe dropped his head, resigned to revisiting the TEG site. "Well, hell."

"We paid Earth First a visit," LeBlanc said. "Young Mr. Westburg was sweetness and light until he asked for a warrant, and we produced it. As well as explosives, we found a cache of marijuana and a fridge full of edibles."

The revelation adjusted Gabe's assessment of BAM. Perhaps they were into more things green than they let on. "How much weed?"

"Let's say Craig has some explaining to do. Thanks for the lead. Any more information you have, feel free to share."

"I don't know, LeBlanc. As enjoyable as our relationship is, it's kinda one-sided. I'm doing all the talking. Seems to me you'd want to give me the occasional hint. We're both trying to figure out the same thing. Like who the victim is. I heard a blow to the head killed him."

"I'm not giving you any hints. And you don't need them. Stay in touch."

Gabe smiled and crossed LeBlanc's name off his list. It wasn't much and Gabe wasn't sure it mattered, but LeBlanc had indirectly confirmed the cause of death.

Gabe felt a tiny uptick in his mood, an easing of his prickling conscience about the Glenfiddich. If he ever envied Catholics, it was times like this. A distinct downside to being brought up Protestant was the lack of a confessional booth. While Catholics could leave their guilt at the feet of the priest, Protestants dragged their conscience around like reeking sneakers.

He was staring into his almost empty mug, thinking LeBlanc might be redeemable, when Horace Minken and Dreadlock Phil paused by his stool. Minken's face creased with a wide grin. "You look like you've been to hell and back."

"Not so sure I'm back yet."

"I hear ya." Minken focused on Gabe's rock. "That's a great charoite specimen. Get it at a mineral shop?"

Gabe handed it to Minken. "Nope, found it. What did you call it?"

Minken inspected it. The purple shimmered. "Charoite. The sole deposit is in Russia. I've seen pieces at mineral shows. Yours is up there with the best."

"Is it worth anything?"

Minken laughed and tossed the rock back. "Maybe fifty bucks. Hey, heard that kid from O'Malley's ranch who got smacked in the head yesterday is your brother. He gonna be okay?"

Gabe nodded. "Yeah, lucky boy."

After Minken and Phil left, Gabe moved to Jacobson's booth, claiming the seat opposite him. "Hey, Bill, how's the misinformation business?"

Jacobson tore off a piece of toast and sopped up some of his sunny-side eggs. Gabe's stomach twisted when he focused on the yellow slime. He looked away and took a deep breath.

"I don't know what you're talking about, *Dee Ess*."

"The baloney you printed about town money coming my way. You should verify your information."

"I merely mentioned a rumor. Speaking of baloney, what's the big deal with your name? Why not tell me?"

Gabe shrugged. "Sure, why not? It's Desert Sun."

Jacobson's lips tightened. He swiped his last piece of toast around his plate, mopping up the glistening yellow ooze. An acidic taste crept up Gabe's gullet. He swallowed twice and took a quick sip of coffee, forcing down the bile.

"There you go again," Jacobson said. "Cracking wise."

Gabe shrugged again. "Have it your way. Who do you think is involved in these explosions?"

"Why would you care what I say?" Jacobson narrowed his eyes. "You called me a liar two minutes ago."

"Nope. I said you should verify information. Didn't they teach that in college?"

"I know how to check facts just fine." He had a challenging look in his eyes, spoiling for a fight.

Gabe nodded and sipped his coffee. "You know how, but you can't be bothered?"

Jacobson sneered. He opened his wallet and counted out bills. "I'm done talking. You're trying to get me to say something you can report back to Chilton."

"Nope, I'm giving you free legal advice. Hire a fact-checker."

Jacobson stood up, almost bowling over David who had arrived with Gabe's Special and hot sauce.

"That's rich." Jacobson's voice reverberated. "Legal advice from someone who got turfed from the profession. A suspect in a brutal murder. How did you get off? Bribe witnesses? Bump them off? Is that what I'll find when I *check my facts* about you, Dead Skunk, or whatever your name is?"

Gabe's head was thrumming, his shoulder ached, and his knee throbbed, but he vaulted from the booth and grabbed

Jacobson's arm, spinning him around. Fear flickered in Jacobson's eyes as he backed a step away.

Gabe relaxed his fists and put a smile on his face for the benefit of the breakfast crowd. "Here's more legal advice, Billy-boy. Tread carefully. Print garbage about me again and I'll sue. I'll end up owning your paper, your truck, your house and everything in it. Have an excellent day."

Jacobson stood still, sputtering and red-faced, as Gabe went to the rack of coffee thermoses and poured another mug. This time he opted for Prince of Darkness. He watched Jacobson leave the café and felt another uptick in his mood. At this rate, he'd feel cleansed in a week.

Gabe nodded at the other diners and returned to the booth. He gazed at his Ain't No Dude Ranch Special—firm scrambled eggs, onions, peppers, and cheese. No ooze. No yellow slime. His stomach relaxed. Rhonda wasn't there to stop him. He added several shots of hot sauce.

Gabe swallowed a forkful of the Special and waited for the heat, counting to three. On schedule, a cleansing fire rose from the back of his throat to his sinuses and out his tear ducts. He wiped his eyes. "Damn straight, it ain't no dude ranch."

As he enjoyed the Special, he thought about the paperweight. Charoite, not a local mineral, Minken said. If not local, then why was it at TEG's site? He could ask Aldercott, but then Gabe would have to admit he took the rock from Aldercott's property. Tangled webs, Gabe thought.

He swallowed the last piece of biscuit and drained his coffee, preparing to leave, when Rhonda entered through the café's back hallway. Gabe whisked the hot sauce out of sight.

She slid into his booth. "Gawd, you must have a killer hangover."

"How can you tell?"

"It's all about pasty skin tones." She studied him. "You're either dead or hung over."

"At this point I'm pretty sure it's a hangover. Before I ate the Special, I was thinking I was dead, but now I'm rejuvenated." Gabe twirled his empty coffee mug. "I had a run-in with Jacobson just now. Is it only me, or does he antagonize everyone?"

"He has a star complex. He doesn't like anyone who might become one. How's your baby brother Jack?"

"Is there anyone in town who doesn't know I'm his brother?"

"Maybe one or two residents of Cemetery Hill."

"Hah. Jack should be okay. He told Mercy and O'Malley that he was helping me investigate. Mercy's had mercy on me —she's not gonna kill me. But O'Malley still might."

"I admire your knack for pissing people off." Rhonda counted on her fingers: "Bill, O'Malley, and BAM, who claim you put the cops on them."

"What can I say? It's a gift."

"And Nicole," Rhonda continued. "What happened last night?"

"I mentioned I talked to her father about the sabotage. She got steamed."

"You talked to him because he lost his investment in that mining company?"

"Yeah. Thought it was worth checking out."

"Kee-ryste. In that case, put everyone in town on your suspect list. High Yield Prospecting Enterprises. What a name. The only thing high about it was our expectations, helped along by laudatory articles in the *Journal*, I might add. Everyone thought it was gonna be the next great score. We were all gonna retire."

"Who else invested?" Gabe said.

"Everyone. Cheryl, Bill, Harris and Kate. My hubby and me. Almost everyone in town."

Chapter 43

JACK COULD NOT WAIT to get out of hospital. He'd been awake since six, when a young, smoking-hot but all-business nurse—a total tyrant—rousted him so she could shine a piercing light in his eyes. Seven times during the night, someone had shaken him awake, poked and prodded, when all he'd wanted to do was to zone out.

"Are you feeling rested?" the Tyrant had said, when he'd jerked awake at six.

"Musta got a solid hour of sleep. Can't understand how you let that happen."

Her face flushed pink and her eyes darkened, their blue becoming almost purple. "We're so lucky the smack on your head left you with a working brain so you could entertain us with your smart mouth."

"Glad to oblige." Jack smirked, and her pink flush deepened.

She checked the dwindling level of fluid in the IV bag. "Looks like I can unhook you. This won't hurt a bit." She removed the needle from his forearm, put a piece of cotton over the spot, and told him to press down. He relaxed. It hadn't hurt.

In the next instant, she grasped the tape securing the IV tubing to his arm and ripped it off. Jack's eyes bugged. He yelped. A bracelet of red, stinging, hairless skin wrapped itself around his arm. He rubbed at it, his eyes tearing. "Ow. Geez. That hurts."

She smiled. Her eyes were icy blue. "Glad to oblige."

Jack turned away, gingerly rubbing the tender strip. He tried to sleep, but it was hopeless. Who knew what other mean tricks the she-dragon would pull if he let his guard down? He had no TV, no books, nothing to do but stare at the walls. The only relief from the boredom of the dragging morning was a visit by the newspaper guy who wanted to interview a local hero.

Then more boredom until Tyrant appeared mid-morning and said he was being discharged. "Your brother's coming to collect you. Stop lollygagging, get dressed."

Jack frowned at her. She didn't look so old—mid-twenties maybe—but she acted like a teacher. Or someone's crotchety grandmother. No people skills. That was her problem. Didn't they teach that in nursing school? He sat upright and a piercing pain shot through his brain like an arrow. He clutched his head. "Ohhhhhh."

"Headache?"

He squinted at her. He nodded, moaning as the pain juggled around in his brain. She handed him water and two white pills. "Take these. No alcohol for twenty-four hours."

"I don't drink."

"Sure."

When his headache eased, Jack slid from the bed and dressed. Blood spotted his sweatshirt; grass and mud stained his jeans. He looked at the blood splatter on his new jacket. "Mom's gonna kill me."

"Hey, Jacko. How're you feeling?"

Gabe stood in the doorway, his face pale except for one bruised, puffy cheek.

"Sore," Jack said. He touched the bandage on his head. "Got thirty stitches up here. What happened to you?"

"I'll fill you in on the road." Gabe hugged Jack for a long moment and then moved to the window and leaned against the sill. "Mom phoned just now. The cops are at the ranch with a search warrant. She says it lists paint and explosives."

Jack grabbed the edge of the mattress. His knees felt unpinned from his legs. He sat on the bed and hung on.

Gabe fixed his eyes on Jack's face. "I told her to call Harris. Will they find anything?"

"No way." He met Gabe's gaze and held it. "There's nothin' for them to find. Honest."

Gabe watched him for a second and then nodded. "Okay, good. If there's anything we need to know, you gotta tell us. Understand? Better we know about it than be ambushed."

Jack swallowed.

"You scared the hell out of us, Jacko. What were you doing in that pasture?"

Jack hesitated and kept his eyes on the floor. Finally, he said, "I was heading for the Valley of Horses, y'know? And I saw a guy in the pasture. Near the rig. I skirted around and hid my ATV in the trees. By then he was gone, so I went to see what he'd been doing."

"Didn't he hear your engine?"

Jack blinked. He hadn't thought of that. "Guess not."

He raised his head. "I thought he was the driller. Then I saw the burning fuse. I thought I could help solve the case. I tried to stomp it out, but it just kept burning. I tried to rip it out of the dynamite but couldn't."

"What happened when you couldn't extinguish the fuse?"

"I got scared and ran for the trees. Full speed." Jack brushed at his jeans. "I fell twice, skidded on wet grass. I remember a boom and something pinging, like a chime."

Jack frowned and tried to remember. It was fuzzy. "I think I crawled through the brush. Next I know, it's dark and cold and I'm lying near my ATV. I couldn't find the keys. I wasn't sure where I was, y'know? I wandered around and then found the trail and followed it. When I reached Harris's paddock, I got my bearings."

"Do you remember what the guy looked like?"

"Huh?"

"The guy, Jacko. The guy who lit the fuse."

Jack closed his eyes and tried to bring up an image. It kept skidding away from him. "He was far away. I can't see his face, but there was something weird. It's right there, I just can't grab it."

"Don't try to force it. When your head clears, it might come back. When it does, tell me." Gabe's eyes flicked toward the door.

"Jack Diamond?" A deep voice, coming from the doorway.

Jack turned at the sound. A tall Mountie entered the room, glanced at Jack and then at Gabe. "Jesus, Gabrieli, look at you. Been brawling?"

Gabe gave the cop a quick grimace. "Yeah, with a horse. Jack, this is Sergeant LeBlanc. He's working on the sabotage too."

"What's your connection with Mr. Diamond, Gabrieli?"

"We're brothers."

"Mmmmm." LeBlanc faced Jack. "Jack Diamond, you're under arrest for property damage and possession of explosive devices."

Jack's stomach heaved. If he hadn't been sitting on the bed, he'd have fallen to the floor.

LeBlanc pulled his handcuffs from his belt as he recited Jack's rights.

Gabe exploded from his perch at the window. "What? Are you out of your mind, LeBlanc? Look at this kid, he just got beaned trying to *stop* an explosion, damn near died, for Chrissake."

"Or, he was injured when he set the explosives and messed up. That's the truth, isn't it, Mr. Diamond?"

Gabe sliced the air with his hand. "Don't say anything, Jack." Glaring at the cop and pulling out his phone, Gabe said, "He's not talking to you, LeBlanc. I'm calling his lawyer right now. This is the stupidest damn thing I've heard since Ambrose threatened to charge me with assault. What do you guys do all day, sit there in Trail and dream up bogus charges? It's no wonder people get away with murder in Canada. We have goofballs for cops. Complete goofballs."

Jack sat slack jawed. He was petrified by the words "under arrest" yet reveled in watching Gabe in apeshit mode —incredible.

"Stand up," LeBlanc said to him. "Hands behind your back."

Jack's knees wobbled, but he managed to stay upright as LeBlanc cuffed him.

Gabe yelled into his phone. "Harris, drop everything, I need you. Hang on." He lowered the phone and glared at LeBlanc.

"Don't ask him any questions, LeBlanc, because he won't answer. Jack, not one word. Zip it, stay cool and we'll get you out."

LeBlanc led Jack to the door and stopped. "You can tell his lawyer we have your brother nailed on the property damage and possession charges, Gabrieli. Those are for starters. I believe we can connect him to the TEG explosion. And someone died there, so you know what the charges will be then."

As LeBlanc pulled him through the doorway, Jack fought hard to still his quivering lips. He looked back at Gabe, who was speaking with Harris but watching Jack. Gabe winked. The same signal he'd used when Jack was a little kid and needed reassurance that things would be okay. Please God, let Gabe be right.

Chapter 44

SHORTLY AFTER NOON Gabe drove toward TEG's site, somewhat calmer than he'd been at the hospital when LeBlanc hauled Jack away. Harris was on his way to Trail to spring Jack. He'd refused Gabe's offer to tag along, saying, "You'll do more good by solving the case and clearing him."

Gabe would have been completely relaxed had he not phoned O'Malley's ranch, intending to tell Mercy about Jack's arrest. Seamus answered the phone, a sign The Frikkin Comedian was back on the scene. "Mercy's indisposed. What's up?"

When Gabe filled him in, Seamus let out his trademark "cheeez-ussss." Then he said, "When the Mounties confiscated a bag of stuff from the tack room, I figured trouble was coming. Hoped I was wrong, but lately, hoping's useless with Jack. He's just like you. Trouble."

The remark pumped an unhealthy amount of adrenaline into Gabe's bloodstream, pushing his heart rate into three digits. He clamped his lips shut, breathed in to the count of five, and squeezed his phone until his hand hurt. When he could speak without yelling, he said, "Jack's a seventeen-year-old kid who's been farmed out to an asshole who pretends to know something about parenting. I'm surprised Jack's doing as well as he is."

"Sure, blame it on me. I'm trying to give him some spine so when life happens, he'll man up, not be a gutless wonder and fall apart."

"You mean like I did."

"Shoe fits."

"As always, nice talking to you, O'Malley," Gabe had said to dead air.

Now, he drove along Highway 41 in the sunshine, listening to Willie Nelson and Toby Keith sing about beer for their horses, and gradually regaining his equilibrium. He climbed Timberline, passed Deception Ridge Viewpoint with its usual couple dozen trucks and trailers, and bumped up the logging road.

Except for skiffs of snow, the turnout was empty, an excellent sign. He donned his gloves, zipped his down jacket, and hiked the trail. When he reached the clearing, he stared in disbelief. Snow blanketed the entire space.

No chance he could look for graffiti now. He cut a path to a hump in the center of the site, which he guessed was the remnants of the burned shack. He kicked at the snow covering the debris. When a sharp pain lanced through his knee, he switched legs and attacked the snow with his left leg, finally uncovering part of the debris. If core samples were there, they would be somewhere under the piles of crud. He booted the ruins aside, searching for cylinders of rock like those he'd seen at Minken's site, and finding nothing more than burned wood and blackened metal. No core samples.

Gabe studied the rest of the snow-covered debris. No way could he clear the snow from all of it. He picked three areas at random, cleared the snow, and then toed the debris aside to see what lay beneath. And came up empty every time.

He was amazed by what the fire had done to the shack.

Of course, this fire had been helped by a few gallons of accelerant. Ubrowski, the fire chief, had speculated the arsonist used gasoline. Not very helpful for identifying suspects, because everyone in Cheakamus had a can of gas kicking around their garage.

He slapped at his jacket and jeans in a futile attempt to rid himself of the soot that covered him. As he turned to leave, a reflection from the hillside caught his eye. He isolated the glint —sun bouncing off glass midway up Rimrock. Remembering the pictures he'd taken here yesterday, Gabe scrolled through the photos on his phone until he found what looked like a vehicle in about the same spot on the hill.

His skin prickled. Strange that someone would be there again today. Perhaps a trail rider, perhaps not. Adrenaline kicked in. If he could see the vehicle, whoever was in it could see him. Gabe turned and walked out of the clearing. When he hit the trail, he broke into a limping run, moving as quickly as his swollen knee allowed.

He hustled into the truck, put it in four-wheel drive and roared up the logging road. Whoever was there would hear the engine whether Gabe drove full out or half-speed. He opted for speed, hoping to reach the guy before he could escape. Or load a weapon.

When he rounded a hairpin curve, the truck skidded in the snow and Gabe slowed to a crawl. The road was white from side to side and as far ahead as he could see. Pristine snow, broken only by rabbit tracks. No one had driven this section today. He stopped the truck and decided to cover the rest of the trail on foot.

The steep pitch made Gabe's hike a struggle. His knee reminded him with every step that it was swollen, bruised, and unhappy. He was breathing hard and sweating harder by the time he could see the vehicle, a brown Ford Ranger. It sat in a turnout at the top of the trail, snow on its roof and hood. The tailgate was down, and two ramps extended to the ground. ATV tire tracks ran from the ramps, past the Ranger and along the trail. The snow around the pickup was trampled. Someone had been in or near the truck recently.

The truck bed held a wooden crate and a large cooler. The crate held one frying pan, one saucepan, and a few dishes. The cooler held condiments and bottled water.

The truck's license plates were missing. When Gabe tried the driver's door, it opened. That made sense. If someone had stolen the pickup and dumped it here, why bother locking it? Plus, this was Cheakamus. No one locked anything.

The Ranger's interior was a study in good housekeeping: pillow and sleeping bag on the passenger seat; a cache of soup-in-a-cup, crackers, peanut butter, and Maynards Wine Gums on the driver's seat. The glove box held nothing more than the owner's manual; the console held CDs, a tire gauge, and gas receipts. Gabe found the keys under the driver's seat.

Why would someone steal a truck and ATV, dump the truck here, stash the keys, and drive off in the ATV? Maybe the owner had engine trouble and intended to return, but still took his license plates with him? No way.

Gabe snapped pictures of the Ranger, and trekked back to his F-150. He sat in the truck and opened his notebook. He added "Ranger," then crossed TEG off the list and felt another uptick in his mood. Sometimes nothing was something. The TEG scene stood out because of what wasn't there. Core samples.

As Gabe drove along the logging road, he asked himself three things: Why would someone steal core samples? Who owned the Ranger? Who was camping in it?

Immediately after he turned onto Highway 41, his in-cab phone dinged, signaling messages. "Back in civilization, Three," he said, and punched the message button.

The first message was Harris: "Good news. Call me."

The second message was Minken: "Got an interesting fish story for you."

The last message was Bethany, who sounded subdued: "I'm at Heathrow. Please call."

Relieved that Bethany had surfaced, Gabe returned the call, but was punted to voice mail. "Bella, glad to hear from you and that you're almost home. Sorry I missed you. Call me."

Then he punched in Harris's number. "LeBlanc cut us some slack," Harris said when he answered. "He released Jack on a promise to appear."

"What happened to the uptight cop we know and love?"

"I'm a superb lawyer. Plus, Mercy sweet-talked him. She and Seamus agreed to keep a tight rein on Jack."

"Ahhh, poor Jack. So, what now?"

"Stop by the bar and I'll fill you in. I'm waiting on Cheryl McMillan. She says a potential buyer's arriving tomorrow."

Gabe pulled over and phoned LeBlanc. "Thanks for letting Jack out," he said when LeBlanc answered.

"I'm a reasonable guy."

"And my mother is a force of nature."

"That too."

"I was up Rimrock today. I found a Ford Ranger at the top of the logging road past the TEG site. No plates, no papers. Looks like somebody's camping in it. I thought you'd want to know."

"I'll send someone. That it?"

"Now that you ask, did your guys remove the core samples from the TEG site? Cause I didn't see any there. Nor did I see graffiti. Did you?"

LeBlanc's sigh was long and loud. "Just because I released your brother doesn't mean he's off the hook."

"The kid's innocent, LeBlanc. Compare his graffiti to the stuff at the bombsites. It's different."

"We found explosives and aerosol paint in his tack box. We'll test for prints, but even if he's not good for the sabotage, he's not lily white. We found his ATV in the bush by Mayor Chilton's pasture. Along with a bag of aerosol paint cans. And I hate to tell you this, several empty vodka bottles."

Chapter 45

SHORTLY AFTER TWO o'clock Gabe parked his truck in Greta's garage. Since eight o'clock this morning, when he'd opened his eyes, hungover and on the floor, he'd checked two items off his list: LeBlanc and TEG's exploration site. Progress, if not significant.

Harris wanted him to stop in at the bar, but first Gabe needed to dump his soot-stained clothes and take a shower, try Bethany again, and talk to Greta.

When he finished his shower, he realized his hangover had disappeared. His shiner was fading, and his cheek had lost some puffiness. Except for his bruised shoulder and swollen knee, and the heaviness he felt about LeBlanc's revelations concerning Jack, he was almost right with the world. Well, as right as he got these days.

What had happened to Jack since he'd moved to Cheaka-mus? Gabe understood Jack's anger at being shipped off to O'Malley's ranch. Granted, Mercy's reaction to Jack's school situation wasn't great, but she'd sent him to someone she trusted would do his best—proof of her insanity in Gabe's mind, but nothing he could change.

What confused Gabe about Jack was something he'd

never experienced in Eau Claire. Back there in Alberta, Jack was always up front with Gabe. Now, Jack was evasive at best, a flat-out liar at worst. Take the graffiti, for instance, or the ATV at the museum. Any doubt Gabe had that it belonged to Jack disappeared when he'd seen the unlocked door barricading the mine tunnels. Teenagers, tunnels, and partying. No-brainer. And now LeBlanc's news about the stash of vodka bottles confirmed Gabe's suspicion that Jack was drinking. Not merely having an occasional illicit beer with buddies. Drinking. He added Jack to his list of things to worry about.

When he phoned Bethany, her voice mail once more kicked in. "Hey, it's me," he said. "Over to you. Love you."

Gabe hauled on clean jeans, boots, and his favorite sweater: a gift from Bethany, in a gray she said made his eyes darken. Shrugging into his jacket, he headed to Greta's door.

"I was going to pop over in a bit, see how you're taking it," Greta said, swinging the kitchen door wide and waving him inside.

She'd obviously heard about Jack's arrest. "It'll be okay," he said.

He sat at her kitchen table, straightened his right leg, and massaged his knee. "I'm wondering about core samples. Are they valuable, worth stealing?"

After a moment's thought, Greta shook her head. "Their only value is they prove what came out of the ground."

Gabe tilted his head, not getting it. "How so?"

"The basic idea is you split the core in two lengthwise, keep half and send the rest to the lab for assaying. You can retest results with your saved half. I'm not an expert. Horace or Ed Gwinn could tell you more."

"I phoned your Indiana Jones, a.k.a. Ed Gwinn the super geologist, a couple times. No response."

"I'm waiting on him too. He has several long-distance calls on my phone bill. He always sends me the money, but this time it seems he forgot. I'm glad you're not upset about today's paper."

Gabe blinked. "What?"

"Good grief, what else?" She passed him the *Journal* and there he was, front page once again.

Two pictures were above the fold. The first showed Kate and Gabe by Tornado Callie's stall Tuesday evening, smiling at each other, Kate's hand on his arm. The caption read, "Sometime P.I. Gabrieli and close friend, Kate Chilton."

The second picture was of Jack. The caption read, "Gabrieli's brother and bombing victim, or more?"

He scanned Jacobson's article. A paragraph about the town hiring Gabe to investigate the sabotage, another about the slow investigation, and the sucker punch:

"Some say if D.S. Gabrieli spent less time tossing sugar cubes into whiskey glasses, bullying honest citizens, and cozying up to women, he might unearth a clue and solve the heinous crimes ripping the fabric of our town. Others say Gabrieli is ill-equipped for the job, being nothing more than a rube from Haystack, Alberta.

"To be fair, Gabrieli has done more than spin his 4x4 wheels. He helped rescue horses near the mayor's ranch. He was on scene with our pretty vet, Dr. Nicole Mitchell, so people are uncertain how much of the hard work Gabrieli did.

"While our Lothario was charming the town's women, his brother, Jack Diamond, was apparently investigating the sabotage for Gabrieli and was injured by the explosion at Chilton's pasture last night. At press time young Jack, who's known to be a graffiti artist and environmental activist, was resting comfortably in

Cheakamus Hospital. Does he have more to do with the bombings than we think?"

Gabe shook his head. "I shoulda remembered the advice I used to give clients: never get into pissing matches when the opposition has a gun or a newspaper column. Either way, you'll lose."

"Everyone knows you're working hard to solve the case," Greta said.

"It's Jack I'm worried about."

———

GABE PARKED outside Tiffany's and collected an extra-large Mudshark to go before strolling across the street to The Peak. Inside, Tom Mitchell stood by the beer taps and a waitress leaned her hip against a barstool. Both focused on sports highlights on the TV.

"Harris here?"

"Running errands."

Gabe moved to a small table next to the massive river-rock fireplace at the back of the room. He called Lucy and was punted to voice mail.

"Hey, Luce," he said to the machine. "Reporting from fireside at The Peak Bar where it's mid-afternoon, mid-week, and things are mid-busy."

Harris blew through the doors, carrying a Tiffany's to-go cup. Gabe finished his message: "I hope you shipped my shoes. I need them for Saturday."

Gabe followed Harris to a tiny office tucked next to the men's room. He sat in the spindly metal guest chair designed to encourage guests to be gone. "Should you be drinking the competition's coffee?"

"The bar's coffee sucks," Harris said. He loosened today's bolo tie, a square black stone, and sipped.

Gabe leaned forward. "I just saw today's paper. That picture—"

Harris waved it away. "Don't sweat it. The usual Jacobson innuendo."

"The stuff about Jack pisses me off even more."

"I called Bill and told him he was opening himself up to lawsuits. And that Seamus might not be the right person to get on the wrong side of."

"Or you and me."

"Yeah. But Seamus petrifies him. We don't."

Gabe relaxed. He tilted his chair back and placed his feet on Harris's desk. "So, what's next for Jack?"

"The Mounties are testing the paint and explosives they found in his tack box. He swears none of it is his. The results should be back tomorrow."

"I hope Jack's being straight with us."

"Me too."

"I haven't heard diddly from Ambrose about the incident in Tiffany's," Gabe said. "I don't like assault charges hanging over my head."

"Relax," Harris said. "If he charges you, the case is so weak, a first-year law student could win it, and you've got me, ace lawyer, on your side."

Harris was probably right, but Gabe disliked trials where he was the accused. An assault charge would be his second appearance in court as an accused, and the second unfounded charge against him. He was beginning to take it personally. "I can't figure out why Ambrose is so antagonistic. Sure, maybe I mouthed off a bit. But LeBlanc seems to be able to let things like that roll off. Not Ambrose. It's like he was looking for a reason to charge me."

"Perhaps," Harris said. "But you do have a distinct knack of pissing off cops."

"Me?" Gabe said. "Maybe Ambrose is just an unhappy guy. I googled him and of all the pictures of him online, there was only one where he looked remotely happy. And that was seven years ago when his nephew joined the Calgary cops."

Gabe thought about that picture and said, "I keep thinking there's something familiar about Ambrose's nephew. And then I think, nah it's just a family resemblance. It's driving me up the wall."

"Try sleeping on it. Tell your brain to check your mental files and deliver the answer in the morning."

Gabe stared at Harris. "When did you get into that woo-woo stuff?"

Harris grinned and shrugged. "It works."

"Uh-huh." Gabe rocked back and forth in the metal chair, taking in the cramped, windowless office. The toilet in the adjoining men's room flushed, burping, gurgling and hissing. "As offices go, this would make a superb storage room. Still, The Peak's a fine establishment. Why sell it? Suppose I rene-gotiate that business loan for you?"

Harris sighed and shook his head. "It's not the loan. It's the upcoming balloon payment."

"So?"

"It's complicated."

Gabe waited. Harris grabbed a pencil and tapped a slow, even rhythm on his desktop. "The loan has several balloon payments. We've already borrowed to cover the first one. From Seamus. The second balloon payment is due at the end of the month. If we can't meet it, we could lose the ranch."

"Seamus won't make another loan?"

"I don't want to ask. We haven't repaid the first one yet." He smiled a half smile. "Never borrow from family, or worse yet, your wife's family. It makes for tense dinners."

"What about extensions?"

"The bank's extended three times already. They told us last time that was it."

"And refinancing is out?"

Harris tapped his death-march rhythm and nodded.

"Well, hell." Gabe rose, stretched, and moved to the door. "Back to Plan A. Solve the sabotage. Make the mayor a hero and the town an inviting place to buy a bar."

"Soon would be good." Harris removed a check book from a drawer. "I need to pay a few bills and then I'll be out to relieve Tom."

A few more patrons were hanging out when Gabe re-entered the bar. Carl Dochmann from Solomon's Choice Ranch perched on a barstool, sipping a beer, eyes fixed on the TV. Craig Westburg from BAM and his sidekick Frank Palmer occupied a table by the windows with the petite chefs, Pinky and Green Goddess.

"Did Horace Minken reach you?" Carl asked Gabe. "I ran into him, and he said he was looking for you."

"Oops." Gabe called Minken's number and left a message. "Horace, call me back." Gabe nodded at Carl. "Thanks for the reminder."

"I heard your brother was injured in last night's explosion. Is he okay?"

"Pretty much. Out of hospital but in deep shit with his mother."

"Kids. Trying to be detectives. Lucky he didn't run into the bomber. Then again, if he'd seen the guy, he could ID him and we'd all rest easy."

Gabe opened his mouth to respond when a sharp finger poked his sore shoulder. "Gabester. Big-shot private eye."

When Gabe turned, Craig Westburg stood a handsbreadth away. The toothpick in his mouth twitched up and down as he worked his jaw.

"Craig. Nice to see you."

Craig poked Gabe's shoulder once more. "You sic'd the cops on us. What's up with that?"

Carl turned his attention away from the TV and watched Craig. Tom stopped wiping down the counter.

Gabe winced and rubbed his shoulder. "Think a minute,

Craig. If you saw the story in the paper about the supposed food fight, you know I'm not the Mounties' friend. So why would I sic them on you?"

Craig frowned and leaned forward. "All I know, everything was fine. Then you visit us and suddenly, so do the cops. Now it's totally screwed up."

This time he poked Gabe's chest. Gabe grabbed Craig's hand and squeezed his fingers. "Don't do that. This is my best sweater."

Craig wrenched his hand away and clenched his fist. Frank grabbed his arm and pulled him back a step, saying, "Don't do anything stupid."

Harris came out of the back hallway and hurried over.

"Listen to your friend," Carl said to Craig. "Be smart."

"What's going on?" Harris said.

"Misunderstanding," Gabe said.

Craig shook off Frank and glared. The toothpick flicked from one side of his mouth to the other. "Someday someone's gonna screw with *your* life. See how you like it." He flung his toothpick to the floor, stomped to his table, slumped into his chair, and chugged his beer.

"I'll take over," Harris said to Tom. "You get going."

"Big date?" Gabe asked Tom.

"Nah. Greta asked me to seal the tunnel mouth at the Valley of Horses. 'Use spikes,' she said, 'to keep the kids out.' Gotta do that now 'cause tonight I'm driving one of the wagons. Not that the Percherons need a driver. They could do the route blindfolded."

"I'd forgotten about the wagon rides."

"That's because you're new here and don't have children," Carl said, draining his beer and sliding off his stool. "The little kids wait all year to ride in the wagons. Greta called me about the tunnels too. One comes out somewhere on our land. I'll make sure it's sealed."

After Tom and Carl left the bar, Harris said, "What was Craig on about?"

"The cops raided his place. He thinks I had something to do with it."

"Imagine that. You're having your usual effect on people. Bill...Craig." Harris paused for a beat. "And Nicole. What did you do? When I mentioned your name today, her face pinched up."

"I interviewed her father about High Yield and the money he lost. She thought I was out of line." Gabe shrugged. "I can live with it."

"Lots of people lost money on that company."

"I heard you had a few shares."

"Kate and I lost twenty-five hundred bucks." Harris flashed a wry smile. "In case you're wondering, not enough to make me plant bombs."

"Never crossed my mind. I'm guessing someone has a grudge against mining companies. Other than Wally Mitchell, is there anyone you can think of who hates mining? Or Aldercott specifically?"

Harris shook his head. "Nope. I've got no clue."

"That makes us even." Gabe turned to leave. "I'll keep you posted as I spin my wheels."

"Come by the wagon rides at the museum tonight. Everyone will be there, suspects included."

Greta phoned before Gabe could start the truck. "Anders Thorvaldsen is alive. He's here, looking for you, and not happy."

Chapter 46

GABE PARKED on Lookout Road behind an ATV so mud-spattered he could barely pick out its faded yellow paint. He limped along Greta's walk, thinking about his various aches and bruises. If Reverend Beam had a problem on Friday with the shiner and cuts, too bad. Gabe had a legitimate explanation for all of it. But if Beam was like the clergy in Eau Claire Gabe had known during his teens, explanations would mean diddly squat.

Greta ushered him into the kitchen. A runt sat at her table, staring at the teapot and holding his unkempt white head between his hands. He looked up when Gabe entered, his eyes astonishingly blue beneath bushy white brows. Gabe thought, "So this is what a Viking looks like when he gets old."

The Viking frowned. "About time. I got a bone to pick with you."

"Good grief, Anders. Settle down." Greta poured him a cup of tea. "Drink this. Herbal. Calming."

The Viking sniffed the liquid and sipped. Grimacing, he pushed the cup away. "Cat piss."

"This crotchety old geezer is Anders Thorvaldsen, a long-time friend," Greta said. She introduced Gabe as, "D. S. Gabrieli, a new friend. You can call him Gabe."

The Viking pushed himself from his chair. "You're bigger'n me, and a hell of a lot younger, but I was Golden Gloves. I can whup your ass."

Gabe studied the short, skinny, geriatric fury in front of him and bit his bottom lip to stop from laughing. He relaxed against Greta's counter. "Why would you want to whup me?"

Thorvaldsen stabbed the air with a bony finger. "They took my home 'causa you."

"Who took it?"

"The cops."

"Huh?"

"It's your fault," Thorvaldsen said. "I saw ya snooping around, poking through my things. Taking pictures."

Trying to follow the man's words made Gabe's head hurt. He pulled out his phone, clicked on his photos, and said, "Show me."

Gabe scrolled through the pictures until Thorvaldsen jerked and said, "There," and pointed at the picture of the abandoned Ford Ranger.

"You own this truck?"

Thorvaldsen's eyes flicked to Greta, then back to Gabe. "The Dark Knight gave it to me."

This time Gabe couldn't suppress the laugh. "Like Batman?"

"Don't get snot-nosed. He wore a long dark coat. I don't know who he is, so I gave him that name. He left me a truck."

"He just drove it up the mountain and said, 'Here you go, Anders, live it up'?"

"He left it there. Keys, the whole shebang. I can't drive it 'cause the tank's sitting on empty."

"Instead, you've been driving the ATV that was in the bed."

"Hah, you want me to say 'yeah' so you can call the cops

again." The Viking folded his arms and reclaimed his chair. When he next looked at Gabe, his face was morose. "I had a tent till a bear trashed it. Now this. Where am I gonna sleep?"

Greta said, "Would you like to bunk in here until we get this sorted?"

Thorvaldsen shook his head. "Gotta have daylight and fresh air."

A sentiment that resonated with Gabe.

"I'll sleep outdoors," Thorvaldsen went on. "Even if it's becoming dangerous after dark. Look what happened to that kid the other night."

"In the pasture? Did you see it?" Gabe said.

"No. Heard about it."

"That kid is Gabe's brother," Greta said. "He was trying to extinguish the fuse."

Thorvaldsen's face softened. "He's okay, right?"

Gabe nodded. "Seen anyone else around the area? Someone up to no good?"

"Nah, and I've been watching. He shoulda cut the fuse."

"Pardon?"

"Can't extinguish it otherwise." Thorvaldsen rose from the chair. "I'll be going." He pointed his finger at Gabe. "You do the right thing. Get me my home back."

After the Viking left, Gabe said, "I'm glad Thorvaldsen's not dead. He makes a great suspect: wanders around the mountain, knows about explosives."

"That's ridiculous," Greta said. "Anders is old school like Pierre was. Too much respect for mining to blow up things. If he has a beef he says so, flat out, like he did with you."

———

GABE SAT at the table in his suite and checked his list. Still not dealt with: Gwinn, Aldercott, High Yield. He opened his laptop. He could squeeze some research in before the wagon rides at the museum.

But first, he placed his daily call to Gwinn and sent his daily email. Where the hell was the guy? In a remote part of Nevada, with no access to phones? Or hiding out in the mountains near Cheakamus, planting explosives? He drew a circle around Gwinn's name.

When Gabe searched High Yield Prospecting Enterprises online, he found the usual dry corporate information, along with three articles written by Jacobson. The first two discussed the company in optimistic language, lauding the potential of some Nevada mining claims it acquired from Big Score Ventures. "There's gold in them hills," one article crowed.

Jacobson's third story mentioned disappointing assays and focused on High Yield's decision to abandon what had proved to be dud properties. The headline read: "High Yield Prospecting Enterprises: Hype?" Gabe admired Jacobson's creativity. "Hype" was both an acronym and a criticism.

Alerted by his rumbling stomach, Gabe checked the time. Five o'clock. He'd need to hustle if he wanted to eat before checking out the kiddies' wagon rides at the Evergold Museum.

Even though he wore his down jacket, Gabe felt the chill in the air as he hurried to his truck. How low would the temperature drop overnight? The Viking must have as much aversion to confined spaces as Gabe did if he slept outdoors this late in the fall.

He crept along Main Street, searching for a parking spot near Tiffany's, and hit the brakes when he spotted a pickup backing out from a spot a couple car lengths ahead. "Our lucky day, Three," Gabe said, patting his dash,

As he waited for the vehicle to leave, he thought again about Anders Thorvaldsen and grinned when he remembered the Viking's references to the Dark Knight. "Don't get snot-nosed," he'd said, when Gabe had asked if he meant Batman.

When the pickup at last vacated the parking spot and sped away on Main Street, Gabe kept his foot on the brake. "You do the right thing," The Viking had said to him. "Get me my home back."

It would take a miracle for the police to release that Ranger. If Thorvaldsen didn't want to sleep indoors, he would have to rough it. For an old guy, The Viking seemed to be healthy and fit. But how many nights in the cold on a mountain, with no shelter, could a person withstand?

Gabe couldn't retrieve the Ranger for The Viking, but there was another solution. He took his foot off the brake and stepped on the gas. Dinner could wait a bit.

Chapter 47

GABE DROVE along Main Street to Joe's Hardware Emporium and parked in the lot. Every Canadian small town worth living in had a store like Joe's—offering nuts and bolts and tools, camping supplies, beach balls, Red Flyer wagons, and doohickeys.

By the time he'd found everything he needed, Gabe had trekked the length of the store three times, gradually building a pile at the check-out: up-in-a-minute tent, camping stove, sleeping bag, cooler, small propane canisters, bear spray, and two gas cans.

While the clerk rang up the order, Gabe studied the store's selection of flashlights, which ranged from small penlights to behemoths that would light an average hockey rink. He chose an old faithful: sturdy metal case and a choice of low or high beam.

The clerk pointed to a display of LED flashlights. "If you tire of buying batteries, or don't want to use your phone, these are the way to go." He selected one not much larger than a good cigar, lifted a lever on its side and cranked. The high-pitched revving sound reminded Gabe of the toy cars he played with as a boy. He would prime them by running their wheels several times over a hard surface, then set them on the floor and let them bash into Lucy's dollhouse.

Ten cranks of the handle charged the flashlight. When the clerk flicked the switch, a piercing light shot out. A guy could never have too many gadgets. Gabe added the wind-up cigar flashlight to his pile.

THE DINNER RUSH at Tiffany's hadn't yet started, allowing Gabe to snag his favorite booth at the back. He sat facing the door, a gunslinger in a western, and checked out the special on the chalkboard: *boeuf bourguignon over pappardelle.*

Rhonda was on her way to his booth when he spotted Aldercott through the café's windows. "Be right back, Rhonda." He hurried outside. "Manfred."

Aldercott glanced over his shoulder, raised his hand and walked back. Gabe said, "I was out at your site a while back, looking at the damage from the explosion. I didn't notice any core samples."

Aldercott stared at him, silent.

"I wondered what happened to them. Someone rip you off?"

Aldercott laughed. "That would get them a sore back and maybe a hundred bucks on a good day. No, I store my core off site. More secure."

"Ahh, okay. I'm having dinner and could use a mining lesson. Join me?"

"I'll have to pass," Aldercott said. "I'm double-booked and late to boot. Another time. Take care now."

When Gabe returned to the café, Rhonda stood by his table. "I'll be damned. You came back. I thought you were up to your old tricks. Want the special tonight?"

He slid into his booth. "*Boeuf bourguignon.* Isn't that stew? A commoner in a king's robe? And what's *pappardelle?*"

"Kee-ryste, I'm cooking for a heathen. *Boeuf bourguignon* is to stew like *chateaubriand* is to roast beef. And what kind of Italian doesn't know *pappardelle* is noodles?"

"Just testing you. Okay, I'll have stew and noodles. And *café noir*."

"Hah. You think I don't know what that is. The coffee's where it always is. Prince of Darkness tonight. A force to be reckoned with."

While he waited for the stew to arrive, Gabe sipped coffee and thought about his research into High Yield Prospecting Enterprises. Five years ago, it was a small company with a promising mining property. Frequent positive news releases moved the stock price consistently higher over two years. Investors were enthusiastic, evidenced by Jacobson's glowing words. Then came several disappointing assay results, and the stock price cratered. Soon the company announced it was discontinuing operations. Its shares became wallpaper. Darling to dog.

Suppose several investors were responsible for the explosions in Cheakamus, each independently taking their frustration out on miners? In Agatha Christie's world, perhaps. High Yield looked to Gabe like a dud of a lead.

He doodled in his notebook, printing the company's initials. H-Y-P-E—not a logo you'd want to promote. Why didn't the company think about the initials when it chose its name? Gabe's devious side kicked in. Was the company aware of the acronym, a hint hidden in plain sight?

He jotted down Big Score Ventures—the company that sold the dud property to High Yield. A cynic would make that BS Ventures. Gabe knew of other initials as well: TEG, for The End Game.

Suppose High Yield was Aldercott's company? Perhaps the fascination with hidden meanings was his. Gabe shook his head. People here had invested heavily. They would remember if High Yield was Aldercott's company. Gabe aimed his pen at

Aldercott's name, about to cross it off, when he decided to first find out what Ed Gwinn knew. He left Aldercott on the list, added Big Score Ventures, and closed the notebook.

Rhonda delivered his dinner at the same moment as Nicole slid into the opposite seat. "Can I join you?"

Gabe pocketed his notebook. Nicole asked Rhonda for a slice of maple sugar pie, and Gabe's mouth watered. "Maple sugar pie?" he said.

"A fan?" Rhonda said. "I'll bring two slices."

"My treat, Rhonda," Nicole said. "Paying off the bet over his name." She leaned back, cleared her throat, and looked around the café.

Gabe wondered why Nicole was here. The last time they'd shared a booth, she'd stormed off in a snit. Sometimes it was best to duck your head and let things be. Gabe focused on his meal. As Rhonda promised, it was much more than stew.

Nicole played with her cutlery and filled him in on the filly's recovery, which was going well. Gabe took his last bite and asked, "Will you release Junebug and her buddies to Solomon's Choice?"

"Yeah, next week sometime. I checked out the ranch. Their animals are all healthy and happy. I guess forgetting the herd on Rimrock was Nestor's sad mistake."

Rhonda brought their pie, topped with hefty mounds of whipped cream. She watched while they tasted. It was sweet, maple, creamy, and perfect. Gabe told her so. "I knew that," Rhonda said.

When Rhonda walked away, Nicole admitted why she'd shown up. "I want to apologize for overreacting before."

Gabe waved it off, his mouth full of whipped cream.

"I know you have a job to do," she said. "My dad didn't blow up anything. He *was* out of town. In fact, I picked him up at the airport."

"You're his alibi?"

"Yes." She looked feisty again, prickly.

"Okay, good. That's that, then." They finished their pie in silence, then Nicole said goodnight, slid out of the booth, waved to Rhonda, and left the café.

Gabe watched her walk away. If Nicole hadn't overreacted when they first talked about Wally, he might have learned Wally's story was legit sooner. If she collected him at the airport, that took the two of them off Gabe's suspect list. It still left her brother, Tom, whose education was sidelined when Wally lost the family dough. Tom, who was nearby when the explosion in Harris's pasture occurred. Nicole had been with him. Was she his alibi too? Or was she covering for him?

Chapter 48

ON HIS WAY to the Evergold Museum for the wagon rides, Gabe made two stops: one, a service station to fill the gas canisters; and two, the top of the logging trail above TEG's site where the Ranger used to be.

There, he stood in the semi-dark, hoping for the sound of an ATV but hearing only the chatter of chickadees. He unloaded the two gas cans and most of his Joe's Emporium purchases, keeping the flashlights.

When he was back on Highway 41 and in cell range, his in-cab phone rang. He punched the receiver button. "Gabrieli."

A slight pause, then a raspy, whispering voice. "Go home, asshole."

Finally, someone was reacting to something Gabe had done. He wondered what it was. "Wrong number. No asshole here."

"You're a comedian, asshole. Go home or we'll get you where it really hurts."

"Calling names is impolite. You shoulda asked politely. So, nope. I'm sticking around."

"Hayseed. You're gonna regret messing with us." Whispers broke the connection.

————

THE PARKING LOT at the museum held at least fifty vehicles. Most of the activity centered on the machine shed at the far end of the lot. Light spilled onto a crowd of adults near two small concession carts inside the open overhead doors. Gabe bought hot spiced apple cider and popcorn, and entered the building.

Jack stood beside a dark green wagon with three bench seats. His skin had regained enough color that Jack appeared almost his normal self—if you didn't focus on the sutures in the center of a jagged white strip on his head where the surgeon had shaved his hair. Small price to pay, Gabe knew, when you considered the damage the fly rock could have done.

The green wagon Jack guarded would hold six adults or nine of the wired kids who formed a twitching line alongside. There were maybe forty of them, ranging from pipsqueak to preteen. The little ones jostled and giggled, and every thirty seconds sent runners to the stall to check the whereabouts of the horse.

Gabe noticed Mercy and O'Malley standing near a trestle table that held coffee urns and pastries. Mercy smiled and waved. O'Malley frowned.

"They're coming!" a pipsqueak shouted, charging past.

Gabe heard jingles from a harness and the solid clop, plop of hooves. Kate appeared, leading Hollywood Hank, who sported red ribbons in his braided mane. His saunter proclaimed, "I'm so cool even I'm amazed." The kids cheered.

Hank was unfazed. He bobbed his massive head toward the screeching children, some of them not quite reaching his belly. They stared goggle-eyed as he plodded past. An "ooohhhh" replaced the shrieking.

Kate stopped in front of the wagon traces and pulled back on Hank's halter. He clopped back between the traces. Kate dropped the reins. Hank stopped and waited patiently while she and Jack hitched the wagon traces to the girth and collar of his harness. Gabe was impressed. His little brother made it look simple.

Kate swung into the driver's seat. Hank tossed his head and snorted. The kids forgot their awe and shrieked. Jack helped eight children into the wagon, tucked blankets around them, delivered a lecture about sitting still and not leaning over the edge, and claimed the last seat.

"Okay, Hank," Kate said, flicking the reins.

Hank and the wagon moved forward, out of the machine shed and into the parking lot.

Gabe joined Rhonda near the snack tables. Harness bells jingled again, and a red wagon pulled by Blackberry, with Tom Mitchell holding the reins and Roxanne supervising the small passengers, entered the shed.

The pipsqueaks in line screeched and Roxanne whistled them down. "Blackie needs water and a breather. You'll leave in fifteen minutes. So, pipe down."

"That's my take-charge baby," Rhonda said, grinning in Roxanne's direction.

Gabe offered Rhonda some popcorn. "I wonder where she gets that no-nonsense attitude."

"Beats me."

Gabe strolled over to the coffee urns. He kissed Mercy's cheek and nodded at O'Malley.

O'Malley grunted.

Gabe balled his popcorn bag, tossed it and the dregs of the apple cider into a garbage can, and said, "How's Jack doing?"

O'Malley frowned. Mercy said, "He's restricted to the

house unless he's with someone we trust or is doing chores at Kate's."

"Don't even think about asking him to help you on the case anymore," O'Malley said.

"Jesus, Seamus. I never asked him in the first place."

"For reasons that escape me, Jack idolizes you," O'Malley said. "Please discourage him from trying to *be* you."

Gabe kissed Mercy's cheek again. "Love you, Mom. Gotta go find some suspects."

He selected a Nanaimo bar from the pastry tray, dropped a loonie in the donation jar, and worked the crowd like a politician, but doing more listening than talking. The wagons made several trips in and out of the machine shed with their tiny passengers while Gabe made the rounds of people in the building.

Midway through his hobnobbing, when Hollywood Hank and Blackberry were enjoying a brief break in the action, Gabe noticed Jack and Roxanne standing by the far wall. Roxanne's fists were balled, and her head bobbed as she talked. Jack made a pleading gesture just before Roxanne spun on her heel and marched away. Jack punched the wall. Young love. No easier than old love.

After forty-five minutes canvassing the crowd, Gabe knew nothing of value. No one had seen or heard anything suspicious. Most believed the bomber was a madman, a tree hugger, or both.

———

THE WAGON RIDES HAD ENDED, and the parking lot was emptying fast when Gabe sought out Jack. "Walk me to my truck, Jacko. I need to talk with you."

On the way across the lot, Gabe filled Jack in on his meeting with The Viking. "Crusty old guy. Itty-bitty too, yet he said he was gonna whup me."

"Oh shit!"

"Relax, Jacko. The guy was blowing smoke."

"No, I mean your truck."

Even in the poor light from the distant lamppost, the graffiti shimmered. HAYSEED had been sprayed across the driver's side panel in fluorescent orange letters.

"Son of a bitch!" Gabe ran a limping, lurching gait to the truck. A sharp, jagged line carved the gleaming black paint from the front fender to the taillights. He walked around the truck. More keying and another orange HAYSEED on the passenger side.

Gabe groaned. "Ahhh, man. Who attacks a defenseless truck?"

He popped the hood. The engine was intact, no unwanted explosive accessories. He grabbed the old faithful flashlight, slid under the truck, and checked the underside. Clean.

When he crawled out and brushed himself off, Jack was rubbing at the keyed scar.

"It won't come off," Gabe said. "It's gonna need painting. Christ, not even a month old." Gabe paced back and forth, focusing on pushing the anger aside. He needed to be calm when he broached things with Jack.

When his breathing was no longer ragged, Gabe leaned against his driver's door, gazed at the sky full of stars and said, "Listen, Jacko. LeBlanc told me about the vodka bottles stashed by your ATV in Harris's pasture."

Jack started, his eyes wide, his face flaming. "What about them? They're not mine. Could be anyone's."

"But you admit bottles were there?"

"Uhh. No. But if they were, they aren't mine. I don't drink."

"Don't waste time lying. I don't expect you to be a goody-goody, but what's going on? Saturday at O'Malley's ranch, I suspected you were wasted. Now LeBlanc says you stash booze in the bush?"

"You don't know anything."

"I know this: That ATV I saw at the museum is yours. You and your crowd party in the tunnels. You were hungover last Saturday, and you were buzzed in Harris's pasture."

"What do you care?"

"I wouldn't be on your case if I didn't care. Jacko, get smart. You have a great life ahead of you if you cut out this stuff."

"I got a life. You stayed out of it for the last year. Why not keep doing that?" Jack turned away and shouted his parting shot. "I'm not supposed to be with people Mom doesn't trust. See ya."

Gabe watched Jack return to the machine shed. That hadn't gone as he'd hoped. In the perfect version, Jack would admit he'd messed up and promise to straighten out, thanking Gabe for caring enough to raise the topic. Gabe figured he should research how to talk to teens, or better yet, wait until Jack turned thirty and talk to him then.

He settled into the driver's seat, took a deep breath, and started the engine. Nothing exploded. Gabe was grateful. Small mercies.

Chapter 49

BACK IN CHEAKAMUS, Gabe considered hoisting a couple pints at The Peak. Then he thought about Jack and instead bought a Mudshark to go and returned to the apartment where he consulted his list: Gwinn, Aldercott, High Yield, and Big Score Ventures. He alternated between sipping coffee and twirling the purple rock on the desk while he hunted around online.

No matter how often he searched Aldercott's name, he found no mention of any involvement with High Yield or Big Score. However, practicing law had taught him where to find information about a company's management and operations. He accessed the online database of public companies and found both High Yield and Big Score. Aldercott's name was not among either company's management.

He bored himself scrolling through Big Score's list of public documents, accomplishing nothing except blurry eyes, before turning to its financial statements. Soon he had something: the notes in Big Score's last set of financial statements before it disappeared from public life described the company's sale of the once-promising mineral property to High Yield.

Big Score had purchased that property from Manfred Aldercott, in exchange for fifty percent of everything Big

Score earned from the property. Along came High Yield, which paid Big Score one million High Yield shares, worth about one hundred thousand dollars at the time. Aldercott would get half the shares, worth fifty thousand dollars. Peanuts.

Gabe accessed a database of trading information and was searching for High Yield when his phone rang. The display flashed "Andrews."

"Hi bella, I couldn't reach you."

"I was on a plane," Bethany said. "The station asked me to return to Calgary early." Her voice was lifeless. "I just met with the manager. They may let me go."

"What?"

Her voice became squeaky, the way it always did when she was trying not to cry. "They're worried ratings will fall if they put me back on the local broadcast." Her voice broke.

"That's bullshit."

She sniffed and said in a shaky voice, "They're going to do a poll or something. Unbelievable. No matter how long it's been, they say I'm still the wife of a suspected killer."

Gabe wanted to tell her to stuff the job, say screw them, and come back to him. But she loved her job.

She said, "I'm sorry to dump this on you."

"I love you. Never be sorry for talking to me, babe. When will they decide?"

"A week maybe. However long it takes to do the poll and have their ass-covering meetings. In case I'm thinking of suing."

He heard the hint of backbone returning to Bethany's voice. "Good for you, babe. Keep that thought. I'll send you names of some lawyers to phone."

She promised to stay in touch and ended the call. Gabe stared at his reflection in the balcony slider. More than a year and it still came down to Drake's death.

He sat in the recliner, wallowing in his bummed-out mood

for an hour, maybe more, before his phone rang again, the display showing "H. Chilton."

Harris spoke in a rush. "Another explosion. At the museum."

"On my way. Call the cops."

"Done. They'll be awhile, gotta come from Trail. Fire truck's on its way. Ubrowski said someone called it in. Kate and I are heading over. We're worried about the Percherons."

On his way out of Cheakamus, Gabe called Greta and filled her in. "It's probably safer for you to stay at home, Greta," he said. "I'll stop by after we assess things and talk to the cops."

Chapter 50

WHEN GABE COULDN'T SEE smoke or flames after he screeched through the turn onto the museum access road, he hoped it was a good sign. He skidded around the last curve and saw the fire truck in the parking lot, its crew packing away hoses.

He parked by the machine shed and took a moment to stick his head in the door. The Percherons stood in a clump in their stall, eyes fixed on the entrance and ears pricked forward. "Everything's cool, guys. Kate will be here soon."

This explosion's aftermath was benign compared to previous ones. The museum building was intact, but its door had been kicked in. "No MINING," with the telltale starburst dots, had been sprayed across the door and walls with red paint. The explosion had reduced the headframe to a pile of rubble.

Ches Ubrowski separated himself from the cluster of firemen and joined Gabe by the debris.

"No fire?" Gabe said.

"Nothing to speak of," Ubrowski said. "Some charring. We wet things down as a precaution."

"Who phoned it in?"

"Mr. Anonymous."

Kate's white Escape roared into the lot, followed by Bill Jacobson's Ram 1500. Bill parked and climbed from his truck, camera in hand. Gabe's anger at the morning's news article about Gabe-the-Lothario and Jack-the-Kid-Criminal resurfaced, fresh and strong. "Excuse me, Ches. I need to see Jacobson."

Despite his sore knee, Gabe reached Jacobson in five quick steps and, when Jacobson offered a gee-whiz smile and salute, Gabe punched him in the jaw. The man landed on his ass. Gabe's fist tingled, then throbbed. It felt great. He stood over Jacobson. "You print garbage about me and people I care about again, I'll do more than tap you on the chin, you jerk."

Jacobson scrambled to his feet and ran to Ubrowski and his crew. "Did you see that? He hit me for no reason. That's assault and you're all witnesses."

"Didn't see that," Ubrowski said. "Did you guys?" His crew shook their heads.

"You didn't see it?" Jacobson's voice squeaked. "He walked right up and hit me."

"No, I'm pretty sure you made a move to strike him first," Ubrowski said.

Jacobson sputtered. "I made a move?" His face was almost purple, spittle on his lips. "I *greeted* him, you ignoramus."

Gabe entered the museum where he found trashed display cases. Tools and mineral specimens littered the floor. In the gift shop, dishes were broken, chairs upended, and the postcard and souvenir map display overturned. He left the building and approached the fire crew, scanning the lot for Jacobson.

"Bill got tired of screaming at us ignoramuses and left," Ubrowski said.

"Thanks for the support."

"Our pleasure." Ubrowski grinned. "Made our day."

While they waited for the cops, Ubrowski and Gabe

helped Harris and Kate load the Percherons into the horse trailer.

"We can't risk leaving them here," Kate said. "We called Greta. She's closing the museum and canceling the wagon rides."

Gabe pulled Harris aside. "I found a link between Aldercott and High Yield. He had a connection with the company that sold High Yield the dud property. He received half the shares they paid for it."

"Worth much?"

"I need to do more digging. But if I could find the link, so could others. High Yield's investors, for instance. I think Aldercott's operation was the target."

"What?"

"Just like the movies. The real target is hidden in the midst of similar crimes, to make the cops think they're dealing with a nutjob or serial offender."

"Or we have a copycat."

Gabe thought about it. "Yeah, a copycat would explain why the TEG scene differed a bit from the others. This makes my head hurt."

Sergeant LeBlanc pulled into the lot just as Kate closed the door on the horse trailer.

He approached the group. "Anything to tell me?"

Ubrowski filled him in.

"Jacobson flagged me down," LeBlanc said. "Claims you assaulted him, Gabrieli."

"My crew and I saw it differently," Ubrowski said.

"He said you'd say that."

Everyone was quiet. A standoff. Gabe held his breath and tried not to think of courtrooms and trials.

"I invited him not to pursue things," LeBlanc said.

Gabe started breathing again.

LeBlanc told the group they could take off. No one argued. Gabe followed the fire truck and Kate's Escape and horse trailer down the hill. He flexed his throbbing hand and enjoyed a momentary rush of satisfaction. Then he thought of Bethany and her angst, and Jack and his troubles, and Cheakamus with a nutjob on the loose, and his smile died.

———

WHEN HE PARKED in front of the guesthouse, Greta stood in her living room, looking out the window. She met him at her front door. "Is the damage bad?"

"The headframe is wrecked. They tossed stuff around inside the museum, broke some dishes, sprayed graffiti on the siding. Nothing you can't fix."

Tears ran down her cheeks. Jesus, he thought, what now? He touched her arm. "Do you want some water?"

"Maybe tea?"

"Coming up." Gabe headed to the kitchen.

Greta sat at the table while he filled her kettle and set it on the stove. She blew her nose and sniffed. By the time the kettle boiled she was calm. She pointed at a canister. "Tea's there."

When Gabe put the teapot and a cup on the table, Greta said, "Sorry I'm a crybaby."

Gabe poured the tea and pushed the cup toward her. "Would it make you feel better if I told you I punched Jacobson?"

Greta's eyes brightened. "Really? Why didn't I hear that?"

"What? The grapevine isn't invincible?"

"Ahh, it doesn't miss much. For instance, it's buzzing about the fact you've been seen twice with Nicole. Is a romance starting?"

"No way. I'm trying to get back with my wife."

"Oh, I see. It would be lovely if Nicole could find someone worthwhile, like you." She was quiet for a moment. "I feel so sorry about Wally, her dad."

"Losing his money, you mean?"

"No, about his wife."

Gabe stared at her.

"That's right," she said. "You're new in town, you don't know. Wally got married again after Nicole's mom left him. His second wife is in long-term care in Vancouver. Wally visits her every two weeks, never misses. My friend goes for treatments in Vancouver on the same schedule. She and Wally take the bus together every time."

"Really? Interesting."

THURSDAY

Chapter 51

THURSDAY MORNING GABE awoke confident things would get worse. It was more than intuition. He had facts to back it up: a whispering idiot's threats, Bethany's career crisis, his vandalized truck. And topping the list: two explosions in the last two days.

He grabbed his phone and checked email. A thanks from Bethany for the lawyers' names he'd sent. Nothing from Gwinn. It was early; perhaps he'd catch Gwinn at home. He tried Gwinn's number; the machine told him the mailbox was full.

He flexed his right hand, relieved to see only minimal swelling between two knuckles, and thought of last night's conversation with LeBlanc. Just when you're sure cops will always be uptight pukes, you meet a guy like LeBlanc. He placed a call.

"Gabrieli, what have you got for me?" LeBlanc said.

"Three things. One, Wally Mitchell has an alibi for the TEG explosion. Two, damn near everyone in town invested in the same scam he did. And three, someone wants me gone, making threatening calls, vandalizing my truck."

"Any idea who'd want to harass you?"

"Sergeant Ambrose comes to mind."

"I doubt it's him. He's not in town."

No sense of humor, LeBlanc.

Gabe said, "They called me hayseed."

"Hmm. Maybe it *was* Ambrose. Stay in touch." LeBlanc clicked off.

Gabe headed to the shower. "Maybe it was Ambrose." He laughed out loud. LeBlanc was shaping up to be a guy you'd want to share a beer with. If there was nothing else to do. And you were the last two people on Earth.

Before heading for breakfast at Tiffany's, Gabe checked his list. High Yield's name twigged his memory. He accessed an online database of trading information, found High Yield's data, and jotted it down. As he flicked through his notebook searching for his earlier notes on High Yield, he heard someone outside calling his name.

Braving the cold, Gabe stepped onto the balcony and saw Greta framed in her kitchen doorway, arms akimbo, a look of amused exasperation on her face. The Viking stood in the yard and waved a bright blue book at him. "Got something for ya."

Gabe went downstairs, let Thorvaldsen in, and waved him toward the stairway. The old guy stared at the graffiti emblazoned on Gabe's truck and shook his head. He climbed the stairs like a teenager and stood on the landing looking back at Gabe, who was midway up. "C'mon, I don't have all day. You're climbing like an eighty-year-old. Ya need an exercise program."

"Bum knee."

When Gabe closed the apartment door behind them Thorvaldsen said, "I saw you drop the gear by. Thanks."

"Glad you can use it."

"When I hit it big, I'll pay you back. Meanwhile, I have this for you." He handed Gabe a vibrant and eye-catching royal blue journal, its cover tooled leather, its pages dog-eared.

Gabe flipped through the book. It was full of notes, phone numbers, symbols. He recognized the phone number written inside the front cover. He'd been calling it regularly. He also recognized the name inscribed on the facing page: E.W. Gwinn.

Thorvaldsen said, "That there's a gold mine of data about mineral deposits all over the world."

"Ed Gwinn gave this to you?"

Thorvaldsen shook his head. "Nope. I don't know Gwinn, but I know of him. None better at his job. That's why I was gonna hang on to it. You can take his opinions to the bank."

"How did you get this?"

"Well, dang, how d'ya think? That Ranger the Dark Knight left me. Found it under the seat, pushed way back."

"When was this?"

"Lemme think." Thorvaldsen squinted his eyes and scratched his head. He stared out the window, motioning with his fingers as if tracking some invisible action.

Gabe resisted the urge to tell him to think faster and instead focused on trying to remember when Gwinn had left for Nevada. Perhaps a week and a half ago?

"Now I got it," Thorvaldsen said. "Monday. The day before Greta took you to the mine. The truck arrived in the wee hours, and I found the book soon as it got light."

"Huh." Why would Gwinn tell everyone he was heading to Nevada a week and a half ago and then abandon his truck on Rimrock three days ago? Was he roaring around the hills on his ATV planting bombs? Gabe corrected himself. The Viking was roaring around the hills on Gwinn's ATV. Maybe Gwinn preferred to walk.

Thorvaldsen snatched the journal back. "I *was* gonna keep it." He flicked to a turned-down page and gave the book back to Gabe. "Then I saw this. You're looking into the explosions, so here you go."

Gabe saw "TEG" scratched amongst names, phone

numbers, and chemical symbols. "What did the Dark Knight look like again?" he said.

"It was pitch-black, and I was in the trees. I only caught a couple glimpses when he climbed in and out of the trucks. Sharp nose, short hair."

"Beard? Mustache?"

"Don't think so."

"Tall? Fat?"

"Average."

Gabe accessed Gwinn's website and pointed at his picture. "Is this him?"

Thorvaldsen shook his head. "Nah, too big. Nose isn't right." He peered at the picture of Gwinn leaning on his yellow ATV. "But that sure looks like the ATV."

"The ATV you didn't unload from the Ranger. The one you're not using."

"Yeah."

Gabe thanked Thorvaldsen as he showed him out. Standing on the landing, Gabe said, "Might need to turn this journal over to the cops."

Thorvaldsen dismissed the comment with a wave of his hand as he descended the stairs.

"How did you know Greta took me to the mine?" Gabe said.

Thorvaldsen hesitated, his hand on the doorknob. "It was Tuesday. There are always groceries for me in the machine shed on Tuesday. I saw ya."

He waved and went out the door.

Chapter 52

SHORTLY AFTER NINE o'clock Gabe drove to Tiffany's, thinking maybe he was wrong, maybe things would get better. Who'da thought The Viking would hand over key information? Someone Gabe had pegged as a prime suspect turned out to be a prime source. Gabe filed the lesson under "Minds, best when open."

Parking was the usual challenge near the café. Gabe didn't know how many people lived in Cheakamus but figured a quarter of them hung out in Tiffany's at any given moment. He waited for an SUV to vacate a spot next to the dude ranch's orange van, then parked and snatched up Gwinn's journal. He climbed from his truck and noticed big Nestor Clayton and Maggie leaving the café, carrying cardboard boxes and plastic crates. As she passed Gabe, Maggie's stack of cartons tumbled to the ground. He placed the journal on his truck's hood and helped retrieve the boxes, passing them to Nestor, who by then had stashed his load of crates in the back of the van. "Thanks," Nestor said.

"No sweat."

Gabe hesitated once he entered the café, tapping a rhythm on his thigh with Gwinn's journal and planning the easiest route through the customers grouped around the espresso machine. In the end he bulled through, using the journal to cleave a path, apologizing when he jostled Aldercott's arm and again when he stepped on Dreadlock Phil's foot.

When Gabe finally popped through the crowd, Carl Dochmann was lounging against the display case, grinning. "You gotta be one hundred percent committed, like a salmon heading home, or the crowd will never spit you out."

Gabe tucked the blue book under his arm. "Never let them see your fear. You having breakfast?"

"Nope, picking up a latte."

Noticing his favorite booth was empty Gabe said, "Gonna grab that booth."

"Go for it. Hey, tell Greta I located the Evergold tunnel on the resort's property. It's still sealed."

"Sure thing."

Gabe poured a mug of Mudshark and sat in the booth, facing the door. When David came by, he ordered the Dude Ranch Special. "And if your mom's not around, hot sauce."

He waved at Harris who had just entered the café. Harris poured himself a coffee to-go and joined Gabe in the booth. "You're looking optimistic," Harris said. "What's up?"

Gabe patted the cover of Gwinn's book. "The Viking brought me this. I'm hoping it contains all the answers." He lowered his voice. "Remember the High Yield shares that Aldercott received for the dud property?"

Harris nodded.

"At the height, just before it cratered, High Yield traded at five dollars. Aldercott had five hundred thousand shares, so he would have made over two million dollars if he sold at the right time."

Harris twirled his coffee mug. "Think he did?"

"Absolutely."

When Gabe told him about the orange graffiti on his truck

Harris grinned. "Hayseed? That's low. If you need a body shop, Findrich has one."

Shaking his head, Gabe said, "I can't be without my truck right now. Unless someone wants to lend me his Jeep?"

"Not a chance." Harris stood. "Gotta run. Keep me posted."

David set Gabe's order down, steam rising from the skillet. A bottle of hot sauce followed. Gabe punched LeBlanc's number into his phone and shook the sauce over his meal as he listened to the cop's invitation to leave a message.

When the device beeped, Gabe said, "Check out Ed Gwinn. A source tells me the Ranger you towed off the mountain belonged to Gwinn. Word is, it appeared on Rimrock three days ago. Yet ten days have passed since Gwinn supposedly left town."

He didn't feel one whit guilty about not mentioning Gwinn's journal. As soon as he'd read it and made notes, Gabe would relinquish it. An hour. Two, tops.

He flicked through the book as he ate his breakfast. Tiny writing, doodles, and chemical symbols filled the pages. He turned to the page the Viking had dog-eared, titled "Alpine Venture Capital." Beneath the heading was an address in Zurich and a phone number. Then a few fragments: "TEG," "Weiler," "Cheakamus," "exp—Au," "inv $500K + $2MM."

He was reading the notations at the bottom of the page when he sensed someone standing beside the booth. Closing the book, he looked up to see Nicole Mitchell smiling at him, a to-go cup in her hand.

"Hey Gabe."

He smiled at her. "Hey."

"Heard you and Kate are meeting Reverend Beam tomorrow."

"Yeah. Hope I pass inspection."

"You will, I put in a good word for you." She winked, waved, and left.

Gabe scooped the last forkful of the Special and pushed his plate away. He checked his watch and estimated it was around dinner time in Zurich. Maybe Alpine Capital would be closed, maybe not.

Gabe called. Voice mail clicked in: "This is Kurt Weiler. I am sorry I cannot take this call. Leave a message please. Thank you."

Very polite, the Swiss. But just once Gabe would like to get a live person on the other end. He left a message for Weiler, then opened his black notebook and updated his "check into" list. He added Weiler.

And Nicole. Possible liar.

His phone rang, the display flashing "Diamond Lucy."

"Hey, Luce. Tell me my shoes are coming today."

"Yep. Rufus and I have them right here."

"Huh?"

"We're here, at the Parkview Motel. It's grimy, so we're checking out. We thought we'd stay with you."

A cat yowled in the background.

"Hah. Good one Lucy, you had me going. I can hear Doofus, so I know you're calling from home. Tell me you sent my shoes."

"I'm not kidding. I packed your shoes and Rufus. I put them in my car and here we are. Homeless in downtown Cheakamus. Give me directions to your place."

Chapter 53

After Gabe recovered from the surprise that Lucy was in Cheakamus, he told her he was an hour away from town, maybe more. A small, necessary fib.

"Meet me at Rocque & Hound at eleven," he'd said. Then he hauled ass. Into his truck, up Lookout Road, around the corner, and into the garage. Even with the wonky knee and lame shoulder, he'd made the trip in three-point-four minutes, leaving fifty-six minutes and change to spiff things up.

He grabbed Gwinn's journal and then hesitated. It was too large to fit in his pocket and yet he wanted to keep it close by so he could finish reading the entries whenever he had a spare moment. He stashed the book in the console. It would be safe there. Unlike everyone else in Cheakamus, Gabe locked his vehicle.

Once he was in his suite, Gabe phoned Greta and arranged for a room for Lucy. When he mentioned Lucy had dragged Doofus along, Greta said, "He'll have to stay with you. Cats scare Hound."

After the call, Gabe went into overdrive. Dishes, glasses, cutlery into the dishwasher, controls studied, and "quick wash" pressed. All food, perishable or not, into the fridge.

Clothes stuffed in the duffel. Then removed and hung in the closet. Because if there was one thing he hated more than shoveling snow, it was ironing. Bathroom cleaned. Counters wiped. Dishwasher emptied. He finished with five minutes to spare.

When Lucy and Doofus arrived, Greta gave Lucy the second-floor front bedroom. "Your brother's created quite a stir in town. I'll tell you all about it once you're settled."

Lucy raised her eyebrows. "Really?"

"I update Lucy regularly," Gabe said to Greta. "Your version of things will confuse her."

"Did he tell you about decking Bill Jacobson last night?" Greta said to Lucy.

Lucy grinned, shook her head.

"Bill printed garbage in the paper. Gabe knocked him on his keister."

Gabe flexed his hand. "Felt great."

After they carted Gabe's shoes, and Doofus and his para-phernalia, into the apartment, Gabe set the cat bowls on the kitchen floor and introduced the cat to his litter box in the bathroom. Doofus did his business, yowled at Gabe, claimed the recliner and closed his eyes.

"I'm real glad to see you too, Doofus." He turned to Lucy. "Couldn't you kennel him?"

"I asked him—did he want a kennel, or did he want to see Cheakamus? He wanted to sightsee."

"He hates traveling. You brought him here; you can take him back to Eau Claire when you leave. And how about explaining why you're here?"

Lucy smiled. "After I eat. I'm hungry. You're buying."

Twenty minutes later Gabe was back at Tiffany's, intro-ducing Lucy to Rhonda and several of the regulars. They claimed his usual booth and Lucy studied the menu. "Ain't No Dude Ranch Special looks good."

"Yep. Just don't ask Rhonda for hot sauce."

Lucy ate while Gabe drank coffee and filled her in on events since they'd last talked. Then he said, "Gonna tell me why you're here?"

"I thought I'd buy Harris's bar. I'm meeting his realtor at The Peak at three."

"Ahh, you're the interested buyer she mentioned."

"Yeah. What do you think?"

Gabe leaned back and grinned. "It's brilliant. Classic Lucy Diamond. Does Harris know?"

"I called him before I came over to your place."

"He's got a balloon payment due on a bank loan. Plus, they owe O'Malley some dough. Best I can figure, he's selling the bar to cover debts."

She nodded.

"You know how much the bar means to him."

She nodded again and was about to speak when the café door banged open, and George Findrich entered. His appearance stunned Gabe. The man was pale, his eyes bloodshot. He shuffled to the coffee rack and shakily poured a mug. He stared at the counter stools as if confused about their purpose.

"George," Gabe called. "Over here."

Findrich turned, focused on Gabe and raised a hand in greeting. He trudged over, his coffee sloshing about. Gabe introduced Lucy, who slid over to make room on the seat. Findrich didn't move.

"You look tired, George," Gabe said.

"Horace Minken's dead."

"What? When? He looked fine yesterday."

Findrich raised his mug and took a tentative sip. "I found him this morning. At his exploration site in my field. Just lying there." Findrich's lips quivered. "Looked like he'd been shot."

"Jesus. Where was the driller?"

"Gone. The rig pulled out Tuesday. I'd heard Minken was going fishing, so I went to see if he was shutting things down. And I found him."

He ran a hand through his hair and drank more coffee. "The cops are still there."

Gabe called LeBlanc, hoping to find out more, and got his voice mail. As he was leaving a message, he saw Rhonda waving at him from the front of the café. She appeared agitated.

She hurried over when he put down his phone. Words rushed out. "You gotta go home. I just talked to Greta. There's somebody there. I told her to lock up."

"Slow down, what's going on?"

She sucked in a huge breath, exhaled, and started again. "There's someone at your place."

Gabe sat there dull-witted. So what? Let them try again or leave a note.

Rhonda waved her hand in front of Gabe's eyes. "Gabe, hello? Someone is in the apartment. Greta saw your cat outside on the balcony and couldn't understand why you'd lock him out in the cold when you were in the suite. I told her no, you were here."

Chapter 54

GABE SKIDDED to a stop on Lookout Road in front of the guesthouse. He and Lucy leaped from the truck; Lucy joined Greta in the house and Gabe hurried along the side of the house and through the back yard to the garage. The side door was locked and undamaged. He unlocked it as quietly as possible and entered. The garage was empty and cold, the window on the opposite wall gaping open.

Listening for sounds from the apartment, he crept toward the stairs. Heart pounding, palm slipping on the banister, he climbed the stairs, praying they wouldn't creak. When he reached the landing, he paused and took deep breaths.

The apartment door was ajar, the jamb gouged. Gabe moved aside and pushed the door open. When nothing happened, he took another deep breath and peered inside.

A pry bar lay near the door. Gabe crossed the room and opened the slider. Doofus yowled and marched past, his orange and white ringed tail flicking with irritation.

Gabe did a fast scan of the apartment. Aside from the door, nothing appeared damaged. However, his clothes had been tossed on the floor and the mattress upended. His laptop lay partially open on the floor next to the recliner.

When he heard Doofus scratching in the litter box in the bathroom, Gabe stuck his head inside the doorway and glanced around. The intruder had scrawled on the mirror with black marker: "Take a hike hayseed. Take your mangy cat with you."

Gabe grinned. "Doofus, how badly did you scratch the guy?"

This was becoming an expensive job: painkillers, the truck's paint job, and now, the apartment door. Fortunately, his deal with Cheakamus covered expenses.

He pulled the suite door closed and went to check on Greta. She and Lucy stood at the kitchen window. Greta opened her back door as soon as he exited the garage. "Good grief. Is he gone?"

"Yeah. He jimmied the apartment door and tossed stuff around. Are you okay?"

She sat at the kitchen table and patted her chest. "Got my cardio for the day. I thought it was you. I was talking to Rhonda, and I saw the cat outside on the balcony and you moving around inside."

"But it wasn't me."

"I know that now. I said to Rhonda, why has he put that poor cat outside in this cold, and why is he cleaning his apartment when I thought he was out with Lucy, and Rhonda said who, and I said you, and she said no you were in the café, and I said well then who was cleaning the apartment, and she told me to lock my doors, and that's about it." She took a breath and patted her chest again.

Gabe waited until she appeared calm. He squeezed her shoulder and said, "I have bad news. Horace Minken is dead."

"Oh no! What happened?"

"Not sure. Someone shot him. And there's more—about Ed Gwinn."

"He's not dead too?"

"We don't know. We found his truck, but he's missing."

Greta nodded. "Anders told me Ed's name was in that journal he gave you. I've been very worried. Where could he be?"

"Is Ed violent? If something riled him, would he hit back? Use explosives?"

"Of course not."

"Okay. Listen, I should move out."

"Whatever for?"

"Someone's looking for something they think I have. If they come back, they might hurt you."

Worry lines furrowed Greta's brow. Then she brightened. "Lucy's here now, so I'll be safe. And we'll pretend you've moved. It will be our secret."

Secrets. In this town.

Chapter 55

ODDS WERE the wannabe burglar was looking for Gwinn's journal. Gabe tried to come up with a list of who might have seen him with the journal. Of course, he'd been reading it in Tiffany's during the breakfast rush. So that meant the list wasn't too long—a mere couple hundred people.

He called Weiler's number again, was once more was punted to voice mail, and left another message.

How could he figure out what Gwinn's notations meant if he couldn't talk to Weiler? Suppose Weiler was on an extended vacation somewhere?

Gabe needed a mining guy. Like Horace Minken, but Horace was dead.

Perhaps, The Viking.

Gabe returned to his truck and headed for Timberline Road on Rimrock Mountain, certain he'd find The Viking and his camp near the spot the ancient Ranger had been abandoned.

When he turned onto Highway 41, however, Gabe realized it was early afternoon and The Viking was probably roaring around one of the nearby mountains on Gwinn's

ATV, looking for gold. It would be smarter to make a social call on the prospector after sunset.

There were other things Gabe could do in the meantime. Like check out Nicole Mitchell's story about collecting her father Wally at the airport. Greta had said Wally always took the bus. There was one sure way to find out whether Nicole was stringing him a line.

Gabe pulled onto the shoulder, phoned the casino in Singleton, and asked for Wally. Due for his shift in fifteen minutes, they told him. Call back.

"Do you have a number for him?"

"We do not share private information, sir."

He put the phone away and patted his dashboard. "Okay, Three, let's go see if all the tourists are still elsewhere or if they've decided to play a little blackjack."

Traffic on the highway was unusually heavy and slow, primarily because of a hay mower moving at half-speed and a lack of passing lanes. Around mid-afternoon Gabe finally took the exit for the casino.

He parked away from the cluster of vehicles in the casino lot. Less chance of a car door dinging the paint job. Then again, with "hayseed" sprayed across both sides of the truck, why worry about a few dings?

Inside, Gabe spotted Wally at a table halfway down the center aisle. Ches Ubrowski, the fire chief, strolled toward Gabe, wearing a burgundy blazer over gray slacks. Slightly formal attire for a casino, Gabe thought. He raised his hand in greeting and then spotted the nametag on his blazer: "Security —Ubrowski."

"Ches, I didn't know you worked here."

"Going on fifteen years. I manage security."

Wally was alone at his blackjack table. "Talk to you for a sec?" Gabe said.

"I was just going to take a break. Why don't you join me?"

Wally led the way to the staff room tucked at the back of

the casino and motioned toward a set of couches and armchairs surrounding a flat-screen TV. "I'm getting myself some water. Want anything?"

Gabe shook his head. "I'm good." He chose an armchair, sat and massaged his right knee. As soon as Wally joined him, Gabe said, "I understand your wife's in long-term care. That's rough."

Wally opened his bottle of water and sipped. "Yeah."

"That's where you were last Sunday? Coming back from Vancouver? Why not tell me?"

Wally shrugged. "It was personal."

"The nearest airport's what, in Nelson?"

Wally eyed Gabe. "I take the bus." He took another sip of water. "Nicole told you she met me at the airport, didn't she? I told her it was the stupidest idea I'd ever heard. Everyone on the bus would have vouched for me, but she was in a complete state because you suspected me."

"Yeah, she was pissed off. She doesn't mince words."

Wally chuckled. "You know it. I can prove I was on that bus Sunday."

"Not necessary." Gabe heaved himself upright and shook Wally's hand. "Thanks for your time."

Gabe strolled through the casino, stopped to watch two women celebrate a jackpot on a Double Diamond slot machine, and then headed to the exit. Ten feet from the doors, Ubrowski and another guard pushed past Gabe, slapped the doors open and ran into the parking lot. A vehicle alarm whooped.

When Gabe exited the casino, he saw the two men by his truck. "What the hell?" He broke into a run, slowing as pain shot through his knee. He dug his key fob from his pocket and silenced the alarm.

"You won't like this," Ubrowski said.

Scattered on the ground by the driver's door were Gabe's CDs, starbursts smashed across the cases. Zigzags had been slashed across the truck's leather seats. The center console was open, and Gwinn's journal gone.

Ubrowski and Gabe went to the security office inside the casino where a technician replayed the security tape of the parking lot. It showed an old, dirty, beige pickup stop near the F-150. The passenger jumped out, fast-walked over, and popped the driver's door just as the camera panned away. When the camera returned to Gabe's truck, the guy was moving fast, carrying the book, the sun glinting off its blue cover. The man wore a knit cap, bulky jacket, and jeans. He kept his head down and turned away in the few seconds it took him to reach the pickup, and then they were gone.

"Plates are muddy," Ubrowski said. "Of course."

On his way out of the casino the second time, Gabe stopped by Wally's table. "I hear someone broke into your truck," Wally said.

"Slashed my seats, trashed my CDs. Seen a dirty pickup around here lately?"

"Why not ask me if it snows in winter?"

Gabe handed Wally his card. "This one's old, beige, muddy plates, got a couple punks in it. I'd appreciate it if you keep an eye out."

————

THE SUN HAD DIPPED behind the mountains by the time Gabe drove up Timberline Road on Rimrock Mountain. At the top of the logging road above the TEG exploration site, he parked near the spot the Ranger had been abandoned. Gigantic trees hugged the road, casting shadow over the area. The only sound was the swish their boughs made in the slight breeze.

He stood on the trail and peered through the underbrush, searching for the tent. It didn't take long before he spotted a rounded shape about twenty feet into the bush. Focusing on the grasses edging the road, he picked out a narrow path. No wider than a deer trail.

"Anders?"

No response. Gabe pushed along the skinny trail, stumbling, fighting low branches and wrenching his knee. Why couldn't Thorvaldsen have set up the tent at the turnaround? Gabe knew why: because The Frikkin Comedian was at work.

He was sweating when he broke from the path into a small clearing. Tent, camp stove, cooler, firepit. Definitely a camp. He found a bag of Maynards Wine Gums in the cooler. Definitely the Viking's camp.

Gabe shouted Ander's name several times. Silence greeted him. He dropped his head. He should have known Thorvaldsen wasn't in residence when he didn't see an ATV at the turnaround. Refusing to admit defeat, Gabe tore a page from his notebook and wrote a note: "Need help. Be back tomorrow with breakfast. Or call me." He added his number, although if The Viking even had a phone the odds of cell coverage this high on the mountain were zero to zip.

He took a deep breath and launched himself back along the trail, stumbling less, but working up the same degree of sweat. And missing Alberta's open fields and prairie grasses.

Chapter 56

GABE WISHED he had a down quilt in his truck when he parked out front of Tiffany's Café. He would have pulled it over his head and stayed there for the duration. His F150, pristine two and a half weeks ago, now had a broken door lock, slashes in its seats and fluorescent orange graffiti along its sides. He'd added another bruise and cut to his face. His knee constantly reminded him he wasn't twenty anymore. Or even thirty. His kid brother was steamed at him. He couldn't get a handle on the who and why of the explosions at the exploration sites. To top it off, he'd been stupid enough to assume that locking the journal in his truck would protect it from theft. Good thing he wasn't charging the town his usual rate. Was he worth even the reduced rate?

"Should we cue the violins?" Gabe's screw-it self said. Choirboy jumped in with, "Self-pity is not a good look." Gabe sighed. It was rare that the two of them ganged up, but when they did, he tended to pay attention. He climbed from the truck, pushed the door closed, and said, "I'll get you fixed Three, as soon as I find the creeps who did this to you."

As he walked past the counter on his way to his favourite

booth at the back, Rhonda stopped him. "Did you catch the burglar?"

"Not yet. But I will."

"Staying for dinner?"

"Yeah. I'm too tired to decide. You choose, Rhonda, so long as it's comfort food."

Once he was settled in the booth, Gabe checked his messages. One from Lucy: "We are at the Peak. Call. No rush."

Gabe returned her call and when Lucy answered, said, "Hey, Luce. 'We,' as in you and Greta, are at the Peak?"

"Yep. I wanted to check out the bar and refused to leave Greta alone in the house. She's having a fine time playing darts with an off-duty paramedic. What's new?"

"Someone broke into my truck and stole a journal. I'm sure that's what they were after this morning. I don't think they'll be back."

"Good, I'll let Greta know. Gotta run, this place is hopping and I'm having a hard time keeping up with orders. See you tomorrow?"

Rhonda delivered his dinner about the same time as Luce signed off. "Baked ziti," Rhonda said. "As comforting as anyone could want."

When Gabe breathed in the aromas of tomatoes, sausage and cheese, he was transported to his Italian neighbor's kitchen. A place he loved to hang out. He tasted. And groaned. "This is better than a down quilt, Rhonda."

"Hah. Can I use that on my next menu?"

———

GABE HAD SWALLOWED the last bite of ziti when his phone rang. When he answered, a man said, "Kurt Weiler calling. Returning your call."

Gabe registered the man's accent. Switzerland. Gwinn.

"Mr. Weiler, thanks for calling back. A complicated story, but do you know Ed Gwinn?"

"Yes. Ed's doing a project for my company. Is something wrong?"

Gabe filled him in—the abandoned truck, the journal containing Weiler's number.

"What can I do to help?" Weiler asked.

"I'm investigating explosions around the area. One of them was at TEG's site. Can you tell me about your project?"

"Certainly. My company invests in new ventures. Like TEG Mines. We hired Ed to check them out."

"When was this?"

"About a month ago. After the assay results from the second drill program."

Gabe remembered the notations of $500K and $2MM in Gwinn's notebook. "Your five hundred thousand investment?"

Weiler chuckled. "No. That was start-up capital for acquisition costs, prospecting, a drill hole or two. The second drill program was one and a half million."

"Not two million?"

"Originally it was one and a half. Then Manfred, Mr. Aldercott, checked with the doctor who said they needed two million."

"Who's the doctor?"

"I do not know. Manfred's partner."

"Did you question the cost increase?"

"It's an expensive thing, looking for gold. Manfred needed to bring in rigs, drill several holes, crush and assay samples. The costs are normal, nothing unusual. And results were positive, high grades."

"So why hire Gwinn?"

"Because the next stage is fifteen million. We told Manfred if we liked the results of the second program, we'd put in fifteen. A bigger risk, we had to do some double checking."

"Until now you never checked anything?"

Weiler must have heard the surprise in Gabe's voice because he chuckled again. "If we double-checked every investment, we'd get nothing done. Mining's speculative. Manfred sent us the assay results, from a good lab in Vancouver."

"When did you last talk to Gwinn?"

"Maybe two weeks? A Thursday? He called about the check assays."

"What are those?"

"Manfred gave Ed some pulps to send to a lab for independent assays. As a check."

Gabe jotted notes, hampered by his swollen hand. For the first time, he regretted punching Jacobson. "Pulps?"

"Pulverized core, like sand, or finer."

"And the check assays were okay?"

"Yes, Ed said the results were consistent with the other assays."

"So then everything was copacetic?"

"Perhaps. We were waiting to hear more from Ed before we sent Manfred the fifteen million dollars. Ed wanted to do more work. He didn't like that there's no core at the site."

"Aldercott says he stores it off site."

"This is news to me. Ed never said that."

"What work did Gwinn want to do?"

"He didn't go into details. I expected a call early this week. But he was also working on another project, so he could be busy."

"A last question. Did Gwinn ever mention wanting to stop people damaging the environment or to teach crooks a lesson?"

"Never. I hope you find Ed safe. Please let me know."

Chapter 57

GABE PARKED his wrecked truck in Greta's garage and carried his stack of wrecked CDs into his wrecked apartment. After he shucked off his jacket, he sorted through the CDs, looking for his favorite ones. The Tyson CD appeared salvageable, as did his Dylan CDs. Springsteen's *High Hopes* was missing. Had he overlooked it in the casino lot?

When Doofus yowled at him, he put out some food and then headed to Greta's house. As he trekked the back walk, he hummed a few bars from *Not Dark Yet*, his favorite Dylan song. The deadbolt on Greta's back door slid back as his foot hit the steps.

"Glad you're locking the door," he said. "Can I look at your phone bill? I want to see who Gwinn called."

Greta withdrew a stack of bills from a kitchen drawer, shuffled through them, extracted one and handed it over. "You can keep it. I've paid it."

"Which ones are his calls?"

"All of them."

As he turned to go, she said, "Have you eaten dinner yet? You don't look so great."

"I had some pasta at Tiffany's. I'm fine, just a little beaten up from hiking around Rimrock. Make sure you lock up."

In the apartment, he poured a shot of Glenfiddich. He studied it, then dumped it down the sink, and opened a bottle of water.

He sat at the desk and twirled the purple rock on the desktop. Doofus jumped into his lap, flopped down, and went to sleep. Gabe could use a nap too, but that would not find the bomber.

Without Gwinn's journal, he was at a disadvantage where the explosions were concerned. He jotted down what he could recall: something about assays and rejects. He remembered some businesses but couldn't pull the names from his memory. One was an assay company, the second a complete blank.

He studied Greta's phone bill, hoping Gwinn had called the companies. Four calls. Two to Kurt Weiler's number in Zurich, the others to Vancouver numbers.

He checked the time as he called the first Vancouver number: seven-thirty. A message said Millennium Assays was closed for the day. Gabe jotted down the name, now recalling it from Gwinn's notes. Gwinn had phoned it and Weiler on the same day. Gabe would lay odds this was the company Gwinn used for the check assays.

The second number, for a call Gwinn made on the Friday before he left Cheakamus, netted another message, this one for Pemberton Petrographics, also closed. That name rang a bell as well, for all the good it did, but he wrote it down.

Weiler had said he didn't know what Gwinn planned to do, just that it involved more work. Gabe speculated Gwinn hired Pemberton Petrographics for whatever task he had in mind. The earliest Gabe could talk to them would be tomorrow morning.

"Good grief, look at this door!" Greta stood in the doorway holding a covered dish. "You can't stay here. Move into the house."

"Hound is afraid of Doofus. I'll find a locksmith to fix the door."

"I brought you dessert. I hope you like chocolate cake." Greta put the dessert on the counter by the sink and then approached the desk where Gabe sat. She gasped. "He must have forgotten that."

"What?"

"Ed's lucky rock." She lifted the purple paperweight and admired it. "It's from Russia. He always had it."

A picture of TEG's site took shape in Gabe's head. He saw himself standing in the center of the debris. Bending down, plucking the purple rock from the space where the body had been. Now Greta held it.

He didn't have the heart to tell her what he suspected.

FRIDAY

Chapter 58

SEVEN O'CLOCK FRIDAY MORNING, Gabe woke to the ring of his phone. "Gabrieli," he said, struggling from the recliner where he'd fallen asleep a few hours ago.

"Hi, sonny. I'll have Rhonda's Dude Ranch Special, two sides of toast, white. Peanut butter. Orange juice. Coffee, black, extra-large, Prince of Darkness, if she has it. And a wild mushroom and cheese omelet. You writing this down?"

Gabe hunted for his notebook. "Every word. Is this all for you or do you have visitors out there, Anders?"

"What time ya coming?"

"Soon as Rhonda opens. So maybe by eight-thirty? I'm surprised you have a phone."

"I'm a prospector, not a Luddite. I wasn't gonna call 'cause I gotta go down to the highway to get cell service, but I knew if I let you pick out my breakfast, you'd bring yogurt and granola. See ya soon. Don't let my food get cold."

Showered but not bothering to shave, Gabe re-wrapped his knee with the tensor bandage and pulled on jeans and a sweatshirt. Thirty-three minutes, start to finish, including The Viking's call. Nowhere near his best time. He blamed it on the recliner.

———

WHILE HE WAITED for his take-out order at Tiffany's, Gabe sat at the counter and phoned LeBlanc. "I have something for you," he said, when LeBlanc answered the call. "About the body at TEG. I'm positive it's Ed Gwinn."

"Why?" LeBlanc asked.

"He was checking out TEG. He was probably at the site when it blew."

"You know, or you're guessing?"

Gabe didn't want to admit he took a rock, which now seemed to be evidence. "Call it intuition. But something's off kilter."

"Yeah?"

"If I'm right, the guy died from a blow to the head. He was found in the midst of debris from the shack."

"Okay."

"But the shack didn't explode. It burned."

"Correct."

"So," Gabe said, "he had to be dead, or incapacitated, before the fire. And that makes me think someone wanted to cover up the death."

"Adds a whole new flavor to the soup, doesn't it?" LeBlanc said.

"I'll tell you something else about Ed Gwinn that might help," Gabe said. "My landlady told me Gwinn was airlifted off some mountain after a serious fall. Badly broken leg apparently. His medical records may help."

"I'll check it out." LeBlanc said, and disconnected.

Gabe was still staring at his phone, thinking LeBlanc could use a course in communications, when Harris entered Tiffany's. He sat on the stool next to Gabe and plunked the *Journal* on the counter. "Morning. Seen the latest?"

"What now?" Gabe grabbed the newspaper. Jack's picture was on the front.

"The Journal apologizes to Jack Diamond for earlier comments questioning whether he was involved in the recent sabotage. We interviewed Mr. Diamond in hospital as he recovered from serious injuries that were the result of heroic efforts to prevent the explosion that almost killed him.

"The brother of private investigator D. S. Gabrieli, Mr. Diamond has a fuzzy recollection of a person he thinks is the saboteur. However, doctors say he should regain complete recall of the incident once his injuries heal."

"Dammit," Gabe said. "Jack didn't mention Jacobson interviewed him." He phoned Jack, connected to voice mail, and left a message. "Be careful, Jacko. The paper ran a story about you that could make the bombers nervous."

When Gabe lowered his phone, Harris said, "Seamus has Jack under house arrest. And today's not his day to work for Kate. He should be okay."

Gabe nodded, thankful for once that O'Malley was iron-fisted.

Rhonda placed a thermal tote bag, a tray of drinks, and a large paper bag on the counter. Harris watched Gabe pay for the food and then said, "Are you hosting a banquet I don't know about?"

"Hah. The price of a mining lesson from Thorvaldsen," Gabe said. "I'm hoping he can help me figure out a few things."

———

As HE DROVE toward The Viking's camp, Gabe thought about Ed Gwinn, who'd once been on his list of suspects. Now undoubtedly dead. Gwinn had told Greta he had one stop to make on his way out of town. If that stop was TEG's site and Gwinn interrupted the saboteur, it could have sealed his fate. Gabe speculated the bomber killed Gwinn and then set the fire, believing it would reduce the body to ashes and remove any sign of a murder.

Chapter 59

JACK HAD GONE to bed angry Thursday night and was still angry when his phone woke him up around eight o'clock. He'd looked at the screen, saw it was Gabe calling, and let it go to message. Jack wasn't talking to his big brother. Gabe was all part of the plot to make Jack play by everyone else's rules. Gabe had rules. O'Malley had rules. And ever since Jack got hit by fly rock and then arrested, the rules had increased. Well he wasn't gonna sit around at the ranch and play nice.

And first on his agenda, he needed something to mellow him out.

Craig answered the phone with, "Crissakes, it's too early. Don't you ever sleep?"

"Don't give me grief, Craig. My head hurts from all the stitches I have. Take my advice, don't try to stop an explosion."

"That's right, I heard you were out there when that rig blew up."

"Yeah, and to make things worse the cops arrested me! When I kept telling them I saw the guy."

"Whoa! You saw him?"

"Yeah, I was sitting right there in the brush, man,

watching the freaky dude. Listen, I need a baggie. Some papers too."

Craig yawned into the phone. "Okay, gimme till eleven. Same place?"

"Rockin," Jack said and disconnected the call.

Jack tossed his phone on the bed, slipped a flask of vodka into his backpack and left the house. He'd taken no more than three steps toward the garage when Seamus O'Malley bellowed. "Hold it, young man."

Gritting his teeth and jamming his fists into his jacket pockets, Jack faced O'Malley who stood on the veranda, a half-eaten piece of toast in his hand. "Where are you going?" O'Malley said.

"Kate's. My day to work."

"What are the rules we agreed on?"

"Like I had a choice." Jack jutted his jaw forward. "I know the stupid rules."

"Then let's hear them."

Jack's stomach clenched. He wanted to tell O'Malley to stuff it, but if he pushed, O'Malley would yank the leash. Jack would be stuck on the ranch. His shoulders slumped. "Straight to Kate's. Do my chores. No graffiti. No drinking. No riding alone. Straight home."

"Excellent." O'Malley checked his watch. "Home for lunch?"

Jack shook his head. "A dozen horses to groom, so a long day. But I'll be home for dinner. Mom's cooking pot roast."

O'Malley took a bite of toast and chewed. Then he nodded. "I love her pot roast too."

Jack turned toward the garage.

"Jack."

"What?"

"I know the rules irk you. But I signed your release papers. That means I'm responsible for you, son."

Jack nodded and hurried to the garage.

O'Malley was still on the veranda when Jack sped by on the ATV and raised his hand in a desultory wave. "I'm not your son, Warden O'Malley," Jack muttered under his breath.

Could things get any worse? Cops arresting him, saying they found dynamite and spray paint in his tack box. They were lying, or they planted it. How else would it get there? Then O'Malley heaped more idiotic rules on him. Did Mom defend her son? No way. She sided with O'Malley. That's dismal. His own mother turning against him.

And Roxanne dumping him for no reason, complaining she couldn't believe anything he said. And that he partied. So what? Who didn't?

And Gabe, who should be on his side. Where did Gabe get off lecturing about booze? Jack remembered how often Gabe got plastered after Bethany left. Yet he gets all righteous, talking about how you could hurt someone else. Oh yeah, right out of those scared-straight movies. So Jack had a drink now and then. Big deal. He was totally in control. It wasn't like he needed to. He could stop any time. Just didn't feel like it right now.

Once he turned onto Stockman's Road, Jack relaxed. He'd go to Kate and Harris's ranch and get Tornado Callie. He had two hours to kill before he met Craig and he had some vodka, so he and Callie could find a nice bit of pasture. She could graze and he could sip.

Then he and Callie would go up the logging trail, meet Craig, get the weed. And what started out to be a rotten morning would end being superb.

Chapter 60

THE PALOMINO SNORTED when Rocky wrenched on the cinch strap. "Yah, yah. If you didn't push your belly out, I wouldn't have to work so hard."

After he tugged on the stirrups to make sure the saddle on the palomino was snug, Rocky hoisted the second, heavier saddle and half carried, half dragged it over to Lightning, Doc's horse.

Complications. Last thing he needed right now. They were so close. This was the day. Almost all the investors' money would be in Doc's and his bank accounts. They'd do the Skype call with the Cayman bank around noon, take care of all the verification and security shit Doc insisted on, and Rocky would be rich. And out of here.

First though, a complication needed fixing.

"Ooooph." He struggled to lift Lightning's saddle onto the big roan. Of course, Doc wouldn't ride just any horse. Had to have the biggest in the stable. Frankly, Rocky was tired of doing all the heavy lifting in their partnership. Hide the body, steal the Forcite, rig the explosives, burn the shack, get rid of the dead guy's truck.

Rocky should have known things were going to go sideways yesterday morning when he saw Gabrieli with Gwinn's book. How the hell had Gabrieli got his hands on it?

Rocky had taken care of that problem by hiring his favorite criminal entrepreneurs to locate and snatch the journal. It was amazing how a hundred bucks motivated young people these days. Rocky had Gwinn's book several hours later.

Unfortunately, Rocky made the mistake of thinking things would be smooth as a shot of Kahlua from then on.

Noooo.

When he'd read the *Journal* first thing this morning, he damn near stroked out. Front-page news, no less. The Diamond kid had seen him. Rocky hadn't been in that pasture more than two minutes to light the fuse and the punk picked then to be hanging around? Now they had to put the kid on ice until they could deal with the bank.

Plus, there was a second unbelievable news story. A small paragraph hidden at the bottom of the front page: "Mystery vehicle towed from Rimrock. Police refuse to comment whether the Ford Ranger is linked to recent sabotage."

The cops had the truck! He'd paid that Westburg jerk good money to move it.

Doc, true to form, blew a gasket even though it was Craig who'd messed up, not Rocky.

Rocky had phoned Craig not half an hour ago.

"I paid you to move that truck, kid," he had said when Westburg answered. "Now I read in the paper that the cops have it!"

"Yeah," Craig said, "our plans to relocate it got messed up when the cops paid us a visit. We had to be good little boys. It's a shame they got to the truck before we could take care of it, but what're you gonna do?"

"I want my money back. I paid you to do a job. Which you didn't do."

"I'm not returning the money," Craig said. "In fact, I have

information to trade for it. Someone spotted you when you were in Chilton's pasture blowing up that drill rig."

"I already know that. It was in the morning paper. And I know where the Diamond kid lives."

"Yeah, on a ranch with about a thousand cowboys. You'll never touch him there. Frankie and I had a ton of trouble sneaking in there to plant that stuff in Jack's tack box. If fact, that job alone was worth what you gave us for the truck."

"I'll find a way," Rocky said.

"Maybe. But how about if I told you I know where he's going to be, all by himself, this morning at eleven? How much is that worth to you?"

"It's worth what I paid you to move the truck."

"Double that and we can do business."

They had cut a deal and Rocky had come up with a plan. You'd think Doc could say "good job." Oh sure, that's why Rocky was saddling both their horses. Punishment for the screw-up with the Ranger.

He checked Lightning's cinch one last time, then hotfooted it to the house. He pulled the beige balaclava from his pocket and snorted in disgust. Another reason to get this day over. The stupid balaclava was wool, itched like a rash.

Chapter 61

FIVE MINUTES BEHIND SCHEDULE, Gabe reached the Rimrock logging road. He'd stopped on the highway and placed calls to Millenium Assays and Pemberton Petrographics, asking whether Gwinn had hired them. In both cases the response was, "We don't release private information."

When Gabe stopped at the turnaround, the Viking popped onto the road about six yards away from the F-150. Relieved he wouldn't need to haul the food through the bush himself, Gabe unloaded. One thermal tote bag. One tray of juice and coffees. One paper bag containing cutlery, napkins, peanut butter. Marmalade for Gabe.

The Viking took the tray. "Mornin'. C'mon, I'm starved."

He led Gabe to a track that curved into the trees. Wide enough for an ATV. Firm ground. A two-minute stroll and they reached The Viking's camp. "Huh. Didn't see this trail last night."

"How did you get here then?" Thorvaldsen said.

"Through there." Gabe pointed at a skinny path.

"Dang, sonny, that's for deer." Thorvaldsen grinned. "Musta been a hell of a trek."

They sat on logs and balanced the food containers on their knees. Thorvaldsen gestured at his campsite. "Thanks again."

Gabe surveyed the space. "Roughing it is okay, but wouldn't you be more comfortable bunking in a core shack?"

Thorvaldsen's mouth dropped. "What? I'd never do that. Guys would think I was trying to rip them off." He opened a takeout container. Inspected the contents. Went to his cooler, rooted around. Produced a bottle of hot sauce. Shook it over his meal. Lifted a forkful of the Special. "What do you need my help with?"

"Ed Gwinn's missing, might be dead. I've been talking to Kurt Weiler, an investor in TEG Mines. He hired Gwinn to check them out."

"Yeah?"

"Gwinn phoned a place called Pemberton Petrographics in Vancouver. Know it?"

"Sure. They test core samples."

Gabe consulted his notebook. "He also called Millennium Assays. Another testing place?" Thorvaldsen nodded, chewing.

"Why would he call two?" Gabe said.

"Why not ask them?"

"I did. They told me to pound sand."

Thorvaldsen smiled. "Hah. Well, lemme see. Maybe a second opinion, or another job."

Gabe nodded. That's what he thought. One or the other. "Weiler said Gwinn ran check assays that were consistent with earlier results. Gwinn wanted to do more work. If you were Gwinn, what would you do?"

"Do you know how he ran the check assays?"

"Aldercott gave Gwinn some pulps. I guess he sent them to Vancouver?"

"Makes sense. Gwinn got the pulps from Aldercott?"

"Yeah."

Thorvaldsen took a bite of toast. "Next step, if you wanna be extra cautious, is do your own sampling."

"I don't follow. Won't it be the same?"

"Well, you hope so. But you wanna make sure no one's messing with the pulps or fudging results. If Aldercott gave Gwinn the first pulps, Gwinn wouldn't know the source."

"Okay. We do our own sampling."

Thorvaldsen nodded and started on his omelet.

"How?" Gabe said.

"Select some pieces of core. Send 'em to an independent lab for crushing and testing."

"Suppose there's no core?"

Thorvaldsen's eyebrows lifted and his eyes widened. He put down his fork. "No core?"

"None at TEG's site. Aldercott said he stores it off site."

Thorvaldsen frowned. "Yeah, could be. Some guys do that."

"Thing is," Gabe went on, "Weiler said Gwinn worried about the lack of core samples. So even if Aldercott stored them off site, it sounds like they're missing. Could someone have stolen them?"

"Yeah, but for what? No drill core—that's a red flag."

"Why?"

"The core is proof of what came out of the ground, and where."

"Uh-huh?"

"Core comes outta the drill. The miner records details about each piece of core when he stores it. Follow?"

Gabe nodded.

"Now he knows which core sample came from which drill hole, so he can map the mineral deposit. Next, he splits each piece of core lengthwise. Half he sends to a lab for crushing and assays, half he keeps on site. Then people like Weiler can double-check if they want."

He paused and took a sip of coffee. "No core means you don't know the source of the samples being tested."

The lights were coming on. "You're saying your samples, or pulps, could come from another mine?" Gabe said. "You could convince people things are better than they are?"

Thorvaldsen pointed his fork at Gabe. "Right. Or the pulps could be from your site but salted. That's done by sprinkling gold, usually placer gold, into crushed core to skew the assays."

"I thought the core went to the lab for crushing. They salt it at the lab?"

Thorvaldsen shook his head. "That could happen, but it isn't likely." He ate more of his omelet and took a swig of coffee. "Some guys crush core at the drill site and ship the crushed sample to the lab. Not the best practice. But acceptable, if it's all logged." He paused, then added, "And if they keep more core as back-up proof."

Gabe said, "If there's no core, how would Gwinn do his own sampling?"

"Coarse rejects." Thorvaldsen spread peanut butter on his toast.

Gabe remembered seeing those words in Gwinn's blue journal. Right under check assays. "Which are what?"

"This is fun, sonny. Like being back in the classroom. Coarse rejects are bags of crushed drill core kept at the site. If the guy does his own crushing, he'll keep half the core *and* half the crushed sample or coarse rejects at the site. As a record."

"And Gwinn could send some of those coarse rejects to a lab?"

"Yep, and he'd make sure *he* selected the bags. He wouldn't let Aldercott do it for him."

"What stops someone tampering with the coarse rejects?" Gabe said.

"Nothin'. And if the core's missing, I'd be asking that too."

Thorvaldsen smacked his thigh. "And *that's* why he'd call Pemberton Petrographics." Thorvaldsen's face brightened. He grinned. "Sure. Gwinn wanted to see how the gold occurred. I shoulda figured it out sooner."

"What? What's that mean, gold occurred?"

Thorvaldsen leaned forward on his log, intense. "We've been using the same testing methods since forever. Tried and true. Here's your gold lesson, sonny: Gold you find underground is embedded in the rock. Placer gold, you find near or on the surface."

"You mean like they panned?" Gabe pictured a burro and an old prospector, looking just like The Viking. And thought, so what?

Thorvaldsen bobbed his head. "Exactly. The two golds look different. Underground gold shows up as flecks in the ore. Placer gold's rounded 'cause it's been bounced around in rivers. That's where your petrographic scope comes in. Shows whether the gold occurs as placer or underground."

His fork jabbed the air. "I'll tell you this, sonny. If you find placer gold in an underground sample, ya got your basic scam going on."

Thorvaldsen sat back and grinned. End of lesson.

"Huh," Gabe said. Thinking, "So *that's* the so what." He drained his coffee and sat there, putting it together. "If you were Aldercott, and playing this game, would you suspect Gwinn was on to you?"

"Sure. If Gwinn asked for coarse rejects after he ran the check assays, Aldercott would know Gwinn had doubts."

"Would Aldercott know about that microscope test?"

"Without a doubt."

Gabe asked Anders one last question. The answer was no surprise at all.

Chapter 62

AFTER HE LEFT the Viking's campsite, Gabe drove along Timberline Road and after a few miles, turned onto a feeder and passed under the carved archway for Solomon's Choice Ranch. The smooth driveway to the resort curved through tall firs, their branches drooping under fresh snow.

Gabe parked next to Carl Dochmann's white Dodge Ram 3500 near a four-bay garage. He followed the sound of an ax around the corner of the garage, where he found Carl reducing a pile of eight-inch logs to manageable pieces of firewood. "Manfred Aldercott around?"

"Hey Gabe." Carl set a log on end atop the chopping block, steadied it with the blade of his ax. "He checked out late yesterday."

"Know where he went?"

Carl raised the ax above his head and brought it down on the log with a thwack. "Didn't say. He left in a bit of a rush."

"D'you have a number for him?"

Carl dug his phone out of the back pocket of his jeans, fiddled with it, scrolling. "Here you go." He read off a phone number.

Gabe punched it in to his phone. The call clicked to voice

mail. "It's Gabrieli. Please phone me about Ed Gwinn." He left his number, then said to Carl, "Voice mail's all I get here."

"It's the mountains," Carl said. "What's going on?"

"How well do you know Aldercott?"

"So-so."

"It looks like he was faking assay results, conning an investor."

Carl's mouth dropped open. "You're kidding. He strikes me as a straight-up guy." He put the ax down. His gaze slid to the tree line, then returned to Gabe. "But thinking about it, he was real jumpy this last week."

"I think the bombing victim is Ed Gwinn, the geologist kicking TEG's tires. What would Aldercott do if his scam was about to be exposed?"

Carl selected a piece of firewood and threw it overhand in a wobbly spiral toward the pile by the garage wall, then placed another log on the chopping block. "You mean, do I think he killed the guy? I don't know. Anything's possible if you're desperate enough, I suppose. Like I said, he's been antsy, muttering about fixing things."

Carl pitched another wobbly piece to the pile. "You never really know people, do you?"

Chapter 63

GABE HUSTLED BACK to his suite after talking with Dochmann. After a shower and a careful shave, he checked himself in the mirror. His shiner was a mere shadow, the suture scar looked like a frown line, and the cut on his cheek was indistinguishable amid faint yellowish-green splotches. He wasn't pretty but he was clean, sober, and smelled like mint toothpaste. What guy with a Roman collar wouldn't give him an *A* for trying?

He debated about putting on his suit for the meeting with the minister. No, that would just make it look like he was trying too hard. Pulling on jeans and his gray sweater, Gabe was as ready as he could be for the appointment at the church.

The timing couldn't be worse. Minken's death and the theft of Gwinn's journal heightened his sense of urgency. He needed to be working on the case. Instead, he was about to endure an inquisition by a minister.

After an early lunch at Tiffany's, Gabe arrived at the church before one o'clock, ahead of Kate. Parking on the street, he passed the time making a mental checklist of all the things not to say to the minister: don't admit your favorite Scotch is Glenfiddich; don't mention hellraising with Harris as teenagers; don't say religion never helped and you haven't been to church since Bethany left. All that would piss off Kate and make the minister try to save a soul. Two things it was best to avoid.

Ten minutes after one o'clock, he wondered what was delaying Kate. Then the obvious occurred to him. He hadn't thought to drive into the parking lot. Kate would have parked there and would be sitting with the minister, cuddling Devon, and making excuses for his tardiness.

Gabe scrambled from the truck and hurried into the church. He found the office down a short hall and rapped on the door. A man's voice told him to come in. The guy sounded friendly enough. Maybe Gabe wasn't in too much shit with Kate.

When he entered the room, a short, round guy in jeans and a University of Alberta sweatshirt rose and shook his hand.

"Mr. Gabrieli? I'm Joe Beam." He didn't even flinch when he looked at Gabe's face. He went on. "Glad to meet you. Where are Kate and Devon?"

"Kate planned to meet me here. I waited for them outside and finally came in because I thought I'd missed them."

"She's probably delayed. Let's take care of business while we wait."

He gestured at a chair. Gabe sat. Beam settled in his desk chair and opened a folder that held four or five pieces of paper. "Everything we know about Devon Marie Chilton so far. A tiny file for a tiny but thrilling person."

He sorted through the pages and extracted one. "Here we go—her christening." He scanned the page and smiled. "God-father, Desert Sun Gabrieli, Eau Claire, Alberta. Interesting name."

Gabe gave Beam a feeble smile. "I usually go by my initials, or just Gabe."

"Oh, that. I was referring to Eau Claire. It's very musical."

Beam paused. "Your name is not unusual for our generation. But I feel your pain. My middle name is Moon."

Gabe relaxed. "I wonder if our mothers know each other."

Beam laughed. "Could be. Was yours a flower child in Vancouver during the early seventies?"

"San Francisco."

"Close enough. You're an excellent choice as Devon's godfather. Harris and Kate will be wonderful parents, but every child becomes a teenager. And that means angst. When I learned your name, I realized you can probably relate to teenage angst."

"You have that right." Gabe checked his watch. Kate was half an hour late.

"I hear you're looking into the explosions."

Gabe nodded.

"And I hear you popped Bill Jacobson."

Uh-oh, Gabe thought, now it starts. Beam's face was expressionless.

"That just sorta happened. I didn't plan it."

"Do you regret hitting him?"

Hell no, Gabe wanted to say. He stared out the window to the parking lot, still no sign of Kate. He looked at Beam, whose face was bland, that infuriating poker face only clergy, judges, and Wally Mitchell could adopt.

"I regret what he wrote about my friends and my kid brother. I regret I gave him a reason to get even and print that garbage. But hitting him? Not so much."

The first hint of a reaction from Beam appeared. A crinkle at the edge of his eyes, a twitch of his lips. At last, a warm smile. "An honest answer. Admirable. God forgive me, I might have popped him too." Beam looked at his watch. "Not like Kate to be this late."

Gabe phoned her, but the call went to voice mail. "No answer."

"Well, something must have come up. I'm sure she'll call to explain." Beam stood. "It's a pleasure to know you."

Gabe had passed muster. He left the church feeling lighter. Once inside his truck, he called Harris. "Are Kate and the baby with you?" Gabe said.

"No, they're at the church."

Gabe felt cold. "Kate didn't show. Has she phoned you?"

"No." Harris was silent for a moment and then started talking fast. "Maybe her car broke down on the way into town. Maybe her phone's dead. She never charges it. I'm heading home to check."

Gabe put his truck into gear and peeled out.

When he turned onto the highway, he could see Harris's red Jeep ahead ripping down the road. Every time the road curved or the shoulder dropped off, Harris slowed. Gabe knew he was checking for signs Kate's car had left the road.

When they entered Harris's yard, the garage doors rose to reveal emptiness. Harris was out of his Jeep and running to the house before Gabe could undo his seat belt. Harris left the house door open behind him. When Gabe stepped into the entrance hall, he heard Harris running along the hallway upstairs, calling for Kate and Devon. The clock on the foyer wall ticked in the silence that answered his shouts.

Chapter 64

THE SOUND of doors opening and closing drifted down the stairs. Gabe went into the kitchen, hoping for a note on the table, something to tell them why Kate's plans had changed, where she had gone. The kitchen gleamed, its surfaces clean and empty.

Harris appeared in the doorway, his face pale and his eyes wild. "Nothing, nothing. She's not here. Neither is Devon. Sweet Jesus, this can't be happening."

"I'll check the barn and sheds," Gabe said.

"Her car's gone." Harris's tone was sharp. "She won't be in the—" He stopped. His face became ashen. "Oh God, what if some maniac hurt them and stole the car?"

"Don't imagine the worst. Look for a note while I check the rest of the buildings. Then we'll phone people."

Gabe checked the garage, the machine shed, and the granaries, looking for anything out of place or signs of a struggle. The buildings appeared benign, average outbuildings on an average ranch.

The barn was quiet. Things seemed to be where they should. He climbed the ladder to the loft and found nothing but undisturbed hay.

When Gabe exited the rear doors of the barn, he noticed a dull green ATV parked behind the stable. Certain it belonged to Jack, Gabe entered the stable. "Jacko? Are you here?" No response other than a couple whinnies from the resident horses.

When Gabe searched for Tornado Callie, he found her in the paddock, saddled. He climbed the rail fence and called her. She trotted over and nuzzled his pocket. "No treats, today," Gabe said. He ran his hand over her flank. It felt damp. "What's going on? Did Jack ride you and not remove your gear?"

He led Callie into the stable, quickly removed her tack, and shooed her into a stall.

Then he went back to the paddock and did a head count of the horses. Including Callie and the two others in the stable, he had eleven. One short.

When Gabe returned to the house, Harris sat at the kitchen table by the windows that framed a view of the fields. "Anything?" Harris said.

"Jack's ATV is behind the stable. Callie was in a paddock, still saddled and a bit damp. I removed her tack and put her in a stall. I counted eleven horses. Isn't that one short?"

"Yes," Harris said. "Who's missing?"

Gabe shrugged. "Don't know. Could Kate be out riding?"

"Kate doesn't ride unless someone can watch Devon." Harris headed for the door. "Come on, let's check the barn and stable and see what's going on."

Harris jogged to the barn. Gabe gave up trying to keep up with him after several pangs from his knee. By the time he reached the stable, Harris was surveying the paddocks. "So, you're right," Harris said. "Eleven. Hank is missing."

He pointed to the stable. "And our horse trailer is usually parked right beside the stable." He turned and re-entered the barn. After searching through the harnesses, Harris said, "We're missing a Percheron harness."

"Okay," Gabe said. "Where does that leave us? Jack rode Callie earlier, left her saddled, and now he's out for a walk somewhere? And Kate loaded Hank and a harness into the horse trailer? To go where?"

"Nowhere. She was supposed to meet you at the church. That's all she had on today."

Gabe asked, "Did you find a note in the house?"

"No note. Just this." Harris dug into his pocket and held out Kate's Celtic pinky ring. "Someone snatched them. Why?"

"We don't know that. Maybe she didn't wear the ring today. Was she herself this morning?"

Harris's eyes narrowed. "She was fine. What are you getting at?"

"I'm wondering why she'd leave without a note. Anything out of the ordinary happen?"

Harris stared at him, his face suddenly flaming. "You think she left me? Here's a news flash: not every woman walks out on her husband."

Gabe raised his hands and took a step back. He bit back an angry retort. It wouldn't help if they both went off the deep end.

Harris glared at Gabe for several seconds and then ran his hand through his hair. "Sorry, man. I'm losing it." After a moment, he said, "Her ring was on my pillow. She never takes it off. If she left voluntarily, she'd take the ring."

Gabe thought about it. Kate cherished the ring, a gift from her mother just before she died. "You're right."

Back at the house, they divided the calls, Gabe calling Greta and Rhonda, while Harris phoned O'Malley. Gabe's calls were short; neither woman had seen Kate today and would put out feelers.

Gabe heard Harris tell O'Malley they'd phone the police and to tell Mercy to stay calm. Harris ended the call and said, "This isn't good news."

Gabe's stomach dropped.

Harris said, "Seamus said Jack came over here this morning. Jack had said he'd be gone till dinner."

Gabe pulled his cell from his pocket. "You won't reach him," Harris said. "Mercy found his phone on his bed. She's frantic."

"This is because of the story in the *Journal*," Gabe said. "I think the bomber was after Jack. And somehow found him here, with Kate and the baby."

Harris expelled a breath. "God."

Gabe phoned LeBlanc. "It's Gabrieli. Kate Chilton and her baby are missing. No one's seen them since this morning. My brother Jack might be missing too. He apparently went to the Chilton ranch this morning. No one's seen him since."

"Any reason Mrs. Chilton and your brother might leave voluntarily?"

Gabe watched Harris pace the width of the kitchen. "You mean, is Kate helping Jack escape the clutches of the law? Jack's not your bomber."

"I know."

"Huh?"

"The evidence we confiscated from his tack box didn't have his prints. Wiped almost clean except for a partial thumbprint on a paint can. Not Jack's. His stash we found in the bush was covered in his prints. I asked myself, why would Gabrieli's brother wipe only some things clean?"

"So, someone set him up."

"Probably," LeBlanc said. "But that doesn't mean he isn't scared and running."

"After this morning's story in the *Journal*, if he's running it's from the bomber. Plus, Kate Chilton would never leave her husband or their home."

LeBlanc was quiet. Then: "I'll get some guys on it. Stay in touch."

"He'll get some guys on it," Gabe told Harris after the call. "I'm not waiting for the cops. Let's start our own search."

"Excellent plan. Tom Mitchell belongs to Blackstrap Mountain's search-and-rescue team. He can head it up. Maybe Lucy can cover his shifts at The Peak?"

Gabe smacked his forehead. "Christ, I gotta tell Lucy."

While Harris called Tom Mitchell and asked him to start a search, Gabe phoned Lucy, filled her in, and asked if she could run the bar while they searched for the missing trio.

"Anything, you know that," she said.

When Gabe ended the call, Harris said, "You believe this is connected to the bombings?"

"For sure. Either because of the story in the paper or because someone wants to distract me from the investigation."

"Then the rest of us will search while you focus on figuring out who's behind the bombings. A two-pronged approach."

They closed up the house. Harris stared at the door. Then he covered his face with his hands. His shoulders shook; he choked as he sobbed. Gabe squeezed his shoulder. "Hang in there."

Harris raised his head and swiped his shirtsleeve across his eyes. "I couldn't stand if it anything happened before...." Harris stared into the darkness.

Gabe waited. Finally, he said, "Before what?"

Harris exhaled. "Kate and I fought last night. Over money. She had offered to sell the herd to her father. Never talked to me about it. I accused her of making it appear like I couldn't take care of my family."

Gabe stayed silent.

"She said my pride would ruin our marriage. It went downhill from there. We slept in separate rooms. This morning I left without speaking to her."

Chapter 65

WHEN HARRIS and Gabe returned to Cheakamus, Tiffany's Café teemed with people. Tom Mitchell had arrived with his search team, who were huddled with several volunteers, giving instructions and handing out maps of the area.

Rhonda approached them. "Hang in there Harris, Tom's team will find them." She gestured at the crowd. "I turned the place over to Tom for his headquarters. Lucy's at the Peak Bar working his shift."

"Any news?" Harris asked.

"Phil saw an Escape on the highway pulling a horse trailer," Rhonda said. "Eleven-thirty, heading east toward Trail."

"I'm going to check in with Tom," Harris said to Gabe. "Keep me posted on your investigation."

Gabe moved to the coffee station, where a handwritten sign on the antique mirror announced, "Free for searchers." He poured an extra-large Mudshark-to-go and turned to see Phil Livesay entering the café. "Phil," he called. "Got a sec?"

When Phil joined him, Gabe said, "I'm tracing Minken's movements before he died. When did you see him last?"

Phil sighed. "Isn't it a terrible thing? Who'd want to shoot him? I saw him Wednesday, noonish. He was planning a fishing trip to River's End. It's a popular spot so he thought he'd need to drop Aldercott's name to get in."

"Ahhh, right. He mentioned fishing. Did he say anything? Was he afraid of anyone?"

"Nah," Phil said. "I talked to him again late that afternoon. He was upbeat. Said he would come back with good fish stories. Then he laughed and said fishing and fish stories always seemed to go together, and sometimes you didn't even need to go fishing to tell a good one. That's the last I talked to him. I miss the old guy."

"Me too." Gabe got Phil's number from him in case he had further questions and headed for the exit, making a quick detour when he noticed Carl studying one of the search maps at a booth. "Hey, Carl, joining the search?"

"I can spare an hour. Not much, I know, but it might help. I sent Nestor to check the resort's property for any sign of them. He's dumber than firewood but he can recognize human shapes."

"Thanks for helping."

"What the hell is going on?" Carl said. "Hear about Minken?"

"Yeah."

"Convenient how Findrich stumbled on the body, don't you think?"

Gabe shrugged. When he spotted Sergeant LeBlanc talking to Harris, Gabe excused himself and hurried over to the two men.

Harris said, "The Sergeant was about to fill me in on their search plans."

LeBlanc nodded at Gabe and then said, "We are coordinating with Tom Mitchell and the volunteers. I heard ten minutes ago that someone in the Slocan Valley found an Escape and horse trailer in an abandoned barn on his property. Lucky discovery because the fellow is from Calgary and rarely visits the acreage. Because of that news, we are focusing on the general area east of Cheakamus. I've asked the police boat crew to check out the area around nearby lakes. As well, we have two helicopters covering highways and areas we can't access on foot."

It relieved Gabe to hear about the heavy police involvement in the search for Kate, the baby and Jack. He left the café feeling a touch lighter than when he'd arrived half an hour ago. When he noticed Seamus O'Malley rushing along the sidewalk toward him, Gabe paused with his hand on his driver's door.

Seamus waved and approached. "I need a minute. It's important."

Gabe leaned against his truck. "Okay."

O'Malley paced on the sidewalk in front of Gabe's truck. Gabe waited him out.

O'Malley stopped pacing and faced Gabe. "I can't say this in front of Mercy. I know you detest me. But please bring Katie home. And her baby." He sucked in a shaky breath. Tears ran down his cheeks. "And Jack. Mercy's crazy with worry. I'm trying to put on a good show to calm her. But I can't hold it together much longer."

"For the record," Gabe said, "I don't detest you, but you *can* be a prick."

O'Malley nodded, raised a sad face. "Kate and Devon's disappearance made me think about you, and how it hit you when Bethany left."

He ran his hands through his hair. "When Katie's mom died, I wanted to do what you did—rage at the world. But there was little Katie. Only thirteen and no mother. Scared and alone. So, I gritted my teeth and tried to stay sane for her."

Gabe opened his mouth, but O'Malley lifted a hand. "Today I realized you had no one to stay sane for. You only had you. And I knew that if it hadn't been for Katie, I'd have hit bottom. Like you did. Maybe worse."

Seamus swiped the tears from his face, then moved toward the café's door. "Bring them home. I can't go through it again. I can't do it this time."

Chapter 66

JACK SAT on a crate in the Evergold Mine storage bay he and his buddies called party central. He cradled his right arm and tried to stop shivering. The pain in his shoulder from his broken collarbone was overwhelming. Shivering made it worse. He counted the candles in the box at his feet. Five fat ones. How long would they last?

"I shouldn't have come to your ranch," he said to Kate. "I should have headed home."

Kate cuddled Devon and brushed her hand over the baby's soft red curls. "We both made mistakes. I should have phoned 911. But when I first saw you on Tornado Callie galloping flat out and the other two behind you, I thought you and a couple friends were racing."

"They were waiting for me at the trailhead. Tornado Callie saved me. She musta smelled the other horses before we rounded the curve. She changed her gait, flicked her ears, so I knew something was ahead. I was already reining her in, but I never put it together until I saw Freako's goggles. Then I knew it was the guy from the pasture."

"How could they know you'd be on that trail?"

Jack hung his head. "I think Craig told them. I was supposed to meet him there."

"Why?"

He bit his bottom lip to stop it quivering. "I was mad at Seamus and his rules. Mad at Mom 'cause she sent me here and then sided with Seamus. Mad at everyone. I wanted weed."

"Oh," Kate said, her face somber.

Jack sighed. "I screwed up. Craig's a shithead. I trusted him. Never gave it a thought. And then I came to your house. Tornado Callie had them beat. If I'd headed for home, we would have been safe."

He fell silent. Now that I'm counting screw-ups, he thought, what about riding alone? And leaving the phone at home? To make sure Seamus couldn't check up on him. Yeah, that backfired. No phone, no way to call for help. No way for someone to ping him.

Seamus would be beyond steamed. Jack was used to that. His mother, though. Jack wanted to cry. How could he face his mother and see the disappointment on her face again? Like in Eau Claire when he was expelled. How many times would he let Mom down?

And what about his last mistake, or perhaps it was his first one. That he'd been drinking before his ride. That it made his thinking fuzzy. Made him afraid to run home, made him think he'd be safe at Kate's.

Never thinking Kate would come outside and take on Freako. Never thinking they'd grab Kate and Devon. Never thinking.

Kate hugged him. "We all make mistakes. It's what we learn from them that matters. When we get home, we'll both have things we want to do differently."

"Do you think anyone's looking for us?"

"For sure," she had said. "I left my ring behind. Harris will know something happened. He'll notice Hank is gone. He'll start a search. They'll find us soon."

He looked at Kate as she rocked Devon. "Five fat candles," he said. "Good for a couple days, at least."

"I'm glad you're with me and knew about the candles," Kate said. "They'll keep us warm."

"I wish my friends and I had stashed water here too." Instead of weed. His wants had sure changed from what they were a week ago. Even a day ago.

"Hank's here in the tunnels," Jack said. "Do you think he's afraid?"

Kate shook her head. "He's coolheaded. You and I need to stay coolheaded too and start thinking."

"We're hooped. That door is the only way out. We can't push it open or climb through the gap. And Freako just keeps saying it won't be long. Until what?"

"Of the two of them, he's softer. What kind of kidnapper apologizes for the inconvenience? Perhaps we can work on him."

Chapter 67

It was mid-afternoon when Rocky reached the main portal of the Evergold Mine for the third time today. He was breathing hard. Mountaineering was for bighorn sheep and Heidi's grandfather.

Sure, Rocky had spent most of his adult life standing on one rock or another, and in the years since college he'd hiked his share of rugged trails. But that was then. This was now, and he wasn't twenty anymore. When he needed to climb a mountain these days, he used something with a motor.

Which was exactly what he'd done on his first two trips to the mine today. The first trip was in the lady's SUV, towing the horse trailer. After he and Doc unloaded their guests and the Percheron, Rocky had driven the Escape and trailer back to Doc's place where they unloaded and stabled their own horses.

Rocky then drove the Escape and trailer east to the Slocan Valley. He stashed them both in an old barn on a piece of recreational property Doc knew about. Apparently, the owner lived in Alberta and rarely visited the place. It wasn't a long wait before Doc collected Rocky from the drop site and they drove back to Cheakamus.

On the second trip to the mine an hour ago, Rocky towed the snowmobile on a trailer behind the old orange van. Good idea Doc had to use the van as a cover. Rocky had also used it to meet with Craig and his sidekick, Frank, when he needed truck jockeys. Although the van wasn't as smooth a ride as his Sierra, it did the job today.

Even moving the snowmobile through the tunnels had been simple. He hooked the massive Percheron to the trailer and presto. That horse towed that trailer with its load of tools and snowmobile to the tunnel mouth like it was a kid's pull toy, then looked at Rocky as if to say, "Piece-o-cake. That all you got?"

But this third trip was another thing altogether. If Rocky was going to disappear across the border into the US, he couldn't leave his truck or ATV at the mine. People would instantly make the connection between a sabotaged mine and his abandoned vehicles. Then he would be a hunted man. Instead, he left the Sierra and Arctic Cat with Doc, who would get rid of them. Odds were good Doc wouldn't hire Craig's gang of boneheads for the job.

Inside the main portal, Rocky rested for a moment, leaning against the uprights, catching his breath. Why were mountains all uphill? Lucky he wasn't packing weight, or he'd be dead somewhere in the trees back there. The trails were too exposed—being spotting this late in the game would be ironic but unwelcome—so he'd mostly bushwhacked. Uphill *and* overgrown. He'd traveled light: a backpack, the rifle Doc said would be handy if a cougar appeared, and his trusty Swiss Army one-hand knife. He rubbed the smooth casing and flicked it open, admiring the glinting blade. Those Swiss made a wicked knife.

He trekked along the main tunnel to the slatted wood door leading to the tunnel hub. Turning on his flashlight, he slipped through the doorway and turned left.

Things were moving ahead. They'd finished the Skype call

with the Cayman bank an hour ago. Following the security measures they'd set up, Doc and Rocky appeared on screen together, verified their identities, confirmed thirty million of the investors' money was in the account, and issued instructions to send it on to two other accounts. There should have been another fifteen million, but Alpine Capital hadn't sent their money in. Guess they were still waiting to hear from the brainiac they'd hired to check out the operation.

Rocky thought about Doc's split and cursed. Fifty percent. Doc owned thirty percent of Rocky's operation but was getting half the take. It rankled. Rocky kicked a rock on the walkway. Doc had him over a barrel. "Want to get away, have the chance to enjoy your riches? Pay up," he'd said. Damn, damn, damn.

Rocky rounded a curve and spotted the boulder they'd used to block the door to the storage bay. The door was wide enough to allow a forklift through, and well over six feet high. There was a gap along the top of the door, maybe a handsbreadth. Not big enough for anyone to crawl through. No lock, but the door opened into the tunnel so once they rolled the rock in place, nobody was getting out of there. Moving the boulder would have been impossible without the horse. It was Rocky's idea to grab the Percheron when they snatched everyone. Thinking ahead to moving the snowmobile. Typical of Doc though, not to even acknowledge Rocky's brilliance.

Hollywood Hank, the lady said. What a name. What a horse.

Thinking about the awesome animal calmed Rocky. So what if he gave up half the take? Get over it and get on with life. The next company would be all his. He wouldn't need Doc's money.

He heard the baby crying and her mom soothing her. The lady's voice made him feel happy. She could sing a lullaby to him any day. He stopped by the boulder. "Not long now, you'll be out of here."

"Please, can we have water?" she said.

"Don't have any. You gotta wait."

"We've had nothing to drink since we got here. There should be water in the museum. Please have a look?"

"Lady, I've been traipsing all over this mountain for most of the day. I got lots to do yet. No time to hike back through the tunnel."

The baby cried again, and the lady shushed her. "It's okay, Devon, Mommy's here."

He heard her sob. Her voice quivered when she spoke again. "Jack's in poor shape and I'm feeling faint. Who will take care of my baby if I pass out? It won't take you long. Please?"

Ahhh, geez. Why hadn't they thought about water when they brought everyone here? Because they hadn't counted on the woman and the baby, that's why. Their planned quick grab-the-kid-and-go had turned into a logistical nightmare.

Smart kid. He spotted them on the trail and in less than two seconds had wheeled his horse around and split. And man, could that horse run. Then, at the ranch, suddenly they had a firebrand of a woman to contend with. She fought like Wonder Woman, kicking, punching, trying to pull off the balaclavas, screaming. The kid, too, until that bone snapped. Two against one after that, but the lady wouldn't give in. Finally, it was Doc who won the day. Threatening the baby. The minute Doc did that, the lady stopped fighting. Rocky still wanted to puke when he remembered her expression. You shouldn't do that to a person, make her face losing everything.

"Okay, okay. I'll go see."

He leaned the rifle against one of the upright timbers and hurried along the tunnel. At the entrance he stood for a moment, squinting against the bright sun. The parking lot was empty. He donned his mountaineering sunglasses, scurried through the chain-link enclosure, and sprinted to the museum. Inside, he waded through the mess he'd created when he trashed the joint Wednesday night, and approached the cooler in the gift shop. He grabbed water, four bottles for them and two for him, and shoved them in his backpack. He spotted muffins and tossed some in his pack. Then he thought about babies, went to the kitchen and found something that might work.

The parking lot was still empty. He put his head down and dashed to the mine, through the gate, across the fenced area and into the tunnel. Once inside, he slowed to a fast walk, panting, pleased with himself.

"Your lucky day," he said when he reached the boulder. "I'm gonna toss some stuff through the gap." He climbed atop the boulder and dropped the muffins and water through the gap.

"Thank you. You're wonderful."

"Not done yet. In case your baby needs changing? This is the best I could do." He dropped a roll of paper towels through the gap, then two dishtowels.

"You're very kind. What about Hank? Does he need water?"

"Geez lady. Gimme a break. He looked okay to me."

"Take one of these bottles back. Pour some into your palm and let him slurp it."

"I have extra. But if you think I'm letting him chomp me, you're nuts."

"He's gentle. Please don't hurt him."

"Hurt him? Hell, if I could, I'd clone the big guy. He's poetry. Saved me a ton of grief yesterday. You probably won't thank him, but he moved the boulder blocking this door."

Rocky recalled his first efforts to remove the planks from the tunnel exit. He needed to remove them so he and Doc could exit the mine onto the plateau where the ranch herd had been pastured. Greta Rocque must have wanted the boards to stay put because they had six-inch nails in them. Didn't matter whether Rocky used the hammer or the crowbar, nothing worked to pry those spikes out. And did he have anyone to help him? No. Once again he got to do all the hard work. "I'm the brains, not the labor," Doc said.

Rocky had been dripping wet and wheezing like a dying man, thinking they'd have to find another route to the trail, but knowing there wasn't one, when the Percheron snorted and tossed his head. As if to say, "I'm the answer to all your dreams."

Rocky had looped a rope around one of the planks, tied it to the horse's harness and said, "C'mon, Hank. You can do this."

The horse moved forward lazy-like, almost sauntering, and the board came away from the timbers in an instant. "All right! Hank, what a star you are. Poetry."

In less than half an hour he had a hole big enough to move the snowmobile through.

"Speaking of the horse," Rocky said now, "I'm running late. Hank's gotta finish removing the planks from the tunnel exit. Can't catch the evening train to good times if I can't get outta the mine."

"Wait, don't go. Can't you move the rock, let us out of here? Your friend doesn't need to know you helped."

"Soon. I promise I'll call it in. People will come get you."

Rocky jumped off the boulder and hurried along the tunnel. He'd see if the horse looked thirsty. Nice that the lady was so worried about him. Class act, through and through. He was glad he didn't tell her that once upon a time they used horses and mules in mines to haul the ore. Lowered them down the shaft. Left them there when mining ceased, a death sentence.

That wouldn't happen to her horse though. Soon Doc would arrive. They'd finish removing the planks from the tunnel exit, shoo the horse onto the field, wait for nightfall, light the fuse, and take off.

Doc's plan was close to perfect. They'd ride tandem on the

snowmobile to a secluded spot just north of the U.S. border, the drop site for the dope and people Doc smuggled over the line. Rocky would sneak through the trees and lose himself in the great United States of America. Land of the free. He'd call the cops and tell them to look in the tunnels for three hungry and cold people. Then, off to Grand Cayman.

And the lady, kid and baby? They'd be fine. Rocky was a pro. Knew exactly how much Forcite he needed to blow the tunnel exit and nothing else. Besides, the explosives weren't anywhere near the storage bay.

Doc? Doc would take the snowmobile back to Cheakamus. Carry on as usual. Be astounded to hear about the explosion in the mine. Be even more amazed when searchers rescued the people in the tunnel and found another horse on the same field as the first bunch. Say, "Hard to believe this is happening so close to home."

Chapter 68

GABE SAT in his truck on Main Street, letting it idle while he sipped his coffee and tried to sort things through. Both he and Harris believed the sabotage and Gwinn's death were linked with the disappearance of Kate, Devon, and Jack. Harris wanted him to focus on the sabotage case while everyone else search for the missing trio. Although it felt like he wasn't doing enough, Gabe knew Harris was right. If they found the trio, that would probably tell them who was behind the bombings. If Gabe solved the case, that would probably lead them to the missing trio.

Was Horace Minken's death also connected to the sabotage? If so, how? Gabe took a sip of his coffee. He wished he'd spoken to Horace when he phoned about his fish story. If only to learn why a non-fishing fish story made him think it was something Gabe would be interested to hear. He put the truck into gear, but paused before backing out of the parking spot. He grabbed his phone and called Phil Livesay. When he connected with voice mail, he asked Phil to chase down some information.

When his phone beeped to indicate an incoming call,

Gabe checked the screen. Andrews. He quickly ended his message to Phil, and picked up Bethany's call. "Hey bella." He put the truck into park once more.

"Hi, I thought I'd check in to see how things are going."

"Not so great. Kate, her baby, and Jack are missing."

"Oh no! What happened?"

"Someone snatched them. My guess is the bomber thinks Jack can identify him. And somehow Kate and Devon got mixed up in it. Everyone else is searching for them and I'm trying to solve the sabotage case, in case everything is connected."

"Is that what you think?"

"Yeah. But I have almost no leads and can't figure out the ones I've got."

"You are whip smart and stubborn, handy qualities to have right now. I have faith in you. I'll be pulling for you. Keep me posted."

After he said goodbye, Gabe sat rooted in his driver's seat, blindsided. Faith in him, she'd said. But not enough to stay with him, to trust him. A year ago, when he raged against the injustice of the murder charge and her decision to leave him, she'd said the angry man he'd become frightened her. She claimed not to recognize him anymore.

"I'm still me, babe," he'd said. "The guy who loves you, the one you said keeps you safe from ogres."

She had said, "I don't know any more how far you'd go to keep me safe from men like Drake."

He wanted Bethany to believe in more than his investigative abilities. He wanted her to believe in him again. He wanted to save her career. Proving he wasn't Drake's killer would accomplish both. But time was running out.

His gut told him time was also running out in Cheakamus. He hated to think he might lose people he loved. And that people he loved would lose people they loved.

He thought of Harris and Kate's wonderfully warm home on the hill. Welcoming and full of love. He knew what happened to a home when its vital spirit disappeared. It became a brittle shell, spotlighting your loneliness and loss. The warm kitchen became a sterile storage space. Soft lighting became harsh, glaring. Pictures became accusatory. The house was no longer a refuge from the world but a place you could not bear to be. It drove you out and away from those who might help you.

If they didn't find the trio alive, Harris's home would become a house Gabe knew too well. No place to live.

Gabe's phone rang, wrenching him away from dark thoughts. The screen flashed "unknown." He answered. "Gabrieli."

"It's Wally Mitchell. That truck's here."

Gabe immediately put his truck into gear and backed out. "Are you at the casino?"

"Yeah, I was coming on shift, saw them parking. Two young guys, playing blackjack."

"Your table?" Gwinn's book must have brought a hefty reward.

"Nah, a two-dollar table. I got the license plate, but it's the only beige shitbox in the lot."

"On my way. Keep them warm for me."

"I'll do my best. Their dealer looks ready for a break. I'll tell Ubrowski you're coming by." He clicked off.

Gabe made the turn from the Rocque River Bridge onto Highway 41 and put his foot down hard, propelling the F-150 forward. The highway was dry and any other day he'd revel in the scenery and the sensation of driving along a superb road. Today, however, he had one of his private chats with the Head Honcho. "Keep Kate, Jack and Devon safe. And if you could toss a few hints my way, I wouldn't turn them down."

On the way to the casino, he replayed his conversation with Weiler Thursday evening. Aldercott had a partner, a doctor. He thought about Carl's comment. Findrich found Minken's body. Findrich used to be the town doctor. Gabe wondered how many other doctors were in the area. He tapped his fingers on the steering wheel. At least one. Nicole Mitchell. Doctor of Veterinary Medicine.

Chapter 69

WALLY WAS RIGHT. The pickup was the only beige shitbox in
the casino lot. Gabe parked beside it and spotted his *High
Hopes* CD on the dash. Like almost every other vehicle around
Cheakamus, the driver's door was unlocked. He snatched
the CD.

When Gabe entered the casino, Wally was dealing
single-deck blackjack at a table near the cashier's cage. He
glanced up, his eyes sliding to Gabe and past in one smooth
motion.

Gabe recognized the two young players at Wally's table by
their corporate-hemp wardrobe. His old friends from BAM:
Craig and Frank. They each had a beer and a few stacks of
chips on the felt. Gabe watched Wally bust four times in a row,
to Craig and Frank's delight.

Gabe found Ubrowski at the security desk. "I need to talk
to the guys at Wally's table. I'm sure they trashed my truck."

"Be gentle," Ubrowski said. "I'll tell my guys not to bother
you unless you break something."

When Gabe reached Wally's table and stood behind Craig
and Frank, Wally barely glanced up before he dealt the next
hand.

Gabe slapped the Springsteen CD onto the felt. Craig jumped. Frank scrambled off his stool.

"Sit down, Frank. No one's gonna hurt you," Gabe said. Frank reclaimed his seat.

Gabe turned his attention to Craig. "I woulda lent you the CD, Craig, if you'd asked. But no, you had to steal it. Stupid."

"I didn't."

"And then you slashed my truck seats. Colossal mistake. I might get over the CD, but I won't forget the seats."

"It was Frank."

Frank squealed and stared at Craig.

Gabe shook his head. Thugs and thieves. Solidarity was a foreign concept. Corner one, he'll blame it on his buddy nine times out of ten.

Gabe pushed their poker chips toward Wally.

"Hey, what're you doin'?" Craig reached out to paw the chips back. A red scratch ran from his knuckles to elbow. No question which ornery cat put it there.

"Tipping the dealer for you. So, who put you up to it?"

Craig slid from his stool. "No one. What's the big deal? Frankie did something stupid. You got your CD. Frankie'll pay to fix the seats."

Frank stared at Craig like he'd never seen him before. Probably that was true. Frank was just now learning a few truths about his leader.

"It's bigger than a filched CD and slashed leather. Bigger than selling weed. Bigger than a stolen journal. You're in deep shit."

Frank whimpered. Craig glared at him.

Gabe turned his attention to Frank. "*Deep* shit. To start, kidnapping. A young mother, a teenager *and* a baby."

Frank moaned.

"He's full of shit," Craig said. "C'mon Frank, we're leaving." He walked away without looking back.

When Frank moved to follow, Gabe said, "Listen to me,

Frank. I'm not blowing smoke. When you help a guy who commits crimes, you get to pay for those crimes too. And you helped a very bad guy. So far, we've got kidnapping. Vandalism. A murder. Maybe two."

Sweat popped out on Frank's hairline. He rubbed his palms on his jeans and swallowed.

Gabe smiled. "Relax. I figure Craig took my CD and trashed my truck. Help yourself here, Frank. Who put you up to it?"

Frank looked toward the exit. Craig was long gone. Frank drew in a shaky breath and then said in a burst, "His name's Rocky."

The name rang a faint bell in Gabe's memory, but he couldn't place it.

"Rocky paid us to find the book."

"So you broke into my apartment."

Frank nodded and rubbed his palms on his jeans again.

"And when you struck out there, you tried my truck." More nods and wiping of palms.

"You found the book, and took it to Rocky."

"Craig did."

"Do you know where?"

Frank shook his head, no.

"Who's Rocky?" Gabe said.

"Dunno."

"What'd he look like?"

A shrug. "A guy. Freaky. Dressed in black. Weird sunglasses. Drove an orange van."

"Who keyed and sprayed my truck?"

Another shrug. "Not me."

"I'm guessing Craig. Now tell me what you know about the explosions."

"Nothing. We got nothing to do with bombs."

Maybe he was being straight, maybe not. The RCMP

could figure that part out. Gabe had what he needed. Orange van. Nestor Clayton.

"Well done, Frank. In a few hours I'll call Sergeant LeBlanc of the Mounties and tell him all this. Try to call him before I do. It will make you look like the good guy I know you are."

On his way out of the casino, Gabe stopped by Wally's table. He was fanning cards across the felt, shuffling and flicking them to an internal rhythm.

"Remind me not to play poker with you again unless I have both eyes on the deck."

Wally grinned. "I don't know what you're talking about. It's against the rules to deal from the bottom."

Chapter 70

ROCKY WASN'T HAVING fun anymore. A couple hours ago, when he was trudging over the mountain, he suspected he wasn't enjoying himself. Now, as he faced Doc near the tunnel exit to the plateau and listened to his words about witnesses, he was certain.

Doc had shown up, brandishing the rifle in his gloved hands. "I found this back by the storage bay."

"Guess I forgot it."

"Careless." Doc had glanced around and then gestured at the timbers along the tunnel wall. "Why did you place the explosives behind the timbers and not just on the ground?"

Rocky shook his head. For someone smart, Doc could be dumb. "Because if they're on the ground, the blast goes upward and does nothing. We want to blow the uprights and collapse the rock they're supporting."

"If we did that all the way down the tunnel, everything would cave in?"

"Well yeah, but we only want to block the mouth here to make it hard for anyone to follow us. Put explosives along the tunnel? That'd bring the mountain down on the lady and the kid. And the baby."

"It would remove witnesses."

"They never saw our faces. Why else did we wear those stupid balaclavas?"

"To make you believe," Doc had said. "Would you have grabbed them if you knew they were gonna die?"

Now, Rocky stared at Doc. What the hell was he talking about? Of course, they weren't going to die. That wasn't the plan.

"I didn't think so." Doc laughed and aimed the rifle at Rocky's chest. "Rocky, Rocky. It's been great being partners. The return I got from my investment in your venture is wonderful. Thank you. But the partnership ends now. Things got too hot when you killed Gwinn."

"Don't point that at me. It might go off. I didn't kill him. It was an accident."

Doc tossed the rifle onto the discarded planks by the tunnel exit. "Right. The rock pick accidently jumped up and smacked him in the head. Who's gonna believe that?"

"Doesn't matter. We'll be in Grand Cayman enjoying the good life."

"Nope. I'm gonna cut you loose." Doc grabbed the crowbar and swung it, connecting soundly with Rocky's shin.

Rocky felt the bone snap, and he crashed to the ground, screaming in agony.

Doc stood over him, waving the crowbar. "I'd shoot you, but you were so kind to put your prints on the rifle. It killed Minken, did you know that? He told me he'd discovered you weren't at that fishing lodge. Good-bye alibi! It makes sense you'd kill him."

"I never did!"

"You and I know that. No one else does. When I had to kill Minken because of your idiotic lie, I realized the big flaw in my plan was you. I can't be sure you won't do something else stupid. It would be fitting to push you off Deception Ridge. But it's easier to leave you here."

Rocky dragged himself toward the tunnel exit. Doc stepped forward and swung the crowbar, glancing it off Rocky's head and ear.

"Don't rush off. Stay for the party. I could shoot them, but I'll let your handiwork do the job. I'll plant a few more explosives behind the timbers like you recommend. The whole mine will come down. Everyone will think you got caught in your own escape plan, blew up the tunnels along with your hostages and yourself. Me, I'm gonna go home, relax, have a beer. Maybe tomorrow or whenever, I'll help clear the bodies out of the mine."

"Don't do this, Doc. I'll give you an extra share of the money."

"You jeopardized my end game. I make fantastic money moving things over the border. Dead people attract cops. That's attention I don't need. And now that I've got your money, I don't need you to complicate things anymore. Enjoy your last hours."

Rocky pushed himself to one knee and shook his head, fighting to push nausea down, trying to get his eyes to focus, willing the ringing in his ears to stop. His vision narrowed, swirled, and he collapsed onto the ground once more.

Chapter 71

ON THE HIGHWAY back to Cheakamus, Gabe took advantage of cell service and checked for messages. There was one from Harris, his voice cutting in and out. Gabe recognized three words in a stream of static: bikers, Slocan, and LeBlanc.

When Gabe called Harris, voice mail cut in. "Call me," he said. "Your message was garbled." He clicked off and called LeBlanc. When he once again got voice mail, he ended the call. "Where the hell is everyone?"

Finally, Gabe had a few answers to his many questions.

Thanks to Frank, he knew who was behind the theft of the journal. Rocky, a.k.a. Nestor Clayton. Gabe searched his memory for a connection between the name Rocky and Nestor and came up blank. It didn't mesh.

Why would Nestor want the book? The Viking had said there was a gold mine of information in it if you were into mining. Perhaps Nestor was tired of herding the dude ranch horses all over Rimrock.

That thought triggered a memory of Nicole's comment about the herd entering the tunnel like old hands. If Nestor moved the herd to pasture via the tunnels, that would explain the horses' nonchalance. But Carl Dochmann had said the tunnel exit on the Solomon's Choice property was sealed. Not certain it mattered, Gabe shook his confusion away and focused again on why Nestor needed Gwinn's journal.

Perhaps Nestor wanted it out of circulation. A guy would want that if he were running a scam and thought the book incriminated him. That felt right to Gabe. And because the notations in the journal could be linked to a scam by Aldercott, that meant Aldercott, or his partner the doctor, was behind the theft.

Was Rocky/Nestor the mysterious doctor? Carl said Nestor was dumber than firewood. He shook his head as he pictured Carl pitching wood in a wobbly spiral. No Peyton Manning there.

When his synapses finally fired, Gabe stepped hard on the brake, pulled over, and dug out his phone. Unbelievably, he had four bars and when he placed the call, Weiler the Swiss investor picked up in person. "Tell me again what Manfred Aldercott said when he talked about his partner. His exact words," Gabe said.

Three minutes later, Gabe was online, revisiting research he'd done very early in this case, specifically two pieces of information from the University of British Columbia that he hadn't connected until now. And just like that, two more pieces of the puzzle clicked into place. Goes to show you, he thought, you just don't know who you know.

Before he could punch in LeBlanc's number his phone rang. When he answered, The Viking said, "Hey sonny, I saw him again. The Dark Knight."

"When?"

"Couple hours? Hot footing it from the museum into the mine."

"You sure it's the same guy? Is he huge? Or average?"

"Average. Same guy for sure. I only caught a glimpse the other night when he got into his fancy truck, but it's him. Except today he's wearing small black goggles."

Rocky, Gabe thought. Not huge. Not Nestor. Which Gabe had figured out when he'd double checked his online research. Then he focused on the rest of Thorvaldsen's words.

"What fancy truck?"

"Dang sonny, his Sierra. Shiny black. The one he got into after he dropped off the Ranger. What did you think he did that night, walked away?"

Gabe stared at the snow-laden pines and shook his head. He could have used the information about the Sierra a day or two ago.

"Is the Sierra at the museum?"

"No. Only vehicle I've seen is Mrs. Chilton's Escape. It was here earlier this morning. Towing a horse trailer. I think she dropped off a horse."

"Why do you say that?"

"Because the Dark Knight has a horse with him in the mine."

"He has a horse there?"

"Yeah, I was on the ledge above the plateau where the horses were stranded? And I heard the guy say 'Hank, you're poetry!' Then I definitely heard a horse. But when I looked at the plateau, I couldn't see one, so it had to be in the tunnel."

Kate's SUV and horse trailer. Hank, in the tunnel. And Rocky.

"Anders, you're great. I owe you a steak dinner."

Chapter 72

GABE PRESSED down hard on the accelerator. "Don't worry about tickets, Three. All the cops are east of town, searching for our friends in the wrong place." He called Harris, and again voice mail cut in. "I got it, I got it. Tell LeBlanc to check out a Sierra, black. They're at the Evergold. Mine. Hurry."

Then he called Lucy. "Where's Harris?"

"He and LeBlanc went to some biker hangout in the Slocan Valley, near that property where they found Kate's Escape. They got a tip that's where Kate, Jack and Devon are."

That didn't mesh with The Viking's information. Or did it? He'd only said Rocky was at the mine. Conceivably Rocky was unconnected to whoever snatched the trio. Gabe might believe that, if not for the fact Hank was there too.

"Someone's feeding them bullshit, Lucy. Tell them to get to the Evergold Mine."

Before Lucy disconnected, Gabe told her the names of the two people he suspected were behind everything. "Tell LeBlanc," he said.

His phone rang again almost as soon as he disconnected. Gabe answered, heard what Phil Livesay had to say, and grinned. "Got it thanks. Can you pass this on to LeBlanc? Tell him Minken knew it and it killed him."

As he neared the access road to the Evergold Mine, he debated about driving to the museum lot. If Rocky was nearby, he'd see Gabe coming. The lot would be empty because Greta had closed the museum. Gabe's F-150 would stand out, both on the access road and in the lot, especially with its fluorescent orange "hayseed" graffiti.

There was an alternative: the back way in along the logging road Greta's husband used back in the day. He could park near the top and walk to the museum. His knee tensed in anticipation of another hike through the bush.

The logging road was a narrow, rutted trail that snaked up the hill. Its crest came into sight as Gabe rounded a sharp bend. So did the enormous trunk of a downed pine that stretched across the road. Too large to drive over. Too heavy to move. He parked.

Collecting his two flashlights, he clambered over the tree and hiked the trail. He arrived at the museum parking lot with aching lungs and a knee that felt like it belonged on an eighty-year-old. The lot was empty.

He pushed open the wrecked museum door and listened to the silence. The gift shop looked the same as it had after the explosion on Wednesday—the floor and counters a trashed jumble of inexpensive gifts, postcards and prospecting equipment. He walked through the room, moving the mess on the floor aside with his foot, keeping an eye out for the souvenir maps of the mine tunnels. He found the rack of maps on its side behind the cash counter, snatched up a copy and left the museum.

The gate on the wire cage around the mine entrance was closed, its padlock missing. As Gabe approached the portal, cold air wafted toward him from the dark tunnel. He stopped. His chest felt tight.

"It's only a tunnel," he told himself. "You did this before with Greta."

Gabe took a deep breath, gritted his teeth, and entered the tunnel. He walked ten steps forward to the end of what little light spilled in from outside. He forced himself to breathe. Deep, slow breaths. Still, his face tingled, and his heart raced. He looked overhead at the tons of granite waiting to drop and encase him. He told himself to stay calm. He told himself there was an exit. He told himself not to think about mine cave-ins.

The LED flashlight had a stronger beam, but Gabe couldn't risk the noise of cranking the handle. He turned on the old faithful and when its comforting light pierced the tunnel's gloom his anxiety eased a notch. Keeping the beam focused on the ground, he walked the length of the tunnel to the large slatted-wood door that he and Greta had passed through on his tour. It was ajar, just enough room to slip through. He doused the light and moved through the opening, stood in the semi-circular tunnel hub, and listened. Nothing.

Gabe switched on the flashlight again and swept it to the right. It illuminated part of the tunnel that Greta had told him ran towards Solomon's Choice Ranch. Refusing to think about the millions of tons or granite above his head, he walked as quietly as he could along the tunnel, straining to hear sounds of horses or humans. He'd walked about a mile, he figured, the tunnel curved to the right and Gabe's flashlight illuminated a jagged gray wall in front of him. Was this a dead end? Couldn't be, because Greta had told him that the major tunnels all ended at pastures or the plateau. He took a few steps forward and played the light across the wall and up to the top of the tunnel, where he noticed a gap between the wall and the ceiling.

Gabe's skin crawled as he realized the wall was not a wall at all. It was hunks of rock and boulders filling the tunnel. Greta had said TEG's exploration site was more or less above this tunnel. Had the tunnel collapsed here when the saboteurs set off their explosives at TEG's site?

He turned on his heel and ran back along the tunnel, not caring about being quiet, not paying attention to the twinges and aches of his knee. All that mattered was getting back to the relative safety of the slatted door leading to the main Evergold tunnel.

An anxious ten minutes later he was about twenty feet away from the tunnel hub, and slowed to a walk. Once he reached the slatted door, he stood in the center of the tunnel hub and tried to calm his breathing. He pulled the map from his pocket and studied it in the flashlight's beam. A second tunnel a few yards ahead and to the right appeared to move in a northwesterly direction. The map showed one offshoot. The Valley of Horses tunnel was to his left. He vaguely remembered Greta's finger tracing the principal route. The more tunnels and offshoots he explored, the bigger the chance he would end his days wandering lost and panicked in pitch-black tunnels.

He should have bought a ball of string at Joe's Emporium.

He decided to check the second right-hand tunnel. He'd traveled for ten minutes along its curving length he reached another pile of fallen rock blocking the way. A cold sweat broke out on his forehead. He shone the light overhead. "Get serious," he thought. "Like I could tell if it was planning to cave in."

Returning to the tunnel hub, Gabe studied the map and focused on the Valley of Horses tunnel. The map showed three offshoots at various points along the tunnel's length before it ended at the exit onto the plateau. With luck, Kate, Jack and Devon would be in the first branch.

His chest tightened when he realized he might need to check every offshoot of every offshoot. The thought of going down more tunnels and discovering more rockfall made Gabe's knees weak. He might have to go deep inside the mine, walk perhaps miles along the tunnels. How long would the flashlight battery last? He shook himself. Only children were afraid of the dark.

It was more than the dark that made his skin crawl. Just because something looked rock solid didn't mean it was. Didn't mean it wouldn't have a fault deep inside that chose to collapse the very moment you were playing where you shouldn't. Didn't mean it wouldn't bring chunks of concrete, substandard rebar, and rotten plywood down around and on top of you, pinning you in the dark. Didn't mean you wouldn't end up alone listening to the rubble groan and shift, waiting for someone to come.

He leaned against the tunnel wall, light-headed. This sensation of disconnecting from things, this narrowing of his vision, were the first signs he was hyperventilating. Next stage: losing consciousness.

"Relax, dammit," he whispered to himself. "Stay calm for their sakes."

Gabe bent over, lowering his head, hoping to move blood into his brain. It would be much better if someone were here with him. Greta, perhaps. The Viking. Harris. But he was alone.

He remembered the time, thirty years ago. Under concrete. Waiting for someone to come. Waiting alone. In the end, the only person he had was himself. And he'd found, in that puny seven-year-old self, a will to survive. The grit to fight his way over, under, and through the rubble, to push the pain and excruciating fear down and away, to turn the fear into anger at his predicament and the anger into strength.

Gabe straightened. Breathed in. He'd done it when he was seven. He could do it now. He felt strength returning to his body.

He turned left and walked along the valley tunnel, limping but moving with assurance.

He checked the first branch and the second, both times

coming up empty, but gaining confidence in his ability to see the search through.

He moved on. As he entered the last branch, he decided if he came up empty-handed, he'd return to the main portal and call in more searchers.

The tunnel curved slightly and as Gabe approached the bend, he heard a baby crying. He quickened his pace and rounded the curve. An enormous boulder sat against a wide wood panel.

Chapter 73

GABE CALLED OUT. "Kate, Jack. Are you here?"

Jack shouted from the other side of the panel. "Gabe! We're here in the storage bay. We can't open the door."

"Jacko. Are you all okay?"

"My collarbone's broken, but Kate made a sling."

"We're fine," Kate said. "Can you get us out?"

"There's a boulder in front of the door," Gabe said. "With a rope around it."

"They used Hank to drag it into place," Jack said.

"Ahh, okay. Thanks to The Viking, I know where Hank is. I'll get him."

"Gabe?" Kate said. "Be careful. There were two of them."

"Okay. Hang tight, I'm going to get Hank. I'll be back."

Gabe knew Hank must be to his left because he'd checked all the other tunnel branches on his way to the storage bay. He picked up the old faithful flashlight, aimed it down the Valley of Horses tunnel and followed the beam. He crept along, hoping to avoid surprising anyone.

The tunnel was silent. Foreboding.

Gabe shook off thoughts of falling rock and played the

light over the walls. He spotted a bundle of dynamite lodged behind a support timber. A fuse ran down, across the walkway, and up the other side where he saw another bundle. His stomach flipped. The tunnel was rigged.

He sped up, reminding himself that so long as the fuse wasn't burning, he had time. What had Horace Minken told him? Eight feet a minute? No, six. Five? What did it matter? Any time would be too short if he couldn't find Hank and move the boulder.

He rounded a curve and risked calling. "Hank. Hank?"

Nothing.

"Hank!"

An answering whinny. The best sound in the world. Then, a low moan.

Gabe ran, his knee throbbing more with each step. At the tunnel mouth he noticed the bottom half of the planks across the exit had been removed. Hank was tethered to the back end of a small trailer. The best sight in the world.

A rifle lay atop a pile of boards near the wall. A knotted bundle of fuse lay between the trailer and the tunnel mouth. The fuse from the explosives Gabe had noticed along the tunnel connected with the fuse bundle. Two additional lengths of fuse, about seven yards long, ran from the fuse bundle to more explosives stuffed into crevices near the boards covering the tunnel exit.

Manfred Aldercott lay on the far side of the fuse bundle, his right leg bent awkwardly below the knee, blood pooling on the ground near his head. Next to Aldercott was a shorter length of fuse. Burning.

Gabe's eyes fixed on the sparking end of the fuse, tracked it toward the fuse bundle. "Damn."

He stomped on the fuse. It hissed and burned on. He remembered The Viking's words. To stop a burning fuse, cut it. "You got a knife?" he said.

Aldercott sucked in a gasp of air. "Doc took it." His

slurred, lazy speech made Gabe take a closer look at him. His left eye was swollen shut, blood streamed from a gash in his scalp that would need serious stitching, and his right ear was mangled.

The opening in the planks across the tunnel exit was too small to accommodate a horse, never mind one the size of Hank. Any hope of exiting the tunnel to the safety of the Valley of Horses vanished. Even if he ripped off the remaining boards, Kate and Jack waited in the storage bay for him to return with Hank and hook the Percheron to the boulder and pull it out of the way, freeing them.

If he couldn't extinguish the fuse, the only answer was to move Aldercott and Hank through the tunnel and get everyone, people and horse, out of the mine before the fuse burned its way to the explosives. He gauged the length of the burning fuse that led to the fuse bundle to be about six feet.

"How long before the explosives blow?"

Aldercott panted. "Plenty of fuse in that bundle. I did that to allow us time to get off the mountain. Maybe two minutes."

"Are you kidding? A couple minutes till they explode?"

"No." A rasping breath. "To the fuse bundle." Another pause. More gasping. "Three, four more to burn through the bundle. Then, four minutes to these explosives." Aldercott gestured at the explosives around the tunnel mouth.

"An extra minute maybe to the tunnel." Aldercott closed his eyes and lay on the ground, panting and groaning.

Gabe did the math—ten minutes to the first explosives, a total of eleven to the explosives in the tunnel. Maybe.

Maybes were for dead guys.

Chapter 74

GABE SET his watch alarm at ten minutes, grabbed Aldercott's arm, helped him sit, and then hauled him upright. "Lean on me. Hop to the trailer."

A short minute and a half passed before the burning fuse ignited the fuse bundle. Aldercott slumped in the trailer, gasping, bleeding, and looking pale.

Eight minutes remained.

Gabe took a moment to catch his breath before turning to Hank and fumbling with his tether, his fingers cold and stiff. He shook his hands to get blood moving and talked to the horse. "No problem, Hank, we're gonna stroll down this tunnel, move a small boulder, then head for daylight. Kate's waiting for you. Lots of alfalfa for you once we get out of here."

He undid the tether, grabbed Hank's reins and led him to the front of the trailer.

When he dropped the reins, Hank stood in place, relaxed. Gabe blew on his hands again to warm them and then secured the traces from the trailer to Hank's harness, thankful that the harness was already attached to Hank and that he'd watched Kate and Jack hitch Hank to the wagon in the machine shed. He picked up the rifle, nestled the flashlight under his arm, and grabbed Hank's reins.

"Okay, Hank, let's go." Gabe fast-walked along the valley tunnel, toward the storage bay. Hank followed, pulling the trailer.

"You should thank Thorvaldsen, Rocky. I was on my way. But if he hadn't seen you this morning, I might have been late getting here."

Silence.

"Rocky? You listening?"

Aldercott moaned.

"Good man. For a while I thought Nestor Clayton was the guy called Rocky. Until I took a second look online at your university days and read the speech the football coach made thanking a tutor called Rocky Aldercott for his work with the team."

Gabe checked his watch. Less than six minutes. "Yep. Thorvaldsen helped me figure out your scam. Gwinn figured it out too, didn't he? That's why you killed him?"

Aldercott groaned. "Didn't."

"And Minken. Yeah, Minken used your name when he tried to book into River's End. They'd never heard of you. You weren't fishing last weekend. You were here, planting explosives."

"Not true."

"Sure it is. I told Thorvaldsen you claimed he slept in your core shack. Know what he said? 'He's a damn liar.' I gotta say I believe him. You are a liar. You killed Minken to keep him quiet."

"No. Doc did."

Gabe shook his head. Thugs and thieves.

They turned the last corner, and he could see the boulder. He checked his watch. Five minutes. He hollered, "I'm back. With Hank."

Gabe moved Hank and his load past the boulder. He

snatched up the rope that was wrapped around the boulder and tied it to the trailer. "Pull, Hank," he said, tugging on the reins.

Hank plodded forward, the rope stretched taut, and the boulder scraped across the tunnel floor. Three steps by Hank and the boulder had cleared half the door. "Good, Hank, keep pulling."

Four more steps and the door sprang free.

Jack rushed into the tunnel, his arm encased in a makeshift sling. Kate followed, carrying Devon, who appeared as unfazed by it all as Hank.

Tears ran down Jack's face. "Gabe. I screwed up so bad."

"It's okay, Jacko. We need to get out of here, fast." He turned to Kate and said, "Want to ride Hank?"

"I can walk," she said. She cuddled Devon to her chest with her right arm, grabbed the flashlight and Hank's reins in her left hand and headed along the tunnel. Hank followed easily behind her, pulling the trailer and a moaning Aldercott.

Gabe checked his watch. Maybe a couple minutes left. "Don't stop for anything, Kate."

"We'll be home free soon." Gabe said to Jack. He cranked the LED flashlight, turned it on and passed it to Jack. "Hang on to this if you can, Jacko, and light the way for us."

Gabe grabbed the rifle, and they hustled along the tunnel, trying to catch up with Kate. He checked his watch. A minute, if they were lucky, before the mountain came down.

Gabe heard rapid footsteps, voices echoing. He tensed, clutching the rifle tightly. Then, Ches Ubrowski and Harris appeared, carrying lanterns, and Gabe relaxed.

"We're here, we got you," Ubrowski said.

"Kate, Jesus, Kate," Harris said, hugging her, kissing her.

"Harris, run!" Gabe said. "Take Kate and Devon and run. Jack, you too."

Ubrowski grabbed Hank's reins, and the Percheron's

hooves clopped faster. If Hank's family ran, so would he. The wheeled trailer bounced behind Hank. Aldercott moaned.

Gabe checked the time. Forty seconds. Maybe.

When they reached the tunnel hub, Ubrowski pulled back on Hank's lead to slow him. Gabe maneuvered the trailer around the curve while Ubrowski guided Hank past the slatted door into the main tunnel. When they were inside the main tunnel, Gabe flapped his arms at Ubrowski. "Go, go. I'll catch up."

He pushed the slatted door closed. It would probably do nothing to cushion them from the force of the explosion, but it was worth a shot.

Fifteen seconds.

Gabe raced to catch up to the others, his knee cramping with every step on the uneven tunnel floor. He was twenty feet from the exit, when the percussion smacked. The slatted door at the tunnel hub blew open from the force of the explosion.

Hank reacted by doubling his speed.

Through the tunnel's exit, Gabe could see the slate and purple sky that marked the beginning of evening in the mountains. Never had something looked so welcoming.

Hank galloped through the exit, almost dragging Ubrowski along. Hank didn't stop until he reached Kate and Harris, who stood alongside LeBlanc near two ambulances parked outside the wire enclosure.

Gabe and Jack reached the group at the same time as four more explosions boomed, followed by the rumbling, crashing, grinding of falling rock and timbers. Clouds of dust billowed from the tunnel, swirled around the group, and drifted to the ground.

When the dust settled, LeBlanc stood beside Gabe. "You cut that one close." LeBlanc's grin didn't quite mask the alarm in his eyes. "I was almost worried about you."

Gabe handed LeBlanc the rifle. "Found this in the tunnel."

He pointed at Aldercott, lying in the trailer. Aldercott's

hair stuck up in spikes caked with drying blood, one eye was crusted and swollen shut, and blackish-red rivulets of more dried blood streaked his face and neck. Halloween had come early. "This guy's got a story for you, don't you, Rocky?"

Aldercott groaned. "Yeah. Someone clobbered me. Next thing I know, I wake up in there with a burning fuse and a horse."

LeBlanc called an officer over. "Get the medics to put this guy on a stretcher. Then cuff him to it. The rifle's evidence, treat it that way."

LeBlanc turned to Harris. "Can you make sure everyone who was in that mine gets checked out by a doctor?"

When LeBlanc moved away, Gabe pocketed both flashlights and pulled Harris aside. "My truck's up the logging road. I need your Jeep."

"Are you crazy? You heard LeBlanc."

"I need to check something out."

Harris shook his head. "Sorry, man. Whatever it is will have to wait."

Gabe tried every tactic he knew to convince Harris that his mission was imperative. No matter what he said, even when he revealed who he wanted to talk to and why, Harris refused to budge. "Not happening, Gabe," he said. He turned to leave. "The only vehicle you'll be in tonight is an ambulance with everyone else."

Frustrated, Gabe watched Harris approach the group clumped by the emergency vehicles. He stared at Harris's Jeep, parked a mere twenty feet away. If he squinted, he bet he could see the keys Harris always left in the ignition.

Chapter 75

GABE LET voice mail pick up the calls flooding his cell phone as he drove along Timberline Road. At least one message would be Harris registering dismay that he'd borrowed the Jeep.

"You mean stole it," Choirboy said.

"Borrowed to avert impending disaster," his screw-it self said. "Every minute in an ambulance or hospital is a minute for Aldercott's partner to get away." Gabe nodded. Yes.

"Should let LeBlanc handle this," Choirboy said. Gabe nodded, and then shook his head. First, they'd almost killed Jack. Second, they'd kept Kate, the baby and Jack in frigid tunnels. Plus, Hank. Third, a shitload of explosives and a lit fuse.

It was pitch-black when the Jeep bumped over the cattle guards at the driveway entrance to Solomon's Choice Ranch. Gabe sped up the drive and slid to a stop in front of the house. He jabbed the doorbell. Then he jabbed it again. After a long moment Sol Phoebus opened the door.

"Carl around?" Gabe said.

Sol scratched his head. "He was. He said a tractor needed work. Check the machine shed."

Gabe's phone rang as he walked along the well-lit path to the shed. He checked the display. LeBlanc.

"I'm busy, LeBlanc."

"Harris told me what you have planned. Where are you?"

"At Solomon's Choice. About to have a chat with Carl Dochmann. Nothing to worry about."

"Gabrieli, are you an idiot or what? Do nothing until I get there. *Rien*. Understand? Or I will throw you in jail for interfering with a police investigation. I'm five minutes away. Meanwhile? I meant what I said. Do. Not. Engage."

LeBlanc ended the call. Gabe stood on the pathway, shoulders slumped. LeBlanc meant what he'd said. More than he wanted to confront Carl, Gabe wanted to avoid spending time in a jail cell. Fine. He'd wait for LeBlanc.

Before Gabe could put his phone away, Carl opened the shed door and stepped onto the path. When he noticed Gabe, his eyes registered shock and then relaxed.

LeBlanc had said not to do anything. Hoping it would help convince LeBlanc he had no choice but to at least talk to Carl, Gabe turned away from Carl, hit "call return" on his phone. When he heard LeBlanc answer, he punched the speaker button and said, "Pay attention. And step on it." He left the call engaged, stashed the phone in his jacket pocket, turned to face Carl, and walked toward him.

"Hey, Gabe," Carl said, extending his hand. "What's up?"

Gabe ignored Carl's outstretched hand. "Couple things, Carl. First, I've been thinking about horses and tunnels. I believe you move the Solomon's Choice herd through the Evergold. Why lie about it?"

Carl shrugged. "Not our mine. Don't want hassles."

"Maybe. Second, you put just enough of a spiral on that firewood this morning to make me think about football, and college, and how people like your buddy, Rocky Aldercott, earned extra money tutoring the school's athletes. Including a star quarterback called The Doc."

Carl shrugged again. "More than twenty-five years ago. So?"

Gabe watched Carl's eyes. "Rocky's still alive. You didn't quite kill him. He's talking. All about his scam, about Gwinn, about your involvement in it all, Doc."

"He's lying. He's a con artist. You gonna believe him?"

"Oh yeah. The cops will too. Especially when they test that rifle they recovered." Gabe let his gaze drift to Carl's clenched hands.

"Aldercott had a rifle," Carl said.

Gabe nodded and looked Carl in the eyes. "Sure your prints aren't on it somewhere?"

Even though Gabe was watching for it, the speed of Carl's punch took him by surprise. One second he was standing there, gauging Carl's reactions to the conversation. The next he was on the ground, listening to Carl's hurried footsteps. He rolled over and struggled to his hands and knees.

He heard an engine roar. When he pushed himself upright, he spotted Carl on an ATV, heading along the gravel drive toward the barn. He shouted to make sure LeBlanc could hear him, "For the record, LeBlanc, Carl punched me and is now making a run for it on an ATV. Going past the barn, heading for who knows where."

Gabe ran to the Jeep, jumped in, and gave chase. He yelled above the engine noise. "I'm leaving the phone on. I'm trying to follow your orders, LeBlanc. Not engaging. Merely keeping Carl in sight until you get here. Pronto would be good."

By the time Gabe reached the barn, Carl had a significant lead. He could see the ATV's light bouncing across a distant field. He shifted into four-wheel drive, turned onto the open pasture and stepped hard on the accelerator. "He's crossing a field directly behind the barn," he said, hoping LeBlanc's phone was still connected.

The Jeep leaped forward, the old faithful flashlight

bouncing on the passenger seat. Gabe soon cut Carl's lead to roughly one hundred yards.

Carl turned sharply, the ATV lights picking out split rail fences. Gabe drove parallel to Carl, lurching over the uneven ground. He was calculating how best to unseat Carl when his passenger-side wheels hit a rut and the vehicle tilted. Gabe eased up on the gas and tried to coax the tires out of the rut. Instead, the Jeep stopped, its wheels spinning.

The vehicle was stuck. Gabe shifted between reverse and first, which only dug the tires deeper into the rut. "LeBlanc, I'm stuck in the field. I'll leave the lights on so you can find me. Hurry."

Gabe hauled himself from the Jeep. When he focused on the ATV engine's whine, he saw a headlight dead ahead. It took a few seconds to realize the light was getting closer, the ATV coming straight at him. He scooted behind the Wrangler, to the passenger side.

Carl stopped the ATV and dismounted. His voice growled. "I'm gonna finish this, right now, right here." He flicked open a knife.

From the corner of his eye, Gabe saw headlights approaching from the ranch house. He opened the Jeep's passenger door and reached for the old faithful flashlight, his only option for a weapon.

"First Rocky. Now you, messing up my game," Carl said, advancing.

Gabe moved around the Jeep, trying to keep the vehicle between him and Carl's knife.

Carl shouted at him. "You wanna know about the tunnels? They're my highway. For dope, for people. I move it all. Can't let you ruin that."

"Give it up, Dochmann. Cops are coming."

Carl glanced over his shoulder. "Nah, I think that's Sol's Navigator. He'll want to protect me; protect the cut he gets from my business."

Gabe took a second look at the oncoming vehicle. Was there another one behind it?

Carl took advantage of Gabe's momentary distraction. He vaulted over the Jeep's hood and slashed with the knife. Gabe felt his jacket give way, then fire rippled across his left shoulder. He took a step backward and swung the flashlight like he was trying to hit a one-handed homer. It whistled harmlessly past Carl's head.

Carl laughed. "Puny effort. You shoulda left well enough alone. Shoulda just left your punk, smart-ass brother and Kate Chilton in the mine. Along with that screaming baby. Now you get to die instead of them."

LeBlanc's voice boomed from a speaker. "Drop the knife, Dochmann."

Two RCMP vehicles skidded to a stop a few feet from Dochmann. LeBlanc leaped from the driver's side of one and trained his gun on Carl.

Carl froze.

Two RCMP constables exited the second police SUV and approached Carl, guns drawn.

"Now, Dochmann. Drop it now."

Carl's shoulders slumped and he dropped his knife. The constables grabbed and cuffed him and then escorted him to their vehicle.

Gabe collapsed against the side of Harris's Jeep. "Cutting it kinda close, weren't you, LeBlanc?"

"Hah. Unlike you, I waited for backup. Which caused a momentary delay." LeBlanc glanced at the Wrangler. "Gonna need a tow truck to get that out. You want a ride?"

"Forget it, I'm not sitting in the back of any cop car."

"The back seat's for thugs. Get in the front. We'll call it a tag-along. The others are on their way to emergency. Aldercott will be in hospital awhile, but the medics say he'll survive. Everyone else can sleep at home tonight. I'm betting you can too, but I insist you have a doctor look at you."

"Yeah, okay. I think he cut my shoulder. First though, I'd appreciate a ride to my truck."

———

REUNITED WITH HIS TRUCK, Gabe drove himself to emergency and sat around trying to stay awake, until finally a doctor stitched his shoulder, gave him painkillers and told him to get some rest.

Back at his apartment, Gabe pushed the broken door closed, fed Doofus, and headed for the shower. He was revelling in the sensation of hot water pouring over his sore body when the face of the mysterious young Calgary officer flashed before him. And just like that, Gabe knew who the cop was.

Cutting his shower short, Gabe opened his computer and accessed the *Calgary Herald* archives. It didn't take him long to find an article about city police grads in 2002. He found Ambrose's nephew in the accompanying picture and read the captioned names. Frederick Shymkos. And that told Gabe everything about the animosity he felt coming from Ambrose. He made a mental note to tell Harris tomorrow and flicked on the late news.

The drama at the mine was the lead story. LeBlanc delivered a polished account of Aldercott's and Dochmann's suspected involvement in smuggling, fraudulent mining ventures, sabotage, and murder. He thanked "Private Investigator D. S. Gabrieli, who was instrumental in enabling us to break the case."

Gabe laughed out loud. Ambrose would pitch a fit.

Lucy called as soon as the newscast ended. After she told him how glad she was to know everyone was alive and safe, she said, "I talked to Harris. He's agreed to sell a two-thirds interest in the bar. He can repay their loans and then some."

"That's great, Luce."

"Yeah, so I thought you could invest. What d'ya say? You, me, and Harris, partners?"

Lucy, Gabe thought, his brilliant little sister. Finding a way for Harris to keep his bar. They would have a solid investment; Harris could manage things from Cheakamus; Lucy and Gabe could visit once a year to check things out.

"How much?"

She told him. He fumbled the phone. "Christ. Now *I* need to talk to Seamus about a loan."

Lucy laughed. "I'll front it. It will be good to have you beholden to me for more than cat-sitting." She said goodnight and clicked off.

Gabe sat in the recliner, staring out at the night and the sparkling lights of Cheakamus. He'd pushed his fear away today, turned it into energy. In the process, he'd realized he needed to remove the rubble of hopeless dreams from his life, to clear away the piles of impossible wants, needs and desires, to make room for a new reality. One that, if not entirely happy, could at least be hopeful.

Which brought him to Bethany. If he could solve Drake's murder, she might trust him once more. Stop being afraid. Love him again.

But time had run out. To make things right for her, Drake's murder needed to be solved today. And since that wasn't happening, Gabe saw only one answer.

He loved her, always would. Time to prove it.

He placed the call. "Ciao bella, I'm sorry it's late." He told her everyone was safe and that they'd caught the bombers.

"I knew you would do it," she said. "I'm proud of you."

"Beth, love …" He stopped, his throat tight.

"What?" Her voice was anxious.

He took a moment, then said, "Listen, about us. I want you to divorce me."

"What? Where did this come from?"

"It's the best we can do right now. If you divorce me, your

network won't have an image problem. They'll have a woman who took charge of her life and righted it. That's why you gotta start the proceedings, not me, understand?"

"I don't know what to say."

"I'm not saying I'm out of your life. I will find Drake's killer. When I do, maybe we can try again. Until then, you need to be done with me."

He stared at his reflection in the balcony slider. He didn't look like a man who'd just stuck a knife in his own heart. "It's late, sweetheart. Goodnight."

He clicked off, climbed into bed, and pulled the quilt to his chin. Doofus jumped onto the bed, found a spot on Gabe's chest, kneaded the covers and curled up, purring.

Gabe wrapped his arms around the cat and closed his eyes.

THE SECOND SATURDAY

Chapter 76

MIDAFTERNOON ON A SUNNY SATURDAY, bandaged and bruised, Gabe pulled onto Main Street of Cheakamus. He'd spent the last hour in church and needed coffee. He angled his truck into a shady spot in front of Tiffany's Café. He waited for the Dylan song to finish and punched off the CD player. "Catch you later, Bob."

On the sidewalk outside the café, he flexed his bum knee and rubbed his stiff shoulder. He'd dressed in his finest suit and gleaming black city shoes. He'd tied the perfect Windsor knot in his most sedate tie, all the while hoping the trappings would camouflage the bruises, sutures and scars he'd collected since arriving in Cheakamus a week ago.

Despite his aching body, Gabe felt upbeat. The baby hadn't cried during the christening. He'd hummed Tyson's *Barrel-Racing Angel* to her. She'd gripped his finger and blew raspberries while Reverend Beam blessed her: "Devon Marie, may you have your godmother Nicole's compassion for God's creatures and your godfather Gabe's courage and honor."

Beam smiled at Nicole and Gabe. "God doesn't expect us to be perfect. He merely asks us to try to do the right thing, realize we all stumble now and then, and keep forgiveness in our hearts. For others and for ourselves. As godparents, remember the mistakes you've made on the road of life, recognize that Devon Marie will take her share of missteps, and help her find her path through the potholes along the way."

Beam pointed a finger at Harris. "And Heaven knows there are a few impressive ones out front of the church that perhaps Mayor Chilton can order the works crew to fix."

The minister winked at Nicole and Gabe. "God helps those who help themselves."

————

STILL SMILING at Beam's comment, Gabe opened the café's door. A blast of energetic voices hit him. People shouted, "Gabe!"

Streamers, balloons, and banners decorated the café. Trays of sandwiches, pastries, cookies, pickles, and thermoses of Oso Negro coffee covered the counter. Devon occupied the booth of honor, decked out in her white christening dress, propped in her carrier on the tabletop, grinning and waving tiny fists at anyone who stopped to chat.

The front page of a national newspaper hung on Rhonda's antique mirror. It showed two pictures: a woebegone Manfred Aldercott and a belligerent Carl Dochmann. The caption beneath the pictures said, "Mining promoter and dude ranch manager charged with murder and sabotage."

Tiffany's was jammed. Most of the town had turned out for the post-christening, post-crime-bust celebration that Rhonda and her kids had pulled together overnight. Bill Jacobson was absent. Some said he was pouting because LeBlanc hadn't offered him an exclusive on the story.

Mercy, O'Malley and Jack formed a small pod in the middle of the room. "Sunny!" Mercy waved him over.

O'Malley grabbed his hand and pumped it, then hugged him. "Thanks for everything."

Gabe clapped O'Malley on the shoulder, then hugged his mother and kissed her cheek. He tousled Jack's hair. "How you doing, Jacko? Sore?"

Jack shrugged and then winced. "The part that sucks is I can't ride for a while. The good part is I'm alive and so's everyone else. Sergeant LeBlanc says they're dropping the charges. I'm thinking maybe I should stop being a jerk."

Gabe hugged Jack. "That's an excellent plan. I'm proud of you."

Jack's eyes glistened, tears threatening to spill. He swiped a hand over his eyes as Roxanne joined them. "Guess I have to do your chores for a while," she said, taking Jack's hand in hers. She kissed his cheek. "Don't think it won't cost you."

Jack's expression said exactly how much he'd enjoy paying the price.

O'Malley cleared his throat and broke the spell. "We— Mercy, Jack, and I—were talking after the christening. Reverend Beam's words hit home. Like he had us in his sights."

Gabe said, "Yeah, there's a course in theology school called Pointed Comments 101."

He spotted Greta entering the café. She'd changed out of her church-going clothes and now was back to leggings and a tunic — thick and fuzzy leggings with black and white swirls, and a flowing white knit tunic. George Findrich and The Viking trailed behind her. When Gabe waved them over, Findrich handed Gabe an envelope. "Heard you're buying into the bar. Fortunately, you earned that bonus."

Thorvaldsen flipped a key fob in his hand and studied Jack. "I recognize you. You're one of the kids who partied in the Evergold tunnels."

Jack reddened and flashed a sheepish grin at Greta. "That was a different me."

"Hope so," Thorvaldsen said. He turned to Gabe. "Hi, sonny. The cops took Gwinn's ATV away."

Gabe raised his hands. "Wasn't my doing, Anders."

"Yah, yah. Doesn't matter." He dangled the key fob. "I got a new one. A Polaris. Someone left it by my camp with a card thanking me for helping solve the case."

"Huh. How about that?"

"Was it you?"

Gabe smiled over The Viking's head at Findrich. "Not a chance. I said I'd buy you a steak dinner for helping. That's about all I can afford."

A few minutes later Gabe grabbed a coffee and joined LeBlanc who stood with Lucy, examining the offerings on the dessert trays. "Carl talking yet?"

LeBlanc shook his head. "No. But Aldercott is. Gwinn was going to expose his faked assays. They started fighting and Gwinn fell and smashed his head. Aldercott panicked and went to Carl, who was his partner in the whole con. Carl devised the plan. They hid Gwinn's body in Aldercott's core shack and started blowing up drill rigs, figuring everyone would blame environmental activists."

"Sounds plausible," Gabe said.

"Carl wanted the sabotage to look amateurish, so Aldercott complied. But things got complicated when the TEG explosion caused the mine tunnel to collapse, cutting off their escape route from the resort."

"I can't figure why they didn't use one of the trails," Gabe said.

"The sole access to Carl's secret trail to the US was from that plateau where the horses were stranded, and the only way there was through the mine."

"And when the resort's tunnel collapsed, they had to use the main tunnel, which meant The Viking spotted Aldercott."

LeBlanc nodded. "Aldercott may be trying to save his own hide, but he claims Carl killed Minken. Unfortunately, Carl's prints are not on the rifle. But we've got Aldercott's story and yours. Could be enough."

"Could Gwinn's death be accidental? Weiler planned to invest fifteen million. Would Aldercott deliberately kill someone for that?"

"Here's proof of the power of television," LeBlanc said. "The calls started coming in right after last night's newscast. Aldercott had more marks on the line than Weiler. He stood to rake in about forty-five million from investors on this one scam. So even without Weiler, he'd make thirty million."

"Wow," Lucy said. "A ton-o-dough."

"Yeah. We have doubts about Aldercott's story. Sergeant Ambrose is coming to town tomorrow to interview him, Dochmann, and Phoebus."

"Miserable Milton," Gabe said.

LeBlanc's lip cricked up. "He's decided not to lay assault charges against you."

Gabe felt lighter. "What changed?"

"It wouldn't be fair play to send you to jail after you broke the case for Ambrose."

Lucy flashed a wicked smile. "Gee, Paul. Cops and fair play. Do those words actually go together?"

Gabe gazed at them. Paul? LeBlanc on a first name basis with Lucy? Huh.

LeBlanc studied Lucy. The corner of his mouth twitched. "Yeah, you're Gabrieli's sister all right."

Lucy made a comment about a coffee refill and strolled to the thermoses. LeBlanc watched her. She ran her hand through her hair and tossed her head. Gabe hadn't seen that move since Lucy's last fling two years ago. LeBlanc was done for.

The Mountie turned back to Gabe. "Even if we don't get Dochmann for Minken's death, we should be able to prove he was smuggling and that he tried to kill you. Assuming we can enhance the recording I made of your call."

Nestor Clayton had been hovering nearby. He interrupted and said, "Um, I can tell you about Carl's smuggling."

LeBlanc's eyebrows shot up. "That'd help. Why come forward now, not earlier?"

"He said he'd fire Etta. She needs her job. I couldn't risk it." Nestor focused on Gabe. "Just so you know, I never forgot that herd. Carl sent me to Trail on an errand and said he'd round up the herd. He never did."

"Greta said it didn't sound like you," Gabe said. "I have to ask—were you following me?"

Nestor grinned. "Now and then. I was gonna tell you about Carl, how he moved more than horses through the tunnels. But you got friendly with him. Wally said he thought you were okay, but I wasn't sure."

"Wally's a friend?" Gabe said.

"Yeah. And my tutor. I'm working on my high school diploma."

"Good to hear," Gabe said, as he caught sight of Harris motioning him over. He excused himself and joined Harris by the jukebox.

"So, about your Jeep."

Harris waved it off. "Hey, I'm grateful you didn't total it like you usually do when you drive my vehicles." He grinned. "And so you know, I no longer leave the key in the ignition."

"Point taken. Listen, remember that cop in Calgary who was so fixated on me as a suspect in Drake's murder? Shymkos?"

Harris nodded. "Yeah. How could I forget?"

"He's Ambrose's nephew."

"Really?"

"Yep. And I'm betting when Ambrose checked me out, Shymkos was his source."

"And would have told him all about how you threatened to report him to internal affairs and to sue for false arrest."

Gabe smiled. "Without a doubt."

Harris grinned. Then he loosened his silver bolo tie and put his hand on Gabe's shoulder. "I don't wanna get all weird on you. But thanks for bringing Kate and Devon back to me. That enabled me to throw myself at Kate's knees and promise to spend the rest of my life making it up to her for being a fool."

"Sounds like a plan."

"Funny thing. Kate said she spent a lot of time in the tunnel regretting the things she said to me."

"Spending time underground does that to you."

"I think Reverend Beam was talking directly to Kate and me today. About mistakes and forgiveness. Anyway, thanks. For saving them. And for the bar."

"I'm ecstatic I own a share of The Peak. Now, I'm gonna go see my goddaughter." Gabe clapped Harris on the shoulder and joined Kate and Devon in the booth. When he chucked the baby under her chin, Devon gurgled and pumped her fists and tiny feet, making the carrier rock gently.

"Did I say thanks for everything?" Kate said.

"Only a hundred times. You know Harris loves you very much."

"Yes." Kate shook her head. "We got all tied up about money and pride. Said some awful things to each other. But facing mortality makes you realize what matters."

Gabe put his finger out to Devon, and she wrapped her tiny hand around his swollen knuckle. Her fierce grip made his heart slow, and his stomach feel warm. He took a deep breath. Time to say it out loud. "I told Bethany to divorce me."

Kate sat quietly, her face full of compassion.

"The only way she can keep her job is if I'm not her husband. We can try again when I catch the guy who killed Drake."

"I think you did the right thing. And I'm glad you and Lucy are investing in the bar. It's a perfect solution."

Gabe looked up as Lucy and Harris approached the booth. "Lucy knows a solid investment when she sees one."

"And I know you'd be perfect to run it," Lucy said.

Gabe stared at her. What was she talking about?

"Tomorrow we can go over the schedule for deliveries by suppliers," Harris said. "Show you what you have to do as manager."

"I'm not managing anything. I'm leaving tomorrow for Eau Claire."

"You can't leave," Harris said. "You may have a court case coming up."

"Not anymore. LeBlanc said they aren't laying any charges. I'm free to go."

"I'm sure there's some paperwork yet. Besides, you can't drive your truck back to Alberta with ripped seats and 'hayseed' sprayed down the side. That's pitiful."

"Nice try. It's nothing a little duct tape and black spray paint won't fix until I can get it to the shop."

"Bar patrons are talking about a pool on when you'll miss with the sugar cube toss."

"Never."

Lucy said, "Both Harris and I want you to manage the bar. He has a town to run. I have the bar in Eau Claire."

"Findrich has a body shop," Harris said. "But he might need awhile to fit you in."

"Your cat hates to travel," Lucy said.

"Nice try, Luce."

"Just sleep on it, okay? Tomorrow, meet us here for breakfast. We'll talk about it."

———

AFTER THE CROWD thinned out at Tiffany's, Gabe returned to the guesthouse and parked in the garage. He limped up the stairway to his suite and paused at the top. He looked down at his truck and saw "hayseed" in its orange-spattered ugliness again. Harris was right, it was pitiful.

He fed Doofus before sitting in the recliner and staring out at the lights of Cheakamus. Soon Doofus leapt onto Gabe's lap and curled into a ball. Gabe listened to the cat's contented purr and thought about the decision facing him tomorrow.

He would meet Harris and Lucy for breakfast in the morning. They would ask him again to manage The Peak.

The bar had a good supply of sugar cubes.

Jack could use a big brother nearby.

Tornado Callie had nickered when she first saw him.

The Tiffany's crowd had called out his name. With gusto.

Devon could use help with teenage angst.

He owed The Viking a steak dinner.

A guy could feel comfortable in a place like Cheakamus.

He had all night to decide.

The End

Acknowledgments

I love writing about Gabe Gabrieli and the quirky people in Cheakamus.

All the characters, and the town of Cheakamus, are imaginary. Now and then, for the purposes of story, a character in authority may act dishonourably, but this is not intended as a reflection on real-life people in those positions.

I was a mining and corporate finance lawyer for a couple decades, which helped immensely with the authenticity of this novel. But more than that, I'm married to a geologist who was "in to" this book enough to take me to exploration sites, show me how drill rigs work, walk me through a mine tunnel, explain explosives, and drive all over Washington and British Columbia in search of the perfect setting. Any errors, of course, are mine alone.

I am grateful to all my family, friends and writing colleagues who have lived with this novel almost as long as I have. And to organizations like Crime Writers of Canada and Sisters in Crime for all they do to support writers of crime fiction.

Heart-felt thanks to Kobbie Alamo, a great writer and an even better friend, who has been cheering for Gabe from the first moment he pulled his F150 into Cheakamus; to Marcelle Dubé and Karen L. Abrahamson, prolific writers who, more than once, found time to brainstorm, read pages, and haul me over the bumps in the road; and Sisters in Crime-Canada

West, one of the most collegial and fun places for a Canadian crime writer to hang out.

If you'd like to hear more about Gabe (and you are not already a subscriber), please sign up for my monthly newsletter. You'll receive updates on my short stories and novels, as well as occasional free stories. I never sell your contact information, and I promise to try very hard never to bore you! You can sign up on my website: https://charlottemorganti.com.

And of course, I'd love to hear directly from you. Send comments to me at cam@charlottemorganti.com.

Thanks so much for reading *The End Game!*

Charlotte Morganti

About the Author

Charlotte Morganti is a Canadian writer of crime fiction. She has been a burger flipper, beer slinger, and a corporate finance/mining lawyer. Charlotte writes novels and short stories, ranging from gritty investigations to lighter capers. She usually sets her stories in small towns that miraculously harbour both villains (often cunning, occasionally inept) and the sleuths who pursue them.

Charlotte's works have been short-listed for various awards. She is a member of Sisters in Crime and Crime Writers of Canada, and is a past president of Sisters in Crime-Canada West. Charlotte and her husband live in a small town on the Sunshine Coast of British Columbia.

Website: https://charlottemorganti.com

Made in the USA
Middletown, DE
10 September 2023

38291910R00239